A Final Resting Place

By Tim Tormasi

Best Wishes!

Tim Tormasi

ISBN 0-7414-4478-X

Published by:

PUBLISHING.COM

1094 New DeHaven Street, Suite 100
West Conshohocken, PA 19428-2713
Info@buybooksontheweb.com
www.buybooksontheweb.com
Toll-free (877) BUY BOOK
Local Phone (610) 941-9999
Fax (610) 941-9959

Printed in the United States of America

Printed on Recycled Paper

Published April 2008

for Rachael

Prologue

Bill Summers didn't usually take walks at night, yet here he was at two-thirty in the morning in the middle of nowhere. The sound of crickets filled the air, cool for late August. Fall was coming early.

The forest surrounded him, and by the time he reached the pond's edge, he knew what he would do. The answer was in his car a mile back, in the glove compartment.

He had been driving up county road 203, a narrow two-lane that weaved through southeastern Ohio. The road markings were barely visible, being torn away by time and the elements. Potholes had gone unrepaired. 203 was a bad road all right, and these days most people just took the interstate to get where they were going.

Bill had ignored the warning signs and drove without caution for eight miles until he parked halfway off the road. It hadn't broken down; it wasn't a flat tire. He wasn't even worried that another car might come along and hit it. He knew that out here at two-thirty on a Wednesday morning, he was the only man who existed. No one would be coming through for another four hours.

He held his emotions in as long as he could, the tightness at the base of his throat trying to keep them down. When his eyes filled with tears he slammed his hands against the steering wheel. He was being weak when he should be strong—again. He shouldn't be sitting here; he should be *doing* something, and he knew what that something was. You could call it revenge, you could call it justice, you might even call it redemption, but there was no other word for it—it was murder.

1

He thought the fresh air would do him some good, so he got out and started walking. The sound of his boots crunching into the gravel was amplified in the stillness of the night. He depended on the rhythm of his steps for his sanity, trying to clear his mind of what had already happened tonight.

By the time he reached the path, his mind stopped racing. She had led him down this path not long ago and now, without realizing it, Bill was going back to this place. This had been her secret place. He had been going here all along.

When he reached the pond, he turned 360 degrees. Everything was dark blue or black, and strangely motionless—there was no wind moving through the trees, and the water was stagnant. It seemed like this place had been frozen in time since he had last been here. There was one thing missing, though—Julianne. He had known, of course, that she would not be here, but he had come anyway. He didn't know where else to go. He needed a place to sort everything out, and this was perfect.

He sat at the water's edge, tossing stones into the pond. With each *plunk*, he got closer to convincing himself that there was no other way. He'd thrown only ten before he stood and headed for his car.

In the driver's seat now, Bill opened the glove box. He knew that once he touched it, this whole thing would seem more real somehow, and that by picking it up he would be putting a plan in motion that he wouldn't allow himself to stop. He knew if he thought about it too much, he would chicken out and then regret it. He'd been there before. He would have to do this quickly, without deliberation. He only hoped tonight would be like closing one's eyes and ripping off a bandage, and that in the end, he would find it really hadn't been that bad after all.

He wrapped his fingers around the nickel-plated .38 snub nose and took it out of the glove compartment. He felt the weight of the gun in his hand, and opened the cylinder. There were five bullets in it. He tried to line it up so he would have five consecutive shots and realized he wasn't even sure which way the revolver rotated. He'd never owned a gun, never liked them, and never paid much attention to them.

And now he would use one to take another man's life.

He tried to imagine the bullet entering Dale's chest, and the wound it would cause. The dark red glistening wound. He imagined the satisfaction he would get from seeing his surprised look, and from seeing him drop to the floor.

He would never be completely satisfied, however. There was still one thing that none of this would change—Julianne was gone now, and there was nothing he could do to bring her back.

Part One

Chapter One

When Julianne Case walked into Bill's office for the first time he could tell that she'd been crying. Her eyes were red and puffy and she looked like she hadn't slept for days. She was pale—her black hair straight and unwashed. Some of the women who came through his door tried to hide their scars with makeup; some didn't. He had seen it all before. There were two physicians on call to treat the bumps and bruises, the broken bones, and the concussions. Bill was one of four therapists who treated the emotional pain. As part of the shelter's program, everyone who stayed there, even for one night, had to participate in four sessions of counseling. Sessions were to be held once a week for a month, a sort of probationary period to hopefully ensure no one was going back to the same abusive life. Like it said on the pamphlet: at Clarksdale, they didn't just want to help a girl for a night; they wanted to help her for a lifetime.

There was one thing that set Julianne apart from all the others, though. Immediately, Bill saw in her a quiet beauty, a humble beauty. It was the kind of beauty that other men probably didn't see, and that made her all the more special to him.

He stood and walked around his desk when she came in. His secretary was with her.

"Bill, this is Julianne Case." He extended his hand and after a slight pause, she shook it. "Julianne, this is Mr. Summers." The secretary looked at Julianne, who said nothing, and then looked at Bill before leaving.

"Miss Case, it's nice to meet you."

"Thank you," she said, not making eye contact.

Bill took his seat behind the desk.

4

"Please, have a seat," he said, and she slowly sat in the wooden chair, clutching onto her purse.

Bill focused on her file in front of him. "Says you've been here before."

"I was here about eight or ten months ago." She looked past him out the window. "Where's Susan?"

"Susan?"

"Yeah. I talked with her last time." She was wringing her hands and still had not made eye contact.

"Oh, Susan Moore? She no longer works here."

"Did she do something bad?"

"Susan?" He smiled. "Of course not. She got married and moved to Montana."

"Why did she do that?"

"Because she was in love, I guess, same reason anybody gets married."

"No—why did she move to Montana?"

"Her husband has family out there."

Julianne looked at the floor and smiled. "I liked her. She was nice."

"Yes, she was. So tell me—how are things with you?"

"Not too great, I guess."

"Why don't you tell me about it?"

"Okay. I'm not really sure where to start other than what you probably already know. My boyfriend hits me sometimes. This last time wasn't that bad, but I just needed a place to stay, you know?"

"That's why we're here. Why does he hit you, do you think?

"There's lots of things, but it's usually when he's drunk. Sometimes he's had a bad day at work, sometimes when the Steelers lose he gets real mad. Other times I think it's just because he's bored. I'm not real sure. I try to figure out what I said or did, and sometimes I just don't know. Hits me pretty regular, though."

"You shouldn't be asking yourself what you did wrong. You are not to blame. Your file says the cops have been out to your place four times in the last year and you never press any charges. Why is that?"

"I know; I'm sorry. You must get girls like me in here all the time who just let this happen. I must seem pretty stupid."

"Of course not."

"I just want him to stop. I don't want him to go to jail. And every time the cops come out, believe me, he stops. Behaves like a perfect gentleman for them and after they're gone he takes off."

"Where does he go?"

"Who knows. But he's usually gone for most of the night. Has me worried sick about him. Sometimes I think he does it just to get back at me. You know, for calling the cops."

Bill couldn't believe she could worry about a man who had just beaten her. "Doesn't he hate you more for calling the cops?"

Julianne pondered this. "I don't think he really cares one way or another. He's got a cousin on the police force so he knows he'll get a break. And besides, he doesn't hate me. He loves me, and he always says it's the last time."

Bill didn't know how many times he'd heard that, or how many times that promise had been broken. "Do you honestly believe that?"

"I don't know...I guess I want to believe it. It's good to have faith, right? I do know that when he says it, he means it. He's the one who has the problems."

"Yes, but as long as you stay with him, his problems are your problems, and he's going to keep beating you if you don't do something about them."

Julianne finally looked him in the eye. "Are you a religious man, Mr. Summers?"

"Not really. Maybe—I don't know."

Julianne set her purse on the floor and folded her arms. "I was born and raised Catholic. When I was younger I took that for granted. I lived without the Lord for so long that I forgot what it meant to be blessed.

Recently I became reacquainted with my faith and it has turned my life around. It really has.

"I don't believe in cutting people loose when they have a problem. It's just not very Christian. Leaving Dale is probably the worst thing I could do for him. He'd be much worse off without me. He needs me and I'm going to be there for him no matter what. Divorce is simply not an option."

Bill shuffled through his papers. "I didn't know that you were married. It says here that you just live together."

"We've lived together long enough to be man and wife, by law. He doesn't know that, but I like to think of him as my husband."

"I respect that, but if you're not going to leave him, you need to get him some help, because I don't want to see him hurting you anymore."

She smiled at this. "That's so nice of you to say. Maybe I could bring him here to see you."

Bill shook his head. He had experience with trying to treat the boyfriends, and it never went well. They never wanted to be there, and refused to be helped. He thought of Phil Oliver in particular, who had been suspicious of Bill to the point of threatening him. "No, that's not my field. I don't do any marriage counseling or outside psychoanalysis."

"How much does therapy usually cost?"

"In Columbus it's at least seventy-five an hour," he said. "But there are groups in Cambridge that are pretty cheap. I'll get you a list of names."

"Dale makes nine-fifty full time and I make minimum wage part time. It's not going to be easy coming up with extra money. I also don't think Dale would go for it. That's another reason I don't want to see him go to jail. If he goes to jail, I'm out on the street."

"Oh, come on, there's got to be someone—a friend or a co-worker? Any family?"

She grabbed the back of her hair into a ponytail and ran her fingers through it. He imagined her black soft hair and the feeling of her neck trembling under his lips.

"—no one."

"Pardon?"

"There's no one. There's nobody at work that I feel close to; my sister lives in Westerville but she's a total snob. I asked her once for a loan for my birth control pills, because I didn't have insurance, and she said she couldn't help me. She said I shouldn't be taking them if I was a good Catholic anyway. I guess she's right, but she's got four kids under seven. No way I could handle that. No way.

"There's no one except Dale. He thinks I'm sexy; he makes me feel special and wanted. I wouldn't trade it."

Bill couldn't believe what he was hearing. The girl seemed smart enough to know better—smart enough to stay away from an abusive man. With all the horrible things in the world that we can't control, Bill could never understand why some people didn't avoid the horrible things they could. "Do you think he thinks you're special and sexy when he's hitting you?"

"I guess not. But like I said, he's got some problems, just like the rest of us, and I'm not going to leave him. Don't you have any problems?"

He thought about Karen. He knew she didn't love him anymore, and even though they still lived in the same house, it was about the only thing they shared. Their lives were almost completely separate. Their love had been so alive, so passionate, but like watching the hour hand on a clock, that time had passed without them realizing it. "Sure, I've got problems," he said. "You're right; we all have them."

There was a long silence. Bill could feel himself wanting to open up to her, but he had too many reasons not to get involved with Julianne. First and most obvious, she was a patient. He had heard the warnings about therapists sharing too much about their own lives. It was an easy thing to do, because she is pouring out her secret fears to you, and many times it made her feel better to know that you were a human being with problems, too. A good therapist, however, was supposed to "care from a distance," and always be professional. You had to be professional if you wanted her to respect your advice.

Secondly, there was Dale, who he was sure was not the type of guy you wanted on your bad side. Maybe Bill did have a little crush on Sandy Oliver last year, and maybe Phil Oliver's suspicions were right. The ways, though, that he beat her...he had to get involved. Bill knew getting in the middle was a bad idea, possibly a dangerous one. When he looked at her, though, none of that seemed to matter. He knew he had already crossed the line.

"Tell me about Dale. Where did you first meet him?"

She looked at her watch. "Oh! Speaking of meeting him, I'm supposed to meet him downtown in ten minutes! Do you mind if we stop five minutes early?"

"No, that's fine." He gathered her papers and put them in the file. "Have you talked to him since the other night?"

"I called him on the pay phone in the hall before I came in." She stood up. "We're gonna have lunch. He's sweet like this sometimes."

Bill smiled and shook his head slightly. He stood up and extended his hand. Julianne, who had been in a rush, calmed for a second. She stopped and gently took his hand. "Thank you so much, Mr. Summers. You're very nice. Thanks for listening to me go on." She slowly let go of his hand. "I'll see you next week then?"

"Yep."

"It's a date," she said, smiled, turned and left.

Bill stood there for a moment, her beauty branding itself into his brain.

Chapter Two

Bill dipped a fork in the boiling pot of spaghetti and took one of the noodles out, putting it in his mouth. It would need one or two minutes longer. He'd practically lived on some sort of dry pasta all through college. That was nine years ago, and he was beginning to feel like a bachelor again.

Karen was a detective for Muskingum County Homicide, able to keep regular hours until two weeks ago, when Mark Cherneau disappeared. Cherneau, 28, was something of a local celebrity. After high school, he had played seven years of minor league baseball, spending the last four years for the AA Sea Dogs in Portland, Maine. Over that time, he was decent, but never spectacular, and when they cut him loose in 2006, no one else wanted him.

He came back to his hometown of Logan, Ohio and worked at the General Electric Plant until two weeks ago when he vanished. The local media was all over it, and when initial searches failed, they increased their fervor.

Karen was immediately assigned the case. If it was a homicide, these first few weeks would be crucial. She and her partner were working from seven-thirty a.m. to eight-thirty or nine at night, talking to anyone who might know anything. They were gathering names of people who had been in The Last Stop Tavern, named that because after the Logan exit off state route 26, there was nothing southbound for 47 miles. Unfortunately for Cherneau, it had a more literal meaning on July 22.

Over the weeks, as leads turned into dead ends and the search continued, Karen became more and more frustrated. The press was watching closer than normal, and Karen was failing in front of them. This bothered her of course, but not nearly as much as the fact that *no one* could find Mark Cherneau. Two weeks with thirty men searching, and so far nothing.

She hardly spoke to Bill these days, and when she asked him how his day went, it sounded obligatory. When Bill would ask about her day, she replied with the stock answer she gave to the media—it was going okay, they had found nothing new.

It was now eleven p.m. and Bill was getting worried. Sure, she had been working long hours, but never this long. And there was no phone call. That was the thing—where could she be that she couldn't call?

Chapter Three

Karen was on her way home when dispatch called.

"This better be good," she said. She had just put in one of her longest days yet, and one of her least productive. Nothing was moving forward in the case; it seemed like one dead end after another. She had a monster headache, and was looking forward to getting home, taking some aspirin and a bath. She would try to forget it for just a little while—try to silence the questions that seemed to be coming from everywhere—from the press, from the chief, and from herself.

"Detective, we have a 919 at the northeast sector of Wayne National Forest. Two miles north of state route 84 on Johnstown road. Take a right at Deer Run. Detective Flanigan has been notified and will meet you at the site."

Karen turned the car around. 919 meant a body had been found. Finally, she thought. It wasn't good news, but she was happy to hear it just the same. It was something to go on. Sure, it would have been better to hear that he had just run off with some girl to Mexico; the truth, though, was that Karen had never expected him to turn up alive. In homicide, you learned to expect the worse, because that's what you usually got.

"Karen, do you copy?"

"Tell them I'll be there in fifteen minutes."

At the scene, she saw five unmarked cars, two squad cars and a truck that had 'Wayne National Forest Parks and Recreation' on the side. Light rain was coming down. A man with an orange hunting vest that said "crew" in big black letters got out of a car. He had a flashlight and was wearing insulated work boots. He walked over to another car and tapped the window. He said something to the man inside and pointed at Karen. The man in the car was Tom Flanagan, her partner.

The two men came over as she was getting into her trunk. She sat on the bumper and pulled rain boots over her shoes. As the two men approached, the man in the hunting vest held a poncho out to her.

"I've got one," she said. She looked at Tom and smiled.

"I was home for a grand total of two minutes," he said.

"Lucky you. I never made it at all," she replied as she pulled the raincoat over her head.

"Karen, this is Ron Fulson. He was part of the search crew that found him."

They shook hands. "How do you do, ma'am," he said. "I saw you on the TV last night, talking to them reporters."

"That was me," she said. "So, Ron, you the one that found him?"

"Yes, ma'am. Almost stepped right on him. I was looking to my right and walking straight ahead when I went down a little step. There he was, white as a ghost. I know it sounds weird, since he was the reason we've been out here almost two weeks, but he scared me, almost stepping on him and all. I'm relieved the search is over, though; my feet were beginning to hurt."

"Are you sure it's him?"

"Oh yeah, it's him. Guy's face has been plastered all over the news—I probably know it better than my own by now. I also seen him play ball a few times. It's him all right."

The two eight-man teams had been searching ten hours a day for nearly two weeks. The first team had been concentrating on the northeast and north central sections of the forest. Fulson's team had been covering the eastern and southeastern sections.

Karen turned to Tom. "Any media show up yet?"

"No, but we're thinking any minute. Of course we're trying to keep it quiet for now, telling everybody not to say anything, but you never know when one of these guys is going to try to make a quick buck."

"I guess we should feel lucky that they're not here already. Who's up there?"

"Head ranger of the park, a couple sheriffs, some guys from forensics. That's about it. Two or three search guys left. I think they're just curious."

"Wilson up there?" She asked. Jared Wilson was the Chief of Police for Muskingum county. When he had given the case to Karen and Tom, he told them to investigate with a "special urgency." That 'special urgency' may have come from the fact that his son had played high school baseball with Cherneau, and it hit him close to home.

"He's not here anymore," Tom said. "He came right out when the body was found. He only stayed long enough to make sure. I got here just as he was leaving. He seemed pretty shaken up. Hardly said a word."

"Anything to you?"

"Nope. Just got in the car and left."

Karen grabbed a flashlight, then slammed the trunk. She paused for a second, taking a long breath. It was already a long day, and it was about to get longer.

"Okay. Let's do it."

After fifteen minutes of walking through thick forest, falling once on the uneven terrain, she saw the spotlights in the distance. It was raining heavily on the trees above them, the big drops making a 'pop' sound on their raingear. The brush underneath was like a blanket over the soil, and as they walked, small branches cracked like dry bones.

The sight ahead was a strange, eerie one; in the middle of such darkness were two flood lights hanging ten feet from the ground. There were flashlights pointing and moving as the men were doing their own tasks. It looked to Karen like something out of a UFO movie. A small group of them was standing in a circle. Twenty yards away there was a fire trying to survive in the rain.

Two men talked and shook their heads as they warmed their hands. They stood beside a stretcher with an empty body bag laid out on it.

"Any idea on the cause of death?" Karen asked Tom.

"One thing's for sure—it wasn't a suicide."

"Why you say that?" She approached the circle and between the men caught a glimpse of the blue jeans on the victim.

"That would be pretty much impossible," he said, one corner of his mouth turned up slightly. She gave Tom a puzzled look.

"You'll just have to see for yourself," he said.

The three of them walked slowly, quietly to the scene. Karen braced herself for the worst. If someone was speaking to her, she certainly didn't hear. Her eyes were fixed on what lay in the middle of the circle.

She put her hands on the shoulders of two men in front of her to let them know she was there. The one on the left, one of the men from the search crew who had stayed, jumped when she touched him. The two men moved to let her through when she showed them her badge.

A forensic specialist was taking blood samples both from the body of Mark Cherneau and from the ground. Another was taking pictures.

Her stomach turned slightly at the sight of the blood, as it always had. She'd wondered before if that meant she was in the wrong profession. In her life, she had only seen three actual murder victims at the scene, but she'd seen thousands of pictures—multiple stabbings, gunshots to all parts of the body, hangings and beatings. She couldn't recall ever seeing any pictures of anything like this. It was *different*, somehow—she couldn't tell how exactly, but something was very strange here. The cruelty this took was beyond her comprehension. She wondered how long Mark Cherneau actually lay like this before he died.

The rain continued to fall. The forensic specialists worked quickly so that the evidence didn't get washed away.

Karen turned away from the scene. She was getting cold, but mostly it was what she'd just seen that made her shudder.

Chapter Four

When the phone rang at eleven that night, Bill was nearly asleep. He was lying on the couch with the TV muted. Four empty beer bottles were on the floor, standing in a row. It was about time Karen called.

"Hello."

"Hi, Mr. Summers, it's me."

"I'm sorry?"

"It's me, Julianne Case."

"Oh, hey! What's the matter?"

"It's no big deal. I'm sorry, but I didn't know who else to call."

"No, that's fine. What's wrong?"

"He left me," she said matter-of-factly.

Bill smiled with relief. Whether Julianne thought so or not, this was good news. "Are you okay?"

"Yeah, I'm okay, it's just that I need a ride. I hardly have any money, not that there are any cabs out here anyway."

"I guess I could come get you," he said. "Have you packed any of your things?"

Bill was already thinking of the problem this would cause. Where would he take her? She's got nowhere to go. He tried to keep his personal feelings out of this. He had a professional obligation to help her. Also, Karen wouldn't want to hear any explanation for a pretty young woman in their house when she got home. Beyond that, Karen was very perceptive; she was trained to see things that others miss. If they were all to be in the same house together, something—a look, a smile, anything—was sure to give him away.

"No, of course I didn't pack anything," Julianne said. "We were only gone three hours."

"Gone, what are you talking about? Where *are* you?"

"I'm at a rest area on 70 a little east of Cambridge."

"What!?"

"I told you, he left me! I can't believe he would do this." She paused. "I'm sorry, but I really need your help. He was in a real mood; he just took off. I was thinking I could probably get a ride with one of these truckers, but I don't know."

"No, no, don't get in the car with anybody. I'm going to come get you; you just sit tight. Now I think I know that rest stop, but are you on the eastbound or westbound side?"

"West. We were coming back from Wheeling, but I had to pee. He just left."

"Okay, okay, you just try to take it easy and I'll be there in half an hour. All right?"

"Okay," she said.

"And you're not going to get in anybody's car, right?"

"Right."

"I'm on my way."

Bill hung up the phone. He moved quickly around the house. It would be best if he could get out of there before Karen got home, which was bound to be any minute. He got out of his cut-off sweatpants and put on a pair of black jeans, the ones Karen said looked good on him. He tucked in his white v-neck t-shirt and took the stairs to the bathroom two at a time. He brushed his teeth twice, to try to get the alcohol off his breath. He put his head under the faucet, the way he used to do in school when he was late for class. He was overdue for a haircut, and his lying on the couch had made it stand up.

He grabbed the towel and dried the excess. As he raised his head and looked at the mirror, he saw that the blood had rushed to his head. He looked at his red face and muttered, "God, what are you doing?" He shook his head, without an answer to that question, and then ran his hands through his hair a couple times. He rinsed the hair off his hands and dried them.

Julianne's face was all he could think of. The dark hair, the large brown eyes. The dimples in her cheeks when she smiled. He grabbed the keys off the table in the foyer, expelled a long breath and walked out the door.

As Bill was pulling out of the driveway, the TV he had forgotten to shut off was showing pictures of a newsman reporting live from Wayne National Forest. It was raining heavily there, and the reporter had no umbrella. The little hair he had was a soaked mess. Raindrops were bouncing off his spotlighted head. In the upper right-hand corner of the screen was a picture of Mark Cherneau.

Chapter Five

Phil Oliver sat on the bar stool, glassy-eyed. His six-foot-two, two hundred-fifty pound frame was clutching the bar like it was a life preserver and he was a drowning man.

It wasn't a very big turnout here for a Friday night—Phil estimated the place was about half-empty. He was a regular here at the Last Stop, and on Friday nights, you could set your watch by his arrival at ten o'clock. But unlike the TV show 'Cheers', there was no one who greeted him with a rousing 'Phil!' when he arrived. Most of the clientele at The Last Stop was under thirty; former high school football players and the girls they've been with since the tenth grade. They came to party—to live irresponsibly as they had back then, so they could pretend that the best parts of their lives were still ahead of them. Phil Oliver didn't come to meet with friends, and he didn't come to party. He had just eclipsed forty, and he had no problem with the fact that he'd hit his prime over twenty years ago.

The only reason he came to the Last Stop was to drink.

And maybe forget about Sandy.

He raised the mug to his lips. The beer slid down easily. His dirty blond hair was still a little wet from the rain, but he didn't care. He wasn't here to impress anybody. He just liked to get out of the house as much as he could.

Hank Peters, the bartender, was talking to a couple of guys who looked like they could still be in high school. They were talking Ohio State football and whether they would be able to make it back to the championship game.

Phil always got free beer at the Last Stop because of his brother Marty, a distributor for Anheuser Busch in

Columbus. He covered Muskingum, Perry and Morgan counties. If Marty's old buddies, Hank and Steve, who owned the place, ordered three kegs, every now and then, they got four. In return, he asked them to just look out for Phil. See that he stayed out of trouble, and drive him home when he was too drunk to drive (which was most of the time).

After his wife left him, Phil wasn't the same. He was never in a good mood, never talked to anyone about it, or anything else for that matter. Marty checked up on his older brother when he could, but between forty hours a week and a wife and two kids, he hardly had any spare time.

The high school kids, who were sitting in the middle of the bar, were still talking about OSU football when one of them stopped and looked at the TV. It was hanging in the corner, right above where Phil was sitting. The boy stopped talking, and his friend and Hank both turned to look. Phil did his best to focus on the screen.

By the time someone said, "Hey turn that up!" Hank was already halfway to the set. He turned it up loud enough to be heard over the juke box; then he decided to turn the juke box off completely. A few people said "hey!" in protest, looking up from their pool tables. Hank turned the channel on the big screen from the baseball game to a man who was reporting from Wayne National Forest. Rain dripped from the man's nose.

"—a search that has gripped Muskingum and surrounding counties appears to be over. The search for Mark Cherneau, a native of Logan and former minor league baseball player, has ended tonight in tragedy. Cherneau, 28, had worked for General Electric in Logan the past two years until fifteen days ago when he disappeared, supposedly from The Last Stop, a bar outside Logan."

This caused one man, who was leaning on his pool cue for support, to say, "Hey! Wow, man!" He was probably the only one there who didn't know that fact, and no one paid him any attention.

"Cherneau did not report to work on Thursday, July 23, and repeated calls to his home and to his family brought no answers.

"This evening, at nine-fifteen p.m., one of the search crews, led by Ron Fulson, a fireman from Zanesville, found Mark Cherneau's body about a mile and a half from where I'm standing. Police have closed off the entire northeast section of the forest as a crime scene. They are working to collect evidence quickly, presumably because of what this rain can do to fingerprints, fibers and the type of valuable evidence they will need if they are to catch whoever is responsible for this death."

The anchorwoman in the newsroom cut into the report. "Jim, any word as to what caused the death?"

"All we know is what the police have told us—the body has been found, and it is definitely Mark Cherneau."

"Any indication that it was murder or suicide? Accidental death, maybe?"

"No, there is supposed to be a press conference first thing in the morning, but for now we just can't say. If I had to guess, though, I've got to believe that this was murder. Hunting is prohibited in these woods, and I don't see why anyone would walk a mile and a half into this wilderness to kill himself. It's the middle of nowhere out here."

"All right, Jim, thank you for that report."

Phil Oliver cracked a smile. He couldn't believe how stupid reporters could sound sometimes. He finished his beer, and raised his glass.

"Hey Hank—can I get another beer?"

Chapter Six

Karen got a drink from the search team's cooler. The coldness of the water made her stomach feel a little better. Seeing the body wasn't the only reason for the queasiness, though—she hadn't eaten anything since one-thirty. The thought of food right now, however, made her feel even more sick.

Tom shook Ron Fulson's hand as Fulson left the scene. It was after eleven now, and most of the people had gone. Two forensics men were still hard at work. The park ranger and one of the search crew men were scanning with their flashlights, looking for something. The two men who had been standing near the fire were still there with their body bag and stretcher. One was telling what seemed to be an amusing anecdote. Tom walked over to Karen and put his arm around her.

"You all right?"

"Yeah, I just needed a minute," she said, wiping one eye. "I just got a little freaked; I don't know why, but it got to me. I tried to act like it was nothing, like it was no big deal."

"It's not 'nothing' and you and I both know that."

"Yeah, but I was hoping it would be, you know? Why can't it be just another part of the job? If the media saw how I reacted, or if Wilson saw, they would write me off as an emotional woman who can't handle the job. This is the biggest case I've ever had; you know I can handle it, don't you?"

"Of course I do. I don't doubt it for a minute."

"Why can't I be analytical about it then, like you?"

Tom held her tighter and looked her directly in the eye. "You think I'm not affected by this type of thing? My stomach's turned too by all of this. The myth that some cops like to create is that 'if you've seen one stiff, you've seen 'em all.' That's total bullshit. I make myself look long and hard at it because that's what keeps me focused. Hell, I can't ever get it out of my head until we find the son of a bitch. Damn thing usually keeps me up nights. You too, probably."

"I always thought I was an insomniac. Too paranoid to fall asleep. You spend all day looking for some monster and not find him and then you can't get him out of your dreams."

"Karen, we react the way we do because we're human and because we care. That's all there is to it. It has nothing to do with your ability. You know my father's seen his share of victims and he said more than a few of them gave him the willies. And you know he's as tough an investigator as they come. Ten times tougher than me, that's for sure."

Karen knew that Tom's father was a legend in the Zanesville P.D., but even if he was ten times tougher than Tom, she still would prefer having Tom as a partner. He could always diffuse a tense situation, and although it was rare, sometimes she needed that. Times like tonight.

He kept his arm around her as they walked back to the body. Karen had seen the victim from the human perspective. Now she would look as an investigator.

The baggy blue jeans on the victim had been secured to the ground by metal spikes, the kind that were used for camping. Three were used on each leg. Two at each knee, and one at each ankle. Whoever had done this, Karen thought, had made sure that Cherneau wasn't going anywhere.

The victim was found without a shirt; wet leaves stuck to his white torso. His nipples were blue, matching his lips. The eyes stared straight up, covered with a bluish gray film. There were specks of soil in one of them. There was no emotion in the face—no surprise, no horror. Absolutely nothing.

Both arms had been amputated, and in the pools of blood and rain and mud lay two branches in place of the arms. They were small limbs, shorter and thinner than human arms. One had been jammed into the shoulder socket and the other seemed to have fallen out and was coated with blood.

Karen walked over to the County Coroner, who was jotting notes into a book. "Hey Fred. Any thoughts about the object used to amputate the arms?"

"Whatever it was, it sure wasn't very sharp. You see how the skin on the shoulders was ragged? My guess for now is that the arms weren't hacked off; I think they were *sawn* off. Takes a sick bastard to be able to do this. It's not easy to saw off an arm. Takes some time. You can't just slice through it like a loaf of bread. Takes some work. I certainly don't envy you, tracking down this nut."

"I don't envy me, either. How long would it take somebody to die after something like this was done to them?"

"Oh, it'd be a matter of minutes. Very quickly. I'd say no more than ten."

"Do you think the victim was conscious for most of that time?"

"Hard to say. I'd think you'd pass out if you saw something like this happening to you, but I suppose it's possible. Doesn't sound like a fun way to go, that's for sure."

She thanked him and told him to give her a call after the autopsy.

She walked slowly back to the scene, looking at the ground in front of her. What could possess someone to kill this way? It had to have been premeditated; no one took walks out here in this area of the forest, and there was no campground for ten miles. How did you do it? Did you knock him out and drag him out here? Did you point a gun at his head and force him to take a walk with you? Did you carry the stakes and the saw out here in a bag, or did you have them already planted out here? Did Cherneau know you?

The park ranger and the crew member continued their search to the north and to the east of the scene. They were looking for the arms.

Karen stood over the body with her arms folded. She watched one of the men from forensics peel the leaves off the body one by one and put them into plastic bags. She absorbed the image she knew she couldn't forget if she tried. There would be no sleeping tonight.

Chapter Seven

Bill set the cruise control on his 2004 Chrysler Se-bring convertible at seventy-five miles an hour. He was driving east on interstate 70, moving toward Julianne, thinking about Karen. He wondered where she could have been and if she was home by now. If she was, she would be furious. She would search the house, and when she didn't find him, it would serve her right. Maybe now she'll know how it feels.

Things weren't always this way between them. They had met at Ohio University in 1995, when they were both juniors. The first time they talked was just before a class in Abnormal Psychology. Bill was taking it for his major. Karen was taking it for fun. She had thought that the course would serve as a good background if she was to become an investigator someday.

Over the course of the semester, Bill sat closer and closer to her. Two guys who sat behind her obviously admired her. They would talk and smile and then look at Karen. Bill tried to sit somewhere near her every day, and toward the end of the semester, he even got up the nerve to sit in the same row as her.

"Hi." She turned to him and he felt a sudden rush of fear. Why did he think he could do this? His mouth dried up.

"Hi," she said. She was wearing a flowered dress that she'd worn once before. She looked very pretty in it.

"I was wondering if you had the notes from last Thursday."

"I think so," she said, sounding unsure. "Just a second." She shuffled through her notebook papers. She licked a finger to get a better grasp on the papers. He looked at her face, and how her hair fell around it. She was so beautiful. She was out of his league, and he knew it.

"Ah, here it is," she said, and handed the page to him. Only one page, he thought. She must not be much for note-taking. He usually took about four pages of notes. He didn't care, though. Notes were about the last thing on his mind right now.

"Do you mind?" he asked, holding up the page, indicating that he wanted to copy it.

"No, go ahead if you can read my writing."

There was still five minutes before class. "I'm sure it's fine. Thanks." Bill began copying the notes. The two guys who sat behind Karen came in and sat down. One of them laughed. Bill pretended not to hear them. He was busy writing words, and busy concentrating on Karen. He got to a word he couldn't make out. He had wished he could think of something, anything to say just to make conversation, and this would have to be it. He turned to her and noticed that she'd been watching him.

"It's about time you made it over here," she said.

Bill was speechless.

"It's okay," she said. "I don't mind or anything. I'm going to be a cop when I get out of school, and last semester I took a class that taught us to be more observant in our daily lives. So I'm training myself to always be observant of little things, like slow advances from stalkers."

"I'm sorry...I just...I...." He tried to think of a plausible lie that might ease his embarrassment. This was a HUGE mistake, he thought. I should have just stayed in the back.

"Do you have class after this?" she asked.

"Not until three".

"Maybe we could get some lunch. We could talk about my sloppy handwriting and maybe *your* abnormal psychology." She started laughing and at first he didn't know if she was laughing at him, but then he started laughing, too. For the first time since he had come over, Bill felt at ease.

The lecture that day focused on monomaniacal madmen, from Captain Ahab to Adolf Hitler to Charles

Manson. It dealt with some of the most disturbing facets of the human psyche, but Bill was smiling through the whole thing.

He saw a state trooper in the distance and turned off the cruise until he'd slowed to the speed limit.

Cold air drifted through the convertible top where one of the latches had broken a year earlier. It was a constant annoyance, but he refused to pay the four hundred dollars it took to replace it. In the winter, he had to have the heat on high just to try to cancel it out. Instead, he was usually sweating and shivering at the same time.

He had loved the idea of buying that convertible, even though it was only a Chrysler. It wasn't a Porsche or a Mercedes. He had always dreamed of having a convertible, and as soon as he was able, he bought one.

That whole first summer, the top was down nearly all the time. He had just gotten out of college and was engaged to marry Karen in the fall. He would be starting at Clarksdale at the end of August working in his chosen field. In short, life was good.

By that third summer, however, long after the new car smell had faded, the convertible top was up almost all the time. A two minute trip to the grocery store didn't seem to warrant the trouble of taking it down anymore. Even during long trips in the warm sun he kept it up. He didn't like the sun beating down on him as he drove, and having to squint to see. Summers in Ohio seemed to be getting hotter and hotter, with many days reaching the nineties. Riding with the top down felt like you were opening an oven at high speeds. So the top stayed up.

This was not unlike his marriage. In what Karen's aunt Jean had called their 'courtship,' Karen had been very affable; she was interesting to talk to on nearly any subject, funny and definitely beautiful. Bill couldn't really understand what had made her go out with him, and he worked at the relationship with a passion that Karen had never seen. He had been funny and romantic, never broke a date, and was always a gentleman. He simply wouldn't allow there to be any reason for her to break up with him. He tried to be the 'perfect guy'. He discovered that her confidence had a way of rubbing off on him, and he fell in love with that confidence. He fell in love with her.

After the first few years of marriage, though, his confidence had eroded. The adoration she once felt for him was gone; she no longer seemed to think he was the charming, funny man she fell in love with. She had plunged into her work, and he into his, and their relationship reached a standstill. There were just the two of them—separate individuals now living separate lives. He could still feel a deep love for her, but it was buried by indifference. There was something there that felt lost; something he couldn't get back. It confused him. Was this how love ended? Did love fade? And that love he could still feel underneath everything else—was he just being sentimental?

He drove on in the night, trying to brush his thoughts of Karen away like cobwebs.

Chapter Eight

Karen came in the house and put her briefcase on the floor. She had fought sleep on the drive the whole way back from the crime scene. Although her mind was racing at one hundred miles an hour, her body had run out of gas. She couldn't remember a day as long as this in her career, or one this stressful.

She hung her overcoat on the handrail and slowly went upstairs. At least the reporters didn't give her too much grief. They had been upset that they weren't allowed closer to the scene, but seemed satisfied with the answers she had given—yes, there was a body, yes it was Mark Cherneau, and yes, they suspect foul play. They had pressed for details, and had surprisingly backed off when they didn't get them. After two weeks of not knowing anything, maybe tonight they were happy to have anything new to report.

She was exhausted. She couldn't believe it, but she actually might get some sleep tonight. If she could just go for five minutes without seeing his face. What was it about this victim that had been so horrifying to her and seemingly not to anyone else? Something about what she'd seen was strange; it struck her on an almost personal level. She hadn't known Cherneau—she only vaguely remembered his being in the news as a ballplayer. But still, something lingered.

The irony about the whole scene with the reporters was that their biggest desire was to see the body—'why can't we see the body?'—'when will we be allowed to see it?' It was Karen's *job* to look at it, and now she wished she'd never laid eyes on it.

She took off her clothes except for her underwear and found one of Bill's t-shirts on the floor. She picked it up and put it on. Wait a minute. Where was Bill, by the way? He wasn't in the bed; he wasn't anywhere upstairs.

She *did* say hello to him when she came in, didn't she? She couldn't remember. Wait. She remembered seeing the television flickering in the living room. He had probably fallen asleep down there again. This would be the third time this week. He was either asleep when she came in or too lazy to get off the couch and come upstairs and say hello. Either way, that was fine with her. She really didn't feel like telling the story of her day in full detail. For some reason, Bill kept asking questions about the case. He was almost becoming a live-in reporter. Tonight she could do without it.

She sat up in the bed and turned to the alarm clock. She had almost forgotten to set it. It read 12:47 a.m.

She would be getting up in five hours.

Chapter Nine

Bill got to the rest area at exactly midnight and didn't see Julianne. He got out of the car, went up near the restrooms and still didn't see her. Maybe she was in the ladies room.

"Mr. Summers, over here!" She was at a picnic table, sitting in the darkness. At first, he couldn't see her. She stood up and waved and he began to walk toward her. She was smiling at him, looking embarrassed. Bill had his hands in the pockets of his jacket and was caught by surprise when she came up and hugged him. He could tell she'd been sitting out in the rain.

"Thank you so much," she said. She was wearing jeans and a sweatshirt that was dark gray from the rain. The sweatshirt had grease stains on it.

"God, you're soaked," he said. Without fully realizing what he was doing, he put his arm around her as they walked back to his car. "Are you all right? Aren't you cold? You know you could've waited inside."

"I know. I was fine out where I was. I like the rain sometimes. It just makes me feel... better, you know? Anyway, I didn't want to miss you. I'm so thankful you're here." He opened the car door for her and then hurried to his side of the car. When he got there, she had already unlocked it for him.

As they got on the highway, Bill looked at her and smiled. He thought he would feel uncomfortable with her in his car, but he wasn't. He was simply happy that he could help her and that she had thought to call him in a crisis. He felt a little guilty; he wondered if he would have responded so quickly if she weren't so beautiful. Over the years of helping battered women, he had grown to dislike men in general— all the ones he ever heard about were slime. They beat and raped their wives and girlfriends; some even tried to kill them.

Bill's suspect motives now made him feel a little like slime himself.

"So tell me again why you were sitting in the rain?" He was unable to think of anything else to say.

"After I talked to you, I was sitting on those benches in front of the bathrooms. It was under the roof, so I was out of the rain at least, and I could still look for you. But I was very cold, because I only had on a t-shirt. So I was sitting there with my arms folded, shivering probably, when this big burly guy comes up to me and says, 'You all right, darlin'? You look mighty cold. You run away or something?" She was making her voice deep trying to imitate the man, and she laughed. So did Bill.

"Do I look like I'm seventeen or something? Do I look like some teen runaway?"

"I guess you could pass for seventeen, but I don't think so. Sounds like a pickup line to me."

"The guy seemed nice enough anyway. I told him I was waiting for a ride. He said he could take me where I wanted to go. I said 'no thank you' to the guy and then he took off his sweatshirt and told me to put it on. He told me to wait for him, because he had to go to the bathroom, and that when he came out, we would go wherever I wanted to go. He winked at me and then went into the men's room.

"Well, there was no way I was going with this guy, but at the same time, I was cold. So after he went in, I hid behind a tree in the picnic area. When he came out a few minutes later, he looked around for me a little, but then he left. He didn't seem upset. I hope he didn't mind losing his shirt, but I think I needed it more than he did. Besides, it was a little small for him." She grabbed the neck of the shirt and pulled it up to her nose. "Smells, though. I couldn't tell when I was outside as much, but now you can really tell."

"Yeah, you sure can," Bill said, smiling. "Probably doesn't help that it's wet, either. You're probably still cold, aren't you? You're soaked."

"Lot better now, though. Thanks again for coming to get me."

"Believe me, it's no problem. You'd probably get dry faster if you took off Burly Man's sweatshirt, though." He couldn't believe what he just said. She's in your car five minutes and you're asking her to take off her clothes, he thought.

"I...don't think I should."

"That's fine," he said. He felt he'd offended her.

She paused for a minute. "It's just that it's a white t-shirt that I'm wearing underneath this. You know, I was riding along with Dale and sometimes I just wear one of his t-shirts. I didn't expect anything like this to happen. Plus, I'm not wearing a bra. I don't really have much of a chest, so a lot of times I just don't bother. I'm so embarrassed."

Bill felt himself blushing. He kept his eyes on the road. "It's fine." He looked in the back seat. There was a lot of junk back there—cups, junk mail, a couple books, a couple CDs and a flannel shirt. He grabbed the shirt. He noticed Julianne get a chill. "Here, I know you're cold and you shouldn't be wearing wet clothes." He was trying to convince himself as much as he was trying to convince her. He gave her the shirt. "After the guy left, why didn't you go back to the bench that was sheltered?"

She laid the shirt across her legs. She put her hands on her shoulders and began to take off the sweatshirt. "I guess I was afraid of other guys coming up to me and doing the same thing. Before this guy gave me the shirt, two other guys had smiled at me and said 'hi.'

Bill wasn't surprised. She had been putting on a one-woman wet t-shirt contest back there. Funny thing was, Bill didn't even think she had realized she was doing it.

She pulled up on the shoulders of the sweatshirt and when her head was in the shirt, Bill looked at her. The sweatshirt was pulling up the t-shirt underneath, exposing her bare skin. He checked the road and looked back at Julianne. The t-shirt was up over her ribs as she struggled with the sweatshirt. "Man, this shirt does stink!" She said from inside the shirt. Then it was off and he watched the t-shirt fall back around her.

Bill felt the guilt again. She has no one to count on, including you, he told himself. You just want her like every other guy. Like every other slime.

"Mr. Summers?"

"You can call me Bill, you know. It's not like I'm the school principal or anything."

"Okay...Bill. I said I was just kidding. It was just a joke."

"What was just a joke?"

"I said that the rain had stopped and we should put the top down. I was just kidding." She put on his shirt. "That's much better, thank you."

Bill drove on, not speaking, paralyzed by the differences between his personal and professional feelings.

"So," she said, "is it fun having a convertible? I've always wanted one."

Chapter Ten

Although her mind was incessantly turning, Karen was exhausted. She felt drained like never before.

She took a Benadryl to help with her allergies, which were bad this time of year, and made worse by where she'd just been. It would also help her sleep. Taking a Benadryl always knocked her out, and that was what she was hoping for.

After half an hour of lying in bed, staring at the ceiling and seeing Mark Cherneau staring back at her, Karen finally felt herself caving in. She would give up for now. The drug took its effect, and she drifted to sleep.

Karen was eight again, playing in the yard with Lucky. She would toss the big orange ball to him, and he would try to catch it in his mouth, but it was too big. Little Karen thought it was funny, because Lucky would try anyway, so she kept throwing it to him.

The sun was beating down on the backyard, which was surrounded by pines. There were also two cherry trees that the birds were always picking at, and in the back corner of the yard was a huge oak, at least fifty feet tall—bigger than any other tree in the neighborhood. In fact, it was bigger than any of the buildings in town.

Karen was wearing her special Sunday church dress, the sunflower one that made her feel pretty. She always made sure to play with Lucky a little before they had to go.

Her father came to the back door and rapped it from the inside.

"Karen, it's time to go!" and then disappeared into the house again. It was the third time he'd called, which meant it really was time to go. She turned back to Lucky, who was waiting for her to throw the ball again. She held the ball high and hit it like a volleyball. It eclipsed the

*sun for a moment before the brightness hurt her eyes.
Never look at the light, she could hear her mother saying.
The ball hit the grass and bounced up. Lucky ran after it
and batted it with his front paws. It rolled down closer to
the large oak.*

*Karen stood frozen. She turned back and there
was no sound coming from the house. The dog stood
looking at Karen. She took three steps toward the tree.
Then she heard something behind her; it was a high-
pitched noise.*

*She faced away from the tree and looked around
the house to the front yard. Her parents' car appeared
driving very slowly up the hill to the main road that went
into town.*

*It was difficult for Karen to make it out, because
the windows were starting to fog up, but she could see
her father in the car behind the wheel. His head was
bleeding and she could see him saying her name,
screaming her name, over and over, but she couldn't
hear him.*

*She hadn't seen it at first, but now she could also
see her mother, sitting in the back seat directly behind
Karen's father. She was motionless, and stared straight
ahead the whole time. Her face showed no emotion, no
sign of the danger that her father seemed to be aware of.
Her mother's hair was wet, and because it was normally
dark brown, Karen couldn't tell if it was blood or not.*

*The car got to the top of the hill and turned to-
ward town. Karen slowly turned back to the tree. The sun
had become obscured by clouds, and the wind was
beginning to pick up. The branches at the top swayed
back and forth. Lucky barked at them.*

*Karen approached the ball slowly, and as she bent
to pick it up, she stopped. The top two branches were
waving at her, bending towards her, reaching,
reaching—*

*There was a flash of light and she was now in
Wayne National Forest, standing above Mark Cherneau's
body. No one else was there. She was the age she was
now, wearing a white slip without shoes. She stood there,*

perfectly still, her legs on either side of his waist. His dead eyes turned to her, and the branches he had for arms reached up for her. She felt one scrape against her leg. It moved up her slip and scratched at her thigh.

Karen tried to scream, but she was unable to exhale. The air in her lungs had turned stale, and was trapped inside her. She felt her lungs burning, suffocating, desperately needing oxygen.

The air was as dead as the man lying beneath her.

Chapter Eleven

Dale Parker took out the key to *his* house and put it in *his* lock on *his* door. Inside, he would get a beer out of *his* refrigerator and sit in *his* chair and watch *his* TV.

That crazy bitch.

After the kind of day he'd had, too. You drive all the way to fucking Wheeling, with a deal already made, and they say there ain't no deal. Sure, they bought a hundred bucks worth—gas money was what that was. "Here's something so you're not sorry you came," they had said. Like hell. You tell somebody you want all of it, all fourteen hundred bucks worth, and then you drop a single 'c' note? No.

Fuck that.

And then on the way back, Julianne talking up a storm like she's on some fucking field trip in the seventh grade.

It wasn't true, what she said, was it? He never heard nothing about people being legally married after they live together for so long. That was bullshit, right?

And her talking about it like it's a good thing, like they'd be happier. Maybe she's thinking I'm gonna treat her like some fucking queen now. Well, she's wrong. Ain't no way some little twenty-five year old Jesus freak is gonna think she owns half of my stuff. No way she's getting half my stuff, I don't care how hot she is.

No.

He should have dumped her at a rest stop a long time ago.

Dale gave up on the stupid TV, got another beer and went downstairs. When he got angry or worried (not that he would be worried about *that* crazy bitch), he went downstairs. He could throw himself into his work and not be concerned with anything else, not even think of anything else. It was like therapy. Not that he needed therapy. She did, not him. He would become trance-like and work down there for hours and hours, not sensing that any time had passed.

This was his work, his *true* work, and he knew it. It wasn't some bullshit factory that for forty hours every week tried to suck the life out of him.

This was where his talent was.

This was something he loved.

Chapter Twelve

"So, why don't you tell me your life story?" Bill said, as they passed a sign that read 'Zanesville 25."

"You're always on the clock, aren't you?"

"Just making conversation. I'm used to asking these type of questions."

"So is this like, off the record?"

"I'm not a cop or anything, but yeah, if you want to look at it that way."

She looked out at the open fields passing by. "Let me see...I don't know, what do you want me to say?"

"I don't know. I just want to find out what would make a nice girl like you end up with someone like Dale."

"You don't even know Dale."

"I know what he does. I know how he treats you. I have to ask myself why you would stay with him; I mean, maybe something happened to you when you were young."

"My childhood was just as happy as anyone else's; it doesn't have anything to do with Dale."

"Really?"

"Yeah," she said defiantly. "I met Dale at a bar one night and we started talking. We talked for a long time. He didn't even try anything that night when he took me home. He was a gentleman that first night, and I really respected that. A couple nights later, we went out."

"And how did that go?"

"We went back to his place and we had sex. But it was more than that. It wasn't like the type of sex we have nowadays, hard and fast. No, that first time, he was so gentle. It almost seemed like he was afraid. Or nervous or something. It was almost like he worshipped me. That first time is still probably the best time we ever had. At least for me, anyway.

"I felt a little guilty after we did it, though," she said. "I had just been dumped by my boyfriend, who never really thought we were boyfriend and girlfriend, but we were. At least I thought so. That was my senior year of high school—four years ago. He was the first guy I ever loved. With Dale, it may not have been love at the start, but that's what it became. He treated me special; it wasn't until we were together for a while, I'd say a year or more, when he first hit me. I knew I shouldn't have stayed with him, that I should have left him right then and there, but by then I was...where I was. You know what I mean?"

"Tell me about the first time he hit you."

"We had just had sex, and I wasn't really into it. He'd been out that night and came home drunk. He tried to force himself on me, and I acted like he was just kidding around, you know, to get him to stop. He asked me if I thought he was funny and I said no. He kept asking me over and over, and I kept saying, 'No, no!' He grabbed both my arms and took me into the bedroom. He made me lay on the bed, face down, and put my hands up over my head. Then he pulled down my shorts and underwear. I didn't know what he was doing; I thought maybe I should just let him...f.u.c.k. me, like he said he did to girls who laughed at him. I thought maybe he was just really horny, and he would get it out of his system or whatever, and then everything would be back to normal. We'd had sex a bunch of times before this, what's once more? No big deal right? He leaves, then comes back in, breathing heavy. I couldn't see what he was doing, and then he starts smacking my butt with something. It really stung; my eyes watered up every time he'd hit me. And then, after he tried to put his thing in there and just made a mess on me, I turned over and saw what he'd been hitting me with. It was a flyswatter. Sometimes when he gets angry with me, he says he's gonna go get the flyswatter."

"Damn it, Julianne! You let him do that and then you let him rape you? For God's sake, why do you stay with him?

"That was the only time anything like that's happened. He's never forced himself on me since. And he only *tried* to rape me. Like I said, he made a mess on me and then he was done."

"He still hits you though."

"Not with the flyswatter. There's one thing that's good about it. There's always a bright side to everything. He could hit me much more often and much worse, but he doesn't."

"I'm sorry, Julianne, but that isn't a bright side. The fact is that he hurts you. He shouldn't be hurting you in any way, and I think you should leave him."

"I already told you; I love him despite his faults. I have to. That's the way I am. Things are okay between us ninety percent of the time, and because of the other ten percent, you want me to walk out on him? I just can't do it. Plus, where would I go?"

"Well, I certainly don't want you going back there tonight. I think you should go somewhere and consider the possibilities. Do you have any cash on you?"

"Why?"

"I'll take you to a motel, and then come get you in the morning."

"That's not necessary. He probably won't even be back tonight. Nights when he's like this he takes off and usually doesn't come back for a day or two. I'll be fine if you take me home."

Julianne directed Bill to the house that was out in the country. There was a forest beyond the back yard, and a big front yard. It was a bland little white house, one story with crimson shutters providing the only bit of color.

"There it is," she said. Bill saw an old truck that didn't look like it actually ran parked in the driveway. He also noticed the living room light on.

"The light's on—do you think he's here?"

"Yeah, he's here," she said, sounding a little disappointed. "That's his truck in the driveway. I was hoping to have the house to myself tonight."

Bill didn't pull in the driveway. He kept driving. He knew he should have let her go back to her life, but he couldn't. He decided that she would never have to deal with Dale again.

Chapter Thirteen

"Where are we going?" Julianne asked.

"I'm sorry Julianne, but I just can't let you do this. You have to let me help you. I'm going to take you to the Holiday Inn up the road. I'll come back in the morning to pick you up."

"Look, Mr. Summers, I really appreciate you trying to protect me and all, but I have to go back there sometime, and I don't see any point in spending money on a room when we know that tomorrow night I'll be going home. Dale might hit me every now and then, but I ain't scared of him. I'm not."

Bill thought about this. He didn't have any other way to explain it but to tell her the truth. He often felt the need and desire to get involved in the lives of the women who came to Clarksdale. Growing up in a home where his father abused his mother, and his mother telling Bill that she 'bruised easily' gave him a deep passion for his work. Bill could never let go of the rage he felt for his father, but every time he helped an abused woman, that rage would be momentarily suppressed. This desire, this need, to get involved was magnified by the almost overwhelming affection he felt for Julianne.

"Julianne, let me try to explain something to you. I see a lot of girls who are in your situation, some worse, and every time I talk with them, it hurts me to hear about the abuse that goes on in their lives. It hurts. Believe me, I treat all my cases with sensitivity and compassion. I want to help every single victim who comes through my door."

"And now you're helping me, and I thank you, but you don't have to. You've already done so much to help me."

"No, but it's more than that. What I'm trying to say is that...you're special to me." Bill started to feel uneasy.

"I don't know if it's just that I have seen so much of this abuse lately that I'm not going to stand by anymore and let it happen, or just a professional lapse on my part—"

"What are you trying to say, Mr. Summers? I'm not following you."

Bill knew he was rambling. Just come out with it, he thought. "Here's the thing, Julianne. Ever since you first came into my office, I've had a certain...affection for you." His hands were beginning to sweat as he grasped the steering wheel. "You such a smart and attractive woman and, more than any other woman, the thought of you getting hit by some stupid, ignorant jerk really gets under my skin. I don't think I can tolerate him doing you harm. I can barely tolerate hearing you talk about it."

"Oh," she said. "I don't know what to say."

"You don't have to say anything. I know that I shouldn't have said that; you just needed a ride home tonight and I had to go and complicate everything by dropping this on you. I'm sorry and it won't happen again."

Julianne turned to face him. She put a hand on Bill's forearm. "No, listen," she said, her voice barely above a whisper. "It's okay. It's nice to know that someone really does care, that someone's there when I need them. You don't know how long it's been since I had anyone I could depend on."

"Next week I'll assign you to someone else at Clarksdale. I'm afraid my advice would be biased. You don't need this on top of everything else that's happened."

"No way. *You* are my therapist, and there's no way I would trade that. It's good to know that you're also my friend."

They pulled into the parking lot of the Holiday Inn ten miles north of Logan. There were only a few cars strewn about.

"The last thing I wanted to do was to make you uncomfortable. I just wanted you to understand that my reasons for bringing you here extend beyond my professional duties."

At the front desk of the hotel was a man sitting on a bar stool watching a baseball game on a small television.

"Help you folks?" He asked without taking his eyes off the game.

Julianne had told Bill to do the talking. "Yeah, she needs a room," he said. Bill got out his wallet.

The man looked up from the game. "Just her?"

Bill liked the feeling of someone thinking he and Julianne were together. "Yeah, just her. How much?"

"Okay, single room, we have one queen size or two full. Your choice."

Bill looked at her. "Whatever," she said to Bill, looking unsure whether she should be doing this.

"Queen," he said.

"Smoking or non?"

"Non," Bill said instinctively, and then remembered the room wasn't his. "I'm sorry. Do you smoke?" She shook her head.

"Non," he said to the man.

After entering her information, the man said, "that'll be $46.94."

Julianne got into her purse and pulled out a ten dollar bill. It's all she had, she told Bill. He told her it had been his idea and he would pay. She let him.

"You gonna be all right?" he asked as they drove around back.

"Sure, I'll be okay," she said, "but I still say you don't have to do this."

"I'm glad to do it. This is probably the extent of how much I want to get involved here, short of going over and having a talk with Dale."

"Oh, you don't want to do that," she said with a laugh, "he'd kick the shit out of you."

"No, I wouldn't want that to happen," he said, smiling uneasily.

They pulled up to the room. "Well, this is it," he said.

After a long pause, she said, "Yep. This is it. You want to come in? It's more your room than mine, you know."

"No, no," he said slowly. "That's not why I did this, Julianne."

"Okay, I know. And thank you." She extended her hand to him, and he shook it. They both smiled.

"I'll see you in the morning," he said.

"Okay."

Bill was still smiling as he drove away. He had a good feeling in his chest. He put the convertible top down and turned up the radio louder than he had in years. He felt no guilt about what he'd just done, as he'd expected he would—nothing but the feeling that comes from genuinely helping someone in need.

This is what it was all about.

Chapter Fourteen

Julianne left the light off after she got into the room and put her purse on the table. She sat on the edge of the bed, staring straight ahead into the darkness. She could barely make out the TV and dresser in front of her at first. She stayed there as her eyes adjusted. She couldn't think of the last time she had been in a hotel room as nice as this. In fact, she could hardly remember the last time she'd been in *any* hotel room. She recognized the smell, though. It was a smell she liked, and she didn't think you could get that smell anywhere else. It was a good smell.

It was a clean smell.

As her eyes continued to focus, Julianne sat up straight on the bed, and then gasped. Someone was looking right at her! She stood up and went for the light, and out of the corner of her eye, she noticed the figure did exactly what she did.

She had been looking in the mirror.

She laughed at herself. She wasn't surprised she was a bit paranoid; this was a strange place, and she was alone. It was something she wasn't used to. There had always been a man around.

She took off her clothes and got into bed, loving the feeling of the cool sheets on her bare skin. The comforter and blanket were heavier than the ones she had at home. Plus, they didn't have air conditioning at home, and this time of year, about all you could stand was a sheet. This room was cool, though, and she went over to the air conditioner and set it even cooler.

She made sure the door's locks were fastened, and went into the bathroom. When she turned on the light, she was surprised at how big the room was. This bathroom was actually a *room*, not the size of a closet, like the one at home.

She was happy to see the small bottle of bubble bath on the sink. She loved taking bubble baths, even though she hardly ever got to take them. Dale didn't like her just sitting in the tub doing nothing. He told her when she first came to live with him to "get in, get clean, and get the fuck out."

Julianne shut the door to the bathroom and turned on the shower.

She sat on the toilet and rested her head on her hands. She laughed, and the sound of it made her feel lonely. Maybe Bill was right, she thought. Maybe I should think of leaving Dale. Bill had said a lot of nice things about her, like saying that she was smart, and maybe she should believe him. She didn't know, though. Maybe he just said that because he wanted to have sex with her. That was all boys ever wanted.

And then she'd gone and thrown herself at him like a whore. You ought to be ashamed of yourself, she thought.

She spread a towel on the floor and lay down. After a while she would take that bubble bath, but for now she would just lie here.

She watched the steam roll over the shower curtain and fill the upper half of the room, fogging up the mirror. She was glad now that he had brought her here; she did need some time to think. Was Dale going to get any better, or was he getting worse? He had always been the same old Dale; she didn't think he was going to get better or worse. Of course, nothing's really happened that would make him change. He's had the same job, the same house, the same truck as long as she'd known him. No, what Dale needed was something positive to happen in his life. But what?

She changed the water from the shower to the faucet, got the bubble bath from the sink and poured all of the little bottle in the tub. She put her hand in the water and stirred it around.

She got in the hot water and let out a little groan. She loved the water. She'd always loved the water—from the swimming hole as a kid, where she would go with her sister, to bubble baths, to the soothing sound of the shower, even rainy days. Rain covered the world, quieted the world; the clouds were like a blanket over everyone. She couldn't really put her finger on it, but there was something about water she loved, that had always made her feel good.

It made her feel clean. It made her feel pure, and purity was what she wanted more than anything.

Chapter Fifteen

Karen put her briefcase on the table in the hall behind the conference room at the police station. Tom was eating a bagel and Jared Wilson was talking to some media people nearby.

"Hey, got another one of those?" she said to Tom.

"As a matter of fact, I do," he said and handed her a bagel. "So, boss, what are we going to tell these people?" he said.

"What can we tell 'em? We don't know anything. Any word from the coroner yet?"

"He called about twenty minutes ago. He said they're doing the autopsy at eleven. Said they'd be done by one if we wanted to stop by."

"Yeah, just what I need to see after lunch. Okay, Tom, give him a call back and tell him we'll be there. As far as what we tell *them*," she said, nodding towards the press in the next room, "we tell them what we always tell them—'it's the beginning of the investigation, we're leaving our doors open.' If they ask, and they will, we don't have any particular suspects."

"Are we withholding anything?"

"The stakes in the pant legs. The arms we can talk about. Did you stay after I left last night?"

"Yeah," he said. "I was one of the last to leave. It was like a Stephen King novel out there."

"Did they find the arms?"

"Nope. I stayed with a couple of the crew guys after everybody left, but we didn't find anything."

"Jesus, Tom, how late were you there?"

"Three-thirty. I knew I wouldn't get any sleep anyway."

"Well, at least you could try! From now on, no putting in longer days than the lead investigator, got it?"

"Got it, boss. So, did you get any rest?"

"Yeah, I was exhausted. Took a Benadryl. That's probably why I feel like shit now."

Tom got up and threw the little paper plate and Styrofoam cup away. "I was too afraid to sleep. Thought I might see the boogeyman." He checked his watch. "See you out there; we're on in about ten minutes."

"Okay."

Karen hadn't remembered until Tom mentioned the boogeyman. She'd had the dream again. Since her parents had died in an auto accident when she was 12, Karen had been having the same dream. The trees had arms and her parents slowly going up the hill to their death. Those first few years it came quite frequently, once or twice a month. She would wake up sweating and crying for a mother who would never come.

By the time she was in college, she only had it once or twice a year. She would have it when she was under a lot of stress. Sometimes during finals week, which was probably the worst possible time. She hadn't had the dream for two years until last night. Was Cherneau in the dream? She seemed to think he was. No wonder, considering the way he'd been killed.

She went to face the media knowing that Mark Cherneau was firmly lodged in her subconscious.

Chapter Sixteen

Bill was able to take Julianne home without anyone noticing because Dale had already left for work.
They didn't say much on the way, just Bill asking if she
was okay and her thanking him again.

He went to work and tried not to think of her,
which was difficult because it was a slow morning. He
only had two appointments scheduled, and one of them
didn't show.

He decided to take an early lunch at 11:30. He
went across the street to the sandwich shop and got his
lunch to go. He bought a newspaper, folded it under his
arm, and went back to the office.

He put the bag on the desk, along with the drink.
He let the newspaper fall to the desk, and it was then he
saw the headline: "Cherneau Found Slain." Underneath
the headline it read: *Fifteen Day Search Ends In
Tragedy.*"

Bill read the whole article before he ate his sandwich. The story didn't give any details, simply noting that
the body was found the night before and that there
would be a small press conference this morning. It was a
big headline, but there were only a couple paragraphs on
the front page. On the continuation on page 8, there was
only one additional paragraph.

Bill turned back to the front page and looked at
the picture of a man named Ron Fulson, the man who
found the body and Jared Wilson, Chief of Police for
Muskingum County. They were at the site, and there
were many people in the background, mostly people
from the search crew. Bill looked closely, but he couldn't
see Karen in the crowd.

As he took a bite of his sandwich, there was a
knock on the door. He tried to say "come in" but his

mouth was full. Nothing happened, and there was another knock, this time more forceful.

"Come in," he said, wiping his mouth with a napkin.

The door opened. "Bill, are you in here?"

"Hey! How are you?" He stood up, walked around the desk and gave the woman a quick hug.

"I'm good, how are you?"

"I'm just fine, have a seat," he said. The last time he had seen Sandy Oliver was almost six months ago when she moved to Columbus. She had come in with very little self-esteem at first, and after a few sessions, he knew she had a lot of potential. Even though she had worked at the IGA as a checkout girl and was in an abusive relationship, she was very bright. He had been glad to hear that she'd moved to the city, because there were so many more opportunities there. Columbus was a good step in reaching her potential.

"You got your hair cut," he said.

"Yeah, 'chopped' is more like it. Part of the new me."

"It's classy," he said. "So tell me about the 'new you.'"

"I'm studying to be a paralegal."

"A legal secretary."

"We prefer to be known as 'paralegals', thank you very much."

"Excuse me, 'paralegal.'"

"That's better." They smiled at each other. Bill was so proud of her and what she'd accomplished in the last year. A year ago, she was a mess—mentally, physically, and emotionally. She had reached a breaking point on a night last June, when she had run away from her husband, Phil. The people from the local hospital had taken her to Clarksdale at three in the morning. When someone answered, she had said, "I can't go home—he wants to kill me."

This was the reason Clarksdale was there, and of course they took her in. The next day, she had two black eyes, bruises on her back and on her legs, a cut on her forehead where he'd hit her with a bottle, and a broken right pinkie finger. She said that she had punched him in the face, and it had probably hurt her more than it had hurt "his thick skull."

"So what else are you doing—are you working somewhere?"

"I'm at a law firm, just doing odds and ends. I deliver the mail, work in the copy room, and I also do some secretarial work, typing up depositions. Whatever I can."

"'Secretarial work?' Don't you mean 'administrative assistant' work?"

"No," she smiled, "you can call me a secretary for now. But when I get my degree, it's 'Paralegal', got it?"

"Sounds great, Sandy. I'm thrilled to see you doing so well."

"Thanks. I owe a lot to you for that. You gave me the strength and courage I needed."

"Don't tell me you came all the way from Columbus to tell me this," he said, although it would have made him happy if she had.

Sandy's demeanor changed. She now looked quite serious. "No, it's actually because of these." She pulled two letters out of her purse.

"What are those?"

"Letters from Phil."

"God, when did you get those?"

"I got the first one about six weeks ago. Then a couple weeks ago I got this one. He mailed them to my mother since he doesn't know where I am. He is practically closer to my mother than I am, and he knew that if he sent them there, I'd get them. In the first one, he said he wouldn't write again, and in it he said he'd changed, that he still loved me, and that everything would be different this time."

"You don't believe this do you? Tell me you're not considering this."

"Are you kidding? Hell no, I don't believe him. Maybe he has changed a little, but he's always, *always* going to be the guy who almost killed me. No, if he turned into Prince Charming *and* won the lottery I still wouldn't go back with him.

Bill was glad to hear that. She was a strong, independent woman now, and it was good to know he'd had something to do with that.

"So, what are you going to do?"

"That's why I'm here. I'm not exactly sure what to make of this one," she said, holding up the second letter. "The first one's pretty normal, but this one's just weird."

"Is it a threat? Do you think he might come after you?"

"I'm not worried about that. I changed my name—now it's Sandy Kelley."

"'Sandy Kelly' what?"

"Just 'Sandy Kelley.' My middle name is now my last name. I wanted to use my maiden name, but he could find me just as easily that way. And just to be safe I added an extra 'e' in the name. Now it's K-E-L-L-*E*-Y."

"So you don't think he'll be able to find you? I mean, this isn't a game of hide and seek we're talking about here."

"He'll never find me. In the Columbus phone book, there are two *Sandy Oliver*s, four *S Oliver*s, and two *S Mullen*s, my maiden name. For one thing, he's too lazy, and another, he's stupid. He would look up the two *Sandy Oliver*s and then quit, believe me." She put the letters on the desk. Bill looked at them and then at Sandy before picking them up. "I want you to read them," she said.

"Do you think this is my business? Don't you think you should show them to the police?"

"I can't even tell if these are *threats*, Bill. That's the thing about them. Like I said, the first one is pretty normal, but the second sounds like he's on edge. I'd like for you to take a look and give me your opinion. You can call, e-mail, or fax me." She handed him a card. "Here's my contact info."

"You're going to make a great paralegal. I'll be in touch in a few days."

They shook hands. "Thanks, Bill. I really appreciate this."

As he watched her walk away, Bill thought of the letters she'd entrusted him with, and how she couldn't tell if they were threatening or not. It was so curious. The anger welled in him. He didn't care how 'vague' these letters were; he knew what Phil Oliver had done to her. As far as Bill was concerned, any letter from him was a threat.

Chapter Seventeen

After having easily digestible salads for lunch, Karen and Tom got to the county morgue a little after one. An assistant was finishing up the Y-shaped stitches in the victim that started at the pubic hair, went up the stomach, and branched out at the chest, to each shoulder.

"Hey, Nicky, where's your boss?" Karen asked.

"In his office, recording his notes," he said, looking at Karen, still suturing.

"Don't you have to watch what you're doing?" Tom asked.

Nicky stopped. "He ain't gettin' no sicker," he said to Tom, smiling. "I know—old joke. Still funny, though. I could do this is my sleep. Almost have on some nights when I work third shift."

Karen and Tom walked over to Dr. Fred Barnes' office. They looked through the window and saw him scribbling away on a legal pad. His desk was a mess, and he bore a slight resemblance to Albert Einstein. He stopped his tape recorder and rewound the tape for a second, hit play, and began scribbling again. To Karen, he always put a great deal of energy into his work, and seemed like a mad scientist on the verge of discovering something great. Finally, Karen knocked on the door. He motioned them in.

"Ah, yes, Detectives Summers and Flanagan. Come, sit down." They did. "Guess what? Mr. Cherneau died of loss of blood. Shocker, isn't it?"

"Speaking of shock, had he gone into it, from what you could tell? You said something like that to me at the scene."

"Yes, there was also that, but it certainly wasn't the cause of death. This man lost over half his blood; Made Nicky's job a little easier, too. He didn't have as much to drain."

"What about the murder weapon?" She asked.

"It's definitely something with teeth."

"What do you mean?"

"Like I suspected, the arms weren't hacked off, or sliced off. They were *sawn* off. That's why you have the jagged skin around the shoulders. We found traces of rust in one of the shoulder sockets."

"So what we're looking for is—"

"An old saw, I'd say. The kind you can run down to Sears and get for $5.99. The kind that is in just about every garage in the county. Sorry, but unless this maniac is so stupid as to not clean up the saw, I don't think you folks are going to have a weapon on this one."

Karen sighed. This was what she'd been afraid of.

"Find anything else?"

"He had a kidney stone forming, if that's what you mean. Also, there was a build-up of fluid in his lungs. Looks like he might have had pneumonia coming on." He looked out at Nicky, who was covering up the victim.

"A lot of fluid? Could someone have tried to drown him, and then had a better idea?"

"No, no. Not that much fluid. Also, I checked his records, and there were no bronchial problems in his past. This was probably just mild pneumonia."

"Did you take a sample of the fluid?"

"Sure, we always take samples. We'll run the usual tests; they'll be done in a couple days."

"Could it have just been the rain?" Tom asked. "It was raining heavily that night."

"No, this fluid was there before he died. Unless a body is submerged in water, the windpipe contracts upon death, and nothing gets in there. You should have seen Nicky there on his first corpse five years ago. When we rolled it on its side, and air came out, it sounded like the body was exhaling. I had to let Nicky go home to change his underwear," he said, laughing and watching Nicky through the glass. "We'll do the tests, but to me it just looks like your common pneumonia. The start of it at least. Aside from the obvious cause of death, there seemed to be nothing too out of the ordinary. That was until half an hour ago, when the tox screen came back."

"What'd it show?"

"Diphenhydramine. A lot of it."

"And that is?"

"An antihistamine. Commonly known as Benadryl. He could have been taking it for the cough he no doubt had from the pneumonia. If he did, though, he sure didn't read the label."

"Why's that?"

"First of all, it says to not take with alcohol. And there was quite a bit of alcohol in his system. He was an alcoholic by the looks of his liver. Benadryl is a strong sedative, and combining it with a depressant is dangerous. And secondly, we estimate there was over three hundred milligrams in his bloodstream. That's six times the suggested dosage. Even one dose can put you out for the night and make you feel tired the next day."

"Tell me about it," Karen said. "So when would you say he took them?"

"I'd say just about an hour before he died. The drug takes about a half an hour to take effect, to be absorbed into the bloodstream. The effects of the drug were in their first stages, according to the tox screen."

"An hour before he died, huh? Tell me, Fred, if I wanted to drug somebody so that they couldn't put up a fight, enough so that I could stash him in my car, take him up to the woods and cut his arms off, would twelve benadryls and some beer be enough to do it?"

"Oh, definitely. The dozen benadryls alone would be enough to do it. The beer would just be a bonus."

Chapter Eighteen

Later that night, after Karen had gone to bed, after the usual small talk that made no mention of Mark Cherneau, Bill got out the letters Phil Oliver had sent to Sandy. He went into the den and sat in the leather chair where he did most of his reading.

Dear Sandy,

Hi. How are you doing. I've been doing o.k. but I miss you something awful. It's not the same without you here around. I wanted to write to you to tell you that I've changed my ways. I ain't gonna hit you no more. I been thinkin a lot since you left, and I know that what I done was wrong, and I'm sorry. Hank says that I been expressin myself phisicly, you know, like with my fists. I'm sorry to say he's probably right. He says I should use my mind instead. Says I shoud know better, and he's right about that too. I don't know what I can say to convince you, other than telling you that I never been as serious about anything as I am about this. I know it's easy to remember the bad things I done, and it's probably just as easy to forget all the good things. I guess that's another reason why I'm writing to you. We had so many good times, like that time we went to Niagra Falls. You remember how we just took off one day? How about that time we went to Cedar Point and I got sick on that roller coaster. You

thought that was pretty funny, even though
I wasn't too happy about it. I can laugh
about it now, though. And then there were
all those times we went camping. You know
how much we both loved camping, and I
don't know about you, but I miss it. I'd
like to go, but it wouldn't be the same
without you. Nothing is the same without
you. Please just give it some thought, and
remember that I love you. I won't write to
you again.

                                        Phil

Bill thought about Phil, and wondered what kind
of person he was. He couldn't remember asking Sandy if
he'd graduated high school. It seemed he may not have
even gotten to high school. The letter he'd just read
seemed honest and heartfelt, but wife beaters, he had
found out, made pretty convincing liars.

Bill took a sip of decaf. He put the first letter down
and turned his attention to the second letter:

Dear Sandy,

        I know I said I'd only write to you
one time, but what the hell. I'm bored. I
need somebody to talk to an there ain't no
body around. Have you given any thought to
what I wrote you about last time? Are the
doves flying in your head? I got to tell
you, lately I got nothing but crows
picking at my brain. There's this and
there's that, a rat a tat tat. We go back
so long, you and me. You think you could
ever get rid of me? You know I'll always
be there, in your mind, in your memories,

in your brain, the crow among the doves. I'm that one that you can't never shed, as long as you live. I remember when I was in the fourth grade, and we went on a field trip to a space museum. This one girl, I can't remember her name, she sat next to me during the planetarium show. And there was this one kid, his name was Carl Young, and he liked her. Now I didn't even know this girl, other than she went to our school. I sure as hell wasn't after her, I know that much. But still. He got real pissed at me and the next day, during recess, he came up to me and hit me. He hit me on the arm, which was strange, but it hurt like hell anyway. My arm tingled for about an hour. I still got this red mark on my arm to this day. It's like a tattoo or something. Anyway, my point is that I don't remember that girls name, but I sure as hell remember Carl Young. That's what I'm talking about, is all. Much as you try, you ain't never gonna forget me. Oh come all ye faithful, for richer for poorer, for better or worse.

TILL DEATH DO US PART.
You do remember, don't you?

Your loving husband.

Bill was unsettled by this letter. Phil Oliver was definitely losing it. Did he really want to get involved, though?

Chapter Nineteen

Dale woke up in his workshop with a new blade in his lap and a hangover. He had stayed up until three in the morning, measuring, calibrating and sharpening. He would put this one in the ebony handle that he'd made last year. He was saving it for a blade that was worthy. So many of those damn Japanese blades had nice pretty handles and a piece of shit for a blade.

This one, though, he was really proud of. He didn't usually make nine inch blades; he usually stuck to four and five inches. That length was short enough to be really strong and long enough to do some real damage—whatever kind of damage you were into.

When he picked out the piece of metal at the shop, he knew it was special. There was something about it—the feel, the look, the density of the metal—he knew he had a winner. He had waited until the right time to forge it, though. The right time had been last night.

He always worked better when he was angry. Angry at someone, something, it didn't matter. This time it had been two things. Those bastards in Wheeling who weren't buying and Julianne, who wasn't shutting up about it. When he was angry, he worked aggressively with the hunk of metal until it became a work of art. Dale believed the blade could reflect the mood of the person who made it. The best blades were made with precision care and a little bit of aggression. He looked at the blade next to his right hand. It had turned out perfectly.

The workshop now had ninety-five knives hanging from magnetic strips on the walls. They were all his. Having so many knives on his wall was not, however, something to be proud of. It meant business was slow—very slow. The knives ranged in size and shape, ones with straight edges and ones with serrated edges, some sharp and some not so sharp. The only thing they all had in common was that they were all made with his two hands.

Dale was on his way up the stairs when he heard the front door opening. He stopped, and quietly went back down the stairs. He got one of his two knives that had twelve inch blades. It was old, a knife that his dad had helped him make when he was sixteen—a real monster. The way Dale felt when he carried this knife, he would almost prefer it to a pistol.

He walked slowly up the stairs and heard foot-steps coming towards him. He got to the kitchen first and waited on the other side of the refrigerator.

The footsteps were closer, now in the kitchen. Just as Dale was about to strike, he heard the voice.

"Dale, baby, you here?"

It was Julianne.

Dale quickly put the knife on the table, knocking over a couple beer bottles. Julianne's smile faded when Dale grabbed her by the shoulders and pushed her to the wall.

"Why you sneakin' around, huh?"

"I was—"

"You was what? You just come and go when you please, is that it?" He placed the palm of his left hand between her breasts and his right hand around her throat. She tried to swallow. "You think you can just come and go like you own the place? But you don't own the place, do you?"

"No."

"No. I own this fucking place, and when you want to come in, you better knock from now on, you hear?"

"Dale, I didn't even think you were here! What are you getting so crazy about?"

"Crazy?" He tightened his grip around her throat. "You ain't seen me crazy," he said, his mouth clenched as he said it. They looked at each other for a moment. Julianne managed to get the word "sorry" out of her mouth and Dale released her soon after.

She deserved a beating then, but he didn't give her one. He went to the bathroom, then came back to the kitchen and got a beer from the fridge.

"Baby, you shouldn't be drinking. Come on, I'm gonna make some eggs. Would you eat some eggs if I made some?"

"Sure, I guess."

"Ain't you workin' today?" He looked at her and for a second, Julianne thought he might come after her again, but he didn't.

"I ain't going in."

"Won't you get in trouble?"

"Fuck them. When they call, you can tell them I'm sick."

Dale went into the living room, now holding onto the knife he had put on the table in one hand and the beer in the other. He sat in the recliner and watched the Channel 9 news, which was talking about the finding of a body.

Chapter Twenty

The next week, Bill got a call five minutes before his appointment with Julianne.

"I can't make it." Her voice was soft, and to Bill, it sounded unstable. He hadn't spoken to her since the morning he picked her up from the hotel and took her home.

"Okay," he said reservedly. "Is anything wrong? Are you all right?" He'd been looking forward to seeing her again. He'd thought about her often in the past week, wondering what she was doing, and how she spent her time.

He'd hoped she would come in and tell him that she'd had it with Dale. She would say that she'd been thinking about what he'd said that night, and how it made sense. She would come in twice as strong as she'd been the week before, saying she'd been liberated—no longer would she fear the men in her life, no longer would she tolerate abuse, mental or physical. It would be because of Bill.

Because of him, she would be free.

"I'm fine. I just forgot I've got a doctor's appointment today."

"A doctor's appointment? Are you sick?"

"No, this is a regular checkup sort of thing. I'm really sorry. I plum forgot about it until yesterday when they called."

"I've got some afternoon spots open if you'd like to come by later."

"I'm sorry but I can't. I'm busy all day."

"Tomorrow then?"

After a pause, she said, "Can't. Would it be okay if we just made it for next week at the same time? I'll make up the session, though, I promise."

"Okay, but I hope you're all right. If you're at home with bruises on your face, you should call the cops. You should also let us help you. That's what we're here for. He shouldn't be allowed to get away with that."

"I know, I know," she laughed. "I don't have any bruises on my face. Dale's been really good to me lately. I told you before that he hardly ever hits me. You gotta believe that. If you must know, my doctor's appointment is of the female nature, if you get my meaning. It's a standard annual checkup. There's nothing wrong with me."

"That's good to hear," he said. "You would tell me though if he were beating you, wouldn't you?"

"Of course I would, you know that."

As he hung up the phone, Bill wasn't so sure.

Chapter Twenty-One

Julianne was happy this Monday morning. She and Dale had a good weekend together. He was being sweet to her lately, and on Saturday they had even gone out to a restaurant. Dale had Thursday and Friday off this week and they were planning on spending a couple days camping.

She also liked it when Dale was in a good mood because everything in their relationship changed, if only for a while. She could say things she couldn't normally say, and she could do things she couldn't normally do. Even the sex was different.

After canceling her appointment, she started back the hallway toward the bedroom. Today would be the day; she could feel it. As she walked, she pulled the slip over her head and dropped it. It felt good to be naked, to feel the air against her skin. Her nipples stiffened. She put her hands in her hair and caressed the back of her neck as she walked into the bedroom.

Dale lay on the bed, wearing a white t-shirt and no underwear. She could see that he was ready for her. She loved this. It didn't happen often, but every now and then Dale was in the mood to give up control. Go get the rope, he would say, and she would know.

He had said it this morning, and that was why Julianne was happy. It was perfect timing, even if he didn't know it. She got on top of him, straddling his stomach. She removed his shirt, exposing the three inch tattoo on his chest. It was a picture of a knife—a replica of the first knife he had ever made, the one he'd made with his father. The tip pointed to his heart.

With the shirt now off, she took his hands and put his wrists together. He moved his hands to the upper right hand corner of the bed. She finished tying the wrists together, and tied the other end of the rope to the post on the headboard. Neither of them said anything, just occasional grunts from moving around and getting everything in place. Sometimes Dale asked her to tie his feet together, too, but today he didn't.

She got off him and stood there for a second before leaving the room. She came back a minute later with a small bottle of baby oil. She put some on her hands and put a couple drops on his penis. She began rubbing it, up and down again and again. He moaned and she straddled his knees. As she continued caressing him, she pushed her breasts together with her upper arms. She knew he liked it when she did that.

After a minute, she bent down and got the bottle off the floor. She put more than she usually did in her cupped hand and threw the bottle on the floor. She rubbed it on her breasts and closed her eyes. He didn't like it when she looked at him when she did that, and she knew it. It was during times like this that she knew that she could be just as sexy as those strippers he would go see with his friends. She knew she was just as good looking, and had just as good a body as they did. She started moaning quietly, and the more she loved her own body, the louder she got. She knew she was ready, and knew from experience that soon he would want to get inside her.

As she moaned louder, he too began to moan. She could see that he was breathing rapidly, and watched the knife tattoo on his chest rise and fall. "Now fuck me," he said. On command, she put her hands on his chest and moved up toward him. She lowered herself on his penis, which felt warm and hard inside her. He slipped into her easily. Even though this was what she thought of as 'one of the good times,' she still had the same feeling—it was almost equal parts pleasure and repulsion. It felt good, but at the same time, she didn't like having anything inside her, violating her. She knew where that part of her came from, and perhaps that was why, once she started having intercourse, she liked to get it over with.

She started rocking her hips toward him and away from him, moving her body like she thought the strippers would. She sat straight up and ran her hands through her hair. She knew that if she did that, Dale would think he was fucking a wild woman; it would make him come more. She rocked faster, and as his grunts became louder, she knew he was close. "Not yet, baby, not yet," she said. She also thought that if he held it in longer, he might come more. Dale could wait no longer, though, and Julianne felt the warm fluid inside her.

She untied him and smiled. She kissed him quickly and made her way into the bathroom. She knew he would be asleep within five minutes.

She turned the water on so he wouldn't hear, and took out of her drawer a zip lock baggie. She hadn't thought of how exactly she would do this, and every way she tried was awkward. Finally she squatted down and held the baggie open between her legs. She was nervous, and was holding the semen inside her. She got on her knees, put the open baggie under her, and tried to relax. After a few seconds, the semen began running down her leg. She got as much of it in the baggie as she could and hoped it would be enough.

Chapter Twenty-Two

Karen and Tom showed up on the doorstep at nine-thirty in the morning. They knocked three times over a minute until the door opened.

Standing in front of them in cut-off sweatpants and a shirt which read "Don't Worry, Be Happy" on it was Phil Oliver. His eyes were red and puffy. Karen smelled the alcohol when he opened the door.

"Yeah?" he said, squinting.

"Mr. Oliver, I'm Detective Summers and this is Detective Flanagan."

"Yeah?"

"Sir, we're here to ask you a few questions regarding the night of August third, the night Mark Cherneau disappeared."

"Yeah?"

"Mr. Oliver, do you mind if we come in?" Karen thought he might still be a little drunk.

Phil looked at Tom and then at Karen. He looked past them and squinted as if sunshine was unfamiliar to him. "If you want to."

Karen and Tom stepped into the house. Karen almost inadvertently kicked a beer bottle that was lying on the floor. It wasn't the only one; there were at least ten empty bottles that she could see, some on the coffee table, others on the floor. There was a potato chip bag that looked empty as well that was on the floor. She sat on the couch and leaned back. Next to her on the couch was a sweatshirt that said "Champion" in small letters.

"You want some coffee? I was just going to make some."

"No, thank you, Mr. Oliver."

"My daddy's dead."

"Excuse me?"

"Mr. Oliver—he's dead. You can call me Phil if you want to. Or 'Trigger,' even. Some people used to call me that. But I ain't never heard nobody call me 'Mr. Oliver.'"

"Why did people call you 'Trigger?'"

"Back in my twenties, me and some friends used to go shooting every Sunday before football. I had this .9 millimeter—not that many people had 'em back then, not the way they got 'em now—I'll tell you what, I could shoot the damn lights out with that thing. Every time I squeezed one off, BING! Bulls eye. Or damn close. I guess that's why everyone called me Trigger, on account of me being such a good shot and all."

"You still have that gun, Mr. Oli—Phil?" Karen asked.

Phil got up and went to the kitchen to get a cup of coffee.

"Worried about me having a gun in the house? No. Sold it. Got good money for it, too. People would see me going BING BING BING, right in the heart, and they think it's a magic trick or something. Like the gun's got eyes of it's own. It was a hell of a gun, that's for sure, but it's like I used to tell them: ' it's the gunman hits the bulls eye, not the gun.'"

"So what kind of gun do you have now?" Tom asked.

Phil looked at him as if he'd intruded on a secret conversation. "Ain't got no gun no more, officer," he said emphatically. "Why you asking me about some gun, anyway? I heard Cherneau got himself hacked to pieces."

"So you and your friends don't go shooting any-more?" Karen asked.

"Nope." He sat down and put the coffee cup on the table.

"So what do you do nowadays?" she asked.

Phil reached over the arm of the chair and without looking got a bottle of Jim Beam from the floor. He poured as much as he could into the cup without it spilling over. "Oh, not much. My wife and I are separated now and I'm trying to get it together, you know."

Karen looked at Tom as the silence filled the room.

"Okay, Phil, if we could, I'd like to get to the night of August third, the night Mark Cherneau disappeared. It was a Friday night, and from what we know, he went to the Last Stop at about 10:00. That's the last place he was seen alive.

"Now, Phil, we know that you're a regular at the Last Stop—"

"I want to tell you right now, before you go any further. I was *not* there that night. You probably know I'm there almost every Friday night, every *night* almost, but I wasn't there on the third."

"We know."

"So what you come here for, then?" He gulped his coffee.

"Mr. Oliver," she said, "you said it yourself. You're there all the time. When we talked to Hank at the bar, he didn't remember too much; he gave us a few other names, and believe me, they will all be checked out. The one thing he *did* remember positively, though, was that you *weren't* there. So our question to you is, why *weren't* you there, and where were you?"

Chapter Twenty-Three

After six months of putting away every spare dime she could without Dale's knowledge, Julianne finally had enough money for the appointment at the Brown-Williams Fertility Clinic in Cambridge. Today would be the day when she would find out the truth.

Julianne followed the nurse into the exam room. The doctor would be right in, she said.

A few minutes passed, and Julianne wondered if the doctor be able to tell what she was trying to do. Would he be able to read it on her face?

"Miss Case, it's nice to meet you, I'm Doctor Levin." They shook hands. "Mary tells me you are trying to have a baby."

"*Mary* told you that!?"

"Yes, Mary—the nurse who brought you in here."

"Oh, yes. Of course; I'm sorry. That's right."

"We're going to see if we can help you. Now the first thing I think we should do—"

Julianne reached into her purse and took out the zippered baggie.

"Oh my, you brought a sample," he said, taking it from her. "You want us to test this, I presume." She nodded. "How long have you and your boyfriend been trying?"

"I stopped taking the pill six months ago," she said, then indicated the sample. "Was it okay that I brought that?"

"Yes. Perfectly fine. It's good because we'll be able to determine more quickly which one of you is having the trouble.

"Okay," he continued, "here are some common reasons couples have for not conceiving: first, and this is the most common, is a low sperm count. The good part about this, though, is that this condition is the easiest to remedy. There are different possibilities here on how to get the count higher, and if those don't work, there is artificial insemination.

"Another could be that he is sterile, or that you could be infertile. These may sound final; that if either of these are the case, then you have no chance of having a baby. There are certain advancements, however, that make this not necessarily the case. In other words, there still is a definite possibility you could have a baby, even if this is the situation. I don't want to get too specific now. It's better we wait and see the results of the test and the results of your exam. From there, maybe we can get Dale in here, too, and we'll sit down and go over what the next step should be."

"How soon will I get the test results, Doctor?" She nodded toward the baggie. "Is that enough?"

"Yes, this is enough. You'll be able to know the results in a couple weeks. When did you get this sample?"

Julianne thought that was a strange was of putting it. "This morning. About an hour and a half ago."

"And how did you go about collecting the sample?"

She looked at him puzzled and didn't respond. "I…"

"Did you have intercourse?"

"Yes."

"That's all I need to know," he said, smiling. "I know that's a funny question, but the lab needs to know."

"Okay."

The doctor put the clipboard down. "All right, Miss Case, why don't we have you hop up on the table, and we'll start with a general checkup."

She got on the padded table even though she wanted to run from the room. She hated doctors like this, the kind that put fingers where they shouldn't be.

"Okay, if you could just unbutton the top two buttons on your shirt, so we can listen to your heart."

Julianne hesitantly obliged. Doctor Levin told her it would be cold for a second, and then placed the stethoscope over her heart.

"Just relax and breathe normally." Julianne knew her heart was beating fast and she was taking short breaths. He moved the stethoscope around her heart. He then took it and put it on her back. He didn't ask her to take her shirt off, and that was a relief. She felt so awkward, in this cold, well-lit room with this total stranger examining her, like some sort of specimen.

"Okay," he said, taking the stethoscope off his ears, "your heart was a little fast, but it sounds good. And your lungs sound pretty good, but I did hear a little wheezing there, and some buildup of phlegm. Do you have allergies?"

"I have hay fever, but it's not bad, usually. I had a little sneezing spell before I came in. That's probably why."

"Okay. I'm going to have Mary come in—Mary *the nurse*—and she's going to get you a gown and get everything ready for the next part of the exam. I'll send her in."

"Doctor, I'm sorry."

"What's the matter?"

"I can't do this."

"Miss Case, I assure you, there is nothing to be afraid of here."

"I know. I feel silly. Maybe we could wait and see what the results are from the test and go from there. Do you think we could do that? Please?"

"If you are uncomfortable, I'm not going to make you do anything you don't want to do."

"Thank you. I really appreciate this."

"No problem. We can reschedule your appointment." He opened the door and took a few steps out into the hallway. Julianne didn't follow him.

"Actually, if it's all right with you, I'd rather wait to hear the test results and make an appointment then. Would that be okay?"

"Sure. Whatever's good for you. This may delay the process, I hope you understand that. We'll call you with the results in a couple weeks, and then it might be another couple weeks before we can see you."

"That's perfectly fine with me. I'm not in a rush. But could you do one more thing? Could you not call me about the results? Could I call you in a couple weeks?"

Doctor Levin came back into the room and shut the door.

"Miss Case, does your boyfriend know you're trying to get pregnant?"

"He knows," she said. The Doctor looked at her and folded his arms. She knew he was waiting for the truth.

"Miss Case, whatever you tell me stays in this room. Everything is confidential."

"Okay. I kind of let Dale think I'm still on the pill. But I know that he would love to have a baby."

"How do you know that? Are you sure of it?"

"I'm not sure, but how could he not? How could he not want a precious little baby, something so pure and so innocent?"

"This is really not my place to say, but I just hope you're careful. I hope you know what you're doing."

"I do, Doctor. Thank you. This is something God wants to happen. I can feel it in my heart."

Chapter Twenty-Four

"All right Phil, stop looking into that coffee cup for answers and tell me the truth." Karen folded her hands in her lap and tried to at least sound patient. "Where were you on the night of August third, the night Mark Cherneau walked out of the Last Stop to his death?"

"I was," he said, clearing his throat, . "at my mother's. I was visiting my mother."

"You were at your mother's. Okay, tell me when you went there and when you left."

"What, you want exact times, to the minute."

"As close as you can get."

"I drove there at about eight forty-five, I know this because it was a few minutes before *CSI* was starting and I was gonna watch it. I sometimes go over there to watch it because she's got this, like, enormous television. Hell of a lot better than that piece of shit, let me tell you.

"After the show was over, I got in my car and was on my way to the bar. I only got about a half mile when that damn truck you saw in the driveway made this clanging noise and started jerking. Then it died. Just left me sit."

"And where was this?"

"Down 203 past the lodge."

"What's your mother's address? We're going to need to talk to her later today," she said.

"Don't believe me? Go ahead, ask her, I don't give a shit."

"The address."

"I don't know it."

"You don't know you own mother's address?"

"It's out off 203; I don't know what the name of that little dirt road is. I don't even think it has a name. You know what road I'm talking about?"

Karen knew the area, but even now after living here for eight years, there were still some areas where she'd never been and couldn't place. This was one of them. There were many 'little dirt roads' around; she didn't know where any of them went, and she never took the time to find out.

"No, you know where it is, Tom?"

"Yeah, I think I know the one he's talking about," he said. "Just before you get to the old schoolhouse?"

Phil nodded. "Yeah, it's the second house on the left. She's got about three hundred acres out there. You can look for an old rusted out 1952 Chevy Pickup; used to belong to my father before he died."

"Tell me everything you know about Mark Cherneau."

Phil smiled. He looked at Tom. "What do you want to know?"

"What I just said. Everything."

"He's dead, I know that much," he said and laughed. "I never knew the guy, you know, on a personal level. I thought he was a hell of a ballplayer. I watched him play for Logan High. Went to a couple games."

"Did you two have any mutual acquaintances? Same boss, same friends, girlfriend?"

"This is a small town, Detective. We're all sort of tied together here. Even if you leave, part of you is still here." Phil looked out the window. "Those are roots, Detective. Roots that you don't know much about. But Tommy here does. Your husband does."

"What does my husband have to do with this?"

"He's lived in Logan all his life, right? 'Cept when he went off to college. Came right back, though. You see, a man knows where his home is. He knows it like he knows his own name. My mother has a picture on her wall that says, 'Bloom Where You're Planted.' That pretty much says it all, doesn't it, Detective Summers?"

"I don't think I follow," she said.

"What I'm saying is that you women don't know about roots. You don't know about having a home, you don't care about knowing where your place is, and staying there. Women think they can go wherever they please, so long as it suits them. But they can't." He reached for the coffee cup, but then reached over the arm of the chair and drank straight from the bottle of Jim Beam. "They can't."

"You telling us everything you know about Cherneau?"

"Yep." He took another drink and smiled. "Would I lie to you?"

"If you have, I'll find out, then you won't be my favorite person in the world—you know that, don't you?"

"You don't scare me, Little Miss Detective."

"Good. Then you won't try running when I come back here to bring you in for further questioning."

"I got no reason to run; I haven't done anything."

Chapter Twenty-Five

That night, just as Bill was sitting down in front of the television to eat supper, Karen came home. It was seven o' clock—the earliest she'd been home since the case began.

"Hey," he said.

"Hey."

"You're home early."

"I'm really tired; we talked to a lot of people to-day. It was like beating our heads against the wall. They all saw pretty much the same thing—nothing. What is that you're eating?"

"My attempt at Chinese. It doesn't look like much, but it's not that bad. There's plenty more."

She took off her coat and her shoes and walked out to the kitchen. A few minutes later, she returned with a plate in hand. She put the plate on the coffee table and sat on the couch. Bill was sitting in the chair adjacent to the couch. It was the first time in over a month that they had eaten supper at the same time.

"Three of the people we talked to said pretty much the same thing, though, so that's something."

"What'd they say?"

"They said Cherneau was an asshole, first of all. They also say they saw him leave The Last Stop at around 12:45 a.m., alone. This is good," she said. She smiled at him. "I didn't know you could cook like this."

"I got tired of only being able to make spaghetti and macaroni. I'd go out to eat, but there's nobody to go with."

"I know I haven't been around much lately, Bill. You know how big this case is, though."

"I know. I just wish you'd let me help you. When you get into cases, you shut everybody around you out.

And this is the biggest case you've had. I want you to be able to come to me for help."

"You know that's how I deal with stress. I internalize it. I don't want you to feel shut out. I have to devote all my time to the case, though." She took a bite. "Your name came up today."

"My name? When?"

"You know a guy by the name of Phil Oliver?"

"I've never met the guy, but yeah, I know the guy. He's a crazy bastard. You talked to him? I hope you had Tom there with you."

"I did. Oliver's a regular at The Last Stop; he's there every Friday night. I heard you could set your watch by his arrival at ten. On the night Cherneau disappeared, he never went there. We went and talked to him. He said that you 'know about roots,' and I don't. The guy hates women."

"Tell me something I don't know."

"How do you know him?"

"His wife was in Clarksdale a few times. He beat her within an inch of her life. Guy's an asshole, not to mention crazy," he added, thinking of the letters.

"Well, that's something he has in common with Cherneau. Did she leave him?"

"She moved to Columbus, changed her name. She's doing real well."

"He told me that they split up, like it was a mutual thing."

"No way. He still wants her." Bill stared straight ahead, looking at nothing. "I'm sure of that."

Chapter Twenty-Six

The next week when Bill saw Julianne again, she seemed more relaxed with him. She sat back in her chair and asked if she could take her shoes off. It was a strange request, but it was perfectly fine with Bill.

"So what do you want to talk about?" he asked.

"I don't know; you're the professional. Let's talk about whatever you want."

"What if I asked you to tell me about your first sexual experience?" Bill was embarrassed to ask, but at the same time, it was a routine question.

Julianne seemed to be scanning the floor, looking for the right thing to say. Maybe she didn't want to say anything at all.

"If you'd rather talk about something else, that's OK."

"I'm just trying to remember...the first experience. You don't mean the first time I did it, do you?"

"No, doesn't have to be."

"Oh, oh—Dean Byars! I'll tell you about Dean Byars; this is pretty funny.

"Okay. It was the last seventh grade dance. Dean Byars had asked me to go with him, and I said yes, but it's not like he could pick me up or anything. The guys just asked the girls and then everybody met there. Even though we were supposed to be 'going together', Dean and I didn't dance, slow that is, until twenty minutes before the dance would end at nine. Those last twenty minutes, though, we danced the whole time. They played all slow songs, and with each dance, Dean got a little closer. I could tell he was nervous; I was, too. Who wasn't back then? Then, during the last song, it happened."

"What happened?"

"By this time we were as close as you could get. In the middle of the last song, I think when he got his courage up, he pulled my hips to his. We were pressed together. I could feel his...hardness against my stomach. It wasn't just a little hard, either. His penis was pointing straight up. I didn't know what was going on! I couldn't believe it; I didn't even know it could go that way, much less get big like that. I was a little scared, but I guess my curiosity got the best of me. I wanted to feel it. So I looked around to see if either of the chaperones were watching, and when no one was looking, I did it."

Bill was staring into her eyes, visualizing every detail. Her eyes were so big and so dark that he couldn't see where the iris ended and the pupil began. They were hypnotic.

"I took my right hand off his hip and put it over his jeans where his penis was. It went almost all the way up to where the snap was. Dean jumped a little when I did that. His breathing became erratic; I could hear it right in my ear. I began to rub up and down and after maybe ten seconds, he stopped dancing. He stood there, and he let out a little groan. I asked him if he was okay, and he said, 'yeah, yeah.' He backed away from me and started dancing again. He and I both looked around the gym to see if anybody had seen us. To our relief, no one had. I took my hand away, and I felt something wet between my fingers. I didn't know what had happened. I thought he'd gotten scared and peed himself. Can you believe that?"

She laughed and the sexual tension that Bill had been feeling was lifted. He was glad to get back to feeling comfortable with her. She brushed her hand across her knee.

"Yeah, those days were innocent fun. We didn't know anything about sex or evil or the big bad world. We couldn't have known what kind of disappointment was ahead of us."

"What do you mean?"

"Life doesn't exactly live up to its promise." She stared out the window behind Bill, her eyes becoming vacant. "We're brought up as children thinking that life is this wonderful thing where everything you believe in actually exists and if we could just be grown-ups then our world could be wonderful. When you're a child, you have all the hope and ambition but no freedom to make anything of it. And then when you are an adult and you have the freedom...well by then it's too late."

"Too late for what?"

"Too late to do anything positive—to late to change the world. I wanted to change the world when I was a child. It's too late for that now."

This was a side of Julianne that Bill hadn't seen. He never knew she had such a cynical view of the world. "It doesn't have to be, Julianne."

"Sure it does. I think that in high school, you start as a child, and leave as an adult by experiencing certain things which turn you into what you've become. You 'find yourself,' as they say. Isn't that what that means? Please tell me if this doesn't happen to everybody."

"Yes, I think it does, sure. But they're not supposed to make you a cynical person, or make you forget your dreams."

"Do you believe in Santa Claus?"

Bill didn't answer.

"It's not rocket science we're talking about here, but it's still a tricky question, isn't it? You want to tell me 'yes, you believe in Santa Claus,' but you also don't expect me to believe that you think that some guy in a big red suit visits every house in the world in one night and squeezes his fat ass down their chimney and gives us presents. But when we're children, we believe in the simplest way that he exists. We don't care about any of that other stuff; we're free of doubt—we're pure.

"Sooner or later, though, we find out that he goes by other names—Father Christmas, Saint Nick—and you start to wonder. You figure out that it's your parents who buy you stuff and put it under the tree. Pretty soon you realize that he only exists in theory; his 'spirit' is out there. After that, he becomes a rumor which we all know isn't true."

"There are some people who choose to believe in him, regardless. Some people can keep those child-like qualities, if they allow themselves. You could be the same way if you wanted to."

"I can't take a lie and convince myself it's the truth. I can't do that, no matter how hard I try. And it's not just Santa, it's everything. You believe in something when you're a kid and it crumbles right in front of your face and they call it 'part of growing up.' I just wish somebody would have told me the truth when I was a kid. I could've been prepared."

"What is the truth? What is it you wish they'd told you?"

Julianne sighed. Her eyes were filling with tears. "That when you're a child, the world is full of magic and they want you to love this magic and then they strip it from you. From then on, life's just a matter of trying to fill your time before it's up. What's the opposite of innocence? Guilt. And guilty is what I am, for the rest of my life. It's like trying to believe in Santa Claus again; you just can't. There's no going back from guilt."

Chapter Twenty-Seven

Sandy Kelley, the former Sandy Oliver, pulled into her apartment complex in Upper Arlington, one of the most affluent of the Columbus suburbs. She got out of her 1996 white Ford Taurus, her arms full with two briefcases, a coffee mug, and five inches of files in manila folders.

It was five till seven, and her paralegal class at Columbus State started at seven-thirty. She would never make it, but she was going to try. If there was one thing she had learned in the last year, it was that making an effort, even in the face of futility, is better than not making one at all. She tried to reach for her keys. She leaned over and tried to feel her pockets when one of the folders fell to the pavement. "Shit." The papers were strewn on the ground, and to pick them up, she had to put everything down. She tried to force herself to calm down, to slow down. She took a deep breath and just looked at the papers before beginning to pick them up.

She lived by herself in the smallest one bedroom apartment they had at Oak Hill Apartments, which was still more space than she needed. Her building was at the furthest end of the complex, through the maze of streets, all named after a type of tree. Willow Run was her street, and it felt about a million miles away from Logan.

Sandy finished taking a quick shower, and grabbed for the towel on the hook. She opened the shower curtain and through the steam on the mirror, she looked at her naked body. She wondered if she was still attractive. It had been six months since she'd left Phil, and seven months since she'd had sex. It's time, she thought. You can't be afraid of men all your life, even if you were married to a psycho. There was one man in her class at Columbus State, Robert, who she thought liked her. She liked him, too. She supposed he was the reason for the quick shower, even if it made her late to class. If he asks you out, you can say yes, she told herself. Maybe "Sandy Kelley" was the type of girl who could ask a guy out. Who knew? She loved the idea of reinventing herself.

As she stepped out of the shower and began to dry off, she heard a single loud 'thud.' She stopped—didn't move or breathe. She listened for it again, and heard nothing. Could it have been the neighbors downstairs?

When she didn't hear it again, she dried off quickly and put on the clothes she had picked out for class, while being as quiet as she possibly could. She realized that she hadn't taken a breath in a while, and coughed at the lack of oxygen. Don't hyperventilate—just take it easy, she thought.

She'd had trouble getting used to living alone the first couple months in a big city. Noises like this happened every now and then. It was no big deal.

Now fully clothed, and not entirely dry, she walked out into the hallway, looking both ways as if it were a busy street she was trying to cross. She walked toward the living room and heard a car start loudly in the parking lot. The sound scared her. She continued to walk to the living room.

The sliding glass door to the balcony was open. She put one hand to her mouth. She checked the kitchen; there was no one in the apartment.

But someone had been there.

She looked around. There was nothing missing. She felt sick to her stomach, her breathing erratic. She looked out the door to the second floor balcony, but couldn't see anything.

Chapter Twenty-Eight

"What's the time line?" Police Chief Jared Wilson asked. He had ordered Karen and Tom into his office first thing in the morning.

Tom got into his briefcase and pulled out some papers. "We have Mark getting to The Last Stop somewhere between 10:00 and 10:30. He wasn't a regular in the bar. He went directly to the bar, and talked to Hank Peters, the bartender there. Hank knew Cherneau in high school—they were both on the baseball team together, but at first Cherneau didn't recognize him. Hank had to tell Cherneau who he was and that they went to school together. He said Cherneau seemed distant. Hank says that he walked in, looked around as if he was to meet someone and didn't see them. Then he said to Hank, 'It must be Old Friends Night—you'll never believe who I saw out in the parking lot.'

Cherneau then ordered a Guinness. Hank gave him the beer, and said, 'Who?' Cherneau didn't know what he was asking. He said, 'who'd you see out in the parking lot?' Just then, a man named Steven Blake, a big guy with a long beard, came up and gave Cherneau a shove that almost knocked him off his barstool. 'Hey dumbass! Didn't you see us waving at ya? Whoa! What is this black shit you're drinking? You want me to get you a Bud? We got a couple pitchers over here.' Blake then reportedly put his arm around Cherneau, the kind that is almost a headlock, and said, 'What other bad habits you pick up in Maine? Drinking that shit.' And then Cherneau went over and sat with them."

"You never found out who was in the parking lot?" asked Wilson.

"Nope," Karen said. "We asked everybody if they had seen anyone suspicious in the lot, but nobody saw anyone outside."

"Okay, tell me what else you know about that night."

"By Hank Peters' estimation, it was close to midnight when Cherneau left. He had asked the bartender if he had any aspirin, but he didn't. He said that Cherneau was glassy-eyed, but he didn't seem drunk. He said he had only had the one Guinness, but he may have had some of his friends' beer. The friends, he says, had probably both had a pitcher each and they *were* drunk. Hank asked him if he was okay to drive, and Cherneau said that he was fine, and that he was just tired. And that was about it. He left. Fifteen days later he's an armless corpse."

Chapter Twenty-Nine

This is bullshit, Dale thought. He threw down the newspaper and got off the couch. Because of the sound of the TV, he hadn't quite heard it clearly, so he turned it off. Twice he'd heard a low *thud*. Julianne was already asleep in the bedroom, so he knew it wasn't her making noise. He knew what his house sounded like and, with all its *creaks* and *thunks* from the basement, this sound didn't fit.

What was that noise? Was it the wind outside? Was someone out there? He heard it again, and stood still in the middle of the living room. That was about as good as he was going to hear it, and he still couldn't identify it.

Dale's hands turned into fists. *What the hell is that?* he thought. *If it's those kids from down the street, I'll fucking kill them for messing with me.*

He went to his workshop in the basement. He grabbed one of the many knives that hung from the wall. He had made this one a couple years ago, and could hardly remember doing it. It had a long blade, and was dull to the touch. Dale made a mental note to go through and sharpen every one of them. For now, though, it would do the trick.

He stopped in the middle of the room, surrounded by the knives he'd made, and listened.

Nothing.

He could feel his heart beating faster now. As he walked up the stairs, his head became filled with hate, a blinding hate that wanted to be unleashed. He would do it, too. They were on his property.

His property.

Room by room he walked, first turning out lights, then checking windows. First there was the kitchen, then the living room, and then he went to the spare back bedroom, which was already dark. He looked out the window in the spare bedroom. Had he seen something out there? He thought he saw something move.

He went to his bedroom and, without turning on the light, took off the white t-shirt he was wearing. He went to the closet and shut the door almost all the way before turning on the light. He reached inside and took out a black t-shirt. He put the t-shirt on and smiled. He remembered, as a child, playing hide and seek late summer nights like this one. He always made sure to wear solid dark colors. He had hardly ever been caught.

He shut the closet door and went into the hallway. He walked in total darkness toward the living room, knowing exactly where he was at all times. He had walked up and down this hallway for nine years.

In this house, *his* house, he didn't even need eyes.

He figured he could get out the back door more quietly. Both doors made noise when you opened them, but the one from the kitchen wasn't as bad. When he got into the kitchen, he heard the noise again. He was breathing audibly now; he wanted to run out the door screaming like a madman, but couldn't. That wasn't how the game was played. He had to keep quiet. The real monsters, the *best* ones, were the quietest.

He went outside as slowly and quietly as possible. There was no moon in the sky. He was surrounded by darkness. He stood there on the back porch for a minute, trying to let his eyes adjust. They never did. It was simply too dark outside. He could be locked in a closet and it would look the same.

He walked into the grass in the backyard, waving the knife back and forth. If anybody were to get in his way, on his property, they were gonna get sliced right through the middle. They would deserve it.

He stood in the middle of the yard and listened for the sound, but heard nothing.

"Eeeee!!!" The noise made him jump. What the hell was that?! It sounded like it could be human, but he didn't think so. A bird, maybe. Then he heard what sounded like the 'thud' coming from the front yard. He walked around to the front, raising his knife. He held the air in his lungs, waiting to strike. He squinted to see, and thought he saw something moving away in the distance. He couldn't make out who it was, or what it was. Maybe they knew the tricks of hide and seek, too.

He stood out there for five more minutes, but he could sense whatever it was had left. Now he just felt stupid, standing out in his front yard with a knife in his hand.

If they come back, I'll be ready, he thought.

I'll be ready to slice each of you in two.

He went back inside and turned on the light to the living room and the TV.

That night, with the knife under his pillow, Dale slept like a baby.

Chapter Thirty

The next morning, after Dale had already gone to work, the telephone woke Julianne up. It was past ten; she had been sleeping a lot lately, at least ten hours a night. She just had no energy anymore. Getting out of bed was the major chore of the day, and if she could get that done before noon, she felt as if she was being productive.

Although they had no answering machine, Julianne had no intention of getting up to answer it. It seemed to ring forever, and Julianne finally got up and walked down the hallway, trying to move quickly and failing.

"Hello."

"Miss Case? Is this Julianne Case?" The voice was energetic, like she'd just won the sweepstakes.

"Yes—who is this please?"

"Miss Case, this is Melanie at Doctor Levin's office. I know you were going to call us, but I wanted to let you—"

"Are the tests back?" Julianne was now fully awake.

"Yes, ma'am, they are. If you'd like to come by the office anytime, the doctor will go over them with you. You don't need an appointment."

"Can you to just tell me the results? I would really appreciate it."

"I don't think I can tell you, but maybe I can get the doctor on the phone for you. I don't see any difference whether you're here or not."

"Oh, that would be great, thank you."

After being on hold for nearly five minutes, Doctor Levin got on the phone.

"Miss Case, how are you this morning?"

"I'm just fine doctor, thank you. You have the test results?"

"Yes, I do. Miss Case, it looks as though you were correct about you and your boyfriend's inability to get pregnant. Unfortunately, his sperm has come back as having a very low count—extremely low. For all intents and purposes, he's sterile. Through in-vetro fertilization, there is the slight possibility that you could get pregnant by your boyfriend, but we would have to have him come down here and give a sample, and we'll see where we can go from there."

"I don't think Dale would be up for something like that."

"Have you told him that you're trying to get pregnant? I really think that he has a right to know about this."

"I'll tell him when the time's right. Thank you very much, doctor, for saving me from making the trip."

"No problem. Do you have any other questions for me?"

"No, I don't think so. Looks like I was taking the pill the past two years for nothing," she said.

"Yes, it looks that way. Are you going to be all right? This can be pretty devastating news for some couples."

"I'm fine. Just wasn't meant to be, I guess." After a short silence, she said, "Thank you again for everything. I really appreciate it."

"You're welcome, Miss Case."

Within fifteen minutes, Julianne was out the door.

Chapter Thirty-One

"I've got a secret I need to tell," Julianne said at the beginning of her third session with Bill. "Can you keep a secret?"

"Yes," Bill said. "I am legally bound to keep secrets. Whatever you need to tell me stays between us. I'm not allowed to tell anyone."

She put her purse on the floor and clasped her hands in her lap. She stared at the floor in front of her.

"I'm trusting you now more than I've ever trusted anyone; you have to promise never to tell anyone."

"Sounds serious—I don't know if I can make that promise. If this is information about a crime, I have to tell the police. And I definitely will if it has something to do with your safety. What is it?"

"Do you watch the news?"

"Yeah."

"So you've heard of Mark Cherneau?"

"Of course. That's all the news *is* these days. And more than that, my wife is the detective in charge of the case."

Julianne looked horrified. "Oh. Never mind, then."

"Why? What is it?"

"No. There's no way I can tell you now."

"Tell me what?!"

"Listen, I have an idea," she said. She picked up her purse and pulled out a small black leather Bible. She set it in the middle of Bill's desk, facing it toward him. She sat back down.

"Put your hand on it," she said.

Bill didn't move; he looked at her with a 'this-is-nonsense' expression. He knew that what she was about to tell him could be evidence to the crime that held the county in shock—a crime that his wife was trying desperately to solve. He was obligated to report any evidence of any crime that he was aware of. If he didn't, there even was the possibility of his being an accessory after the fact. That was not a probability, but he knew that he could be charged if he didn't disclose everything he knew.

"Do you believe in God?" She stared intently at him.

"Yes."

"Then put your hand on the Bible, please. Otherwise, I can't trust you."

"Can't you just tell me?"

"You know my beliefs, Bill. I know that if you put your hand on the Bible and swear never to tell a living soul what I'm about to tell you, you would keep your word. You are an honorable man, and I have the greatest respect for that."

"Then why do I need to swear on the Bible if I'm such an honorable man?"

"Please, just do it to put my mind at ease."

He waited ten seconds that felt like ten minutes. He desperately wanted to know what she had to say, but he also knew she was right—he would keep his promise to Julianne.

He put his hand on the Bible.

Her demeanor brightened the instant he touched the book. "Thank you. Now say these words: 'I will not repeat what I am about to hear, so help me God.'"

He said them.

"I'm responsible for the death of Mark Cherneau."

Chapter Thirty-Two

After getting less than two hours sleep the night before, Sandy Kelley knew she had to do something. Less than twenty-four hours earlier, someone had broken into her apartment. 'Broken in' wasn't exactly right, though; there was no forcible entry. She was almost sure that she had locked the sliding glass door to the second floor balcony.

She wasn't *totally* sure.

Regardless, *someone* had been in her apartment.

Someone had stood there while she took a shower.

She pulled her car into the three story parking garage on 4th street. After she pulled into a spot on the top floor, she pulled the wallet from the purse and checked it. The five hundred dollars was still there.

She walked down 4th street two blocks to Manny's Pawn Shop. She took a deep breath before opening the door and walking in.

There were only three men in the shop; two were customers, looking at the guitars. The other was behind the counter, reading a baseball magazine. Sandy figured it was Manny. He was a little overweight, and had gray hair.

All three men turned their attention to her when she walked in. She felt their eyes on her even as she walked past the men looking at the guitars. They would look at her ass, she knew.

They would think about having sex with her.

"Help you?" the man behind the counter said.

"Yes, I need a gun."

"You gonna shoot somebody?" he said, smiling at her. "Who you gonna shoot—husband? Boyfriend? Your boss, maybe?"

"No, this is strictly for protection purposes. My...apartment was broken into."

"Oh. Most people come in here to buy a gun, they want to shoot somebody. They don't say that's what it's for, but that's it, sure enough."

Sandy said nothing. Maybe this was a bad idea. This wasn't her thing. She thought of how she felt after the break-in, though, and decided to continue.

"I'm just kidding, lady. Don't get scared; Manny gonna take good care of you. Now—what kind of gun you want? Thirty-eight? Semi-automatic? I got 'em all, lady. I even had one of them laser-sighted ones, but I sold it the other day. You realize that there's a waiting period. The Man says you gotta wait, then you gotta wait. The 'Head Start Bill' is what I like to call it. Gives your boyfriend three days to get the hell out of Dodge before you can turn into Thelma and Louise and come out shootin'!"

Sandy smiled. She thought this was mildly funny, but she also thought she should laugh at Manny's joke. He probably wasn't the kind of guy you wanted to upset.

"I think you'll do just fine with this thirty-eight snub nose I've got here. He unlocked the glass case under the counter and took it out. He popped it open and spun the cylinder. "This is a quality gun. Normal thirty-eights go for around four hundred, but this one is nickel-plated. A beauty, don't you think? This one I got to get five hundred out of. It's a solid-crafted gun, and it'll stop anything that moves. You don't need to worry about that."

"I don't have five hundred. Do you have anything else? Maybe something closer to three-fifty?"

"I got a few here that are less than four, but they're all shit. You don't want any of those. Tell you what—how much can you spend? I'm willing to make you a deal on this one here. I think this gun suits you. I think this is the best your going to find for under $600, which is what these babies go for new."

"I don't know. I really can't go over four hundred."

"I'm sorry, but I can't let it go that cheap. You don't have to pay the whole amount now, you know. You can pay me a deposit while we get the waiting period going, and then pay the rest later."

She said nothing. She didn't like to haggle. She preferred to avoid the confrontation. She looked at the gun and said, "four-twenty five."

"Sorry sweets. I absolutely must get four-fifty. And now I'm barely making any money off the gun. You're getting the thing at the price I paid for it. Basically."

"Four forty-five," she said.

She thought this might make him angry, but he laughed. "You are one hard lady, you know that? I pity the guy that pisses you off. Four forty-five it is. Sometimes I think I'm gonna go out of business; I'm just too nice a guy."

Sandy felt strange filling out the paperwork.

She was buying a gun.

Chapter Thirty-Three

"What do you mean you're responsible for the death of Mark Cherneau?" Bill said quietly. He felt a twinge in his stomach.

"Maybe I better take this from the beginning. Do we have enough time to get into this?" Julianne asked.

"We have all the time you need. Start from the beginning, and tell me everything." Could he be sitting across from Cherneau's killer, this woman he'd fallen in love with? Was it because his wife was struggling with this case and here, for once, was his opportunity to help Karen? She had always been so independent, and with this case, that independence was more of a hindrance than an asset. She wouldn't ask for help, but here was Bill's chance to give it. Was his curiosity just that—like looking at road kill when it would be just as easy to look away?

"Okay, I guess I'll start in high school. I went to Logan High—graduated 2001."

"That's where Cherneau went to school. Did you know him?"

"Yeah. He was a couple grades ahead of me. He also lived just down the street from me. You can imagine my surprise, when he was a sophomore in high school, he asked me out. I was only in eighth grade, and here he was, already the star of the varsity baseball team, asking me if I wanted to go up to Ash Cave with him. I was thirteen years old, and there was no way I was allowed to date anyone, much less someone in high school. Back then daddy was still alive and he wouldn't have it.

"It also wasn't the easiest thing for him to tell his jock buddies that he was seeing an eighth grader. Most of his friends were dating juniors and seniors, and here I was, not even in high school. We agreed to keep everything secret. It was better for both of us. Besides, he said that 'sometimes love has to be private.' I was so thrilled he had called it 'love;' it was so romantic—our secret love.

"We were only together for about four months total, but we met just about every day that spring and summer. We would go to Ash Cave and walk the trails. We never went anywhere public—like the mall, I mean—it was always Ash Cave. It was just about the most unpopular place for a teenager to be, which was just fine with us.

"There are six trails to walk out there—four lead to Steiner's Pond in the center. One goes around the park, and the other one is more of a hike up to the peak. For the first week and a half, we would walk one of the four that went to the pond. He would hold my hand as we walked, talking about baseball mostly—how the team was doing, how he was doing—I learned a lot about baseball during those two weeks. He explained things like 'sacrifices,' and what a 'suicide squeeze' was.

"Of course I know it now, and maybe I even knew it then, but he was just interested in my body. He wanted what every high school boy wants. He told me I was a 'babe' and that I had a better body than most of the girls in his grade. It was embarrassing, but I liked it, too. When we would get to the pond, we'd sit in a little clearing, same place every time. It was close to the water but out of the way enough that any people walking by couldn't see us. We'd make out there for hours; he would run his hands over me, mostly over my clothes. A couple times he'd put his hands under my sweater, and that was okay with me. I thought that was what sophomores did.

"The whole time we were doing this, I felt a little queasy. I don't know if I was excited, scared, or feeling guilty. Probably all three. All I knew for sure was that this was the most exciting thing I'd ever done.

"By the end of the first couple weeks, I knew what we were leading to. There was no way around it. There would be a point where I knew just feeling me up wasn't going to cut it. We were going to have sex. Normally for a girl to be in my position, I guess she would be excited to be doing it with one of the most popular kids in school. But I wasn't. I was scared to death. And not only that—for the first time in my life, I really was struggling with my faith in God. I knew that you weren't supposed to have sex until you were married, and I'd always tried to do what God wanted. This was disobedient—willfully disobedient. There are times when you sin, and you don't know you're sinning, or at least you don't think about it as you're doing it, and I guess for some reason these are more acceptable. I mean, we're all human, with weaknesses, and sometimes you make mistakes. But this—this *pushing God aside*— was something else altogether. I didn't really want to do it; it made me feel horrible. At the same time, to be honest, I had never wanted anything more than I wanted to do it with Mark. I thought he loved me, and I loved him. I even tried to find a reason not to have sex with him—he was too old for me, or I was too young, he wasn't good looking enough, I hardly know him—I tried to find a fault, any fault, but I couldn't. He was perfect. He was sweet to me, and he made me feel special.

"One day, we took the trail that went to the top of the hill, not our normal trail that went to the lake. It was a long hike up to Weaver's Peak. You ever been there?"

"Can't say as I have," said Bill.

"That peak is the highest in the county. It's beautiful up there. I still go up there every now and then. Anyway, we went up there one day after school, and I think we both knew we were gonna do it. I even wore a skirt that day to school, something I never did then. He got on top of me and pulled off my panties, and pulled down his pants. My heart was beating a mile a minute. I was so scared and excited, but he went slow, and asked me if I was okay. I told him to be gentle. I don't know if it was his first time or not. He put a condom on, and pretty soon he was inside me. The whole thing only lasted about thirty seconds. He had started slow, and then got faster as he went along. I loved it, even though it was awkward, but I also felt...shame. We were up there, and I was afraid someone might see us. I stared at the sky the whole time."

"Okay, so you and Mark Cherneau had sex when you were thirteen. That was more than ten years ago; what does it have to do with his death?"

"It was something I just remembered the other day, something that Dale said last year. Dale and I were in a bar in Logan, one of those country bars with live music and line dancing. Dale went to the bar to get us a beer, and I was sitting there alone. Some guy—"

"Was it Cherneau?"

"No, no. I'd never seen him before in my life. He comes over to me and asks me if I want to dance. I say 'No, I'm with somebody,' and he says, 'It don't look like you're with anybody,' and he puts his arm around my waist with one hand and tries to put the other hand between my legs. Just then the guy falls to the floor and I'm soaked with beer. Dale had come up and hit him on the head with one of the mugs. The guy was on the floor bleeding, and there was glass everywhere. Of course this got the attention of the whole bar. Dale said, "If you ever put your hands on her again, I'll hack 'em off!" and then he spit on the guy. I'm not even sure if the guy was conscious at this point. We were thrown out of the place; even the band stopped playing for a minute."

"Are you telling me you think Dale killed Mark Cherneau?"

"He's a very possessive man. I know I would never tell him that I had slept with anyone else, but maybe he found out somehow. Maybe he found out and just went crazy, I don't know."

"But that was long ago."

"Don't matter. If Dale just found out, it would be like it just happened."

"Did anyone else know about you and Cherneau?"

"I don't think so, but I really can't say. Mark could have told somebody; I certainly know that I didn't tell anyone. Mark and I made a pact never to tell anyone and

I have stuck by that. I'm scared, Bill. That's why I told you all this. I don't have anyone else to tell, and I'm scared and I don't know what to do. I knew Dale was crazy when it came to me and other guys, but I never knew he was the type who would murder someone."

Bill got up from his chair behind the desk and sat in the chair next to Julianne. They looked into each other's eyes. He took her hand in his. "This is a very serious matter we're dealing with. I think for now you should just go about your life like nothing has happened."

"I don't think I can do that."

"If he knows that you know he might have killed Cherneau, he might do something that will put you in danger. God knows how he will react."

"I don't think he would ever hurt me." Bill gave her a look. "I mean...permanently."

"You didn't think he was the type to kill somebody, either. Listen to me. I'm gonna get you out of this, but for now I just need you to give me a few days."

"What are you going to do?"

"I'll figure something out, okay?"

"Okay." She put her hand on his face. "Thank you."

He leaned in to her, drawn to her by some magical force. They continued to look into each others eyes. They had shared so much and so little. She had told him so much, but what had they experienced together? He looked at the beautiful lips he'd wanted to kiss since they first met. Bill felt a chill along his back as he leaned toward her. Their lips touched softly for just a moment, and after it was over, Bill had to remind himself to breathe.

He couldn't remember if he had ever felt a kiss like that.

Chapter Thirty-Four

That night, when Karen came home, Bill struggled with himself. Should he tell Karen? Of course he should. For the first time since they had begun dating, however, Bill had kissed another woman. Not just that, but he thought he might love Julianne. The kiss had made it real to him, as if up until now the whole thing had been just fantasy. He was so attracted to her, but he never thought that she had felt the same about him. Even when she had invited him to her hotel room, he figured she was doing that out of a feeling of obligation. He was just someone on the perimeter of her life.

But did he really want to be *in* her life? Wasn't this all just a sexual attraction? Did he actually want to ruin his marriage over Julianne? Did he want to get involved—and possibly have to deal with Dale himself? Could he actually do that? He avoided confrontation. Over the years, he had tried to overcome his own fears—fears of failing, of dying without doing anything meaningful in his life, or let's face it—death itself. What lies ahead of us? What is Beyond, if anything? In one of his earliest memories, he was in the back seat of a car, driving in to town with his parents. They passed what had been an empty field the city was turning into a graveyard. He remembered looking at one of the stones, just staring at it, almost trance-like, and thinking of what was six feet under that stone. There was a person down there, trapped. It must have been when he was very young, before he could grasp what a 'soul' was, and that it was separate from the body. At the same time, he couldn't imagine not existing, either. The concept that someone just 'burns out' like a light bulb was also beyond his thinking. So he imagined what that must be like—dark, no air, not being able to move, even if you had an itch that had to be scratched.

How far had he come from that image of death? Sure, he now had entirely different beliefs of death, but could he rule out that first childhood image? Could he extinguish that possibility altogether? It is the Great Unknown, no different from a child's fear of the dark.

The graveyard that had been an empty field when Bill was a child thirty years ago was now full.

Chapter Thirty-Five

As Bill slept, Karen sat on the cold tile floor in the bathroom and tried to cry. She thought it might help. Everything was piling up on her—she could feel the pressure on all sides. From the police chief who was looking for a quick arrest, to Cherneau's mother, who had told her not just that she wanted the whole thing to be over, but that she *needed* it to be, they all wanted the same thing—closure. And it was something that she couldn't give them. The whole town wanted answers, and although she was trained to get them, she had none.

The internal pressures were just as bad. She had always expected the best from herself. How did Tom think she was doing, and Chief Wilson? She could tell herself over and over again that it didn't matter what anyone else thought, but she still wondered if they sat at home and said things like 'she's incompetent.' *That's silly*, she thought. If you were doing a lousy job, they'd let you know. Not to make you feel bad, but to just try to help.

The case had been going on for almost three weeks now, and they still had next to nothing. She tried to get her body to give in, to let go. She couldn't. People cry all the time, so why couldn't she? She made a few whimpering noises, after which she felt stupid. She looked ridiculous and she knew it. She wasn't the type to sit and cry.

She clutched a notebook and a pen. Who knew when something would come to her, right? Karen always felt the need to be writing things down. They would be clearer in her head that way. It was something concrete, something that could be looked at and studied. Something that she could focus her eyes on, and it helped her concentrate.

She wrote down everything she could think of, and when she looked at what she had written, none of it added up.

Chapter Thirty-Six

That morning, before he left for work, Bill got a phone call.

"William, you father has passed away." It was his mother's voice on the other end of the line. Bill felt a warm uneasiness in his stomach. It was strange hearing it from her. His father left when Bill was eleven.

"I don't know what to say," he said.

His mother cleared her throat. "I don't really know what to say, either, other than he's gone."

With those two words, Bill felt as if he was now alone on the earth, that it had only been he and his father inhabiting the planet. That was the sensation, what it meant was unclear—was this feeling a second abandonment, only this time a permanent one? Or was it one of relief, as it had been when he was a boy, of stepping out from a lifelong shadow of darkness?

Bill tried to shut these thoughts out, knowing he tended to intellectualize everything, to sort everything in the file cabinets of his mind. He knew that he shouldn't be thinking of either thing.

"When's the funeral?" he asked.

"I don't know the particulars yet. I have to call the funeral home and make arrangements."

"Why are *you* making them?"

His mother did not reply for a moment, then simply said, "I was his wife."

He kept quiet. His mother was already upset.

After he hung up, he got a glass of cold water. It hit his stomach and felt calming. He felt a lump in his throat, and forced a cough to try to clear it. He thought now of that graveyard that used to be known as Miller's field that was just outside of town. He felt that same fear he had as a child, when he first realized he was mortal. It was as frightening now as it was then, that someday, just like his father, he would be put in a box and be put under the ground.

Someday, he too would be simply described as 'gone.'

Bill sat on the chair in the kitchen and didn't do anything. He was frozen inside, and it scared him. He had always known this day would come, and after he found out that his father had lung cancer, he knew the day would be sooner rather than later. He put his face in his hands, but still felt nothing. He was ashamed.

Bill's father had served in Vietnam, and less than a year after he returned, Bill was born. As an officer in the Army, Bill Sr. was used to giving orders, and he expected just as much discipline from his wife as he did from his soldiers. When things weren't done exactly as he wanted them, Bill Sr. often lost his temper. He felt that his wife should somehow know what he wanted, and when she couldn't read his mind, she would get it. Bill always expected to get used to the yelling and the loud noises that came from downstairs after he went to bed. He never did. One of his first memories was seeing his mother one morning with two black eyes. He had asked her why her face was "purple," and she started crying.

As Bill reached adolescence, he knew full well what was happening. He knew it wasn't normal, either. His mother had told him that "this sort of thing happens to everyone now and then," but Bill knew it was a lie. He would sleep nights with a baseball bat on the floor by his bed, and when he would hear the beatings begin, he would want to grab the bat and go down there and beat his father over the head until he stopped. Stopped beating his mother or stopped breathing, he wasn't sure. He never could, however, bring himself to do such a thing. He knew he didn't have it in him.

The abuse increased in both occurrences and severity, and he knew he had to do something. He couldn't call the cops, because he didn't want the whole town to know how shitty his life was. He certainly couldn't 'reason' with his father. Even the mention of such a thing would ensure that he would be beaten as well.

One day, when Bill was staying over a friend's house, he spotted the solution in a kitchen cabinet. Up on the top shelf, he spotted the black barrel of a handgun. It was hidden behind some old dishes, but he could definitely tell what he was looking at. He made no mention of it to his friend, and late that night, after everyone was asleep, Bill went into the kitchen. He was able to be extremely quiet, something he had learned from having a father who hardly slept and who would beat him if he was up after ten. He grabbed one of the chairs and picked it up. He knew sliding it would wake the whole house. He put each leg down one at a time. He took a deep breath and got on the chair.

The door to the cupboard creaked when he opened it, and Bill's heart pounded. His hands were clammy, and he stopped to take a deep breath.

Luckily, there was enough room on the top shelf to gently slide the stack of old dishes to one side. Even though he grabbed the gun with both hands, he almost dropped it. He had never held a gun before, and it was heavier than he'd expected. He went back to the bedroom where he and his friend were sleeping. He felt around the dirty room until he found his book bag. The book bag was filled with sports magazines. Bill put the gun between some of the magazines so that the bag wouldn't make a *thud* when he put it back on the floor. This would also help to conceal the shape of the gun in the bag.

"What are you doing?" said the friend, sounding not fully awake.

"I had to go to the bathroom," Bill said, and that was enough.

The next day, Bill went home soon after he woke. He went straight to his room, which was normal.

He took the revolver out of the bag and tried to check to see if there were any bullets in it. He had seen it done on TV and after a moment, the cylinder opened. There were three bullets in it.

"Jesus," he muttered. The sight of the bullets made it real to him, the fact that these bullets could actually come out of this gun and go into his father's chest. The .38 trembled in his hands. Inside, a voice in Bill's head kept repeating the words: "have to, have to, have to," and he put the gun under the bed and tried to collect himself.

He put the baseball bat back in the closet.

He was through playing games.

A week passed without any fights between his parents, and Bill began to wonder if God was intervening in some way. It seemed that his parents hadn't gone for a week without at least raising their voices in...well, ever. And now there was nothing but silence. There was a different strangeness to it. Bill lay in his bed awake, waiting for the yelling to start, but it didn't. He had prayed for the yelling to stop many times—were his prayers finally being answered? Were they answered because of the gun? The silence that came from downstairs was downright eerie. They must not even be speaking to each other, he had thought. If they were speaking to each other, there would eventually be yelling. It was the only way they communicated.

He went over it in his head each night—what would Bill do the next time his father lost his temper? He knew it like the back of his hand—first there would be the raising of his voice, but there would be silence from his mother. A short time would pass, and he would hear his father start in again. This time he would hear his mother yell back. Then the arguing would go into high gear and then, like taking a needle off a record, the noise would stop, and there would be nothing. Sometimes young Bill heard the slap, or punch, and sometimes he didn't. But he knew that it had happened just the same.

Bill would go to bed each night with the gun in his hands. It made him feel like he was someone else, someone who didn't fear his father, someone who wouldn't, under any circumstances allow any of his shit. He never would go downstairs after ten, and certainly not when they were having an argument. He now planned on surprising them, waiting until the yelling became unbearable (it had *always* been unbearable, but now he could do something about it), then he would quietly walk down the steps, the gun pointing at him. Bill had even thought of something cool he could say, like he'd seen in Dirty Harry movies. He would wait a second, and then say to his father: "There are three bullets in this gun—do you want two in the head and one in the heart or the other way around?" He knew he could never be cold enough to say that, but it made him feel good to imagine it happening that way.

No, the way it would probably happen, Bill figured, was that he would come downstairs pointing the gun at his father, and the yelling would stop. He would try to steady the gun, but it would still shake. He would look squarely at his father for once and say: "This will stop now. You will not do this anymore." His voice would shake as much as the gun in his hand, and he knew his father would laugh at the whole absurdity of it all—his "little pussy boy is going to shoot the old man, huh? Go ahead then, if you got the guts!" And then Bill expected his father would say that that wasn't the first time he'd ever had a gun pointed at him. There would be a standoff, but not as much between Bill and his father as between Bill and his own nerve. If he could stand there and look at his father's eyes and not cave in, the situation might dissolve somehow and there would be no need for any violence. On the other hand, Bill's father might not be in the mood to deal with his son. It was very possible he would call Bill's bluff, and just try to walk up and take the gun from him.

Bill hoped for everyone's sake that that wouldn't happen. He would not give that gun up for anything, even if it meant pulling the trigger.

On the seventh night, however, Bill heard something downstairs a little after midnight. He had been almost asleep when the 'thud' made him sit up in the bed. He wasn't sure what it was—it could've been almost anything—a door shut, something in their bedroom like a dresser drawer being closed, or even furniture being moved, although Bill didn't know why that would be.

He stared straight ahead in the darkness, not breathing, waiting for the sound again. He grabbed for the gun underneath his bed. He waited and waited, but the sound didn't come. Should he go down there and check it out? Was there anything wrong, or was he being paranoid?

About twenty minutes later, just as his heart rate was getting back to normal, just as his breathing slowed, just as he closed his eyes again, Bill Summers heard a sound he would never forget.

It was the sound of his mother screaming.

"Oh my God, oh my God," he said, sitting up and putting his feet on the floor. In all the times he'd listened to their fighting, Bill had never heard his mother scream. At least nothing as bloodcurdling as this. He bent down to pick up the gun from under the bed, and felt a sharp pain in the left side of his chest. The pain was crippling, and as he grabbed the gun and tried to sit back up straight, it felt as though his chest was hollow. Had something punctured his lung? He couldn't get enough air. He stood up, the gun in his right hand, and walked to his bedroom door. His breaths were short, and as he stood facing the closed door, he knew this was it. Time to do it. His mind repeated its mantra: 'have to, have to, have to.' He put his left hand out to the doorknob and began to sob. His mind could say it, but he knew he couldn't do it. Just like everything else, he couldn't do it because he was afraid. His fear caused this paralysis, and there was nothing he could do. It was over. There was another *thud* from downstairs, although this was much different than the one he'd heard before. This one sounded *unnatural.* His mother abruptly stopped screaming. His knees gave in, and his hand fell off the knob. He was on the floor now, crying and gasping at the same time. It was definitely over.

The hatred was eating away at him like a cancer, and he was infested with it. His whole chest burned. He couldn't bear it anymore. The hate had to come out.

It had to come out, somehow.

Bill put the gun to his right temple.

He would count to three, he told himself, count to three, count to three, don't think about it, don't think at all, just count to three.

He felt the barrel push into his head. He mouthed a silent 'one.' He felt fear coming over him, beginning to feel he might actually do it. He wasn't sure how in control of his actions he was at this point. "Two" came out audibly, and the sound of his voice brought him back from the craziness.

He took the gun from his head and immediately unloaded it. The three bullets were in his shaking hand now, and he dropped the gun noisily to the floor. He didn't care who heard. He didn't care about anything right now. Right now, he couldn't imagine ever caring about anything ever again. He stood up and walked to the bedroom window. He had to get these bullets out of this room as fast as he could. He opened the window. The fresh air felt good. He couldn't believe it, but something actually felt good. He extended his arm out over the bushes that were in front of the living room window, and dropped the bullets.

Good. They were gone. It was a relief. He began to feel safe again but then he remembered that his mother had been screaming only moments ago. He started to shut the window when he heard the front door below him being opened.

There had been other times when his father had left after a fight—stormed out and went to the nearest bar, and sometimes Bill would watch him leave. This time as Bill watched his father leave, he saw something different than he'd ever seen before.

This time, his father was carrying a duffel bag on one arm and a suitcase with the other.

Bill stood at his bedroom window watching him move quickly, putting the suitcase in the trunk and the duffel bag in the back seat. He started the car and turned on the lights, which were facing the front of the house. The car just sat there for a moment, and then his father got out of the car, and headed back inside.

Bill didn't know what was going on. He went to the door to the hallway to listen for him. Was he coming upstairs for him? Not more than a half minute after he came in the house did he emerge again. Bill heard the front door close again and went to the window. He saw his father clutching a football in one arm and an M-16 in the other. The football Bill recognized immediately. It was signed by Tom Landry, one of his father's heroes. Bill had never even been allowed to touch it. Bill Sr. had picked up the M-16 in an Army Navy store. It couldn't be fired anymore, but he bought it because it was just like the one he had used in Vietnam.

He's leaving for good, Bill thought.

Bill's father quickly put both items in the trunk, and was getting back in the car when he spotted Bill in the window. He didn't stop; he just continued what he was doing.

As the car backed out of the driveway, Bill had seen something in his father's face he couldn't remember ever seeing before.

His father had been afraid.

Bill rushed downstairs and saw his mother lying there in the middle of the living room floor. There was a large amount of blood on the tan carpet close to where her head was. He yelled out to her, but she did not respond. One half-open eye twitched. He went over to her and there was a massive wound on the side of her head, and blood was coming out of her left ear. She was unconscious, and hardly breathing.

Bill called for the ambulance. They came and took her to the hospital. There she fell into a coma that lasted two weeks.

The day his mother regained consciousness, Bill found the bullets in the bushes and took them along with the gun to Emerson Lake. He walked to the end of the dock and dropped them into the water.

It was finally over.

Part Two

Chapter Thirty-Seven

Bill and Karen hadn't said more than a couple sentences to each other on the way to the funeral. It was a twenty mile drive, but to Bill it felt more like fifty.

Bill Sr. had lived in Marietta ever since he had left the family when Bill was eleven. They had only seen each other once since, and that was an accident. Bill and Karen had gone to the Marietta County Fair three years ago and had seen him in the crowd. Bill had wanted to ignore him, but Karen wouldn't allow it. She said to Bill that she wanted to meet him.

"So how you been?" his father had said, sounding less than enthused.

"I'm okay. This is Karen, my wife." Bill's father shook her hand and smiled at her.

"You're a good-lookin' woman—what are you doing with *him?*"

He laughed, and this hurt Bill. Karen also laughed, and that hurt much worse. Bill felt a rage run through his body like an electric current. Him touching her, looking at her. He had never wanted his father to meet her. He wanted to scream, *I'm not a child anymore! I'm a man now and I'll make you sorry for what you did!* But he said nothing. He was polite and said nothing.

Bill Sr. and Karen quickly ran out of things to say, and after a brief moment of silence, he turned away, saying, "I got to go. Take it easy." And those were the last words Bill heard his father say.

Other than the undertaker, Bill and Karen were the only ones who stayed at the cemetery. It was an overcast Friday morning, and it had rained the night before. This made the burial process sloppy, and as Bill

122

watched six feet of moist dirt cover his father, he thought he might throw up. Tears welled in his eyes from relief as much as anything else.

They sat on metal folding chairs, and Bill's had become uneven during the burial ceremony. One of the legs of the chair had sunk a couple inches into the damp earth. He had the strange thought that his father was trying to pull him down with him.

"I can't believe my mother didn't show up. She was the one who called and told me, she was the one who paid for this whole thing—I don't know why, but she did—and then she just skips the whole thing. I don't understand. Doesn't she need this? For some sort of closure, at least?"

"I don't know, Bill. Do you feel any sort of closure?"

"I don't know. I don't think so. Not yet, anyway."

"Maybe your mother knew that she wouldn't find any here, either. But I'll tell you what I think—I just don't think she cared. She probably closed that door years ago."

"You can't just 'close a door' and make this sort of thing go away. What you're talking about is denial, and it doesn't do anybody any good." Bill couldn't look at her.

"It's not denial. It's called 'getting over it.' 'Moving on.' 'Living your life.' Maybe you should learn from your mother on this point."

"I can't believe what I'm hearing. My father—the man who nearly killed my mother—the man who tortured my mind until I thought I was crazy—has not been in the ground for an *hour*, and you're telling me to 'get over it?!' Are you out of *your* mind?"

"Listen," she said, slapping her knees with her hands, "I think we better go. Come on—it's over and it's time to leave."

"We are not leaving yet! How can you be so insensitive?"

"I am not being insensitive! I am trying to help you! You need to get up and move on!" She started to get up. Bill's face was in his hands. She sat down again. She lowered her voice to a whisper. "Listen to me, Bill. I love you. Do you understand that? Now you can sit there and cry for your father. You can feel guilt if you want to. Over what, I don't know, but you can. You can go through all the motions of grieving if you want to, but it's not going to change anything. Do you hear me? Your childhood will never be different from how it was. You can't change it. It will always be miserable. There is nothing you can say or do or feel that will change it. You think that by showing up here today, that in ten years you'll be able to look back and have fond memories of your father?"

"I don't think that."

"That's good!"

"I'll always hate him."

"That's *not* good. You've got to let go of everything. Your hate, your guilt, everything. You shouldn't have any feelings at all for him. He's been out of your life for more than twenty years now. There is a point where sensitivity can be a person's weakness, and you've passed that point. You're hurting yourself almost as much as he hurt you, only slower. You won't let it go, and it's eating through you. Years and years go by, and you try to help these women—why do you think you do that? You're trying to save your mother from your father. Over and over again. You're trying to save yourself."

Bill sat back in his chair. He'd had that thought once or twice in his years at Clarksdale and had thought of it as a strength. He had first-hand knowledge. It was what gave him his drive, and it was the only way he could turn a negative childhood into something positive as an adult.

"Your parents died when you were six," he said.

"What's that have to do with anything?"

"You grew up with your grandparents until you went to college."

"Yeah—so what's your point?"

"I don't think you know what you're talking about."

"You don't think I know what it's like to lose a parent?!"

"Not that. I don't think you know what it's like to be abused, over and over again, and to *feel* the abuse inflicted on someone you love."

"I think I'm feeling it right now."

"But you haven't been there. You don't know how it feels, and what's sad is that I don't think you even want to know."

"I'm not sorry I was never abused, if that's what you're getting at. Is there something I'm missing? Why would I want to know?"

"For me. You refuse to even try to understand where I'm coming from—to try to comprehend all the different emotions I'm feeling right now. And you—you don't feel any emotions. Right now, what you're basically telling me is to shut up and quit acting like a baby. That's what it sounds like to me. This is real life, Karen. It is happening to *me*, not someone else. You might see this kind of thing every day, but it's never happening to you. Maybe you're numb to it, but I'm not going to have you sit there and tell me not to feel anything. I can't believe you're so cold. You are almost as cold as *him*," he said, nodding to the patch of fresh soil.

She stared at him. "You're a bastard. A fucking bastard."

"Well, at least now you're showing a little emotion. At least you seem human."

Karen walked to the car. By the time she got there, she was trembling with anger. Bill had the keys, so she waited. He stood at the edge of the fresh dirt and put his hands in his pockets. This was as permanent as it got. If this wasn't the end of it, Bill couldn't imagine what was.

The twenty mile trip up had felt like fifty miles.

The trip back felt like a hundred.

Chapter Thirty-Eight

Dale was on his lunch break at the G.E. plant, sitting with Ray and Harold. Dale and Ray had gone to McDonald's and brought back Big Macs; Harold's wife always packed his lunch, and Harold was almost finished eating when the two men came over to the long cafeteria table and sat across from him.

"Hey, Harold—how was that baloney sandwich?" Ray said. "I would have got you something, but Mickey D's don't serve baloney."

"You're hilarious. Dale—what time you end up rolling in this morning? 8:30? 8:45? We were already halfway done with the first run by the time you showed up."

"You punch me in when you got here?" Dale asked.

"Sure, I punched you in. But it used to be you were only five or ten minutes late, and I didn't think nothing of it. But dang, boy, you come in half an hour late and Big Dave notices." Harold nodded up to the glass office that overlooked the plant. It was the office of Dave Jennings, the shift supervisor.

"Yeah well, Dave can kiss my ass if he wants to. I'm tired of his shit anyway."

Dale considered Ray and Harold as working buddies, but they sure as hell weren't his friends. They weren't smart enough. The only reason he hung out with them at work was because he figured they kind of looked up to him. Ray was twenty-one, Harold a mere nineteen. Dale was close to thirty and had worked in this place when Ray and Harold were still in Little League.

"Besides, boys," Dale said, taking a bite out of his Big Mac, "I had a big score last night."

The boys laughed. "All right! Details—she have big titties?"

Dale stopped chewing, even though there was still food in his mouth. "Is that all you ever think about, Harold? Some day your dick's gonna fall clean off."

"What are you talking about, then?"

"I'm talking about driving to Columbus last night and selling some of my knives, that's what."

"Oh yeah? How much you get?" Ray asked.

"A couple weeks ago, I go to one of those bars on High Street, and I meet up with this guy who just got the shit kicked out of him. Guy's leaving the bar, and his girlfriend's buggin' him and he's telling her to get out of his face. So I go to the guy and I say 'hey, looks like you coulda used some help there.' The guy says 'I'm fine,' and I says 'you don't look fine, you look fucked up.' The guy turns to me and says, 'kiss my ass,' and I say 'I'm just trying to help you buddy,' and I pull out an eight inch stainless steel blade I made. The guy freaks out. He thinks I'm gonna stab him, right? And I say, 'you shoulda had one of these. You pull one of these out and people won't fuck with ya.' I told him I make knives and he asked me how much. Now here's the kicker—I give him this crazy price—twice as much as I would actually take—because I figure, what the hell, we'll haggle a little bit—and he just says 'okay,' and gets in his wallet and pays me cash right there!

"So then the guy's waving the thing around and he says, 'so you made this—that's cool, man,' and I took him over to my car and showed him a couple more I had in the trunk. He says to me, 'these are great knives,' like he knows the fuckin' difference, and he tells me he might know some other people who might want to buy one. He gives me his name and number, and it turns out, he's in a fraternity. I called him back a couple days ago, and he tells me he's got eight people who want to buy. So I go over there last night, to this fraternity—"

"Hey, Parker," someone tapped Dale on the shoulder. It was Stewart Kendall, Big Dave's assistant. "Big Dave wants to see you in his office."

"Is that so?"

"Yeah."

"Now?"

"Yeah, right now."

"Why?"

"I don't know. He just told me to tell you to get your ass up there."

"You tell him I'll be right up, after I finish my lunch."

"He said 'now.'"

Dale looked at Kendall, who stood 5'3". Dale was almost as tall sitting down as Stewart was standing up. "You tell him I'll be up there in a minute, you little weasel."

Stewart walked away without saying anything.

"So you went to the college, then what?" Ray asked.

"Okay. I went there and all these rich little college boys got their money all ready to give to me, like they was handing in their damn term paper or something! I sold ten knives. Made more in one night than I make in two months in this place."

"No shit?"

"And you know what else? The first guy said he knew of maybe some other people who might want to buy. Guy says he'd find buyers if he could take forty percent. I told him thirty, and he said it was a deal. I'll see you guys later," he said, not bothering to clean up after himself.

"Hey—don't let Big Dave get to ya," Harold said.

"I'd only be afraid of him if I was a Twinkie." Dale walked up the stairway that led to his boss' office.

The door was open, so he walked right in without knocking. He didn't know what this was about, but whatever he'd done, he would play it cool and be out of there in a few minutes. He didn't like Big Dave, that was no secret; the man was a fake, a real kiss-ass, and he had smooched his way to the top. Today, however, Dale was in a good mood, and he would be rubber and his boss would be glue.

"Dale, come in. How ya been?"

"Okay."

"Come in and sit down." Dale did. He looked across the desk at Big Dave, who didn't get his nickname from his position in the company—he weighed in at somewhere above and beyond three hundred pounds. In fact, he looked like he was closer to four hundred. He sat in his office chair, a chair that was supposed to have arm rests, but had been removed long ago. Dale felt a strange pity for the chair.

"Hey chief, what was it you wanted?" *Other than a couple of boxes of HoHos, you fatass?*

"Dale, I just wanted to check in with you and see how everything was going—if everything at work, and outside of work, was going OK. Is everything OK?"

"Everything's fine. You know, same old, same old."

Big Dave's face turned from friendly to concerned. "I just wanted to talk to you a minute about your schedule here."

"What about it?"

"You are to come in, from Monday to Friday, at eight a.m., is that correct?"

"You know Goddamn well that's correct, so why you askin' me?"

"We've noticed that, in the past couple months, it has been more like 8:10, 8:15, even 8:30 some days. Like today for instance—I had Stewart out there watching the door this morning, and you came in at 8:32."

"You had that little bastard watching the door? For me? I can't believe you did that."

"It's true, and it's well within our bounds to check up on employees who are more than a little late. And these repeated offenses—they're unacceptable."

"I understand. I'll try to do better, chief." There. That ought to shut him up.

"You gonna have to do better than try, Dale. You're gonna have to be here, every day, at eight. Not 8:02, not 8:07—8:00. Do you think you can do that?" He asked, as if it were a three year-old sitting across his desk. Dale didn't answer.

"We know, Dale, that you've been having Harold Baker punch you in every morning. You know that's against company policy. But we don't want to punish Harold. He gets here on time, and he works hard. Besides, we know how much he looks up to you, and we know that's why he's willing to break the rules for you.

"Don't you have anything to say for yourself? That's why I asked you if everything was all right. I was trying to give you a way out. You've been a good worker here, maybe a bit inconsistent, but by and large, you've done a pretty good job over the years. I've got enough here to have you fired, but I don't want to do that. I'm not going to Petersen on this one. This will be just between you and me. I am going to have to write you up, but that is just to have it in the books for future reference, in case we need it. I hope we don't, but if this tardiness continues, I'll have to have a record of it to show Petersen. Next time, I won't be so lenient. I won't be *able* to be lenient. It's unfair to the people who do get here on time."

Dale had his arms folded, and stared at the piece of shit in front of him. "You'd fire me over five minutes. Being five minutes late."

"It's not just five minutes one day, Dale. Not even two or three days. It's *every day*. Now I don't mean that if you come in at 8:02 tomorrow, you're fired. I'm not that cruel. What I am saying is that, if you're not back on track in a couple weeks, then I'll have to take further action."

I do *not* need this shit, Dale thought. Sitting here, taking this from this asshole. I got my own business, and it's gonna take off here in the next few months.

"You know, I've been here for nine years," Dale said.

"I'm well aware of that."

"And that would mean I've been here about six years longer than you, isn't that correct?"

"I don't see what that's got to do with this."

"You know how many people have sat behind that desk since I been here? Four. Maybe five. Maybe I should count you twice, you're so fucking fat."

Big Dave's face turned red, and he started to say something, then stopped himself. "That's uncalled for, Dale. Believe me, you do not want to go there."

"You want to fire me, go right ahead. You don't need to be doing me any favors, you fat piece of shit. And by the way, how can you look at me and say 'that's uncalled for' when I just called you fat? And you ain't just fat, you're ugly, too. You could lose all that weight, and you'd still be an ugly motherfucker. Ain't you a man? Can't you stick up for yourself?"

"All right, that's it, you son of a bitch—you're fired. You get the hell out of here right now. We'll mail you your last paycheck."

"Naw, you don't fire me, 'cause I quit." Dale stood up and put both hands on the desk and looked down at Big Dave. "I don't need this shit. You can take you crappy $9.10 an hour and stick it up your fat ass, you hear me?"

"Leave—you're fired."

"I said 'I quit,' you asshole!"

"Leave—you're fired."

"You heard me, motherfucker! I said I quit! You want to go out in the parking lot, you fucking pig? Huh? We'll see who's Mister Big Shot out there, okay?"

Big Dave didn't say anything. He pointed at the door.

Dale stood and looked at him. He put his hands back down on the desk, on the papers and the desk calendar underneath. In one clean *whoosh!* he swept it all off the desk, including the banker's lamp.

"There you go, pussy." Dale smiled at him. He turned and began to leave when, standing in the doorway, he turned around and said: "Go eat some more twinkies, you fat motherfucker."

As Dale descended, he saw Stewart at the bottom of the stairs. Dale walked quickly to him and shoved him with all his might. Stewart sprawled out on the floor, and papers were strewn around him. He'd wanted to do that since Stewart's first day two years ago and God, it felt good.

"There you go, you little prick," he said.

As Dale walked out of the G.E. plant for the last time, he could not remember the last time he'd felt so powerful.

Chapter Thirty-Nine

Bill Summers was still sitting on the biggest secret of his life. A couple weeks had passed since Julianne had told Bill about Dale's likely guilt in the murder of Mark Cherneau, and Bill hadn't said a word to anyone. He was rather proud of that fact, and equally ashamed. He had kept his word to Julianne (and to God), something that, even while making the promise, he figured he would not be able to do. The secret was the one thing he *had* with Julianne—it was the one thing they shared. Bill liked this feeling, like they were somehow secluded from everyone else. He felt close to her, and he was not about to give that up. Everyone else could stay in the dark for all he cared.

There was, however, still a feeling of guilt, of shame, that went with keeping such a secret. It had kept him awake nights, but was not equal to his feelings for Julianne. He thought of telling Karen, of doing what he knew was right, but he couldn't. Telling Karen would be the best gift he could give her—he knew the case was tearing her apart. There were times when he was very close to telling her, but in the end, he always gave in to his indecision and didn't say anything.

When he thought about it, Julianne needed him to keep his secret much more than Karen needed to hear it. Karen was a good enough detective, and if this was something relevant to the case, he knew she would eventually find out.

He had just finished watching 'Law & Order' when the phone rang.

"Bill, I need you to come get me. I'm sorry—Dale doesn't want me here tonight."

"What happened?"

"I don't want to say right now. But he wants me gone by the time he gets back."

"I'll be there in fifteen minutes."

"It's hot out tonight," she said as she got into his car. She didn't look at him; she just looked straight ahead.

"Julianne. Julianne, look at me." She turned her head to him. Bill felt as if he'd been punched in the stomach. That bastard had done this to her.

The bruise went from her forehead to her cheek-bone, which was already beginning to swell. Her right eye was bloodshot. Why does this happen? He wanted to scream at the world to *make it stop, make it stop!* He wanted to scream loud enough for the whole world to hear and obey.

"Is there somewhere you want me to take you?"

"We could get a drink."

"I think a bar is about the last place you need to be right now. We need to get you to a doctor."

"What are they going to say? It's a bruise and it'll heal in a week or two. This isn't the first time this has happened to me, you know."

"I know that too well."

Bill could no longer hide the fact that he was in this mess. "Julianne, I think I'm going to have a talk with Dale. All these years I've been at Clarksdale, I've seen a lot of abuse, and I try to instill self-esteem to the women who need it. There have been a few times where I would have liked to intervene, but I wouldn't allow myself. But I'll tell you—I've had it. I just can't take it anymore."

"I appreciate it, but I don't think Dale is going to listen to anything you have to say. I mentioned marriage counselors to him the other day and he just got up and left the room. I guess I'm lucky he didn't hit me. I don't think he'll want to listen to you at all. He doesn't seem to like you."

"What are you talking about?"

"I've probably told Dale a little more about you than I should. Tonight I told him I've been seeing you, and well, you can see the results."

"You mean he did this just because you mentioned my name?"

"Who knows what he was pissed about. All I know is that after I mentioned that I saw you the other day, he flew off the handle."

"When you say you told him you were 'seeing me,' did you mention that I'm your therapist?"

"I might have forgotten that."

"What are you doing!? I was going to try to have a rational conversation with this guy and now he thinks that we're together?"

"Well, he's not the type who goes for 'rational conversation' anyway."

"I'm still going to talk to him. Maybe try to straighten him out a little. You have to understand, Julianne—your boyfriend is sick. He's got a quick temper. You don't want to set him off. He's been beating you for how many months now? Or is it years? And you let him. I can't believe you let him; you're smarter than that."

"What other choice do I have? Seriously—what else can I do?"

"You can leave him!"

"And do *what*, exactly? He'll kick me out, I'll have nowhere to live, and I certainly can't get a job I can live on. I don't have any friends who will help me. Try to imagine how it is for me, then tell me how I should just leave him. Let's face it—Dale's about as good as I'm gonna get—he's good to me most of the time, he doesn't sneak around with any other women, he makes a good living."

"I don't think you're giving yourself enough credit. You're taking the easy way out—"

"You think this is easy?"

"What I'm saying is that you could make something of your life. You're bright enough to make it on your own, but I get the feeling no one's ever told you that before. Am I right? All your life, you've had people telling you you couldn't do this or that, probably because they were bitter. The sad part is that you heard them for all those years and now you believe it yourself. But you shouldn't. Thinking Dale is as 'good as your gonna get' is a perfect example of what I'm talking about. This may be a small town, but I know for a fact that there would be plenty of guys who would love you and treat you the way you should be treated."

"And how's that?"

"With complete respect. Not just that, but there are guys who would *cherish* you, I'm sure."

"Are you one of those guys?"

"I'm married, Julianne."

"I know, but what if you weren't?"

"I think you *know* I'm one of those guys."

They were coming up to Kiplinger's Market, just before route 203. "Ooh! Can we stop here a second?" Julianne said. Bill pulled in. She told him to stay in the car. She was back in a minute, holding a six pack of Budweiser.

Julianne stood outside the car door and held one finger up, as if to say 'wait'.

"What is it? What's wrong?"

"Nothing. Look up there." She was pointing at the sky.

"I don't see anything."

"I know. New moon. This is gonna be great," she said, and got in the car. "Turn right up here at 203. I know where we can go."

Chapter Forty

Sandy Kelley couldn't sleep. She'd been having trouble sleeping ever since the break-in, which she now wasn't even sure actually happened. The sliding glass door to the balcony had been shut when she went in to take the shower, hadn't it? Maybe the whole thing was something she'd made up in her mind. She'd been suffering from the occasional panic attack since she'd left Phil; maybe a little delusion wasn't out of the question.

One thing was certain—the gun she'd picked up last week at Manny's Pawn Shop wasn't giving her any peace of mind. It lay there, every night, on her bedside table. She wanted it close if the guy came back, but who was to say he couldn't come in while she was asleep and take it from her? The *thought* of needing a gun was unsettling, and more than enough to keep her awake. Maybe some self-defense classes would do her some good. No, that wouldn't work, either. If an attacker came into the apartment with a gun, what would she do—a couple karate chops and a 'hi-YAH' to scare him off? She didn't think so. The only defense was having the gun handy.

And of course, never sleeping.

She cursed the break-in. She had been doing so well in the big city. She had been careful, and she had been confident. It had happened anyway. Now she could feel herself slipping back into her old self, from the self-assured Sandy Kelley to the submissive, weak Sandy Oliver.

Maybe she needed to talk to Bill Summers again. That always did her good. It seemed he was the only man in the world she trusted. She had him to thank for getting this new life away from Phil.

Her friendship with Bill had lasted more than half a year, and over that time, she fell in love with him. She tried to tell him this, but he wouldn't listen to it.

"You feel indebted to me, and you may feel like you're in love with me, but you're not, Sandy," he had said. "You just got out of a really exhausting, abusive relationship, and while this may feel like the right thing to do, I assure you it isn't."

Sandy had thought that he was probably right. He was the professional, right? She had, however, detected certain feelings from him back then, and she could tell the difference between professional courtesy and attraction. He had been attracted to her.

There had even been the time when he helped her move to Columbus. She hadn't many things—a few boxes, her clothes, a couch and a chair. After they finished bringing it all in, they sat on the couch together, each drinking a glass of water.

"Do you and Karen get along?" she had asked.

He took a second to think it over. "I guess so."

"You never have any problems?"

"There are problems, but it's not like we argue every night."

"Do you ever wonder what it would be like on your own again? You know, to be single after being married all these years?"

"I think about it sometimes."

"Have you ever thought of leaving her?"

"Sandy, what are you asking me?"

"Well, have you?"

"I guess when I get really mad at her."

"Ever think of moving somewhere outside of Logan County? Like Columbus, maybe?"

"No, I've never thought about that."

"Listen to me, Bill." She took his glass and put both glasses on the floor. She took both his hands in hers. "I think you and I should be together. I need you. I feel safe when I'm with you. I think you're attracted to me, too."

Bill was already shaking his head. "I can't Sandy. I just can't do that. I do think you're a wonderful woman. You're going to do just fine here on your own. You're just worried about being here in Columbus by yourself. You ever need anything, though, or just want to talk, give me a call. I really appreciate what you said, and I'm flattered, but I just can't."

That had been how they left it, until the letters from Phil arrived last month. They were disturbing, and so was this. Laying here, a gun a few feet from her head, staring at the ceiling, not sleeping. She decided she would give Bill a call in the morning.

As midnight turned to one, Sandy was as awake as she would be if it were noon. She tried to relax, but every sound was potentially someone trying to break in. Every sound was magnified in the darkness, and with every one she tried to determine its origin. A car door here, a semi driving by there, the neighbors' occasional arguments. She listened intently, and when there was silence, she waited for the next one.

The silence was broken suddenly with a hard rapping on the door. She sat up quickly. Her stomach turned. The clock on the table said 1:41. She slowly took the covers off and put her feet on the floor. She glanced at the gun but did not pick it up. She would just look through the peephole. Maybe it was someone who needed help.

Again, there was a pounding at the door. Four quick knocks and a voice this time, the low voice of a man, someone who was in a hurry:

"C'mon!!"

She was so startled by this that she thought whoever it was was about to burst in. She picked up the gun with both hands.

She had to concentrate on putting one foot in front of the other on her way to the door. There was a groaning outside the door.

When she was about ten feet away, there was a loud thump against the door. Was he trying to break it down? Sandy took a shaky breath and lifted the gun to the door. She moved no closer; this was close enough.

She heard the thump again, only this time louder, startling her. The gun fell out of her hands.

At first, Sandy didn't know what the loud 'bang' was. Had the man fired a gun? No, she realized; her gun had gone off when it hit the floor.

She heard the man running down the stairs. She stepped over the smoking gun and looked through the peephole to see the hallway door closing. She ran into her bedroom and looked out the window to the parking lot. She saw him run into the shadows and disappear into a patch of pine trees. She watched the trees for five minutes, her stomach in knots. She scanned the parking lot. A van on the other side of the lot, close to the other apartment building, looked a bit suspicious. It had its parking lights on, and she could see by the exhaust pipe that it was running. The van was facing east. Sandy's window was facing north, so she couldn't see the license plate. She watched and waited. Why was this happening? What had she done to deserve this? Had she upset someone at work, or in school? Was someone in one of her classes stalking her? Who did she know that had a van? No one that she could think of.

She saw the man again. He came out from the trees, but in the darkness, she couldn't tell if she'd ever seen him before. She squinted, but there was no moonlight in the sky. The man ran away from her apartment building, toward the van. He ran around the vehicle to the driver's side. She heard the sound of the door closing.

She had expected the van to pull away after the man reached it, but it just sat there.

Then the door to the apartment building facing hers opened and three men walked out onto the porch. One of the men lived there. The other two looked like they were going out. All three were holding bottles of beer. She could hear them talking, but couldn't make out what they were saying. One of them pointed at her building and after a second they started laughing. Could they see her watching them?

The horn on the van sounded, and one of the guys on the porch lifted his beer toward the vehicle and said, "All right, Tommy!! Hold on!" About a minute later, the one with no shoes went back in the apartment and the other two walked toward the van. The two men were laughing at something as they walked around to the passenger side, the side that faced Sandy. One of them got in the front seat and the other got in the back.

She began to feel relief. It had just been some drunken college kids. Maybe one of them was so drunk that he had thought that this was his friend's apartment. She smiled. Must have scared the shit out of him when he heard the gun go off. All the buildings in the complex looked the same. It had even taken her a week after she originally moved in to be sure which building was hers.

She sat on the bed and was suddenly very tired. The whole experience had drained the energy from her. Maybe now she would get some sleep.

She went out to the living room and picked up the gun. The smell of the gunshot lingered. She returned it to the bedside table, and walked over to the window to pull the blinds. The van's headlights turned on, and Sandy wondered where the guys were going. They would probably be going to one of the campus bars, drinking and having a good time with their friends. She wished she had friends to go out with. She'd had the opportunities; there were a few girls in class who asked her if she would like to go out with them, and Sandy politely declined. She made a mental note that the next time they asked, she would say yes.

The van pulled away and she pulled the blind.

Wait.

Sandy got a picture in her head that wasn't right. It couldn't be. Had she seen what she thought she'd seen?

She took a deep breath and opened the blind. What she saw grabbed her by the throat.

Her view had been obstructed when the van had been there, but now she could see it clearly.

It was an old El Camino, the Chevy car/truck hybrid that was popular in the seventies. You didn't see many around these days, that was for sure. Sandy looked very closely at the car, trying to find anything that could give her solace. It was a dark color, but maybe it wasn't black. Maybe it was a dark red, or navy. She couldn't be sure. She looked into the north sky and felt her eyes watering up. It could've been red or navy, but the unsettling truth was she thought it was black. The car faced east, so she couldn't make out the person who was sitting in the driver's seat. There was someone sitting there, though.

Phil owned a 1979 black El Camino.

Chapter Forty-One

Bill didn't think this was a very good idea, but he couldn't resist. He and Julianne were driving east on route 203, getting farther from civilization. The muggy night was especially dark. There were no stars in the sky, no moon to shed any light. Bill thought of one of his favorite books that he had read in college, *Heart of Darkness* by Joseph Conrad. The road got increasingly darker, and the trees crept closer to the road until it was just a tunnel made by the overhanging branches. He was almost beginning to feel as if he were someone else, like the farther into the forest he went, the further from himself he was.

He would occasionally glance at her. Her face glowed green from the dashboard lights. She was excited, and even more beautiful because of it.

"This is nuts, you know."

"Is that a clinical term? This is what life is about. These are the type of experiences you don't forget. Besides, when you see what I've got planned, you'll be as excited as I am, believe me."

They reached the border of the Wayne National Forest. There was a sign saying it closed at dusk. The time was well beyond that. There was a fork in the road. To the right was the main road, the road that went to the Visitors Center and the information station. There was a gate attached to the booth where you paid five dollars a car during normal hours. On the gate was a heavy chain with a lock on it.

"Looks like this is the end of the line," Bill said.

"I don't think so," Julianne said, pointing to the dirt road that went to the left.

"That? Is that even a road? It looks like a walking trail to me. It's barely wide enough for a car."

"It's wide enough."

"That one's got a gate, too."

"But this one isn't locked. Just a second." She got out of the car. Bill saw a rusty chain on the ground. Julianne swung the gate open as far as she could. She motioned for him to drive through. He paused. Now that she wasn't in the car with him, it seemed like he regained some of his senses. Her power over him wasn't as strong. Nevertheless, he felt himself drive past the gate. There was no hope of resisting her. Besides, maybe she was right. Maybe this was what life was all about. He had lived 'safe' for too long.

He drove ten feet past the gate so that she could swing it shut before getting back into the car.

"Okay, just follow the road until it ends," she said.

Chapter Forty-Two

Sandy watched the El Camino just sit there. She kept her eye out the window at all times, even when she had to walk backward to the other side of the room to pick up the cordless phone.

After a long ten minutes of watching and waiting, she saw that he had started the car. It pulled away, not hurrying—it seemed to *creep* out of the lot.

She went out in the living room and turned on the TV. She needed the sound to comfort her. She watched an episode of *Seinfeld*, thinking a little comedy might help the situation. What should she do? Should she call the cops? And tell them what—a man who may or may not have been her estranged husband might have been stalking her, or maybe it was just some drunk college kids? Yeah, she was sure that would bring the cops right out. Cops in a big city like this had better things to do than come out here and let her make a fool of herself.

It *was* him, wasn't it? Phil had tracked her down somehow. She didn't know how, but he had. She didn't think he could stay sober long enough, but he had.

The show was finished and Sandy got up to get herself something to eat. She always ate when she was nervous. It was amazing she could stay as thin as she was.

There was a light knock on the door, and a wave of panic went through her. She thought of running into the bedroom to get the gun, but decided to check the peephole first. As she walked to the front door, she noticed the black hole in the wall about a foot from the base. She looked out the peephole and saw two policemen standing there.

"Ms. Kelley, it's the police, we need to speak with you please."

She opened the door, and standing there in her nightgown, she felt exposed. "Hello," she said, "Come in." The officers stepped into the apartment.

"Ma'am, we had the report of a gunshot being fired in the area, can you tell us anything about that?"

She felt like a child who had been caught playing with matches. "That was me. I'm sorry."

"What happened here, ma'am?"

She sat down and asked the policemen if they'd like to sit.

One officer started to walk to the couch, when the other said, "Harry" and shook his head to him.

"No, thanks, we'll stand," Harry said.

"I was trying to fall asleep; it was about one in the morning, and there was a pounding at my door. I was frightened, so I took the gun, my gun, to the door."

"This gun registered in your name, Ms. Kelley?" The first officer asked.

"Yes. I just got it about a week ago."

"You know how to use it?"

"Point and shoot, just like a camera right?" The two men didn't think it was funny. "I was going to take some lessons."

"We recommend that to anyone who has a fire-arm."

"Absolutely, officer."

"Ok, so you went to the door. Did you look out the peephole?"

"Not until after."

"After the gun went off."

"Right. My hands were shaking, and then he banged on the door again and yelled, 'come on!!' That's when I dropped the gun and it went off."

"And then you looked out the peephole."

"Yes, but I only saw the door downstairs closing."

"Have you noticed anything suspicious around here lately?"

"Yes. The other day I got out of the shower and that sliding glass door was open. I don't remember opening it, but I may have. In fact, that's why I got the gun in the first place."

"Were there any signs of forced entry?"

"No."

"Do you know who this might have been?"

"I think it was my husband."

"Your husband?"

"Yes. I left him. Ran away is more like it. He abused me."

"And you think this was him as well?"

"Yes. I saw the El Camino out in the parking lot. I think it was his."

"Not many of those around these days," Harry said.

"That's true," the other officer said. "Did you happen to get a license plate number on the car you saw?"

"No."

"What's your husband's name?"

"Phil Oliver—he lives at 39 Everingham Place. That's in Logan, Ohio."

"OK, ma'am, we're going to have to file an incident report and we would appreciate it if you could come to the station tomorrow to make a statement. We'd also recommend that you file a restraining order on your husband."

"Won't he have to be notified where I live? So he knows where he's *not* allowed to go?"

"Ms. Kelley, it looks like he already knows where you live."

Chapter Forty-Three

They came up to a section of the path that narrowed to only a few feet wide, and Bill put the car in park after driving nearly a mile. He looked in the rear view mirror and saw nothing.

"Well, now what?"

"Now we get out and walk," she said in the tone of a grade school teacher. She opened her door and got out. She took in the fresh air, and stretched her arms to the sky. "It's only about a half mile from here."

Bill stepped out and by force of habit locked the doors. Julianne was already walking briskly about fifty feet ahead of him and he had to run to catch up.

"So, where are we going?"

"My special place."

"Your special place? Why is it special?"

She stopped in her tracks and turned to face him. "Because this is where I killed him."

"Killed him?!"

"Ah, got ya!" She pointed at him and started laughing. Bill didn't think it was funny. "Oh, come on, it was a joke!"

She continued walking, and Bill followed.

"Just a joke, huh?" he said.

"Okay, the truth is that these woods scare me. They've always scared me. I have to make jokes, even if they are lame."

"If this place scares you so much, why do you come here?"

"Just wait till we get there. It's beautiful, and I don't think that many people even know about it. It's been left untouched by man. Going there is sort of like going back in time." She went off from the path and down a small hill, unable to walk in a straight line because of the number of trees.

"You know what I think?" Bill asked. "I think you make jokes about Cherneau's murder because you're trying to cope with it the only way you can. It's a denial of emotion. Or laughter is the only emotion you can handle. Your boyfriend killed a former boyfriend, and that's a traumatic thing to handle, so you make jokes."

"I don't know. Maybe you're right. The thing is, though, I hadn't even seen Mark since high school. I'd pretty much forgotten about him until he turned up on the news. When I heard they had found his body, I felt...well, it was creepy that's for sure, but I didn't feel happy or sad or anything, really."

"You mean Dale never said anything to you about him?"

"No, why would he?"

"Well, if Dale killed him, I would think he would have to have a motive for doing it. That motive would concern you. I just think he would have said something to you before or after he did it."

"Well, he didn't."

Bill was walking a couple steps behind Julianne, watching his footing. He almost bumped into her when she stopped.

"Here it is. Isn't it beautiful?"

Bill looked up and saw a clearing and a small oval-shaped pond. "Wow. This is beautiful. So this is it, huh?"

"Yeah, I used to come out here and swim when I was a kid."

"This is great out here."

"Well?"

"Well what?" he asked.

"Let's crack open a couple of those beers."

They sat on the trunk of a fallen tree a few yards from the lake. Bill took a sip of his beer.

"I tried to call you last week at Clarksdale, but they said you had the day off."

"Yeah, I took a personal day. I...had to go out of town."

"Really? What for?"

Bill took another drink. He smiled. "No big deal, really. It's just that my father died. I took the day off to go to the funeral."

"No big deal?! Of course it's a big deal! My God, Bill, why would you say such a thing?"

"It's not like I even knew the man—he left my mother and I when I was eleven. I only saw him once briefly after that. He hasn't been a part of my life for over twenty years."

"Still, he was your father! That alone makes it a big deal. If he left you when you were eleven, that must have been hard."

"It was."

"And it's got to be something you've carried around all your life." Bill looked at her then. "And now he's passed away? That is most definitely a big deal. This is a turning point for you. Your life will be forever changed from this moment on."

"What do you mean?"

"You've probably hated him all your life, is that right? Hated what he's done to you?"

"Yes."

"It's all over now, though. You've won."

"I don't feel like I've won anything."

"What I mean is, you've survived him. Isn't that what they say in the papers? 'Mr. So-and-So died, he is *survived* by his wife and one son?' Everything that was done to you, you survived. You have triumphed."

Bill finished his beer and opened another one. "I don't know how to feel. I feel good and bad at the same time, you know?"

"Sure, I know," she said. "I never told you about my father?"

"No."

"When I was younger, just after I'd hit puberty, probably about eleven or twelve in fact, my father caught me in a place where I wasn't supposed to be. I was out in the barn, playing up in the loft. He had told me not to go up there, that it wasn't safe up there, but I was up there anyway. That loft was just such a neat place to play. And when you're a kid, who cares about being safe, anyway? He caught me up there, after my sister and my mother had gone to the grocery store. 'Julianne, you get your ass down here right now!' he said. I went down there and he grabbed me hard by the arm and dragged me into the house. He dragged me all the way up to my room, something he'd never done—usually it was just a spank on the butt in the living room and it was over with. But not this time. He took me up there, and he said, 'You know what happens now, don't you?' and I said no. He said it again, and I said no again. He made me get on the bed and he took my shorts off."

Julianne stared blankly into the lake. "And then he showed me. He showed me what happens."

"Oh God," Bill said, and put his hand on her shoulder. Julianne looked at him as if coming out of a trance.

"Did it a few more times until I was fifteen."

"What happened then?"

"He died in a farming accident. I was shocked and sad, but after the initial shock, I was genuinely relieved. By the time of the funeral, I was almost happy. I sat there at the funeral, and as the priest said 'let no man put asunder,' I thought of how I used to think it was 'let no man put *us under*' when I was younger. I don't know if it was that thought, or if I was glad he was dead, or if it was just the utter *seriousness* of the whole thing, but I had to hold back from laughing. I started to crack up."

"Maybe you were just nervous, or maybe this is how you feel your pain, like I said earlier. You make jokes not really to cover the pain, but to release it."

"All I know is that, when I left that funeral, I felt like I'd won. It was a strange feeling, that's for sure. I don't mean to sound insensitive."

"I know what you mean. But didn't you feel any guilt over feeling that way?"

"Sure, but not for long. Not when I thought about what he'd done to me. What he'd taken from me. I felt sad because that was what I thought I was supposed to feel, but it's not really how I felt. I had won the battle with him, and with myself. It was a survival of the fittest, and I was standing on the earth, and he was now in it."

"That's an interesting way to put it. I had the same sort of feeling last Friday."

"It's okay to feel that way. Don't feel guilty about it. You have no reason to. You shouldn't deny your feelings if they are true. And you shouldn't let anyone tell you how to feel. If you're happy he's dead, or relieved or whatever, you should feel happy or relieved. Not how you think you should feel."

Bill finished his second beer as Julianne finished her first. She took the bottle from his hands and put it at their feet. She stood up and faced him. She put her hands on his shoulders. "You know what you need?"

"What?"

"I think you need to go swimming."

Bill laughed. He reached for another beer, and she stopped him.

"Come on. I think we should both go swimming."

"I don't think that's a good idea."

She took her shirt off and let it drop to the ground. She started to undo her bra and he said "wait" but it was hardly audible. She continued to undress.

She stood naked in front of him, and he wished there was a full moon so he could see her better. She stepped closer, wrapping her hands around his head, pulling his face to her stomach. "This is my special place," she said. "You don't have to be afraid here. It is a place of pure things."

"Julianne, I don't think I should—"

"You don't have to have any doubts," she said. "They can ruin a place like this." He stood up off the fallen tree. "Just release yourself," she whispered. He put his hands around her waist and pressed their bodies together. They kissed.

Without a word, Julianne stepped back from him and smiled. She stepped into the black water. "It's cool. Feels good," she said, and went underwater.

When she came up, she was farther out in the middle of the lake. Bill could barely see her in the darkness. He took off his clothes and embraced the coolness of the water.

It was a strange feeling, being underwater in this abyss, not seeing anything. He had never swam at night, least of all in a pond in the middle of nowhere. He surfaced, wiped his eyes and waited for them to adjust to the little light there was on the pond. At first he didn't see her, but then he realized she was right in front of him. Only her head was above water. Her face glistened.

He felt her arms slide around his waist. They kissed with great passion for a long time, drinking each other. She swam to the other side of the pond and he followed her.

When they were both out of the water, they stood and kissed again. Bill now wanted more than anything to be inside her, and when she lay down on the cool ground at the edge of the pond, he did just that.

Although he'd had only two beers, he felt intoxicated as he entered her. It didn't just feel good; Bill felt as if his senses were awakened. Suddenly he was aware of the sound of the crickets, and the smell of the pines. The night had become a bit lighter. It was euphoric. He knew at that moment that he would do anything to keep that feeling.

Anything.

He ran his hands over her breasts and up to her shoulders. She rolled her hips toward him, and he pulled her shoulders down. He wanted her to completely cover him, to envelop him—he pushed himself into her as far as he could, and it still wasn't enough.

She took each of his hands and pulled them to her breasts again. Her hands were now guiding his—she took the forefinger and thumb of each hand and put them over her nipples. She took her hands off his and put them on her thighs. He gently rubbed her breasts, feeling as if he might explode at the touch.

"No, come on," she said to him through her teeth. Again, she put her hands over his. She guided them as they pinched her nipples. He didn't know what she wanted him to do—he pinched and released them and she muttered her approval. He slid his hands between her breasts and up toward her neck. She put her hands and arms over her head and arched her back. When she brought her hands down, she grabbed his hands again. She held them both so that his palms were facing the sky. Then she took one of his thumbs and put it in her mouth. Her tongue twirled around it a few times and then she did the other thumb. She ran his hands, starting below her naval up her body, between her breasts and to her shoulders again. She slid his hands onto her neck.

"No...Julianne," he whispered, shaking his head.

"Yes...please, yes," she said, and pulled each of his thumbs down so that they covered her windpipe. "That's it," she said, taking her hands off his. He made sure not to apply pressure. "Oh, come on, just squeeze me a little bit."

He felt primal, grunting as he pressed into her neck with his thumbs and gritted his teeth.

Julianne seemed taken by surprise: "Ooh, there you go...come on...it's okay, squeeze me," and he did. He released her and a few seconds later she said it again: "Squeeze me."

There was something in those words, something in the way she said them, that drove him beyond excitement every time she said them, and she seemed to pick up on it.

"Come on, squeeze me a little harder," and he did.

As his penis began to convulse, he imagined himself falling through space. Sinking. This was freedom. He could do anything.

She gasped the words to him over and over, faster and faster, until the command was barely audible: "Squeeze, squeeze, squeeze..."

And he did.

Chapter Forty-Four

Tom had been gone most of the morning, and Karen still didn't know where he was. It wasn't like him to not tell her. She tried his cell repeatedly, but it kept going to voice mail. She had asked around the station and no one knew where he was. Cecil Moore, one of the cops she asked, had said, "I think he had a lead." No shit, she thought. But why hadn't he taken her with him?

She tried to clean up her desk. There were papers everywhere, virtually all of which pertained to the Cherneau case. She wanted to arrange them somehow, but the papers all seemed to be unique. There was nothing linking them together—just random facts. The papers might as well have been pieces to a huge jigsaw puzzle that even when put together, wouldn't produce a clear picture of anything.

There just seemed to be something missing, and she knew what that something was—a motive. Some thought the guy was an asshole, but even those people didn't seem to have a specific problem with him. Cherneau did nothing that affected them personally, anyway. Nothing that could be considered cause to kill him. He only had a few friends, and none of them seemed to know him well enough to provide anything insightful. Other than that, the general consensus was that most people had no opinion of him at all. Some people had even said that until they heard the news of his disappearance, they didn't even know he was back home and that they hadn't heard his name for years.

Karen thought Phil Oliver knew Cherneau more than he let on, and thought there was something he wasn't telling. She had to consider him a suspect, but not really because of anything he'd said. It was what he didn't say. He seemed so suspicious, so *guilty*, when they had spoken about Cherneau. He wouldn't answer certain questions about the night of the disappearance, and she had detected an underlying hostility toward him. It seemed to say that there was a past there, one he wasn't willing to even admit to, much less comment on. He wasn't being fully honest with her, and in her experience, that reservation was a sign of either fear or guilt. And Karen didn't think that Phil Oliver was afraid of anything.

Someone tapped her on the shoulder and startled her. It was Tom.

"Where have you been for the last two hours?" She asked. "I've been trying to get a hold of you."

"I didn't want anything to interrupt the conversation I was having."

"With whom, might I ask?"

"Phil "Don't Call Me Mister" Oliver and I just had a little one on one."

"Oh, really? I would have liked to have been there—you couldn't have let me in on your little male bonding?"

"Actually, that's about right. I got some interesting info this morning before I got here, and so I gave him a call. He said he would talk to me but only if I didn't bring that "low-down skinny bitch.""

"Who, me?" she said sarcastically.

"I don't think he likes you much."

"Yeah, yeah, so what is this interesting info?"

"I got a call from a guy I used to work with in the police force says there's been a restraining order filed against him. Oliver's not allowed to come within a hundred yards of his estranged wife, Sandy, who now lives in Columbus."

Tom took Karen into one of the interrogation rooms and shut the door. He told her the whole story of Sandy Kelley's hellish night of the seventeenth. He told her how she had left Phil, changed her name, and had moved to Columbus. Karen had heard that part of the story from Bill, but didn't bother letting Tom know.

"She had successfully disappeared," Tom said. "As far as we know, he hadn't been able to contact her for the six months since she moved to Columbus. We're not even sure he wanted to. And then he shows up at her apartment complex and scares her half to death."

"So you went and talked with him?" She asked.

"Yeah. I got him to admit that he was there that night. He wouldn't tell me exactly why he was there, just says he was there to see how she was doing in the big city."

"And how did he know how to find her?"

"He said that someone told him where she lived."

"Who?"

"Your husband, Karen. He said that Bill gave him the address."

Chapter Forty-Five

Karen parked under a sign that read 'No Parking Fire Lane' at Clarksdale Center for Abused Women. She didn't even bother turning off the car; she would only be a few minutes.

When she got to Bill's office, a woman was leaving. She looked like she had been crying, and didn't look up as she walked past. Karen went in without knocking.

"Another satisfied customer?"

Bill looked up and while he looked surprised to see her, he didn't look particularly happy. "I don't think that's very funny, Karen. That woman's had seven bones broken in the last two years. I don't think you realize how tough these women are."

"I don't think you need to have bones broken to be tough. My heart goes out to these women, these *stupid* women, but you'll pardon me if I don't worship them."

"Are you saying I worship these women?"

Karen closed her eyes and sighed. "I'm here because of one particular woman. One it doesn't seem like you worship at all. Not any more, that is. I think we should have lunch."

Just then the receptionist came into Bill's office. "Mr. Summers, your next appointment is here," she said.

"I suggest you cancel," Karen said to Bill.

"Can't it wait? It's only 10:30."

"No, it can't. This is official police business."

Bill and Karen drove separately to the park just outside the town limits. They sat at one of the picnic tables under a tall oak tree. It was a beautiful day; the sun was shining, and there was a breeze in the air. A pair of mothers played with their children, who were on the swing set.

Bill opened the lunch he had packed that morning. He fumbled getting the sandwich out of the plastic bag. His eyes went everywhere except on Karen. "So—what's this about?"

"Before we get into that, I want you to promise me you'll be honest with me. This has important ties to the case I'm working on, and it's important you be honest with me."

"Absolutely, of course."

"Don't give me that, Bill. Don't give me 'of course' when I know you haven't been honest with me in the past."

"I don't know what the hell you're talking about."

Karen started to speak, then held back for a moment. She took a deep breath, never taking her eyes off Bill. "This is about Sandy Oliver. That's what we're talking about." She looked at him like she was trying to understand him. "Why—that's what I want to know. Why would you do it?"

"Do *what?*"

"You know, I knew the whole time it was going on that you were in love with her. I knew. I could tell in the way you talked about her, the way your face changed. I heard the rumors, too, you know.

"At first I didn't know how to handle it. I debated leaving you, confronting you, beating the shit out of you, but I couldn't tell what was right. I knew what I wanted to do, but was it the *right* thing? I don't know. Anyway, by the time I knew for sure, beyond a reasonable doubt, she was running off to Columbus. I thought it would end there, and it did. But you still have feelings for her, right?"

Bill didn't answer. He felt as if he couldn't say anything.

"And that's why I can't understand why you did what you did."

Bill was afraid to ask. "What did I do?"

"You gave Phil Oliver Sandy's address in Columbus! Didn't you know he would try to hurt her if you did

159

that? Weren't you listening to yourself when you told me what a maniac this guy was?

"No," he said, shaking his head.

"What do you mean, 'no'?"

"I told Phil no such thing. What's happened? What's he done to her?"

"Oh, don't you worry about it. Your poor Miss Oliver—Miss Kelley, excuse me—is fine. It seems though, that she was terrorized by him."

"Terrorized how?"

"There was an incident—he went over in the middle of the night and was banging on her door, yelling at her, but she scared him off with her gun."

"Her *gun*?"

"Yeah, her gun. A pretty little .38 snub nose nickel-plated gun. Much more lady-like than this." She reached to her side and pulled out her .9 millimeter semi-automatic pistol. She put it down. The weight of the gun made a 'thud' on the picnic table.

Bill sat back away from the gun. "Put that thing away. What's the matter with you?"

Karen ignored the question. "So you didn't talk to Phil Oliver."

"That's right."

"When was the last time you spoke with him?"

Bill laughed. He was starting to feel how criminals must feel under interrogation. "I haven't spoken with him since long before Sandy moved to Columbus, that's for sure."

"Tell me what you're not telling me," she said.

"Tell you what? What do you want to know?"

"Bill, do you remember about four years ago, when your car was in for a tune-up, and I let you take mine? You backed out of the garage and turned the wheel a little too much and hit the front bumper on the door? I didn't know this, of course, and a week later when I finally saw the scrape, I asked you about it. You stood there and looked me in the eye and said you didn't know where it came from."

Bill laughed from the embarrassment.

"You are not a very good liar, Bill. I've had better liars tell me stories and I've still known they were full of shit. My job is to know when someone is lying. I'd have to say it's one of my strengths. You look guilty to me of something and I want to know what. You know what I think it is? I think you know Mr. Phil Oliver a lot better than you're telling me.

"It's either that," she said, getting up to leave, "or you're guilty of something else."

Chapter Forty-Six

After finishing his lunch in the park alone, Bill called the office and said he wouldn't be able to make it for the rest of the day. He told them he needed to see a sick friend.

He drove to Columbus in record time and got there just before noon. He pulled into Oak Hill apartments, and quickly realized he had forgotten which building was hers. It was all the way in the back of the complex, wasn't it? He drove to the last street, Willow Run—all the streets were named after trees—and was pretty sure this was it. He drove around the nearly empty parking lot twice, and didn't see her Ford Taurus.

He pulled into a parking space in the middle of the lot. He cursed himself for his impulsiveness, that he hadn't even got her address before he left. Maybe he could find a phone book somewhere and look her up. He sat for a few minutes contemplating what to do. Finally, when he thought he might have the wrong street altogether, and was getting ready to check Sycamore Avenue, she pulled in.

He got out of his car and walked toward hers, which was just pulling into a space in front of the doors. She shut the car off and still didn't seen him. She was gathering things in the passenger seat—a bag of groceries and a book bag. Bill stood in the middle of the lot while she got her things and got out of the car. He was just thirty feet from her but she didn't see him. She walked to the door and he called out to her.

She whirled around, and the expression Bill saw was fear. It lasted only a second, but it was long enough to break his heart. He had the fleeting thought that she may never fully get away from that fear, no matter how far away she moved.

"Bill!" She said. "What are you doing here?" They walked toward each other and met at her car.

"I came to see you. How are you?"

"I'm just fine," she said. "Come on up."

"Is this a bad time?"

"No, I'm done with classes; I was planning on being bored the rest of the day."

They went into her apartment. It looked much different to Bill than the last time he'd seen it, when it was just a bunch of boxes and a couch.

"So," she said, putting the groceries away, "what brings you here?"

"I heard about what happened the other night."

"Looks like we underestimated the son of a bitch, wouldn't you say?"

"Looks like it. How you holding up? Must have been pretty shaken up."

"I was a bundle of nerves the next day, expecting him to be out there in the parking lot, or even somewhere in the apartment. Cried that night, waiting for him to show up. But I made it through. Last night was better, and hopefully tonight will be even better." She handed him a cold can of Sprite, and he took it without saying anything. They moved to the living room and he sat on the couch. Sandy sat on the chair facing it.

"You know, last night I was nervous about going to bed, and I was thinking about finding a new place to live. I thought briefly of moving back home, but that didn't last long. Then I thought of maybe moving to another apartment in town. You know, this city has about a *million* apartments. I even was digging around my closet to find the apartment guide I used to find this place. I was digging and digging and finally, I stopped. I realized I wasn't going to find it. I was tired. Not just 'go to sleep' tired, but *tired.* Tired of running, tired of being afraid. You know, if I went somewhere else, he would just find me there. I've lost control of my life, Bill."

"Sometimes, that's the best thing. Admitting you can't control everything and everybody. It's good to be smart and protect yourself, but beyond that, I don't think fear does us any good. It's hard to shed, but if you can do it, it's a good thing."

"How'd you find out what happened?"

"Karen told me. She questioned Phil in a case she's in charge of. They're keeping her informed on anything involving him."

"Not the Mark Cherneau case."

"Yep."

"Oh my God."

"What—you know something?"

"Yeah, but I'm not sure I can tell you now. I know you're gonna want to know, but don't push me to tell you right now, okay?"

Bill sat motionless. "Okay, but—"

"You wait right here. I have an idea. I've got something I need to give you."

"Uh, okay," he said, his mind searching for what Sandy knew about the Cherneau case that he hardly heard her. She got up and went into the bedroom.

She came back almost immediately and stood in front of him. He didn't notice it at first.

"What?" he said.

"Here. I want you to have this." She held the .38 caliber pistol out to him. It wasn't pointed at him, but Bill backed away just the same. He hadn't seen it until it was three feet from his nose.

"What do you want me to do with this?" he asked.

"Take it. I don't know. All I know is that I don't want it." She still had the gun in her hand, outstretched to Bill. He took it from her, and only had it in his hands for a few seconds before placing it on the coffee table in front of him.

"Why does every woman I know want to show me her gun today? I don't want this. I hate these things."

She sat down. "I've been thinking about getting rid of it ever since it happened. On one hand, it was that gun that saved me. If it hadn't have gone off and scared him away...well, who knows what might have happened.

164

"But on the other hand," she continued. "I don't know how to use a gun. I was more scared with it in my apartment than without it. It was like, as soon as I bought it, that meant that something bad would definitely happen. It was just a matter of when. So the whole time I had it, I was *waiting*, you know? And what was it we were just talking about? How fear is a bad thing. How it never does anyone any good. I bought this gun out of fear, Bill. And it did nothing but increase that fear. I had wished that buying that gun would make me feel safe. It just didn't work. Hell, I probably would've killed myself with it eventually."

Bill didn't know whether she meant she would kill herself by accident or if she was talking about suicide. "What do you want me to do with it? Do you want me to hang on to it, in case you might want it back?"

"I doubt I'll ever want it back. Put it in your attic. Stuff it in your glove compartment and forget about it. You can melt it down and make jewelry out of it for all I care. Of course, if it's a *nice* piece of jewelry, I might be interested in having it back." With that, she smiled. And then he smiled. "So you'll take it? I just want to be done with it."

"Yeah, I'll take it."

From there, the conversation moved into lighter subjects. She told him about how she was saving up to buy a new car. How she had started country line dancing with some friends from school, and how they went to a place called In Cahoots every Wednesday night to drink and to do something called the 'Electric Slide.'

Bill paid enough attention to her to keep the conversation going, but the whole time he was somewhere else. He glanced periodically down at the gun that would soon be in his possession, and thought of the young boy who couldn't shoot his father and had almost shot himself as a result.

Chapter Forty-Seven

Dale Parker finished his dinner, his lousy TV dinner, and put the silverware in the sink. The dishes were piling up, and the kitchen was beginning to smell because of it. But he was damn sure he wasn't going to wash them. That was Julianne's job.

The problem was that Julianne hadn't been there for three days. If she had, Dale hadn't seen her. He was pretty certain that she hadn't been there, because he had a habit of making a mental picture of the house before he left, just to make sure that no one had been there, and nothing was touched.

There had been other times when she had disappeared, like the time when she went to see her mother die in that nursing home in Dayton. She hadn't told him where she was going then, either, but at least she had called. At least that he could understand. She *was* nuts, though. With her 'religious quests' and her rosary beads. Once, she drove to upstate New York to join something she had called a convent retreat, but to him, it sounded more like a cult. Those people messing with her mind made him angry, and if he hadn't thought she was already nuts before she went there, he might have gone up there and had a little talk with the leader—who by the way, was a guy, for Pete's sake—and he ain't never heard of no convent where there were guys, too.

She had come back and all she said was Mary this and Mary that—talking about purity and innocence all the time. He knew she was overboard when she asked him, begged him, if she could have a little space in the house that she could have to herself. A little holy place, she had said. Even with Dale saying no about a hundred times, and even though she got a few smacks for it, Julianne never quit asking. Just a little place, she would say. Just a little place. Finally, he let her have a corner of one of the rooms in the basement. It was a room Dale never went into anyway, and she set up a little shrine, complete with a painting of the Blessed Virgin and beads and a cushion to kneel on.

Even when she went to her little cult, she had left a note. "I'm going to New York to be a part of this," she had written, and left the pamphlet they had sent her. "I'll call you on Wed. night," it had said. When she did call, it took Dale putting on some major charm to convince her to come back, something he hated to do, and he certainly let her know once she returned.

He wasn't sure why he tolerated this religious stuff, but he figured that if she felt so strongly about something as to risk getting a beating, then she deserved it.

But now there was no call, and there was no note, and it had been three days. There was only so much he would tolerate. This wasn't being a free spirit anymore. This was disrespect, pure and simple.

He picked up the phone and dialed the number of his cousin John on the police force.

"Hey boy, what you doin'? Nothing much. I need to report a missing person. I'm not shittin' ya, man. Julianne's disappeared."

Chapter Forty-Eight

Not more than an hour after her husband had left the same apartment, Karen Summers knocked on the door of Sandy Kelley. Karen heard the footsteps coming to the door, then a pause (probably to check the peephole, she thought), then finally heard the chain on the door being unlocked. The door opened and Sandy looked at her with the slight look of confusion on her face.

"Yes?" she said.

Karen showed her identification. "Muskingum County Homicide."

Sandy put her hand to her chest with surprise. She had never seen a picture of Karen, and she certainly had never met her. "Please, come in. You're Bill Summers' wife. He was my therapist at Clarksdale. He was a great help to me."

"Yes, I know who you are. I'm glad he...helped you." Sandy motioned for her to sit down and she did, although she didn't really feel like it. "I'm here to talk about Phil. We've targeted him as a prime suspect in the investigation we're conducting."

"Oh, my. Is this about Mark Cherneau's murder?"

Karen could tell she was hiding something. "Yes, ma'am, it is." Karen tried to look at her without judgment, without thinking about her and Bill together, and composed herself.

"Mrs. Summers, before we talk about Mark Cherneau and what happened with him and Phil all those years ago, I think we need to discuss something else. To clear the air, so to speak."

"I need to know about your husband and his connection to Mark Cherneau. That's all I need to know."

"Well then, *I* need to talk about this with you. I'm sure you've heard the rumors about myself and your husband."

Karen played dumb "Really? What rumors would those be?" Her voice seemed to tremble with her anger.

"Come on; Logan is a small town. I know that you must've heard how people thought Bill and I had been together. I just want to tell you now that it isn't true. I'm sorry I never came to you earlier to explain, but I was afraid. I'm not entirely innocent, you see."

Karen looked at her with contempt. "I don't think this is the time to be discussing this. I'm here to ask you about this case."

"When is the right time, then? I think this is as good a time as any. It's true; I had feelings for your husband. He was a good friend when I really needed it. He helped me become stronger than I thought I could be. Phil had been so cruel to me—you must have heard stories."

"Can't say that I have," Karen said, which was untrue.

"Anyway, if it weren't for Bill, I probably never would have left Phil. I'm sure I would be dead now if I hadn't left him. Your husband saved my life; that's how I see it." Karen said nothing. All the things she had wanted to say to her back then had disappeared from her mind.

"You understand where I'm coming from, can't you? It was *gratitude*." Sandy waited for a reply but didn't get one. "I did love him, is that what you want to hear? I'm sorry, but it's true. He wouldn't leave you, though. He was always faithful; I swear to God. We never did anything—he wouldn't."

"He wouldn't," Karen said, "but that doesn't mean he didn't *want* to."

"You'd have to ask him about that."

"I don't have to. I already know how he feels about you. You may think that I hate you, but I really don't. Hate wastes my energy. If there was anything going on, and I'm still not totally convinced there wasn't, it's Bill I'd hold responsible, not you. Now, if you don't mind, we'll consider that case closed. Let's move on to talking about *your* husband and why we consider him a suspect in this murder case."

"Okay. Have you spoken with him yet?"

"Yes, I spoke with him last week. Real nice guy. He later called me a 'low-down skinny bitch.'"

"And you wonder why I was looking for someone else."

Karen couldn't help but smile at that.

Chapter Forty-Nine

After work, Dale went to the police station and, with his cousin John's help, filed all the necessary papers for the missing person report. Dale told him how this wasn't like her and that he was, in fact, worried. It took a lot for Dale to admit to something like that, but after he did, he felt a little better.

To keep his mind off things, and maybe to also lift his spirits, Dale hung out with John that night. At John's suggestion, they met at the Last Stop.

It was going on midnight, and John and Dale had been there for nearly two hours, playing pool and drinking beer. The bar was nearly filled with people, which wasn't normal, not even for a Friday night. The Last Stop had gained notoriety since the disappearance of Mark Cherneau.

John had been buying the beer all night, and Dale had let him. Finally, John said that it was Dale's turn to buy the beers. They had been playing at the table closest to the bar, which was about ten feet away.

"Hey, can we get some Buds over here!" he yelled at the bartender. The man behind the bar appeared not to hear him.

"Hey! A coupla Buds over here!" Dale was racking the balls up.

"Do I look like your mommy?" the bartender yelled back. "You want a beer, you come up here and ask for a beer. *Nicely.*"

"Jesus," Dale said, "What the hell kind of place is this?" he asked John. He walked with his cue stick up to the bar. All the seats at the bar were taken. Dale stood between a tall man at the end of the bar and girl who was next to him. The girl was young, maybe even high school young, and didn't seem to know the older man. Dale squeezed through. The bartender was at the other end of the bar, helping someone else. Dale took a sideways glance at the man sitting on the stool, and saw the man looking back at him. He had dirty blond hair which looked like it hadn't been washed in days. The man was looking at Dale with a little smirk on his face.

"And what the hell are you looking at?" Dale said to the man. The man continued looking and continued smirking. "What the fuck is so funny, you fuckin' drunk? Huh?" The man returned to looking straight ahead, and took a drink. There was still a smile on his face.

"Okay, pal, let me guess—you want a coupla Buds, is that right?" the bartender said.

Dale nodded and put the money on the bar. He was disgusted at the service in this place.

The bartender opened two bottles of Budweiser and put them on the bar. "$4.75," he said.

Dale handed him a five. "And I want the change back," he said. "You think I'm gonna tip you, you're wrong, ya fuck."

Dale took his quarter and put it in his pocket. He took one beer in each hand, and tried to grab the cue stick under his arm. It fell to the floor with a *smack*. Dale took the beers over to the table and then came back for the stick on the floor. After he picked it up, he saw the man at the end of the bar looking at him and smiling at him. He was *laughing* at him.

"You don't want to be laughing at *me*, mother-fucker," he said. "I'll knock the shit out of you. Got that?"

The man at the bar turned serious and then faced the bar again. Dale thought he would let the guy off with a warning. He went back to the pool table.

John had won six games in a row, but Dale was having his best game yet; he only needed to sink the eight ball for the win.

"Up in the corner," he said, and pointed with the cue stick. He stood back from the cue ball for a moment, lining up the shot. There were still two of John's striped balls on the table, but Dale knew this would be his only chance to win. John was a better player than he was, and making three shots in a row was not uncommon for him.

The eight ball was in the middle of the table, and Dale lined the shot up carefully. He knew by where the ball was that there was the possibility of a scratch; that was how he had lost the first game.

As soon as Dale struck it, he knew it was a winner—the angle was perfect. He had cut the ball just right, and had struck it with confidence. He smiled as the black ball dropped. The cue ball caromed off two rails and rolled back towards him. Dale stood up, took one step back, and watched in silence. The ball had slowed considerably, but was still creeping toward the pocket directly in front of him.

It dropped in.

"Son of a *bitch*!" He hadn't won a game all night. He was a loser. His face was red. John was laughing. In an instant, he broke the cue stick over his knee.

"Whoa! Shit, Dale! It's just a game, man! Take it easy!" They stared at each other. "Now I'm gonna go take a piss, and when I get back, I want you to be calm. Listen, maybe we shouldn't play any more tonight. I'll be back in a minute."

Dale was only about five feet from the bar, and had his back to it. He bent down and put the pieces under the table.

"Hey! What the hell's your problem?" The bartender shouted.

"What?" He said, turning to the bar.

"I just saw you put that broken stick under the table. You're gonna pay for that."

"Like hell I am," Dale said, he said walking away from the bar.

"Hey! You pay for that right now or we'll throw you out of here. Twenty bucks."

"Twenty bucks for that piece of shit?! The thing was bent, and the tip was worn down. And I'd like to see you try to throw me out of here."

Dale heard a laughing then, a large booming laugh coming from behind him at the bar. He turned around and saw that it was the big man at the end of the bar. He was looking at Dale and he was laughing.

Dale turned towards him. "I told you about that, you fucking drunk. What are you—retarded?"

"You're a little boy," the man said, and continued laughing. The bartender put his hand on the man's shoulder.

"Take it easy, Phil, all right? Son of a bitch ain't worth it."

"It's okay, Hank. I got it under control. You want him outta here, right? I'll take care of it."

"'Little boy,' huh? Well, this little boy's gonna kick your ass. Come on, let's go." Dale began to slowly walk toward the door, watching Phil to see if he was coming. Phil didn't move.

"Come on, you pussy, let's go!"

The man stood up. He was taller than Dale had thought, but that was okay. He'd beaten the shit out of people who were taller than this asshole.

The bartender looked at Phil. "You don't have to do this. I got a shotgun right back here. I don't want you to get in trouble."

"It's okay, Hank. I'm gonna enjoy this—the little fucker needs it, don't you think? Just watch my beer."

"I'm gonna show you what happens to people who laugh at me."

"You talk a lot, little boy." Before Phil even got through saying the word 'boy,' Dale caught him with a quick left jab to the nose. Phil tried to move out of its way, but it still caught him. He grabbed Dale's shirt with his left hand, and twisted it so that only his thumb was visible. To someone looking from a distance, it might have looked like he was tearing his heart out. He threw a hard right hand in his face, and before Dale could recover, he threw another one. Blood began to run from both nostrils. Dale grabbed the man's left fist and tried to pry it open. Phil let go of Dale's shirt and tried to grab his neck, but only grabbed a collar. Dale bent down and grabbed him around the knees and tackled him. As he fell to the ground, Dale fell on top of him, the taste of his own blood in his mouth. This enraged him even more—he was an animal now, blinded by rage. He put his left hand around the man's throat and began rapidly punching with the other. He was still punching when he felt a hand around his own neck.

Then there was a loud blast, and both men released their grips. John had run over and pulled Dale off the other man. Both men were breathing heavily. Dale got to his feet and saw that the shot had come from the bartender's shotgun. A crowd of six or seven had gathered. He hadn't seen them arrive.

"It's over, all right? It's over. Come here," John said, and walked Dale back to the truck. He opened the door and put him in the front seat. He held Dale's head just as he would helping a criminal into his squad car. John walked back to the bartender. "Sorry about him. He was fine earlier today. I think maybe his girlfriend left him."

"He owes me twenty bucks for the cue stick."

John got out his wallet and handed him a twenty. As he was walking back to his truck, he stopped to ask the man who was still on the ground if he was all right.

"Just fine. Just taking out the trash, is all," he said.

Dale got out of the truck. He held the door to keep his balance. "C'mon, John, let's get the fuck out of here! Don't waste your time on that piece of shit—let's go! Hey, I'll see you again, motherfucker!" he yelled, and got back in the truck.

Chapter Fifty

John and Dale sat in Dale's living room, watching the news with the sound turned down. Dale went out to the kitchen and got two beers. He came back and handed one to John.

"You know, it's getting tougher and tougher to cover your ass all the time," John said.

Dale took his eyes off the television and looked at him. "I ain't asking for any favors, Johnny. You want to bust my ass, go right ahead."

"Don't get touchy, Dale. I'm just saying you could stand to tone it down a little. You been gettin' more crazy in the past few months." Dale stood up and turned on the radio. The volume was low, and Johnny Cash was singing 'Folsom Prison Blues.' Dale returned to his chair.

"I ain't gettin' touchy, and I know what you're saying. You don't need to pound it in the ground. I ain't stupid, you know.

"You shoulda let me go for a couple more minutes on that guy. I'm still wired. I had him down and was beating the shit out him!" Dale laughed. So did John.

"You were definitely beating the hell out of each other, that much I know." They were both drinking their beers and watching the TV.

"What do you mean, 'beating the hell out of each other?' I kicked his big country ass! I was wailing on him when you guys stopped us. You can go home tonight knowing you saved someone's life."

"All I know is that your face was a bloody mess! I don't know, boy. Was he even bleeding?" John was smiling.

"I had my hand around his throat! I would have killed the fucker, I tell you that." There was a moment of silence. "Aw, fuck you. I'll be back in a minute." Dale walked back through the hallway to the bathroom. He took his beer with him, and continued to drink as he urinated in, on, and around the toilet.

He seemed to piss for an entire minute, and when he was done, he staggered back into the hallway. As he passed his bedroom, he saw something move. The curtain on the window behind the bed was flowing in the breeze. Something was wrong. Dale never opened his windows. Without bothering to turn on the light, he walked closer to the window. Then he saw a person in his bed.

It was Julianne, alive and well—and asleep.

He stood above her as she slept. He bent down and touched her on the hip. She moved but did not wake up. Dale then sat on the bed, and put his arm around her waist.

"Jules," he said. "Jules, wake up. Where the fuck you been?" He took her face in one hand and caressed her cheek. He bent down and kissed her face. Her beautiful face. He still had his hand on her cheek. She started to wake up. He stifled the urge to smack her, and walked back out into the living room.

"Listen, buddy, I'm sorry," Dale said, his voice barely above a whisper. "I shouldn't have said those things. You're right; I know you're right. I know I need to cool it."

"What the hell are you whispering for?"

"I just got a headache. I think I need to sleep it off."

"Okay, I'll be going then. Take it easy."

"Yep. I'll give you a call in a couple days."

After John was gone, Dale walked back to the bedroom.

"Hey," she whispered, "where've you been? I tried waiting up for you, but I fell asleep."

"Where have I been? Where have *I* been? You been gone for five days, sweetheart. Where the fuck have you been?"

Julianne smiled, reminiscing. Dale grabbed her face, which was sideways on the pillow, and turned it to face up at him. He had four fingers on one side of her face and his thumb on the other side. He squeezed her face. "You don't smile. Okay? You don't fuckin' sit there and smile when I ask you a question, you answer it."

"I wasn't doing anything. I just needed some time to myself, okay? I'm sorry. What's wrong with you? I'm not smiling. I'm glad you missed me. I missed you, too."

"Who said I missed you? Huh? Did I say I missed you?"

"You seem so concerned about where I been, that's all."

Dale grabbed the hair on the back of her head. "You listen to me. You are my woman. You understand that? You are *mine*. And nothing of mine disappears for five days without asking first—you got that? I been too lenient with you already. That's all gonna stop right now." He wanted to hit her so bad he could feel his right hand curling into a fist.

"Dale," she said, "I am not some piece of property—I'm a human being. Even if I was a piece of property, I wouldn't be yours."

"What the hell's that supposed to mean? You got some other man? Is that what you been doing—out fuckin' some other man for five days? Huh?" Dale opened his right hand and swung it across her face. "Huh? Is that what you were doin'? And when you're done having fun, you come back here like some stray dog wantin' food?"

"I'm someone else's *property* now. His spirit is within me. Isn't it wonderful?"

He pulled her up off the bed. They stood toe to toe for a second; Dale had his hands wrapped in her shirt—he made sure he had a good hold on her. He swayed her to his left, and then threw her as hard as he could to his right. She fell over and landed in the corner of the dark room. He threw her so hard and fast that she didn't have time to put her hands out to break her fall. Her head and shoulder slammed into the wall before she sank to the floor.

"You made a fool out of me! You know what I did, you stupid bitch? I filed a missing persons report on you! I went to John and said, 'John, please help me! Julianne's missing! Julianne's missing!' I must've sounded like a damn baby! And here you're out havin' a good ol' time! You know what I thought? I thought you might have been kidnapped! I thought maybe you were dead!" He walked over to her and kicked her on the hip. "*I thought you were dead!*" He was standing over her, almost hyperventilating he was breathing so fast, saliva dripping from his mouth. He put both hands on the walls in the corner and leaned directly over her and spit on her.

He picked her up and smashed her into the corner. She couldn't stand on her own, or at least didn't want to, because when he let her go, she started to sink again. He propped her up by putting his right forearm under her chin. He put his left hand on her breast and pinched her nipple. He twisted it until she cried out.

"Oh, does that hurt? No, that doesn't hurt—no, not at all! Not compared to what you put me through!" He put the knuckle of his first finger in her side, between two ribs. He pressed it into her like it was a gun. He almost wished it was a gun, and he wouldn't need to deal with this shit any more. He pressed hard into her ribs until she cried out again.

"What'd I just say?! That doesn't hurt, does it? Huh? Does it?"

"No," she barely said through her tears.

"No what? No what?"

"No, it doesn't hurt!"

"All right then. You tell me it doesn't hurt, okay?"

"Okay," she said.

"Are you learning your lesson?"

"Yes, I'm learning my lesson." He held her neck with his left hand and reached back with his right hand. She tried to move, but she was trapped in the corner. "I fuckin' hate you," he said, under his breath, and then hit her hard with his fist.

Blood gushed from above her left eye. He dropped her and decided to get a beer from the fridge. He stopped at the bedroom door and said to her, "Hey, you learn your lesson?"

"Yes."

"And did that hurt?"

"No, daddy. That didn't hurt," she said, and lost consciousness.

Chapter Fifty-One

When Julianne came to, she was face down on the bed. Dale was pulling her pajama pants off, standing at the end of the bed. He was moaning something she could not understand. She was still hazy, and her eyes couldn't seem to make out anything. She was in darkness. She tried to open her eyes wider and felt the sting in her left eye. There was still nothing.

He pulled her socks off, and then slid his hands up her thighs to her underwear. He moaned some more. Every now and then, he would lose his balance and let go of her to regain it. Julianne was becoming more alert now, but didn't move. This type of thing had happened before, and she had learned that it was best not to fight.

She had learned her lesson.

Dale took her underwear and wrapped it around his hands like he would the reins on a horse, and started pulling her toward him. Julianne felt herself moving, sliding to the foot of the bed. He pulled her as far as he could by her underwear, then let go of her for a second. He pulled the panties off her awkwardly, pulling at one side, then the other, back and forth until they were around her ankles. He had some trouble getting them around her feet, yanking them until they came off.

She felt his large hands grabbing her legs. She hardly moved. He put his hands around her ankles and began to pull her to him again, further down to the foot of the bed.

Her eyes were taking in the light better now, and she could see the streaks of blood from her face in contrast to the white of the sheets.

As he pulled her, she placed her hands over the head of the mattress. Her arms straightened as he pulled, and when he felt her resistance, he laughed.

"Well, well, look who's awake," he said. He pulled her, but she wouldn't budge. "C'mon!" he muttered through his teeth. Her legs were moving now, trying to get free from his grasp. "You know I love it when you're like this. Go ahead, be a wild woman; you know I like it rough." He pulled at her harder now, and she felt her grasp on the end of the mattress slipping. He yanked at her legs, saying one word for every yank: "I—am—gonna—fuck—you—whether—you—like—it—or—NOT!" And with the last word, Julianne felt her hands pull from the end of the mattress.

She grabbed at everything she could—she grabbed onto the sheet, and it came untucked. She grabbed at the pillow, hooking her left hand over the top of it.

Dale grabbed the back of the t-shirt she was wearing and pulled her. He kept his left hand on her shirt and Julianne could hear him undoing his belt and his pants. His voice was hoarse when he groaned, and he sounded like an animal that was enjoying what he was eating. He sounded like a hound from Hell.

He then said with a chuckle, in a deeper voice from him than she'd ever heard:

"Now tell me if this hurts."

He held on to the t-shirt, and with his right hand, he put his thumb close to her vagina. He pulled at it, and Julianne felt him push his way into her. He slammed into her, smacking his body against hers. Over and over again, and Julianne's eyes became blurry again, but this time they were from tears.

"Tell me if it hurts," he laughed again, but got no response. Every time he thrust into her, it hurt a little more, until there was nothing to hurt at all. She felt numb.

She was dead inside.

He groaned some more, and what Julianne felt then was so strange, so foreign, she thought it might be her imagination. In the middle of this soft bed, here was a gift from God. She had slid her right hand under the pillow and felt something cold.

Something sharp and made of steel.

Dale's thrusts were getting faster now, and he was grunting with every smack of his flesh against hers. Keeping the knife hidden underneath, she pulled the pillow to her chest, with her left hand still hooked over the top of it and the right on the knife's handle.

As Dale began to moan louder, and pound her faster, Julianne also began to moan. The volume of her voice grew louder and louder, and as Dale let out a long sustained moan, Julianne felt the warm fluid inside her. She was now almost screaming. She opened her eyes and saw the room more clearly. Her tears had dried and her eyes had adjusted to the darkness.

She sat up on her knees, and without pause, spun around and plunged the knife as far as she could into the side of his neck. She had stabbed him so deeply, the tip had come out the other side. The sound of his moaning immediately stopped and was replaced by a low gurgling sound. She let go of the knife, and watched the surprised look on his face. Blood spurted from his neck. Dale grabbed the knife with both hands, but before he was able to pull it out, his hands fell limp to his sides, and he dropped to the floor like a puppet whose strings had been cut.

Chapter Fifty-Two

When the phone rang at just after three in the morning, Karen was still awake. Much of her best conclusions had been made in the wee hours. She had lit a candle and left the lights off. She sat in her chair and drank decaf. The phone was on the table next to her, so she was able to pick it up on the first ring.

"Hello?" Her voice was raspy from lack of use.

"Is Mr. Summers there?"

"He is but he's asleep. Who is this please?"

"Mr. Summers is my therapist. From Clarksdale. Could I please speak with him?"

"If there's an emergency, you should be calling Clarksdale—I can give you the number if you don't have it."

"I'm sorry for calling this late, but it is an emergency and Bill is the only person I can trust right now."

"You can't trust anyone else at Clarksdale? Why is that?"

"I'm sorry, ma'am, but I can't answer that."

"Is that so?" Karen was tired of dealing with this woman. "In that case, I'll get him for you right away," she said sarcastically.

Karen walked upstairs to the bedroom. She nudged him on the shoulder. He didn't wake up, so she pinched him.

"Ow! What the hell are you doing?" he said, sitting up.

"One of your little girlfriends is on the phone."

"What are you talking about?"

"She didn't give her name; says you're her 'therapist'."

"What's wrong?"

"She wouldn't tell me, but she says you're the only person she trusts. You know, she shouldn't be calling here—she should be calling Clarksdale. You tell her to call *them* and wake *them* up next time." She dropped the cordless phone on the bed next to him, on the spot where she was supposed to be sleeping.

He picked up the phone and tried to wake up. He looked at Karen, who was getting into bed. "Do you mind?" he asked, holding up the phone at her.

"Do *you* mind? I'm gonna try to get some sleep."

Bill took the phone and went into the hall with it. "What's wrong?" He could hear her crying on the other end.

"I'm leaving, Bill. I'm leaving for good. I just wanted to call and say good bye. You've been the only man who was ever nice to me, and you've given me a great gift."

"Wait, wait—what are you talking about? You're leaving? Where are you? I want to see you—I'll come to you if you tell me where you are."

"You remember where we stopped to get beer?"

"Yeah."

"That's where I am, but I should really get going."

"No, just stay there; I want to talk to you. There's something you're not telling me, isn't there?"

"Maybe, but I'm fine. Listen, Bill. I'll probably never see you again. Thank you. I love you."

Bill heard a click. She had hung up. He went back in the bedroom and sat on the edge of the bed, putting his socks and boots on. Karen lay there on her side, with her back to him.

"Where are you going?" Karen asked, sounding half asleep.

"Something's wrong. There's been an...emergency." He said the last word with a touch of fear in his voice—a fear of finding out what had happened that had made Julianne leave. But even more than that, he was afraid of never knowing.

He didn't know whether Karen was falling asleep or pissed off, but she didn't make a sound.

He raced toward Kiplinger's Market. He needed to make sure she was all right. But he knew deep down that she wasn't. Something was terribly wrong. Through all the abuse she had taken in her life, she had stood her ground. Karen thought it was stupidity, but he didn't see it that way. Sometimes, you just can't turn your back on your problems. Julianne had faced them all her life, over and over. It took strength to endure, and she had. Until now. Now she was standing her ground in a different way—Dale had done something to her that was worse than anything she'd ever encountered, something that had pushed her to a breaking point.

Or maybe even beyond it.

When he reached Kiplinger's, he knew immediately that no one was there. The whole place was dark, other than the sign at the top of the pole out front that said "Kiplinger's" with the words "Drink Pepsi" below it. He pulled in anyway, and walked up to the pay phone at the top of the concrete steps. He hoped to find some kind of clue, but found nothing. He got back into the car. He put it in reverse, but on second thought, put it back in park. He didn't know where to go. He wasn't going home, that was for sure. Maybe he could drive around and find her—hell, how many people are out on the road at this time of night? If he saw headlights at all, there would be a good chance it was her leaving town.

Who was he kidding, though? She was gone. She was gone forever and he would have to deal with that. There was a knot in his stomach so painful that he could hardly concentrate. He backed the car out of the parking lot, pulled out onto the road and started driving. Making turns at random, he ended up on route 203.

Bill's breath became short, and his chest started to hurt. He opened the window, and as he put his hand back on the steering wheel, he thought it was shaking. He should have known he would be like this. He'd always been like this. Any little sign of stress, and his body malfunctioned—headaches, stomachaches, asthma attacks, panic attacks. It was laughable how much his body crumbled during these situations. When would it stop?

He had to face it—he became a psychologist in the first place so he could solve his own problems, and it hadn't worked. Years later and he had helped so many other people, but he couldn't help himself. He had thought that he could bury himself in the problems of other people and that helping them would somehow make his own problems disappear. They hadn't.

Frustrated and angry with himself, he pulled the car off the road. He needed to clear his head; maybe a walk would do it. He ended up walking a mile into the forest, all the way to the pond where he and Julianne had made love. It had been her secret place; now he considered it theirs. He sat at the edge, tossing small stones into the water. He watched the ripples expand, disrupting the glassy surface. With each *plunk*, he thought about how such a small thing could make such a far-reaching and lasting impact.

What he was considering, though, was no small thing.

What he was considering, he hoped, would reverberate warmly through his soul forever.

He stood, brushed his hands against his jeans, and knew what he had to do.

Back in his car now, he drove toward the home of the man who had done this.

As he turned down the dark road to Dale Parker's house, Bill concentrated on breathing slowly. There was a yellow sign that said 'No Outlet'. Only two other houses were close by. One was a farm that was behind him now, across the paved road. It had been owned by the Bennetts when Bill was a child. Bill had been friends with Danny Bennett when they were children. He wondered whether they still lived there.

There was another large field that went with the house across the street. Bill couldn't remember that house being there when he was a young boy—it had been a big empty field. The land surrounding the house was still without a crop, with weeds over a foot high. Bill took the dirt access road and drove past the large brick house.

A couple hundred yards past the other house was Dale's house, in bad need of a new coat of paint. Weeds grew around it, too, but Bill wasn't surprised. He couldn't imagine a monster like Dale to be out mowing the grass.

Tonight the monster would be slain. Good would triumph over evil, and Bill's fears would be erased. His work would do the world some lasting good.

What he was about to do would make everything better.

He turned the lights off before turning into the driveway. He pulled in slowly, and shut the car off. He reached across the seat and opened the glove compartment. Among an old pack of gum, a map of Ohio and a couple old fuses, was Sandy's .38 nickel-plated snub nose revolver.

As he held the gun in his hands, feeling the considerable weight of what his wife had called 'pretty,' his stomach began to quiver. This time, though, it was from rage, not fear, and he knew it was just his subconscious telling him to *do something about it!* instead of just sitting there. He knew the shaking in his body was his lifelong frustration, which he had kept caged all these years, where it had twisted and turned him inside out.

Unchain yourself. Purge this hate, he told himself.

He checked the gun. Five bullets.

His hate would burst out of him like a flood, and he would be rid of it forever.

And for the first time in a very long time, he would be pure.

The front door to the house was unlocked, and Bill opened it and walked in as quietly as he could. There was only the yellow light of a small lamp to light the room. He looked around, his eyes wide and the gun partially held out, pointing from his chest. He'd expected to see him sitting there. He had his finger on the trigger and was already applying pressure.

Dale wasn't there, though. "Shit," he muttered. He'd wanted to come in and do it before he lost his nerve. On a cheap radio in the kitchen, Hank Williams was singing, 'Your Cheatin' Heart.'

He held the gun with his arms extended, and crept down the dark hallway. His mouth was so dry he was having trouble swallowing. The first door he came to was open. It was an empty bedroom—there was no furniture in it except for a twin bed and a dresser in the corner. He stood next to it and looked out the window. Next to the window was a painting of Mary and the baby Jesus.

Across the hall was another door. He stood in front of it for a second, and then turned the knob as slowly and quietly as he could. When he was a boy, it had been a game to him to see how quietly he could move around the house at night. He knew he could walk so as to not make a sound, but there were always two things to worry about—creaky floors and creaky doors. Luckily, this door was silent, and when he opened it, he found it was nothing more than a linen closet. Rows of clean towels and sheets stared back at him.

He continued down the hall to the next door which was wide open. He heard the sound of the wind outside more clearly now. He turned into the doorway quickly, and saw the open window. Outside the trees stirred. There was nothing on the bed, other than the white sheets which had a strange, abstract black polka-dotted design. On the floor was a large mass of something; Bill could not make out what it was. It looked like blankets and comforters. He needed to turn on the light and get a better look.

He flipped the switch and looked at the bed. His stomach convulsed and he put his hand to his mouth. He saw the bed first, saw that the sheets were, in fact, white, and that the abstract polka-dotted design was blood. It was sprayed over the sheets. He dropped the gun to his side. He wouldn't be needing it. He knew then whose blood it was, and he knew who was under the blankets. The comforter, which had originally been white with an ivy design, now also had large spots of dark red. The wet dots gleamed in the florescent light.

Bill bent down slowly, touching as little of the corner of the comforter as possible. He pulled it back and began to see the head. There was a navy-colored sheet underneath the comforter. As he pulled the white comforter back slowly, it pulled the sheet down off his face.

Dale's eyes stared up at him, and Bill felt his stomach turn again. There was surprise in the eyes, the mouth parted just enough for Bill to see a purplish tongue behind dry yellow teeth.

Bill continued to pull the blanket, revealing the corpse. It drew back over his neck and the black knife handle protruded from the right side of his neck. As he looked more closely, he also saw its red tip coming out of the left.

She had killed him. He couldn't believe it, but she'd done it. He didn't care if it was wrong. He was proud of her. She had stood up and done something. A smile actually crept onto the face of Bill Summers, and he wasn't ashamed. Not at all.

He continued to unravel what Julianne had done. It was almost a shared feeling of triumph. Good had won, and maybe Bill had given her the strength to do it. He slowly pulled the navy blue sheet over the shoulders, and the smile disappeared just as slowly from Bill's face. At first, what he saw was so shocking, he had no idea what it meant. But soon enough, Bill felt a horror beyond anything he'd ever experienced. His eyes saw, but he didn't want to see.

He saw the truth, but it was a truth he didn't want to know.

Blanket and sheet were down to the waist now, and there was no mistake, no denying it.

He looked around the room, and saw them under the dresser.

Dale Parker's arms had been cut off.

Chapter Fifty-Three

Bill wanted to get out of there as quickly and quietly as he could, but he also wanted to be careful. Maybe if I made it look like a break-in, he thought. Maybe that would lead them away from Julianne. Why would he want to protect her now, though? Could he still love her after what she'd done? Would he want to? She had murdered Dale *and* Mark Cherneau. She may have been using self-defense with Dale, and that was something Bill could understand, but why would she have killed Cherneau? She said she hadn't even seen him in years, didn't care one way or another when he died. She had always looked back on those early years with him as being full of wonder and joy. What possible motive could she have for killing him? Here's a thought—maybe she didn't kill Cherneau at all. Maybe she was being clever by amputating the arms. She would try to pin it on the person who *did* kill Cherneau. Yes, that was it! She had no motive for killing Cherneau. Dale was probably attacking Julianne, and she had killed him in self-defense, but she was scared. She didn't know what to do, so she thought it all out. She would disappear, they would find Cherneau's killer, pin Dale's death on him, and then she could return. She could return without having to worry about getting caught. She wouldn't have to worry about a trial.

She could return to him.

If he made it look like there was a burglary, they wouldn't suspect her. At least give her a little time to get as far away as she could. Her plan was brilliant.

The house was already a mess—he wouldn't have to do much.

He went to the living room and looked out the windows. The closest house was dark, and a couple hundred yards away. He went over to the television and

191

knocked it over to the floor. It made a loud crash, louder than he'd expected. He still didn't think, though, that they could hear it so far away. He took some magazines off the coffee table and threw them around the room. Then he pushed the coffee table over.

He took the lamp and let it fall to the floor. The lamp shade must have cushioned the fall because the light was still on. Bill stomped on it with his boot and the house went dark.

The radio was still playing so he went to the kitchen. He pulled the plug and the house fell silent.

He tried to think of anything else he could do. He went back into the bedroom and shut the window and put down the Venetian blind. If they wouldn't find the body for a while, he didn't want the smell drifting and giving it away. When he went back into the living room, he pulled the shades to all the windows. They would not see him, and they would not smell him.

And they certainly would not hear him.

He tucked the gun into his jeans, and shut the front door behind him, sealing the white tomb that could use a fresh coat of paint. He hoped he had bought her some time.

He had almost stepped off the dark porch when he remembered something very important.

Fingerprints.

He didn't have a police record, so he knew that even if they found any prints, they would come up with a blank, but he wanted to be careful nevertheless.

He went back into the house and took off his flannel shirt. He rubbed down everything he'd touched— he wiped down the lamp, the plug on the radio, the coffee table, even the magazines as well as he could. He wiped down the plastic piece he held to pull the shades in the living room. This reminded him of the window in the bedroom. He went back to the bedroom and walked to the window, ignoring the body as he passed. He wiped down the clasp he'd touched to close the window, and the plastic rod he'd turned on the blinds.

As he walked out of the room, he had a revelation—there were bound to be prints on the murder weapon itself. He turned around and looked at the corpse. The knife would have prints on it and, even though he knew that Julianne didn't have a police record either, they could still match those prints to the prints they would find all over the house. They could conclude from that that the prints on the knife were that of the person living there. He could do one of two things—he could wipe the whole house down, or he could wipe the knife down. It was a simple choice.

He wrapped the shirt around his hand, making sure there were no loose ends. All he needed now was to get the victim's blood on his shirt.

He bent down and touched the long black handle of the knife very gently. The shirt was only inches, centimeters from the neck and all the blood surrounding it. He wiped the handle clean, and the knife, still lodged in Dale's neck, moved up and down ever so slightly. It felt squishy, like a knife stuck in a watermelon.

As he left the house, he wiped both sides of the knob. He closed the front door behind him, still with his shirt wrapped around his hand. He unraveled the shirt and put it back on. He stepped off the porch, impressed with himself.

He drove slowly with his lights off down the road. He paid attention to the neighbor's house as he drove by. He was glad that his car ran so quietly. The windows were all dark. Bill looked at the clock in his dashboard. 3:14. They were asleep. No one would be awake at this hour.

He turned onto the bigger road and drove for at least a half mile, still going only fifteen to twenty miles an hour. When he got out of sight of either neighboring houses, he turned on his lights and accelerated to fifty-five.

He'd done it. He'd gotten away with it.

More importantly, he'd saved her. And maybe a little bit of himself along the way.

Chapter Fifty-Four

A week had passed and so far the body had not been found. That was longer than Bill had expected, and he considered it a stroke of luck. And maybe a little help from the Man Upstairs. Julianne would be long gone by now, and although he wished he knew where she was, he thought it might be for the best. They would obviously want to speak with her after they found Dale, and if they didn't find her, they'd probably suspect her.

Bill sat in his office, thinking of all these things as a woman named Stephanie Bailey went on about how her husband had almost thrown her down the stairs and how he said he would leave her down there until she knew who was the 'commanding officer' of the household. It was a terrible story, and Bill was entirely sympathetic, but still he couldn't give it his full attention. His mind was running full speed on other things. He guessed there was nothing else he could do now, just sit and wait, but it felt as though he should be doing more. He would have to wait until they found the body, and from there they would lump both murders together. Hopefully, after that, there would be a trial, and the man convicted of Cherneau's murder would also be convicted of Dale's murder.

He only hoped Julianne was somewhere safe, somewhere far away, and that she was watching.

"Excuse me? Mr. Summers?"

"What? I'm sorry, Mrs. Bailey—you were saying?"

"I was saying how my husband never listens to me! Now I have to come here and have you not listen to me?! Is this some kind of joke to you?"

"I'm sorry. I assure you it's not. I...haven't been feeling well, that's all. I'm very tired. Again, I apologize."

"Yeah, well, I just do this because they're making me, not because I need any help from the likes of you. I'm fine—I just needed a place to stay."

"That's fine; that's good. If you don't need any help, then that's good."

The session ended and he was done for the day. He was glad it was Friday. Over the past week, he had grown indifferent when listening to the problems of others. He felt somehow that whatever mission he had been on was over. He thought that maybe all the schooling, all the training he'd had over the years had all led up to this.

He walked into the office of Carolyn Schultz, the Director of Clarksdale, and shut the door.

"Carolyn, do you have a minute?"

"Sure, come in and have a seat." She was shuffling a mountain of papers on her desk. "What's on your mind?"

"I really don't know how to say this—"

"Out with it then. You don't have to beat around the bush with me. You should know that after all these years."

"Okay. You know I think the world of you and what you've built with this place." She stopped shuffling the papers.

"Hold it," she said. "Hold it right there. This doesn't sound good, Bill. Have I done something to offend you?"

"Of course not."

"What is it, then? You're not quitting on me, are you? Tell me you're not quitting on me."

"Not exactly, but I would like to take some time off."

"Okay. That's fine. Like how much time?" She spun around in her chair and faced the filing cabinet. She put a few papers in one drawer, then opened another and pulled out a file.

"I don't really know."

"You know what a valuable asset you are to this organization. On the other hand you've been distracted the last couple months. Something's been bothering you."

"Seeing what we see every day can get a bit frustrating. These women come and go and after a while, they just seem to be...the same, you know? I think I've lost my passion."

"Believe it or not, it happens to everyone. You're just burned out, that's all. You're a good man, Bill, and I know you haven't lost your passion. You just need to have your batteries recharged." She pointed to the file in front of her. She turned it around to show him. "Look at this." It was Bill's personnel file. "You haven't taken any time off in three and a half years." She looked at him and smiled. He smiled back. "You *are* aware that we give vacations around here, are you not?"

"I know. It just never seemed like the right time. Either I would have a heavy patient load that I didn't want to dump on someone else's lap, or Karen would be involved in a big case."

"Right now you do have a lot of women on your appointment list, and I know Karen's got that big case, so why now?"

"Actually, I think it *is* the Cherneau case. She's having a tough time with it, and I want to support her. That case is eating her alive. I'd like to do whatever I can to help her."

"Perfectly understandable. You've got a little over two months' vacation; you can take all of it, and more if you need to. I'm glad that you want to support your wife when she needs you. Pardon me for saying, but the way she stormed in here the other week had me worried you two weren't doing so well."

"To tell you the truth, we're not. That's one reason why I need to be home right now."

"Okay. I hope everything works out. I'll reassign your patients; don't worry about a thing here. You can still stop in and see us, though. Let me know how you're doing. I expect you back here full of that old passion, understand?"

"Got it. Hopefully this time off will allow me to find it."

Chapter Fifty-Five

Bill stood under the hot water and wondered how long it would be before someone would find the body. It was good that it was now nearly two weeks since that night. The longer it went undiscovered, the better. Better for Julianne, that was. Bill, however, couldn't help but feel anxious. He wanted it all to be over, and he wanted to know if he had gotten away with what he'd done. He stood there, letting the water nearly scald the back of his neck, and wondered if fingerprints faded over time. If they did, how long would it take for them to fade? Of course, he had nothing to worry about there—he'd wiped his prints clean. Were there other things, though, that could be traced back to him? Hair and fibers, maybe? They would never be able to trace those things back to him, though. It was possible, he guessed, if they were to think of it, but no one would.

He turned his head to the right until his neck cracked a number of times. He felt the stress lodged in there and it had caused him headaches for the past couple days. He hoped the hot water would help, and it did, however briefly. He had become more stressed by not working than when he was working. He sat around the house, not knowing what to do. He tried reading *Anna Karenina*, but found that he kept reading the same sentences over and over. Soon after putting the book down he would usually sleep. He was sleeping seven to eight hours every night, and around three or four during the day. He watched TV all through the day, paying special attention to the news. The news hardly reported anything on the Cherneau case anymore; there was nothing new to report. He decided he would make more of an effort to help Karen. He would tell her that Sandy had said something that sounded like she knew more about Phil's connection to Cherneau than she originally let on.

He turned off the water, opened the curtain and without looking, reached for the towel. He felt the rack there, and nothing else. He stepped out, dripping wet, and saw that there were no clean towels in the bathroom. One lay on the floor, and Bill thought of using it, but decided to see if there were any in the hall closet first.

He opened the door to the bathroom, and felt the rush of cold air over his naked body. Bill shivered and crossed his arms. He put his hands over his nipples and hunched his shoulders.

He walked a couple steps down the hallway to the closet. His hands were wet, and he had to grip the knob tightly to turn it.

Ah, yes. One towel left. It was an old one they never used, but it was clean and folded nicely on the top shelf. An emergency towel in case all other towels were dirty. It sat next to the emergency roll of toilet paper. Bill thought the idea was strange when Karen had first said to him, 'don't use those—they're for emergencies,' pointing up to the top shelf.

Standing in the middle of the hall, he rubbed the towel over him until he was dry. He looked at the water trail he had made on the hardwood floor. He dried his feet off, and then knelt down and dried the spots of water on the floor. He wiped the trail back to the tile floor of the bathroom.

He was finished with the towel now, and after getting the dirt from the floor on it, he wouldn't be using it again. He walked toward the bedroom to put the towel in the hamper, and saw that he had missed a spot on the floor at the base of the open linen closet doorway. He bent down and cleaned it up and then, with the towel in hand, closed the door. He wiped the doorknob with the towel and thought of the last doorknob he had wiped clean—the front door of Dale and Julianne's house. They had a linen closet in their house, too.

And then it hit him.

Something he'd forgotten.

"What the hell are you doing?" Karen asked. She'd just come home and was coming up the stairs when she saw Bill standing naked in the hall. He was just standing there in front of the linen closet, his nose a foot and a half from the closed door. One hand was wrapped in a towel and holding the doorknob. It almost looked to Karen like he was in a trance.

"Hey—Bill." She snapped her fingers. "What's wrong with you—what are you doing?"

"I was, uh, just drying off. I was in the shower."

"And you were drying off in the hall because...?"

"Because there weren't any towels in the bathroom and I forgot to bring one in with me."

"OK. Is that all? Is anything else wrong?"

"No, everything's fine," he said, and snapped out of it. He looked at her and smiled. "How was your day?"

"It was okay. We're talking to a couple possible witnesses who were at the bar later on in the evening. They weren't there when Cherneau was there, but maybe they saw something; someone had to have seen something. Any new information this late in the investigation would be a Godsend." She followed him into the bedroom and sat on the edge of the bed. "I called your office today. They said you were on some sort of leave of absence. They said you haven't been there for a week. Is that true?"

"Yeah, I'm taking some time off."

"I looked like an idiot, Bill."

"Why is that?" He pulled on underwear and a pair of sweatpants.

"You haven't been to work in a week and I don't even know about it! I have to hear it from them? They probably think we never speak to each other."

"We never do. That's the point."

"What are you talking about? When were you planning on letting me know?"

"I was going to tell you the first chance I got, when I could sit down with you. Do you know how hard you've been working on this case?"

"That's a stupid question."

"I don't think it is. I don't think any reasonable person would knowingly work fourteen hours a day, six days a week."

"I can't back off this case and you know that!"

"I'm not asking you to back off the case. I'm just saying that you've been working all these hours lately, and I think you are suffering because of it. You're not getting any sleep, and maybe it's impairing your judgment."

"What are you getting at?"

"I think you should cut back to eight hours a day. Maybe you could budget your time better and get more done in less time."

"Are you telling me how to do my job? You think I'm not doing a good job? How long have you been a homicide detective?"

"I'm just saying you should try a different approach. All this time and what have you got so far—a couple witnesses who were probably drunk?"

"Go to hell. I don't need this shit from you, too." Karen stood up and began to walk out of the room.

"Karen, wait." She turned around to face him. "I don't want to fight with you. Come here a second." She didn't move. "Look, I know you are doing everything you can, and I think you're doing a great job. I know how hard you're working and the pressure you're under." Karen came back in the bedroom and sat next to Bill on the bed. "Maybe I didn't explain myself like I wanted to. My reason, or at least part of the reason, for taking time off is because you and I never see each other, and let's face it, whenever we do see each other, we're fighting. I want to support you in any way I can because I see what this case is doing to you. It's too much for you to handle alone. I'll do all the work around the house, and take care of whatever else that needs to be done."

"What other reasons do you have for taking the time off?"

"I've been going through a lot of stress at work, too. And lately, for whatever reason, I haven't been able to concentrate. I've been really tired, and I'm just a little burned out. Plus, I ignored a lady who was complaining about how her husband never pays any attention to her." Karen smiled. "The lady complained about me, and I really couldn't blame her. So like I said, I'm going to help you any way I can, even if it means helping you with the case."

Karen laughed out loud. "You want to help me?"

"Yeah—the sooner the case is solved, the better, right?"

"Sure." She was still smiling at him. "But how do you intend to help me, detective? This isn't Sherlock Holmes, you know. It's no game. We're not sure who the killer is, but we do know it wasn't Professor Plum in the library with a candlestick."

"You said 'any new information would be a God-send,' right?" he asked.

"Right."

"Okay, I've got something to tell you. Remember our lunch in the park? When you told me about Sandy, and what had happened to her?"

"Yeah."

"That afternoon I went to see her," he said.

"Oh yeah?"

"Nothing happened, if that's what you're thinking. I was concerned. You'd just told me that she'd been stalked and that she had a gun—it sounded like she was in trouble, so I wanted to see her. You know—see if she needed help."

"She's connected to this investigation, Bill. You shouldn't have done that. At least you should have told me."

"I'm telling you now. I told her that Phil Oliver was a suspect in a murder investigation, and to be careful. She says to me, 'not the Cherneau investigation,' and I said, 'yeah,'" Bill said.

"And?"

"And then she looked at me gravely, and said that she knew something about that, but she didn't want to tell me right then. Did you speak with her?"

"Yes."

"She give any motive for Oliver doing it?"

"No. She said Cherneau and Oliver went to school together, and that was about it. I asked if she could think of a reason why he would kill Cherneau, and she said no."

"It didn't seem like that to me," Bill said. "It seemed to me like she knew something, but she didn't want to get into it at the time."

"I'll have another talk with her then. Maybe she'll feel like amending her statement."

She started to walk away, then stopped. "You really want to help me?"

"Of course. Why wouldn't I? I love you."

After Karen left the room, she smiled to herself. She hadn't realized how long it had been since Bill said those words.

Chapter Fifty-Six

"I'm not exactly sure where to begin," Sandy said. "Do you have some time?"

"We've got all day if you like," Karen said.

"Okay, as you may or may not know, Phil is a couple years older than Cherneau. Did Phil tell you they knew each other?"

"No. He said they went to the same high school, but that was it."

"This was before then. Sixth or seventh grade."

"Sandy—the story you're about to tell me—do you have any first-hand knowledge of it?"

"No, this is a story he told me a couple years ago."

Karen took out her recorder. "Do you mind if I tape this?"

"Go right ahead. First of all, Phil told me this whole story one night when he'd had a lot to drink, and by that I don't mean a lot for normal people, I mean a lot for Phil, which is *a lot*. We'd been married for about four years by then, and we'd had a good night together, which in those days was rare, believe me. We'd gone to Paglio's to eat, then to All Star Lanes with Tommy Herrmann and his wife Trudy. The guys were drinking and having a blast, and over the course of three games and who knows how many beers, they had watched strikes turn to spares, and spares turn to gutter balls. Trudy and I were having fun too, but we decided to sit out the last game.

"Their last game was a close one, and Phil won. After the game we were sitting at the bar, and on the news they were talking about Cherneau. About how he'd hit two home runs that night. They said something like, 'look out, majors, here comes Mark Cherneau!' When I looked at Phil after the story was over, he had this smile on his face. Only it wasn't a happy smile, you know? He was shaking his head. I said to him 'what?' and he just said 'nothin'' and drank his beer. Is this the kind of thing you wanted? I'm trying to be as thorough as possible."

"It's fine," Karen said. "Any detail you can think of, I want to hear it."

"Okay. We said good-bye to Tommy and Trudy, and since we were having such a nice time, we didn't want to go home just yet. We decided to relive some old memories. You heard of Mount Everest?"

"Of course."

"I don't mean the actual Mount Everest; I'm talking about the big hill out past the Robinson Farm on 419."

"I don't know what you're talking about."

"You know how 419 curves out beyond town and goes uphill most of the way?"

Karen nodded.

"There's a place a couple miles before you get to Marietta County where the kids go to make out. Make out and do whatever else. It's the highest elevation in the county, so some of us used to call it Everest. We'd make jokes about it—like calling it the 'highest place on Earth' because kids went there to smoke grass, and we'd also say that it was the place to go if you wanted to 'go all the way.'

"We drove up there—I drove because he was so drunk. He drank some more—we both drank some more, actually—and then we had sex for like a minute and a half. There was a long silence afterward, and for a while, we just sat there and took in the view. Then, as if he's almost desperate to say anything, he goes, 'You want to hear why I was laughing at that guy on the news?' I say 'sure.'

"He says, 'That guy almost killed me when I was thirteen.' I had no idea what to say, so I just kept quiet. So he goes on about how, when he was thirteen, Cherneau and some friends had almost killed him. It was a nasty story."

"Tell me, word for word, as closely as you re-member, what he told you."

"You should know that, when he was younger, Phil had no friends, and the classes he was in were, for the most part, Special Education. To the other kids, the 'speds' were the freaks of the school. They were seen as less than human, and they were treated as such. Now, Phil was and is actually of at least average intelligence, but he's learning disabled. Back then, no one knew what ADD was. He had trouble concentrating.

"One day, the small group of kids in Special Ed were out at recess. They had a recess period before the other kids had recess. They weren't out on the playground entirely alone, though. It was getting close to summer vacation, and the gym classes were meeting outside. The kids from Special Ed were out there playing basketball, and the kids from Cherneau's gym class were in the adjacent gravel playground, playing soccer.

"It was a crude form of soccer; the kids would just mob around the ball, everyone kicking each other more than the ball. The ball would get stuck at the chain link fence, and the kids would grab on to the fence and just kick away. Then the action stopped. A couple kids screamed for Mr. Jenkins, the gym teacher, who had barely been paying attention. He and the recess monitor, Mrs. Hall, both went running over to the fence. The basketball game also stopped.

"Phil could see the blood on the fence from a hundred yards away. One of the kids in the gym class took off his grey t-shirt and gave it to Mr. Jenkins. He wrapped it around a kid's hand, and he and Mrs. Hall escorted the kid, named Eddie Gordon, past Phil and into the school. Phil later found out, and he's not sure how much of this had been exaggerated, that Eddie's finger had gotten stuck on a very sharp part of the chain link fence they had all been clinging to. As twenty kids huddled around a small red ball, shoving and pulling their opponents out of the way, Eddie was caught in the stampede, and was pushed to the ground with his finger still stuck on the top of the fence. It was said that a sharp piece of the fence had jabbed into his finger, and when he fell over, it had pulled the skin off the first two knuckles of his index finger. The rumor was that you could even see some bone. Phil said he didn't see bone; he just remembered all the blood, and the trail of it that had dripped off the shirt wrapped around Eddie Gordon's hand.

"One of the kids from the special education class then kicked the basketball so hard that it went over to the soccer game. He was afraid to get the ball, and Cherneau and his friends weren't throwing it back, so Phil walked over. When he got to the twenty or so kids, they all got quiet. Standing in the middle of the group was Mark Cherneau. He was holding the ball. The kids were all huddled up around the fence, and when Phil asked for the ball, Mark said, 'Come and get it, sped.' Phil was about twenty feet from Cherneau at this point, walking slowly toward Cherneau, who was saying, 'come here, sped, come here, sped.' When he got to about five feet from Cherneau, he held out the ball. Phil took a step closer, and then Cherneau flung that ball back behind his head, over the fence and across the street. Kids weren't allowed to go across the street to get a ball; they had to wait for a teacher to get it.

"All the kids laughed, and Phil started to walk away. 'Hey!' said Cherneau. 'Aren't you going to get your ball, you stupid sped!?'

"Now, you have to remember—Phil was two years older than Cherneau, two years bigger, and he wasn't afraid of some little fifth grader when he was in seventh grade. Plus, being called a 'stupid sped' in front of all those kids just set him off. So, without saying a word, Phil walked right over to Cherneau and hit him square in the mouth. Hit him good, too, I guess. Gave him a bloody nose and a fat upper lip. Cherneau didn't fight back, because just then a teacher had come back out to the playground. She saw Cherneau's face all bloody and asked him what happened. He didn't want to say that this 'sped' had gotten the best of him, so he said that the ball had just hit him in the face.

"After two boys had bled on the same day in gym class, they put away the soccer ball for the rest of the year. Since Phil wasn't in any of the same classes as Cherneau, and it was nearing the end of the school year, Cherneau waited until school was out in June to take out his revenge.

"As it turned out, it was one of Cherneau's friends, Terry Robinson, who had come up with the plan. It would take place on the Robinson farm, and it was something that his older brother, Stanley, had threatened to do to Terry, if he ever stole any of his stuff. They were just kids, and Cherneau and his friends saw it as just another prank. Sometimes kids don't see the cruelty of their actions."

"Tell me everything you know about the actual incident."

"Okay. It was early summer, and Mark had told Phil that he and some other kids from his baseball team were going to play out on the Robinson farm. They said they had a big open area in the middle of the hundred acres that the Robinsons owned. Even though he didn't like Mark, Phil was happy that they included him in the game—he thought he was becoming one of the cool kids. So early one morning, he met up with Cherneau and Robinson and some of the other kids at the Robinson house. It was early, but it was already hot and humid. There were about seven of them, and they went out there and sure enough, there was a huge opening in the middle of the dense forest.

"They played for about an hour and a half, having a good time. Phil thought he was 'one of the guys.' But of course he wasn't."

"What do you mean?"

"It was all a trick. They all decided to take a break and were sitting around, laughing. Then everyone became silent and started looking at each other. They all became serious, and before Phil knew what they were doing, he was ambushed. Phil's arms were held by two guys each, and there was one guy on each leg. Phil

208

struggled, but couldn't move. The two guys on each leg pulled his legs apart and Mark Cherneau stood between them. He put one foot on Phil's chest. 'We're gonna teach you a lesson, you fuckin' retard. We're gonna show you what happens when you fuck with me.' As he said that, one of the other boys gagged him with a handkerchief. They blindfolded him. His hands were tied around his back. They walked him over to the edge of a stump. Phil felt something go around his neck. He still didn't know what was happening. They forced him to stand on the stump, which was only about two feet wide. He was screaming now, and it dawned on him—that was why he'd been invited out here. They were going to kill him. He felt a rope pull at his neck, and heard some of the boys fumbling with it close to him. Then Mark said to him something like, 'Okay sped, now don't move. We don't want you to hurt yourself,' and a couple of the boys laughed. One of the boys stood with him for a short second, and took off the blindfold. Phil found himself standing on the stump with a tight rope tugging at his neck. The rope had been slung over a branch of the closest tree and tied around a lower branch. There was nothing he could do. Any step or the slightest loss of balance meant he would hang himself."

"Oh my God," Karen said. "That's so sadistic. I can't believe a group of young boys would be capable of doing something like that. Then what happened?"

"The boys continued their game."

"You're kidding."

"Nope. They played all afternoon while Phil stood there and watched from literally the brink of death. At one point in the middle of the day, one of the kids said, 'hey, check it out!' and ran over to Phil and pulled down his shorts and underwear. He stood there the whole afternoon like that. The heat was up to the mid-nineties for most of the day. Phil stood there with flies buzzing around him, trying not to faint.

"When the boys left around six o'clock, they pulled up Phil's pants. Mark told him he was proud of him. Phil thought maybe he'd passed some sort of initiation. He thought they'd let him down. But he was wrong. They left him there."

"Jesus. How long was he there?"

"A couple of the boys—not Cherneau—came around that night and let him down. He said he stood there for thirteen hours. I think Cherneau was just going to leave him there until he hanged himself and say it was a suicide."

"And these two boys must have had second thoughts."

"Must have."

"Do you know who these boys were?"

"No."

"Do you think Phil will tell us?"

"Hell, no. He told me the story a couple times, and he told me if I ever told it to anyone else, 'something extremely bad would happen to me.' He would kill me, I think. That's why you have to watch him around the clock. If he finds out I told you, he'll go nuts."

"Sandy, do you think he killed Mark Cherneau?"

"Yeah. He wanted Cherneau dead, that's for sure. And Phil's always been a patient man. He could have waited for years to find the right opportunity to kill Mark. Phil told me that one day he would get him. He said that what Cherneau had done to him was the worst torture he could imagine, and that when he thought of something worse, he would get his revenge."

"It sure looks like he got it."

"Just think about it—you're Mark Cherneau, local celebrity. You go to a bar one night and someone who you recognize buys you a drink. The man says he's a fan and that he's seen you play ball a few times. You don't know the drink's been drugged. Soon you are being dragged through the forest, barely conscious. You don't know why. Whatever's in store, though, isn't good, that's for sure. But you can't do anything about it. You can barely stand from the drugs. So you lay there while some guy holds you down. Through the haze you see him produce a saw. You start screaming when it tears into your shoulder, but you somehow know that no one will be able to hear you. You lose sense of time and place and, if you're still conscious, it is only a partial comprehension of what has happened when the person walks away with your arms."

Chapter Fifty-Seven

"Tell us the story, Phil," Karen said, closing the door to the interrogation room. Karen was standing, and walking around the dingy yellow brick room. In the middle of the room was a stainless steel desk. On one side of the desk was Tom Flanagan. He never took his eyes away from the man on the other side.

"I don't know what the hell you're talking about—"

"You know damn well what I'm talking about. This isn't something you just forget. We know that you knew Cherneau more than you were telling us before."

"I don't know what you're talking about."

"Sandy told me everything."

"I'm telling you—she's gone loco or something. I never spoke to Cherneau until we were both in high school. Whatever she told you, she made up."

"Is that so?"

"Yeah, man. You know, maybe I should go see her and straighten this thing out."

Karen put both her hands on the desk and stared into Phil's eyes. "You're not gonna touch her, do you hear me?"

"I'm not? I thought you'd like that, Mrs. Summers. I wouldn't think you'd mind, since she was fucking your husband and all."

"Fuck you."

"Sandy fucked me, but mostly she was fucking your man. Don't worry about it, though. They ain't doing it anymore. Sandy's probably banging someone else. And your husband's probably on to some other fucked-up broad. I mean, other than you, that is." Phil laughed and sat back in his chair.

Karen looked out the window at the number of empty desks in the homicide unit. She tried to gather herself. "Stop avoiding it; spare us the boyhood story if you want to. Let's just cut right to it—tell us how you killed Mark Cherneau."

"I ain't no killer, and I got proof."

"Oh really? Let's hear it." Karen pulled up a chair and sat beside Tom. Phil hooked a finger at Karen, indicating he wanted her to move closer, as if to tell a secret.

"My proof that I ain't no killer," he whispered, "is that your husband is still alive. You see, detective, if I was a killer, I would have torn your husband's throat out when I suspected he was screwing Sandy. But you see, I didn't. I have restraint. Some people might not have it, but that's what separates men from animals. I'm pretty smart for a former sped. I can control myself—which is more than I can say for your shrink husband."

Tom crossed his arms. "You beat your wife repeatedly. Twice, she was on the verge of death," he said. "You call that restraint?"

"No, I call that 'discipline.' Just teaching her a lesson. And she learned, too. Sometimes she'd forget, but sooner or later, she'd learn. I believe I got one more thing I need to teach her. One important lesson left."

"I'm telling you right now," Tom said, "we're going to watch you like a hawk, and if you get within a mile of her, I'm gonna introduce you to a world of pain."

"I'm shaking, asshole."

"You should be, wife-beating chicken shit," Tom said.

"Why don't you take a few minutes," Karen said to Tom, nodding toward the door. Tom got up, and without taking his eyes off Oliver, found the door and exited.

"So what did Sandy tell ya?"

"I'm not going to tell you what she said. I want to hear it from you. Tell me about what happened between you and Cherneau when you were kids."

"You really should believe me on this. Sandy's lost it. I have to tell you, for the record, that you got the wrong guy. I didn't do nothing. And as a citizen, I have to ask you to stop wasting my tax dollars. They go to pay your salary and I think you should be out finding the real killer."

"Thanks, but I think I know what I'm doing."

"Obviously not."

"Why won't you tell us where you were the night Cherneau disappeared? You're a regular at the Last Stop, but you weren't there on the night of the 23rd. You can help put your tax dollars to use by giving me a straight answer."

Chapter Fifty-Eight

The rain pounded against the windshield as Bill turned the key. He had been sitting in his driveway for twenty minutes, trying to make sure he was doing the right thing. He tried to imagine what other people would do in his situation, and wondered if he was acting rationally. He'd gone there two weeks ago in a blind rage, with murder in mind. That had clearly been an irrational act—and wasn't this just an extension of that?

Tonight, though, he had a much more sane purpose. He hadn't realized it then, but he'd forgotten something that night. He had done everything he could to erase his presence. Wiped his fingerprints clean, except for the doorknob to the linen closet. He remembered now the fear and rage he felt then, before he knew it was a closet. Thinking that he'd gone to a house to murder someone to find him already murdered, Bill could now understand how he forgot a simple closet door.

He had mulled over the question for two days now—should he go back and clean that last print? Was it worth the risk? He didn't have a criminal record, so they wouldn't be able to trace it to anyone. Did he want to risk being noticed? It was strange that Dale's body had gone undiscovered for so long. Didn't this guy have any friends or family? Didn't he have a job?

After two days of internal debate, he couldn't let it go. He decided he would just do it and get it over with. Otherwise, knowing that print was there would drive him crazy. The cops would surely find it, and he couldn't have his fingerprints at the scene of a murder, even if they were untraceable. He had gone into the house undetected once; he could do it again. He would just have to be careful.

Extremely careful.

As he drove, rain pelted the vinyl roof of the convertible. He turned the wipers on their maximum speed, and it still wasn't enough. It was now fifteen minutes past two in the morning. He had been able to sneak out of the house without Karen noticing.

He tried to devise a plan, but a plan implied something complicated; this was not. Get in, wipe down the prints, get out. Simple as that. He just had to make sure he wouldn't be spotted. The whole thing, if it went right, would take less than five minutes.

He tried to prepare himself for what he would smell in there. The corpse had been rotting in the late summer heat. He would hold his breath. Shouldn't take longer than half a minute, and Bill knew if he really had to, he could probably hold it twice that.

Within a mile of the house, the rain lessened. He was even able to turn the wipers down a notch. Each road he took was less populated than the last. First there was I-77, then state route 203, then Wilmer Road. On the three mile stretch on Wilmer, he had passed only one other car. Bill turned onto the next to last road. As far as he knew, it didn't have a name. It was a farm road that connected Wilmer to Ridge Road. Neither Wilmer nor Ridge were heavily traveled roads, which is why Bill never expected to see anyone at this time of night.

He never considered himself a lucky man. His knack for being unlucky always came up in the most inappropriate times. Two winters ago, while sawing up firewood in the backyard, he nearly cut a finger off. The blood ran from his finger into the snow, turning it pink. No one else was at home, so he quickly put a towel around the finger and got in his car. He was half way to the emergency room when he got a flat tire. When he got out to try to change it, someone driving past saw all the blood and let him ride in the back of his truck. The truck owner took him to the emergency room, and they were able to sew up the finger.

Just before he pulled onto the road with no name, he saw a pair of headlights in the distance. Here, at two-thirty in the goddamn morning! What the hell were they doing out here?

He knew he would get to the no-name road before the oncoming truck would. He drove slowly and thought quickly—he would just keep going straight. Whoever was in the truck was probably going to Wilmer, and taking this as some kind of shortcut. Bill would drive on to Ridge, and come back around in a few minutes.

Bill passed the road to Dale's house. The rain was still steady on the windshield as he approached the truck. It was a late model Ford F150, and it took up most of its lane. It was a dark color. As the truck passed, Bill took his foot off the gas. He watched the truck, now fifty yards from the dead end road, in his rear view mirror. He saw the truck's brake lights come on. He turned his head around, disbelieving. The truck turned up the dirt road. Bill looked back to the front and saw he was driving directly over the double yellow lines. He slowly guided the car back into the right lane, wondering what the person in the truck was doing.

There was another house back there, one that could be seen from the road. Dale's was a little further back, out of plain sight. Maybe the truck was going to the first house. Maybe that's all it was. Bill continued toward Ridge Road, which was about half a mile away.

He turned right on Ridge, and began looking for somewhere to turn around. There was a farm up in the distance and a fruit stand pull-off a little farther up, but Bill couldn't stand the wait. Besides, there was no one around. He did a three point turn in the middle of the road and headed back to the road with no name.

Approaching the long driveway, he thought he could probably run faster than the speed he was driving. The rain was steady and light. The dark truck would be hard to see at this distance of about five hundred yards to the first house. As Bill crept along now at idle speed, he squinted at Dale's neighbor's house. He hoped to God to see that truck. The house passed from the right side of the windshield to the passenger window. He still couldn't spot the truck. He put his foot on the brake and stopped in line with the driveway. He had a fleeting thought of going ahead with his plan, not letting anyone or anything stop him from coming here to do what he was here for. He still had the gun in the glove box. The thought was absurd, however; it was simply too dangerous. He reached across the passenger seat and rolled down the window. He felt the cool rain on his forearm. He squinted again, and again he couldn't spot the truck. He had been sitting there for only twenty seconds, but he began to feel self-conscious. If he were to be spotted, sitting out here while someone in a dark pickup was finding a murder victim, he would surely be hunted as a suspect.

He surveyed the landscape one last time, desperately hoping to see the truck.

He didn't.

Chapter Fifty-Nine

When Karen woke to the sound of the phone ringing, she was sweating. She had been having a nightmare, but she couldn't remember what it was about. That was a blessing, she supposed.

"This is Summers," she slurred, still trying to shake off the demons that lay in her subconscious.

"We have a situation here that you should know about." Karen could tell it was Randy Myers, one of the homicide detectives.

"What kind of situation?"

"Body found out by Wilmer Road. After I saw the guy, I thought of you."

"How nice of you." She extended her leg and swept it over to Bill's empty side of the bed. He was probably sleeping on the couch again. "So what's this have to do with me?"

"Look—we're still here at the scene and we're gonna be here a while." He gave her the address. "I think this is something you're gonna want to see first hand."

"You've got me so intrigued, how can I say no?"

Getting dressed, she wondered if what she was about to see would be connected to the Cherneau case. It better be, she thought. She pulled on a pair of jeans that were lying on the floor and an Ohio University sweatshirt.

She walked down the stairs expecting the TV to still be on. Even though the television had a sleep timer on it, he wouldn't use it. He would fall asleep and just let it go. Bill had used the excuse that he fell asleep watching a movie many times. He told her that he loved "those old black and whites," but she thought he just liked the *idea* of liking those old movies.

After he'd worn out the movie excuse, he had said that the couch was so extremely comfortable that he couldn't help it. It *was* a comfortable couch, but it was an excuse. She could tell long ago that he'd lost interest in her. She was afraid he wasn't attracted to her anymore. Her approach was to not push the issue, and hoped that it was just a phase. A really long phase.

When she got to the bottom of the stairs, she slid on her Nikes and glanced over to the living room. The television was not on. She thought she'd better at least let him know where she was going; whether he cared or not didn't really matter. At least not right this second.

She turned the light on in the foyer, which was bright enough to see into the living room. She walked to the back of the couch. She saw the blanket there, but she didn't see Bill. She touched the blanket to be sure. He was gone. She walked over slowly to the small half bath by the kitchen, not wanting to scare him. When she got there, the door was open and the room was dark.

She started to turn on lights on the first floor, and did not see him there. "Bill!" she yelled, but there was no answer.

She took the stairs two at a time before searching the upstairs; still no Bill.

She called for him a few more times.

He was gone.

The strangest feeling came over her that something was terribly wrong. She wasn't sure what, but she did know that the time was now nearly three a.m. and her husband was gone. She checked her pocket to make sure she had the directions to the house, and left.

As she drove, she thought of what Randy had said: "I thought of you," and "a situation you should know about." No way. It couldn't possibly be what she was thinking. Randy would have said something; she was just being paranoid.

Despite these feelings, Karen felt herself driving faster.

At the scene, Karen was more of a panic-ridden wife than an investigator. She ran up to the front porch. Randy was at the door to greet her.

"Whoa, Karen—what's the matter?"

She looked at him and braced herself. In a whisper, she asked, "It's not Bill, is it?"

"Bill? Your husband Bill? No, Karen. No. What's wrong?"

"I'm sorry. Bill was gone when I woke up and those things you said, I didn't know."

"It's all right, Karen. I promise you, it isn't Bill. I'm sorry I sounded so mysterious on the phone; I just wanted you to come down and take a look for yourself."

"Okay." She collected herself. "Okay. I can do that. Is the ME here yet?"

"Yeah. He's working on him now. Why don't we go back."

Karen put on plastic gloves as she walked down the hall. When she got to the door, she side-stepped through the door so as not to interrupt the man taking prints from the doorknob. More than the rest of the house, the room had the heavy smell of death. She walked in and stood above the body. The smell confronted her.

She'd seen this before.

"So, we got a name yet?" she said to anyone who might know.

Randy stood across the body from Karen. "Dale Parker. It's his house. From what we can gather, he lived here with a woman named Julianne Case. Found a couple pieces of junk mail in the trash with her name on them."

"Maybe she lived here before him. I still get the occasional piece of mail for a 'Felicia Waters' in my mailbox and I've lived in my house three years."

"A possibility, but we don't think so. There are some womanly touches here and there. She was probably shackin' up with the guy."

"Been able to contact her?"

"Nope. Don't really know where to start. We just found him a few hours ago."

Karen looked down at the man at her feet. The knife stuck in his neck. The light brown shag carpet had two crusted red stains where the arms had been cut off. There was blood spattered everywhere; Karen thought the victim had probably been standing when he was stabbed, and that the knife had probably sliced the carotid artery. It was one thing to come down in the middle of the night and view the results of such horror, but to try to imagine it happening—to see the blood spurting like a macabre sprinkler, and wondering how long he stood before dropping to the floor, was another.

"Hey Darryl," she said to the medical examiner, "any word on how long this guy's been dead?"

Darryl Cousins was typing on his laptop which sat on the dresser. In the corner of the room, Karen saw what looked like one of the arms. Two men were opening up a large clear plastic bag to recover it. Without turning around, Darryl said, "Pretty damn long," and kept typing.

"Randy, who found him?"

"John Renard, a police officer from New Lexington. He's out there in the living room. Guy's having trouble dealing."

"His first stiff?"

"No, it's not that. This is his cousin."

"Oh. Shit." There was an awkward pause. "Does he know anything?"

"I haven't talked to him at length. I've been trying to calm him down. He told me the basics—they were cousins, and what time he found him. Other than that I haven't been able to get much out of him."

"I'll have a talk with him." Karen walked through the hallway and into the living room. John sat on the far left side of the couch; he had his left elbow on the arm of the couch and his head was in his hand.

"John Renard?" He looked up, and Karen could see the redness in his eyes.

"Yes?"

"I'm Karen Summers, Muskingum County Homicide."

"I know; I've seen you covering the Cherneau case."

She sat on the couch, but kept her distance. "Why don't you tell me what happened."

"My cousin and I weren't close. We only hung out occasionally. Tonight I was visiting some friends in Logan and I thought I would stop by and see how he was doing. I tried to call at around eleven, and there was no answer, so I figured I'd stop over after the bars had closed. When I got here, everything was dark, but his truck was here. I went to the door and knocked before I went around the house and took a look in some of the windows. I saw him sitting there but not moving. I broke in to see if I could help him, and then I called the local P.D.."

"When was the last time you saw the victim?"

"Please don't call him that, ma'am."

"Of course—I'm sorry."

"Almost three weeks ago. We went out to a local bar for a couple beers and to play some pool."

"What bar was this?"

"The Last Stop. He said he'd call me in a couple days, but he never did. I guess that's why I thought to check up on him."

"Tell me about the night at the bar."

"He was depressed. His girlfriend had just left him about a week earlier. She'd done that sort of thing before, just taking off, but this time it sounded like she wasn't coming back. He had me fill out a missing persons report on her, but I think he was just in denial that she had left him."

"And this girlfriend," she started, flipping open a notepad, "Julianne Case?"

"That's right."

"Do you know where we could reach her?"

"I don't have a clue."

223

"Okay. Anything else about the last night you saw him? Anything out of the ordinary?"

"He damn near got in a fight, but that was nothing out of the ordinary for Dale. He was always a pretty hostile person."

"What was the fight about?"

"Dale never needed a reason to fight. I don't really know what it was about. I don't think it was about anything major, but you combine it with the mood he was in that night—he wanted to kill the guy."

"Did you know who the guy was?"

"No. Some big guy. The bartender knew him, though. I think he was a regular."

Chapter Sixty

Bill woke on the couch the next morning wondering if last night actually happened. Had he really gone out there with the intention of breaking in to a murder scene? Had he really seen the black truck, or was it a nightmare?

Of course it had actually happened. He looked at the clock on the television. It was still before nine. He hadn't been up this early since before he took his leave of absence.

Although he thought that Karen must have been gone by now, he heard her upstairs walking around.

He turned on the morning news:

"Authorities won't comment on whether this has any connection to the murder of Mark Cherneau five weeks ago, but from the similarities in the manner in which both victims were killed, we have to believe both murders are the work of the same killer.

"This morning at just before three a.m., local authorities received a call from John Renard, a police officer from New Lexington. He said he wanted to report a murder, and that the victim's arms had been amputated. The victim was in fact Renard's cousin, and he had come by the house when the victim couldn't be reached by phone. The body was taken to the County Coroner's office at five o'clock this morning for an autopsy. We here at channel ten will bring you any new information as soon as it is made available."

Bill watched the video of the scene where he had been just six hours ago. Six hours ago, it was one of the quietest areas in a county that was made up of quiet areas. He had gone there in the middle of the night for a deed that would take no more than five minutes. If he had been there an hour sooner, he would now have peace of mind.

He couldn't believe his bad luck.

"You're awake," the voice from the stairs said. Bill turned to see Karen coming down the stairs, dressed for work.

"Yeah," Bill said.

"I'm surprised after the night you had," she said. She went into the kitchen and got a bowl from the cupboard. She filled it with Wheaties and poured milk over them. She came over to the couch and sat on the chair next to it.

"What are you talking about?" he asked.

"I'm talking about last night. You want to tell me what the hell is going on here?"

Bill couldn't look at her. He never could when he was lying. "Look. I fell asleep on the couch, what's the big deal?"

"In your clothes?"

"I was too tired to go upstairs and change! So what?"

"Cut the shit, Bill," she said. "I know you went out last night. I am asking you what you did and where you went. These are simple questions."

"Don't interrogate me! I don't know what you're talking about! I never left the house last night!"

"Answer me one question, then. When I came home at ten last night, your car was in the garage. It was dry. When I left at 3:15, your car was still in the garage, only then it was wet. It rained last night between 10:30 and 3:30 and you were out in it."

"You're crazy. I think you're becoming delusional. Paranoid. Something."

" Just tell me so we can move on."

"Move on?"

"I know you were out with some girl last night, Bill. I know you're having an affair. Just be honest, for once, and don't insult me. All these nights you're down here sleeping on the couch—how many times have you sneaked out before?"

"You don't trust me at all, do you?"

"Why should I? We both know I have reason not to."

"I never did anything with Sandy, okay? Besides, that was a long time ago. I suggest you get past it."

"You *suggest* I get past it? Well, thank you for that suggestion. Look, whether or not you and she actually did it or not, the point is that you wanted to. You wanted her badly and I know that for a fact."

"You going to condemn me for my thoughts now?"

Karen got up from her chair and went into the kitchen. She put the cereal bowl in the sink, making more noise than usual. "I'm going to work. I'm tired of being married to a child. You could at least be a man for once and own up to what you're doing. You know, I don't need to ask you who you're having an affair with, because I can find out on my own. I can ask around and probably know by the end of the day if I want to. This is a small town, as I'm sure you know, and people in small towns love to talk."

Bill turned up the television, even though the volume had already been sufficient. "You do whatever you want. You will anyway."

Karen was now at the door. She picked up her briefcase and opened the door. "Apparently, the same goes for you."

Chapter Sixty-One

Two days later, Karen met with Ed Pickens from the FBI. He was working with Michael Woods, the man in charge of getting trace evidence from the scene of Dale Parker's murder.

The two men entered the Rose Hill Coffee Shop a little after eleven. Karen was sitting at a table with Randy Myers. After introductions were made, the four sat down at the table in the back of the shop.

"So what have you got?" Karen asked.

Woods looked at Pickens, as if he needed his permission to speak. "We found plenty of prints. Most, of course, belong to the victim. We found four different sets of prints. One is John Renard's, and one is the victim's. Another we believe belonged to the woman who was living there, a Julianne—"

"Case. She lives there," Myers said. "So far, we haven't been able to locate her."

"We assume these prints are hers," continued Woods. He pulled some papers from a manila envelope. On them were enlarged pictures of ten fingerprints. The top page was a printout that positively identified those of the deceased by comparing certain points in each corresponding print. On each were a series of circles made in red marker. They circled small triangular marks the computer had made when it had a match. Woods handed Karen a piece of paper. The page had ten prints, arranged neatly. On this page, however, there were no marks matching the prints to anything.

"This is the second set of prints we found. Like the first set, these were everywhere. In the bedroom on the dresser, in the bathroom on a hair dryer, and on the refrigerator. Like I said, it's pretty obvious these are the prints of the woman who was living there."

"Unless the killer took a shower and had a snack," Karen said.

"What we do know for sure is that the person these prints belong to doesn't have a record."

Randy took sip of coffee. "So tell us about the fourth set."

Michael put the last sheet of paper in front of Randy and Karen. On it was a picture of one complete print and two partial prints.

"These were found on the doorknob to the linen closet in the hallway," Michael said. "It does not match either of the other sets of prints, and we couldn't find any more like this in the rest of the house. As you can see, only one is complete. We guess it's the forefinger, and here's part of the thumb, and this one is the side of the middle finger."

Pickens answered the obvious question. "We didn't come up with anything on that one, either. We ran that first fingerprint in a national database and came up with nothing."

"What about the murder weapon itself," Karen asked, "did you get anything off that?"

"Nope. Wiped clean," Michael said.

"Kind of strange, wouldn't you say?" Randy asked. "I mean, finding one unknown set of prints on a linen closet and nowhere else in the house? What do you make of it, Mr. Pickens?"

"I can think of two possibilities. One is that it's an old one from a relative or guest, and neither the man or woman living there ever use the linen closet, so it was never wiped off. I know that when my wife has guests stay over, she tells them with some strange sense of pride that the "towels are in the linen closet," but we don't use it on a regular basis."

The other three looked at each other. That seemed pretty far-fetched, but no one appeared to want to say anything.

Pickens looked as if he knew they weren't hot for the idea. "Okay, how about this—you have a killer who's never been in the house before. Never mind if this is just a burglary, or murder in the first degree. Let's just say the suspect checks all the doors on his way back the hallway. He finds the victim, kills him, then proceeds to wipe down all the knobs on his way out. Only he forgets one."

By the looks on their faces, the people at the table found that to be a much more plausible explanation.

Chapter Sixty-Two

Phil Oliver felt eyes on him as he sat at his normal bar stool at the Last Stop. At the other end of the bar sat Tom Flanagan. He wore jeans and a t-shirt, as if that would make him undetectable to Phil.

Phil sipped his beer and tried not to think of him, but the more he tried to ignore him, the more he couldn't. He got up and walked to Flanagan. As he approached, Flanagan smiled.

"Why, Phil Oliver! Imagine seeing you here!"

"What the hell are you doing?"

"I'm just having a beer like everyone else."

"You're here to watch me, like I'm some kind of criminal."

"You said that, not me, *Mister* Oliver. I think you're a little paranoid."

"Why ain't you out with your boyfriend, you fucking faggot?"

"I thought I'd come here and maybe meet someone new." Tom raised his glass to Phil and drank.

"Fuck you."

"And fuck you too, you wife-beating piece of shit."

Phil thought maybe Flanagan was a little drunk. "You want a piece of me? I ain't afraid of kicking a cop's ass, you know."

Flanagan stood up, almost knocking over the small table between him and Phil. "There's no way you'd try it, Phil. You know why? Because I'd kick your ass in front of everyone here, and even you have limits on how much personal humiliation you can stand."

Phil stared at him. He wanted to hit him so bad, but he also thought of what Tom had said, and he was right. Cops probably have to learn to fight pretty well, he thought, and even though Phil was half a foot taller and fifty pounds heavier, he wasn't sure he could win. He knew he could never live it down if he lost.

"I'm gonna take a piss," Phil said, pointing at Flanagan, "and don't even think about following me—you hear me, cocksucker?"

Flanagan didn't sit down, nor did he say another word. He watched Phil walk to the bathroom at the back of the bar.

Five minutes later, Tom finished his beer. He was still watching the door to the bathroom. He had not taken his eyes off it.

When he walked into the bathroom, he felt the breeze coming in the open window.

Phil was gone.

Chapter Sixty-Three

Phil drove to Vera Mullen's. He'd always had a good relationship with Sandy's mother. Sandy had not gotten along with her mother since leaving Phil because Vera always downplayed the abuse. In the beginning of the relationship, her mother had mixed feelings about Phil, but Sandy married him anyway. It was part of Sandy's nature to never admit when she was wrong, so when the bruises showed up, Sandy gave her mother the same excuses she would give her friends—that she fell down or that she had been clumsy. It was always bullshit, and Sandy's friends had known it.

Unlike her friends, though, Vera always took Sandy's word. It wasn't that she was naive, exactly—it was just that she felt her daughter would always go to her if something was wrong. She never worried about her daughter unless she gave her a reason. Sure, toward the end of Phil and Sandy's relationship—after Sandy quit her job and after a stay at Clarksdale, rumors began to spread that inevitably got back to her, though not as much as one might expect. Vera was a private person, with very few friends who were close enough to say something. When one did try to confront her with the truth, she became very agitated and asked the person to leave her house. After that, no one spoke of it to her.

When she found out Sandy was leaving and moving to Columbus, and leaving Phil, she was upset at Sandy, not Phil. She demanded to know what was going on, and Sandy didn't want to get into it. She told Vera that Phil was a "bum—a drunken bum and a loser." Vera thought her daughter was bailing out of her marriage. Like so many other things in her life, she had quit when times got tough.

There was a knock on the door. She answered it.

"You don't need to knock, Phil, you know that." He just shrugged. She had the TV on and when he walked into the living room, she turned the sound down.

"You don't have to mute it."

"Don't make no difference to me," she said. It was a baseball game—the Indians and the Yankees. "I can tell what's going on. Besides, I don't like these announcers. The ones on the radio I like, but I don't like these guys. I just keep the sound on so the house doesn't seem so quiet."

"So how they doin'?"

"They might win one as long as they don't blow it here in the ninth. So what brings you by tonight?"

"I've been thinking about Sandy."

"Did you go see her in Columbus like I told you to? Were you able to find it okay?"

"Yeah."

"What did she say?"

"She wasn't home."

"You should give her a call."

"I was sorta hoping you could give her a call. She probably won't talk to me. Probably hang up on me."

"You guys are never going to patch things up by *not* talking to each other. You know that. I don't agree with her just picking up and leaving you, but there were some things you did wrong, too. You still drinking?"

"Some. Not nearly as much as when Sandy left me, though."

"That's good. Alcohol can destroy a marriage—it can also destroy a person. Seen it first-hand."

"So—you think maybe you can call her? Maybe I can meet her somewhere. I want to show her I'm a changed man."

"I could give her a call and bring it up. I don't see what harm that could do."

Chapter Sixty-Four

Dr. Barnes led Randy and Karen to the table. A white sheet was covering a body in the middle of the room. Karen knew it was Dale Parker. She had seen bodies under these sheets enough times to know the shape of them, and she knew the body under this sheet didn't have any arms.

"So Fred, what did you find?"

"The carotid artery was severed. After that, it was all over. It could have happened in an ER and there still wouldn't have been anything that could have been done."

"The guy was dead in a hurry," Randy mumbled.

"You got that right," Fred said.

"Tell us about the arms," Karen said.

"Amputated post-mortem by a very sharp object."

"Post-mortem? Are you sure of that?"

"Yep. You could tell by the amount of blood around the head and neck at the scene versus the blood around the arm sockets. Obviously, there was still a good deal of blood that came out, but what came out *drained* out, it wasn't pumped out."

"And the sharp object?"

"Could be a hatchet, or an ax. Maybe a sharp knife."

Karen wondered what it felt like to actually amputate an arm. It was such a strange m.o. Some serial killers took body parts as trophies, but in this case, they had been left behind. This was different than in the Mark Cherneau murder. In that case, the arms had been cut off with a dull, serrated blade, like a rusty saw. In this case, it was a sharp edge. In addition to that, Mark Cherneau's arms were still missing. It didn't make any sense to cut off the arms in the case of Dale Parker's death. Cherneau was drugged and tortured. The method of killing was to saw off the arms while the victim was still alive. The killer got off on the suffering and torture of that. To do it post-mortem, the killer would get nothing from it.

Karen thanked Dr. Barnes and left with Randy. When they got out of the building, Karen said, "It's not the same guy."

"What are you talking about?"

"I think we got a copycat killer."

Chapter Sixty-Five

Bill was surprised by the letter, but even more by the postmark. He opened it, which had no return address, and saw it was from Julianne. Once he found out who it was from, he noticed the postmark was stamped "Logan Ohio 43138." She was still in town. Maybe she had never left. It seemed odd; as far as he was concerned, she had been long gone. He figured she would be scared; maybe he was wrong. The envelope had some dirt on it, as if the mailman had dropped it in mud, then attempted to scrape it off, which only made it worse. It would have surely gotten Karen's attention had she seen it, but luckily, the mail came after she had already gone to work and Bill had gotten to it first:

Dear Bill,

I miss you. You're all I have left in this world. I've done everything I can to be good, God knows I have. And now look what's happened. I know the police are probably trying to find me, and they will lock me up if they catch me. Lock me up and throw away the key, probably. Please burn this letter after you're done reading it.

I sit out here nights and think of the fun we had that night. I think of the cold water and how it felt so good. It's getting colder now, and swimming probably wouldn't feel as good now as it did then. I don't know.

You're probably asking yourself why I did what I did. Maybe you're not. I mean, if there's anyone who would understand what I did, it would be you. I bared my soul to you, and in some ways, you did the same with me. I feel terrible about what I did, even though I'd probably do it again. I've had trouble sleeping. It's very dark here at night, almost too dark. It's like you can't escape your thoughts, you know? Usually, you can have the TV on and it takes your mind off things. A little, at least. I lie here at night, and it feels like this sin is something heavy, something that sits on my chest and makes it difficult to breathe.

I know you don't think of yourself as a religious person, but I want to tell you that you are. At least in your deep self. You never judged me before, not ever, and I suppose that's one reason I know I can write you this letter and that you won't tell anyone about it. You always treated me like a human being, like a friend even when no one else would. Jesus was like that.

I want to be with you. I need to have you here. We can go far away and never get close to Ohio again. Hopefully, you will want to be with me, too. I hope to God you understand, and I dream of the night we can be together.

I'll write to you again soon and maybe we can find each other.

I love you,

Julianne

Bill promptly took the letter outside into the backyard. He grabbed a pack of matches on his way out.

Outside, he watched as the letter burned, making sure no trace was left. He burned the envelope as well. The paper turned black and shriveled in the flame. He wanted to be with her now, in her time of need. He knew how afraid she must feel; how alone. He wondered what she meant when she said it was dark where she was at night. He had been in that dark place, long ago as a child huddled in his room—afraid, alone, with gun in hand.

238

Chapter Sixty-Six

Sandy and her mother talked on the phone once every couple weeks, and it was usually her mother, not Sandy, that did the dialing. There was the usual small talk and rarely anything else. Sandy's mother would usually just say she was calling to 'touch base', as if she was intruding into Sandy's busy life in the city.

Some nights, the subject of Phil would come up, and Sandy wanted nothing to do with even the smallest discussion. It was irritating to think of her own mother taking his side. Sandy had only gone so far as to say, 'he abused me, mother,' but never gave any details. Mrs. Mullen told Sandy of a time when Mr. Mullen had smacked her around on a semi-regular basis, and that those days only lasted a few years. After that, she said they had a good marriage until he died of cancer at the age of fifty-one. She seemed proud that she'd 'stuck it out,' and told Sandy that her marriage would get better, too.

Sandy knew better, though. She knew that even if she had stayed with Phil, she would have never been happy. She may not have even made it out alive.

She had her cell next to her on the dinner table where she was working on organizing depositions for work. She answered it on the first ring.

After their greetings, Sandy's mother said, "I just wanted to call to see what you were doing Labor Day weekend. I'm going to have a few friends over for a picnic. I know it's still a couple weeks away, but I was hoping to get you before you made any other plans."

"Sounds good. I don't have any plans. When?"

"Saturday evening. Just hamburgers and hot dogs. Probably around six."

"That's fine."

"How's work?"

"It's going really well. They said they might have a full-time position for me after I graduate."

"That's good."

"It'd be nice because I like the people I work with."

"How are your classes?"

"I like them so far. I mean they're okay. We haven't had any exams yet, so I have no idea how I'm doing. But I'm sure they'll go all right."

The conversation continued for another twenty minutes or so. They talked about clothes they had purchased, how Sandy's car had started to make this clicking noise and wondered if she should get it checked out; Sandy asked what was happening on *As the World Turns* and, after her mother's lengthy answer, regretted asking. It was small talk, but that was fine. There was no mention of Phil at all.

Chapter Sixty-Seven

Karen woke up Friday morning at nine-thirty and couldn't remember the last time she'd slept so late. Tom had called the night before and said he was taking the day off. He said that Karen should do the same. He said they both needed a break and they would come back Monday recharged. He said that they shouldn't even think about the case for the weekend, and that by getting some distance, they might gain some new perspective. They should at least try to put it out of their minds. Karen had considered what he said, and decided it was a pretty good idea. She could use a break.

She rolled over and faced Bill, who was still sleeping. He had his back to her. Something was very wrong between them, but she wasn't exactly sure what. She wasn't as sure as she once was regarding his relationship with Sandy Oliver. At the time, she was positive he was having an affair with her—everyone seemed to be saying so, and Bill had definitely acted strange. She knew he had strong feelings toward her, but as far as them being intimate, she wasn't so sure anymore. Sandy had said to her it never happened, and Bill had said the same thing. It saddened Karen to realize it was probably Sandy's word, not Bill's, that she trusted.

From the time the rumors of Bill's affair started almost a year ago, Karen's marriage had been filled with silence. It just hurt too much to bring it up, and she found that if she was able to keep busy with work, she was able to ignore it. In her mind, the trust was gone for good, and from that point on, her attitude toward her marriage was not unlike that of someone grieving a lost one. She took one day at a time, and as the days passed, she hoped the pain would slip away.

She had hoped that by the time a divorce came up, she would be emotionally detached, and would be able to handle the situation.

The pain had not slipped away, however. It had been merely pushed aside. And now, as she looked at the man who was turned away from her, she couldn't feel anything for certain.

She didn't know if the deep sadness she felt was because she didn't love him anymore, or because she did.

It was now one in the afternoon, and Karen was getting pretty restless. She was bored stiff watching television, and Bill got up at eleven, took a shower, ate a bowl of cereal and left the house. He and Karen hardly spoke, and when they did, it was about things like whether the dishes in the dishwasher were clean. When he left, he didn't say where he was going or when he would be back. This irritated Karen, but she understood.

She took a shower, got dressed and left, not knowing where she would go.

As she drove, she thought of the last time she and Bill had really talked. She threatened that she would find out with whom he was having an affair. Come to think of it, she didn't remember him denying it, either. He never said, 'I'm not having an affair.'

She found herself driving to the only place she could think of, the place where he had met Sandy.

She drove to Clarksdale.

As she walked through the parking lot, she hoped that Janice was working. Janice had been Bill's secretary when Bill started at Clarksdale, and they had hit it off from the start. Karen didn't know anyone in town at the time, and soon Janice and Karen were good friends. They saw each other when their schedules allowed, and they told Bill they were doing 'girl things,' and that he should stay home. They would go shopping and out to a restaurant and talk about Bill and laugh.

When Janice was promoted from Bill's secretary to Office Coordinator, she and Karen remained friends. Janice had helped Karen through some of the tough times when many people in the office thought Bill was paying too much attention to Sandy.

Karen asked the receptionist if Janice was in. The receptionist didn't respond; she just picked up the phone. Holding the phone to her ear, she asked who Karen was. Five seconds later, Janice came down the hall, smiling.

"Hey, you!" she said. She put her arms around Karen, and Karen hugged her briefly. "I been seeing you on the news, you know. You're a celebrity! I wanted to call you, but I know how busy you must be, with the case and all. So what brings you here?"

"I took the day off. A much needed break."

"I can imagine. Must be a lot of pressure."

"I'm learning to deal with it. I wanted to see what you were doing later. There's something I need to talk to you about."

Chapter Sixty-Eight

Karen met Janice at Dante's, an upscale restaurant in Lancaster. When Janice arrived at seven, Karen was already there and at a table. They exchanged greetings and had a quick look over the menu. Karen recommended the salmon.

"So, this has been driving me crazy all day—what is it you wanted to talk about?"

"One guess," Karen said.

"I couldn't begin to guess. Is it something to do with your case?"

Karen laughed out loud. "No! What did you think, Jan? I was going to meet you at Dante's to interrogate you?"

"Is it Bill? What's going on?"

"He's having an affair."

"Oh God. Are you sure? How do you know?"

"I just know. We talked about it the other night, and he never denied it. Secondly, Bill's a bad liar; you know that. I can read him like a book."

"That's the truth."

"Then last week, he left the house really late, and he didn't come back until after three. He wouldn't say where he'd been. He thought I would sleep through the whole thing, but that was the night they found Dale Parker's body."

"I heard about that on the news. Wasn't that awful?"

"It sure was."

"Was it the same guy who killed Mark Cherneau?"

"We're not sure."

Janice started to say something, but then stopped, like she was afraid.

"Jan, what is it?"

Janice lowered her voice. "You don't think...*Bill* had something to do with the murder, do you?"

Karen laughed. "Bill, a murderer? You know, we should go out more often, Jan. I could use the laughs. Bill could never do something like that. Anyway, the victim had been dead a couple weeks."

The waiter came and took their order. Karen was thinking of the notion of Bill as a murderer and was smiling the whole time.

"I need a favor," Karen said.

"Name it."

"When Bill became...involved with Sandy Oliver last year, you helped me through that. I think Bill's got some idea that he has to rescue these girls from the Big Bad Wolf. Like he's their savior or something. Sometimes he gets more involved than he should, like when the case is extreme. Sandy's was worse than most, right?"

"She was close to death at one point," Janice said.

"I think when he's attracted to one of these girls, he feels such a connection that he becomes too involved. The girls are probably vulnerable, and he takes advantage of them. He probably uses his own past to establish a relationship with them."

"What past are you talking about?"

"You didn't know? His father used to beat his mother. Nearly killed her. He only hit Bill a few times, but growing up with it was traumatic. When he was eleven, he almost committed suicide."

"I didn't know that. That's awful."

"Maybe you shouldn't repeat that," Karen muttered.

"Of course not."

"I think that's why he is doing what he's doing. He's trying to save his mother."

"That's such a sad story. What do you want me to do?"

"I want you to get me a list of all the women he's had as patients the last year."

"Karen, I can't do that—it's illegal. Everything at Clarksdale is confidential."

"I know. But I know whoever he's seeing would be on that list. I need to know who she is."

"What for? What are you going to do if you find out, go kick her ass?"

"No, I just want to know who it is. I want the whole thing out in the open. The sooner it's out in the open the sooner it can be over. Maybe I'll have a talk with her. Maybe he'll leave me for her, or maybe it can be the start of Bill and I talking about our marriage and working things out."

"Do you still *want* to work things out? After what he's done to you?"

"I don't know."

When the food arrived, Janice and Karen began eating the salmon and didn't say anything for five minutes. When they began speaking again, they talked about less important things. They both agreed it was the best salmon they had ever had.

After the waiter brought the check, Janice looked at Karen and said: "I'm not saying either way right now, but if I decide to do this, how do you want me to get the list to you?"

"Whatever way you're most comfortable with. We could come here and have the salmon again. I'll buy."

Chapter Sixty-Nine

On Saturday night, Tom drove to Columbus. It had been nearly two months since he'd been there. He would go where he always went when he was in town—a place called JD's, in an area of Columbus known as the Short North. Any time life got to the point where he couldn't take it anymore, when hiding his homosexuality in such a small town made him feel practically claustrophobic, he went to JD's and he could relax for a while.

Tom knew there were some people who thought he might be gay, like Phil Oliver did, but then again, guys like Phil thought anyone who dressed nicely and didn't have a girlfriend was a 'fag.'

Tom didn't know anyone at JD's, and that was all right with him. He wanted to go there to be anonymous; to be himself. The people he met there were usually nice enough, and the last time he was there, he met someone who was easy to talk to. They'd had a few beers and talked. It was just what he needed.

Tonight, he was sitting at a table by himself. He had only been sitting there a few minutes when a man walked up with two beers in his hand.

"Would you like one of these or am I going to have to drink them both myself?" the man asked.

Tom smiled. "Sure, I'll have one. Thanks." The man sat and handed the beer to him.

"Do you always do that?" Tom asked.

"Do what?"

"Use that 'am I going to have to drink these myself' line."

The man laughed. "No. I bought this for friend of mine, but then he had to leave suddenly. He just got here and then he had to leave; I hate that."

"I know what you mean," Tom said.

"So you from around here? Name's Joel, by the way."

"Tom." They shook hands. "Nice to meet you. I'm not from around here."

"So where you from?"

Tom paused. "I'd really rather not say."

"Closet man, eh? Perfectly all right with me. I know what it's like, believe me. I grew up in a small town."

"I still live in a small town. It's tough, you know?"

"Oh, sure. I know," Joel said. "Redneckville, USA. If you don't have a big ol' truck, a John Deere hat and five dirty little brats running around the lawn furniture outside, you're a 'queer.' Been there, believe me. You know, I moved here three years ago, when I was 31. I quit my job, came out here, *came out*, and my life has been good ever since. You know what I did before I moved? I was a fire chief. I think sometimes when you're gay and you live in a small town, you take on a macho job to convince the town, and maybe yourself, that you're straight. I even had a wife for a year and a half. I thought maybe I could will myself into being straight. I don't know, maybe some guys can. I sure couldn't." He took a drink of his beer. "What about you? What do you do?"

Tom smiled at him. "I'm a cop." The two men looked at each other and laughed out loud. "I don't know if I could leave my hometown, though. I love it there; I really do. I've lived there all my life."

"If you've lived there all your life, surely the townsfolk must know, right?"

"Actually, I don't think that many people have a clue. I had girlfriends in high school, and people seem to remember that. Plus, I think people know my work keeps me pretty busy. I don't think they would want to believe that a cop in their town is gay."

"You can't just come out and get it over with? Maybe it would be easier that way."

"I think you're forgetting what it's like. If I came out, it wouldn't be over; it would just be the beginning.

All the talk—I would eventually be forced out of my job, there's no way they would let me continue being a cop. And I love being a cop. You know what I do sometimes? Every now and then, I go out on a date with a woman. I take her to a popular restaurant, maybe a movie, just to let people see me with a woman."

"Don't you hate pretending to be someone you're not?"

"Sometimes I think we're all pretending to be someone we're not."

"I don't know," Joel said. "When I lived in a small town, I couldn't stand hiding in a shell. It just about drove me crazy."

"If it's what I have to do to stay in my hometown, doing the job I love, then that's what I have to do. I can come here when I get stressed about it and nice people buy me beers and bring them to my table. That I can live with. As far as the people of my hometown finding out I'm gay, well—that's just something I can't allow to happen."

Chapter Seventy

The knock on the door startled Sandy, especially at this time of night. It was 10:15; in her experience, any knock on the door after ten p.m. was trouble.

This time, however, was an exception to the rule. She looked out the peephole with a feeling of dread, a feeling that she would see Phil's face. She hadn't. She opened the door.

"Detective Flanagan? Is there anything wrong?"

Tom leaned against the railing outside her door. "Nothing's wrong, Miss Kelley. Everything's fine." Tom smiled, looking embarrassed. "I know it's late, but I was in the area—"

"It's okay," Sandy said. "I just freak out every time the doorbell rings these days, with everything going on. Come on in." Sandy locked the door behind him and went to the kitchen. "I was about to have some hot tea—would you like some? The nights have been colder lately. I can't believe it's fall already."

Tom sat on the couch. "Is it caffeinated?"

Sandy looked at the box. "I think so. It doesn't say that it isn't. Is that okay?"

"That's good, actually. I have to drive back home tonight and I feel a little tired."

"It's probably from the beer," she said. She looked up from the teapot and smiled at him.

"Look, I'm sorry. I should go."

"No problem. I won't tell Detective Summers on you."

"I was at a bar here in town, and when I got out on the road I realized I might be a little tipsy. I stopped in a parking lot someplace, I didn't know where the hell I was. I was just sitting there, thinking about the case I'm working on, and how much I *hate* your husband—"

"Soon-to-be ex-husband."

"Okay. He's an asshole, you know?"

She laughed at him. She could tell he was drunk. "I know; believe me."

"Yeah, I guess you would. And I was sitting there in my car, just staring at this big red "Big Bear" sign, and it struck me—I've always hated him. Probably before you ever heard the name 'Phil Oliver.' He was always a bully, even in grade school. Always bigger than the rest of us, on account that he had flunked a few grades." Tom looked confused, as if he'd lost track of what he was saying. "I guess what I want to ask you is this—why did you lie?"

"Lie? What are you talking about?"

"C'mon, Sandy, you know exactly what I'm talking about—that whole story about Mark Cherneau and his friends tying Phil up to a tree somewhere and leaving him to die—that was something you made up."

"No, it isn't! Phil told me that story himself!"

"And you just believed everything he told you, is that it?"

"No, but I can tell when he's lying, and this wasn't one of those times!"

"You know, Sandy, I hear lies almost everyday. Some days I might tell a few myself. I know when someone is lying, and I can tell that you are lying now. But I want to tell you—I'm on your side. It's okay if you lied. I won't even tell if you don't want me to. I think we can work together on this. If you're willing to play the game, then I am. If that's what it takes to lock him up, I most definitely am."

"I don't think I know what you mean."

"Okay. You said that Cherneau and his friends put a noose around Phil Oliver's neck and tortured him when they were in grade school, right?"

"That's right."

"In grade school, I was a friend of Mark Cherneau's. I would have known about this, believe me. It never happened. I mean, some of it happened—the whole part about the playground and Phil hitting Mark. I remember that happening. But after that, Mark was afraid of him. Phil was bigger, stronger, and damn near broke Mark's nose. Mark pretty much left him alone after that. I know the way it actually happened, and I think I know enough about Phil Oliver to know he would never make up a story like that, one that he would be embarrassed to tell. Phil would never make himself look like a victim to anybody, even if he was one. So I know that you made that story up. You didn't even need to come up with anything new; I know you took the torture part straight out of Louis Alvin Beatty's handbook;. You must be a fan of serial killers—he's not even that well-known."

"I...have my reasons—"

"I know, I know. Like I said, I'm on your side. Since this whole thing came up, I knew there was something that wasn't quite right about what you said. Sitting there in that parking lot just now, I figured it out. Let me guess—your ex-husband is stalking you, frightening you, and you don't know what exactly to do about that. You file a restraining order, but working in a law office, you probably know that they aren't really that effective in most cases. You may even know that when a woman files a restraining order against a former boyfriend or husband, a restraining order can push an unstable man over the edge. It can actually be a catalyst for violence.

"Anyway, you may have known that and you figure the only way you're going to feel safe is if he's either locked up or if you kill the son of a bitch. Personally, I would have killed him. You know, invite him over here and then kill him in 'self-defense.' But you've got a better heart than I do, I suppose. You knew that we were looking at Phil as a suspect, and you may have known we were a little weak on motive. So, one night when fear was keeping you from sleeping, you thought up one. Tell me I'm wrong."

The tea pot whistled and Sandy got up and poured two cups. "Sugar?"

"No thanks."

She came back with the cups on a tray and put it on the coffee table. "You're not wrong, detective."

"I didn't think so."

"But you'll help me, right?" She stirred sugar into her tea and took a sip. "You said we could work together on this."

"What I'm going to do is keep my mouth shut. That's how I can help you best. If the other investigators know that the story you told isn't true, they might drop him as a suspect altogether. We were getting ready to drop him just before you told your little tale."

"And you don't want them to drop him, do you?" She asked.

"No, I don't."

"You think he actually did kill Cherneau and Parker?"

"Yeah, I think he did," Tom said. "Just because we can't find a motive doesn't mean there isn't one. And besides, just because someone doesn't have a motive doesn't mean they can't kill. You can call it a feeling, a hunch, whatever—I think he did it."

"Well, you can call *this* a feeling or a hunch or whatever, but I think you want to see him locked up. I mean beyond getting the killer put away. It sounds like you have a personal hatred for him—any truth to that?"

"Let's just say Phil knows something about me that I'd rather not have known."

Chapter Seventy-One

When Karen came into work Monday morning, Tom said that Police Chief Jared Wilson wanted to see them. A couple minutes later, Randy Myers was also brought in the office.

"So what do we know about Dale Parker? Who would want him killed? I heard he had a girlfriend that can't be accounted for."

"That's true, chief," said Randy. "At this point of the investigation, we have to believe she did this and ran. So far no one can find her. We've tried every motel in a fifty mile radius. We've checked her only known relative, her sister—a Danielle Mitchell of Westerville, and she hasn't heard from her in over a year."

"Was there anything at the house that might indicate where she might have gone?"

"No, sir. From what we can tell, she didn't own very many things. She left most of her clothes; they were the only personal belongings we found that we know were hers."

"Keep searching. Widen your search. From what I've heard, this guy was dead for a couple weeks, so she's had a helluva head start. What else you got? Are we sure this was the same one that killed Mark Cherneau?"

"No, sir, we're not sure of that," Karen said. "We think that Miss Case may have amputated her boyfriend's arms to make it look like it was the same killer. Maybe get it pinned on the guy who killed Cherneau. There are some things which make this murder different from the Cherneau murder. Some significant things."

"Such as?"

"Such as leaving the arms right there in the bedroom. Cherneau's arms still are missing. That the arms are still missing was not released to the press. If Cherneau's killer keeps the arms, it is probably an important part of the killer's pathology. Plus, Cherneau died because his arms were cut off—he bled to death."

"He was also drugged."

"Yes, but I think the killer's m.o. involves a great deal of torture before he finally kills them. I think it's the torture he's looking for—the death is just the result of the torture. In Dale Parker's case, however, there was no torture. It was a quick death, probably only took seconds. Cherneau's killer may have even wanted to hear him scream. There seemed to be a whole ritual to it— Cherneau had been drugged, he had tent stakes in his clothing, holding him down. The whole thing sounds premeditated. Parker was stabbed in the throat. There would be no screaming, and very little pleasure would be derived from someone who was looking to torture his victims. To be honest, the only thing connecting the two murders are that the arms had been cut off both victims. Other than that, there's nothing to indicate it was the same killer."

"So you think, Detective Summers, that this woman, the girlfriend, killed her boyfriend, then had the nerve to sit there and cut his arms off after he was already dead?"

"I don't know, sir. One thing I do know is that there is no predicting human behavior in crisis situations. Maybe the whole thing was premeditated, maybe it wasn't. Maybe she found him with another woman and lost it, I don't know. Whatever it was, I think we have two killers out there, not one."

"There is one other possibility we have here, sir," Randy said. "We found fingerprints at the crime scene belonging to the victim and belonging to Miss Case, but we also found a third set of prints that were found on a doorknob in the hallway."

"Weren't they the cousin's, the guy that found him?"

"They were checked against his, sir, and they're not his. In fact, we haven't been able to find a match for them at all."

"All right, for now I want you, Randy, to concentrate on finding this Case woman. She has to at least know something, otherwise she wouldn't have run. Tom and Karen, I want you to remained focused on what you've got on Cherneau. Keep digging."

Chapter Seventy-Two

In the middle of the afternoon, Karen had to go home to get a file. Bill's car was in the garage, but he wasn't home.

She took a quick glance around the kitchen, half-heartedly looking for a note. She knew there wouldn't be one. Bill didn't leave the house much lately, and when he did, he didn't tell Karen where he was going. He was someone totally different from the man she married. He'd slipped through her fingers, and now she realized that, as much as she had thought she could change him, she couldn't. They had gone past the point of no return, and whatever problems he was having, he would have to work them out alone.

She grabbed a bagel and the file and walked out the door. As she locked the front door, she looked at the mailbox. She opened it and found four envelopes—an electric bill, a water bill, junk mail. The last caught her eye. It was a letter addressed to Bill, the envelope hand-written. No return address. She turned it over, hoping to see one, but there was only a smudge of dirt. The front of the envelope had nothing else, other than a postmark of Logan, OH 43138, and a stamp with a picture of Helen Keller on it. Karen held the letter up to the grey sky.

"What're you doing?" a voice said. Karen turned around. Bill was standing on the first porch step. "I said, what're you doing there?"

"I had to get a file. Thought I'd get the mail. What are you doing out here?"

"Just taking a walk."

"You don't take walks." Bill didn't respond. She held the letter up to him. "This came for you." She held out the letter and he quickly took it. "Got a pen pal, do you? Is that from your girlfriend?"

"Paranoid as usual," he said. He examined the envelope. "I don't know what the hell this is."

"Why don't we open it, then?"

"Maybe I don't want to open it right now."

"God, Bill, you sound like a little kid!"

"You think you're smarter than me."

"Where do you get that from?"

"You think you can control me, but you can't. You might be able to control your idiot suspects, but just because you say to open it, you think I'm just gonna do it? You don't trust me now, and you never trusted me before."

"Before what?"

"You have never been able to get close to anyone because you don't trust anyone. Maybe it's your job; I don't know. Maybe you can't separate the two. You are your job. Maybe that's what makes you think everybody has something up their sleeve. I don't know, but even with me, your husband, you were always...cold."

"You think I'm cold, huh?"

"Distant—detached—reserved. Whatever you want to call it, you never, now that I think of it, were a very warm person. You never embraced life—"

"Where the hell are you getting this from?"

"Let's just say I've got a new perspective."

"I know all about your new perspective," she said, pointing to the envelope in his hand.

As Bill turned and walked toward the garage, Karen heard him mutter, "Screw you."

She didn't respond.

Chapter Seventy-Three

Bill put the top down on his convertible and pulled out of the driveway. He knew Karen was watching from the porch, but he didn't look back. He didn't wave. He and Karen had stopped waving years ago.

As he drove on interstate 70, he thought of the night he drove out this way to rescue Julianne. He had saved her that night. Not only did he do that, he had made her strong. And, come to think of it, she had made him strong in return. Julianne had done it—she had reached a point where she said 'no,' that she wouldn't take it anymore. She had stood up to abuse in a way he never had when he was a child. He had encountered so many men over the years he thought deserved to die, and she did something about it. He admired her for that.

He ended up stopping at the rest area where he had picked her up. Once he turned the car off, he figured maybe he hadn't been wandering aimlessly, like he had thought.

He sat at a picnic table and watched the people going in and out of the restrooms. Young children ran through the grass, expending the abundance of energy only children seemed to have. He knew what the letter would say—it would be giving him a time and a place to meet her. After that, there would be no turning back. He had always despised men who left their wives, and he was about to do what he despised. He knew, though, that Karen would be all right eventually. Hell, she was always all right. She had that independence she had learned as a child, and he knew she felt that needing someone meant she was weak. She hadn't even pretended to need him in years.

So here it was, in this envelope. This was his chance, for once in his life, to do something about his pain. Something that would be for the best in the long run. How long had he let his stale, lifeless marriage go on? How long had *he* been stale and lifeless? The way he responded to this letter would forever change his life. And he didn't want it any other way.

He listened to the sound of the trucks flying by on the highway. Felt the breeze from them. He knew before he opened the letter that he would go to her. They had something in common, something much deeper than he and Karen ever had. Something true. He slowly tore open the envelope.

Dear Bill,

I was going to wait another week before I wrote you, but I couldn't. The days are getting shorter now—have you noticed? It's getting cooler out, too. I hope in the past week, you've decided to be with me.

It's taken some time, but I think I'm returning to the innocence I once had. There is only one thing left I need to finish my journey. You. Once you're here it will be finished, and I will be whole again. I will breathe again. I will be clean again. I will bury my past and become a child again. I have thought for many hours about you, and how much I care for you. I don't know how your marriage is going, and I don't want to take you away from your wife, but one thing remains—I need you. We should be together now, and it will all be clear. Once we are together, you will know a joy you have never experienced. I get excited just thinking about it!

I have been spending the last two weeks here at the Hocking Hills State Park campsite. Surprised? I'll bet you thought I was long gone, didn't you? I'll bet you thought I ran. I thought about it more than once, I can tell you. But after thinking on it, I decided that running can be expensive. I been living on crackers and other dry foods. I try not to go into town unless it's absolutely necessary. And when I do, I make sure I go at a time where there won't be much people around. I started out with a hundred dollars, and I knew that wouldn't get me very far. Needless to say, if you decide to go with me, you'll need to bring as much cash as you can. I have my car, but I don't know how much longer it's gonna run. We shouldn't use it anyway.

I was hoping you could come on Saturday night—do you know where the primitive campsites are? That's where I am. It's site number four. You have to walk up a little path to get to it, but it's in a nice clearing. There are some other sites close by, but far enough away so that we can have our privacy. You can come as soon as you like, but I should let you know that I only have the site reserved through Labor day weekend, so if you're coming, it should be before then. We could spend the night here, and then leave early in the morning and start our lives together.

Isn't that a wonderful notion? Starting our lives again. We'll be able to make each other stronger, I just know it. I'm a big believer in fresh starts. Anyway, I hope to see you soon. You don't need to bring a lot of things—just you. And your sleeping bag!

Love,
Julianne

Chapter Seventy-Four

Tom got to Sandy's apartment at seven o'clock in the evening; she wasn't home. He would wait, though. He would wait as long as necessary to make sure he and Sandy saw eye to eye.

After waiting forty-five minutes, her car pulled into the parking lot. He was glad to see that she was alone. What he needed to talk about with her was private. She got out of the car, and so did he. She saw him immediately.

"Have you been waiting for me?"

"Not long. I wanted to go over something with you."

"Something like...?"

"Like a plan to get your husband locked up for a very long time."

She looked at him, and took a deep breath. "Come on up."

She opened the door to her apartment and quickly walked across the room to turn off the alarm. This was a new apartment; she had moved since the incident of the gun going off when she thought she had seen Phil. He may have lucked out once, finding out where she lived, but she wasn't going to let it happen again. This apartment complex was very large, and all the buildings looked the same. Unlike her last place, there was a garage that went with each apartment. Once her car was in there, and she shut the blinds inside, she was able to vanish.

"Nice place," Tom said. "I'm sorry I didn't say so the other night when I was here. It's bigger than your last apartment."

"Thanks. I like it. I feel more comfortable here, and I've been able to get to know some of the neighbors."

"That's good."

Sandy motioned for him to sit, and went to the kitchen. She came back with two cans of Pepsi. Without saying anything, she put one on the coffee table in front of him. "So let's hear it," she said.

The phone rang. "Sorry," she said, walking back to the kitchen. She looked at the caller ID and it showed a number she didn't recognize. It was a local call; probably someone selling something, or a wrong number maybe. She stood beside the phone and let it ring the fourth time. The machine picked it up, but when it was time for the person to leave a message, there was silence, and then a dial tone.

"Did you hear that?" she asked Tom.

"I didn't hear anything. Did they leave a message?"

"No, but they waited until the tone to hang up— does that sound strange to you?"

"Not really. The person probably had to hear your outgoing message to realize they had the wrong number."

"I've got the number right here; should I call it back?"

"Can you tell where the call came from? Was it local?"

"Yeah," she said and wrote the number down.

"Probably a wrong number. If they want something they'll call back." And just as he said this, the phone started to ring. Sandy looked at the caller ID and saw the same number. She picked it up and said a feeble "Hello" into the receiver.

"Hey Sandy." It was Phil.

"How did you get this number?

"Never mind how I got this number." Sandy put her hand over the receiver and softly said, "It's Phil" to Tom.

"Where are you? I know you're not calling from Logan."

"Well, ain't you smart. How about if I told you I was two minutes away from your house? How would that grab ya? You thought you could move and sneak past me? I seen that new apartment of yours, and it looks nicer than the old one. From the outside anyway; of course I haven't been on the inside."

"You're not allowed to be calling me, you know. This is a violation of the restraining order."

"Honey, honey! Is it against the law to tell your wife that you still love her? Huh? I just wanted to call and tell you that you can come home anytime you want. I mean, sooner's better than later, but whenever."

"Why can't you leave me alone? Can't you move on with your life?"

"No, I can't. You might be in some danger, and I wanted to let you know about it. I wanted to warn you about it."

"What kind of danger? What are you talking about?"

"I'm not tellin'. I need to speak to you alone. It can be in a public place if you want. I ain't trying to hurt you, you know."

"What do you want to talk about?"

"It's about that man you got in your apartment right now."

She looked at Tom. "I don't know what you're talking about."

"Don't play dumb with me, Sandy. You got Flanagan in your house right now. Little Tommy Flanagan. There's something you ought to know about him. Something that might make you see what's really going on here. He ain't trying to protect you—he's got it out for me, and he's got a reason. Now, I just want to explain what the hell is going on here. It's not how he's making it out to be. I'm not trying to hurt you, Sandy. I ain't never gonna hurt you again."

She didn't know what to say. "You'll meet in a public place?"

"Sure. Name the time and place, and I'll be there. Just five minutes."

"Why don't you tell me over the phone?"

"Can't. This is something I have to tell you face to face. You'll be able to tell if I'm lying by lookin' at me. You always could."

Sandy knew that was the truth. She didn't know Phil knew it as well. All those times he had lied to her, and she pretended to believe him. He must have known. She looked at Tom, who was now standing five feet from her, watching with great interest. He was shaking his head and mouthing the word 'no.'

"Okay," she said.

"That's great. Time and place, just name it."

"Why don't you let me get back to you on that. Okay? I'll call you in a few days."

"Sandy, wait. Be careful. Flanagan's got a screw loose."

"Okay. I will." She hung up and walked past Tom into the living room. She took a sip of the soda and let out a little chuckle. Tom followed her back into the room and sat across from her.

"What did he say?"

"He said you had a screw loose."

"Why did you say you would meet him?"

"I thought whatever plan you had to lock him up could include this little meeting. You want to trap him into doing something, right? Maybe get him to come over here and then arrest him?"

"Yeah, I guess we could do something like that. I'll have to think about it. What'd you talk about?"

"He said he wanted to meet in a public place, a place of my choosing, to discuss you."

"Me? What about me?"

"He knew you were here. He said he was close by. He also said he knew something about you, that he wanted to warn me about you."

"He's trying to scare you, pure and simple. Can't you see that? He's trying to confuse you. He doesn't want you to trust me."

"Tom, the other night you came over here at ten-thirty at night and you were drunk. *You* told me that Phil knew something that you would rather not have known. I don't know what that is, but when you said that, it was awful mysterious. I'm in the middle of all this, and I think I should be given all the facts. You're not helping me by hiding anything."

Tom sat back in the chair. "You're absolutely right. There is something I should have told you. I've been protecting myself when I should have been up front with you. If you want to know this big secret he's planning on telling you, I can tell you and save you from seeing him. It's not a big deal, really. I just don't want it getting back to Logan and the people there."

"I won't tell anyone, if that's what you're worried about."

"I'm gay. That's really all it is. Phil is one of the only people in Logan who knows it."

"So you're gay—what's the big deal?"

"Here's what I'm afraid of—if the whole town knows, I'll probably be out of a job."

"No you won't, they can't do th—"

"Come on, Sandy! How many years did you live in Logan? You know that town as well as I do, and you know they wouldn't stand for having a homosexual on the police force. They wouldn't. Phil might be the town drunk, but if he tells enough people, pretty soon the whole town is talking about it, including my bosses. They wouldn't fire me right away, but they would make my life a living hell until I quit."

"How long have you...known you're gay?"

"Since puberty, I guess. I went out with some girls in high school, but it always felt like I was doing what I *should* be doing, not what I *wanted* to be doing."

"But why would he want to warn me about you?"

"Maybe he thinks all gays are perverted freaks, I don't know. There are lots of people in towns like Logan who think that. That's why I can't have anyone know that I'm gay. I love my job; it's my life."

Tom got up and took his keys out of his pocket. "I'm gonna head back to Logan. Be careful. If you need anything, give me a call. You have my number?"

She nodded. "Thanks. I'm sure everything will be fine."

"I don't want you talking to him without me there."

"He said he wanted to talk to me alone."

"Well, I want to be close by at least. I'm probably going to be in town on Saturday evening. I'd like to stop by to check on you if that's okay. Maybe even take you out to dinner—how does that sound?"

"That sounds fine—no, wait! I can't. I'm going to Logan on Saturday. I'm going to eat at my mother's at six. Labor Day picnic. Sorry."

"Okay." Tom went to the door and opened it. "You lock this after I leave, okay? And be careful." He gave her a little smile.

"I will, detective. I promise."

Chapter Seventy-Five

Tom was going to be late for work, but he didn't care. This was too important to put off. He knocked on Phil Oliver's door at 7:45 a.m. As expected, there was no answer. Oliver would be sleeping like the dead at this hour. Tom refused to go away, however, and after what seemed like five minutes of pounding, he finally heard footsteps approaching the door. There was a small thud against the door. The door had no peephole, but to either side of the door was a vertical window with a curtain. Tom saw one of the curtains fall back into place and then heard footsteps getting further away.

"Open this goddamn door or I'll break it down, I swear it!" He pounded his fist repeatedly until he heard the footsteps come back. There was a pause, and then the 'snap' sound of the deadbolt. Phil stood there in boxer shorts and an oversized white v-neck t-shirt.

"Man, what the hell you want?" Phil asked. Tom pushed past him and walked into the living room. Phil shut the door. "Where's your boss? Queen Bitch out on another assignment?"

"I came here alone because this is between you and me. I want to know what the hell you think you're doing, calling Sandy? I could lock you up right now if I wanted to."

"Why don't you then?"

"I'm gonna wait. I got a special plan for you. I'm here to tell you to stop calling her and to keep your mouth shut."

"You know, I think she wants to see me. I think she misses me. I think she wants to get back with me. She's probably flunking all her classes in that school of hers and finding out that she ain't smart enough for no college. I knew one day it would happen and she'd come

268

back to me. That's why she ain't even filed for a divorce. She probably knew deep down, too."

"I don't think you could be more wrong about that."

"We're gonna meet somewhere soon."

"If she meets with you, you remember that it's because I let it happen. You're a murder suspect and I can haul you in whenever I want."

"That's a joke. You ain't gonna haul me in, 'cause you got nothing."

"I've got at least four witnesses that say you got in a fight with Dale Parker just days before his murder. You don't think that's something?"

"I know enough about the law to know that don't mean shit. You got no 'direct evidence.' If you did, I'd already be locked up."

"If you talk to Sandy, you keep your mouth shut."

"What? You mean that little thing you had for Mark Cherneau back in—"

Tom leapt at Phil and slammed him against the wall. He had his hand around Phil's throat. "Now you listen to me, asshole. You will not say a word about that to anyone, and if you do, I'll settle our differences myself." He let go of his throat.

"Gee, detective, that sounded like a threat."

"Consider it a police officer's advice concerning your safety."

Chapter Seventy-Six

It was six o'clock on a sunny Friday evening when Sandy Oliver watched the man who had almost killed her half a year earlier walk back into her life. The worst part was that she was here by choice. There had been something about the way that he had pleaded the other night on the phone—she thought there might be something to Phil's claim. Tom Flanagan had visited her more than once while he was supposedly 'off the clock,' and she didn't really understand why. She knew there was something, some sort of history between Phil and Tom, and when asked about it, Tom had answered vaguely. She knew Phil wouldn't be vague. He had never been vague about anything.

Besides, she didn't trust anyone completely, and she figured whatever information she could get on Tom, the better. It never did anyone any good to be ignorant.

They were meeting at a place in Columbus called Rockin' Robin, a fifties-style hamburger joint, complete with nickel juke boxes. Over the speakers, Elvis Presley sang 'Heartbreak Hotel.'

The place was packed, and Phil sat down in the booth across from her. At his request, she had come alone.

She was still afraid of him, watching his every move even though they were in a public place. He smiled at her in a way he hadn't smiled since before they were married.

"Hey, sugar," he said.

"Hello, Phil."

"How's your job? Must be going pretty good, with you moving up in the world and all. That new place you got seems pretty expensive."

"My job's fine; I like it very much. And yes, I have been moving up in the world ever since I left Logan. Since I left you."

"Aw, it hurts me when you say things like that. I know I wasn't good to you; I know I didn't treat you with the respect you deserve and there ain't no apologizin' for it. I mean, I *am* sorry, but I know that something like that can't be made up for."

"Tell me what you want to tell me."

"That don't mean, though, that you can't maybe forgive me, and the things I done. You were always forgiving. You always were giving other people second chances. I was just hoping you would be able to give me a second chance, you know? What do you say?"

She started laughing in a way that could have easily turned to tears. "What do I say? What do I say?" She put her elbows on the table and leaned closer to him. She thought she smelled alcohol on his breath. She looked around to see if anyone was listening. "You beat the hell out of me, Phil! Do you understand? Do you know how ridiculous it would be for me to let you back into my life? Do you know how hard it is to even be sitting here, talking to you?" She put her finger into the side of her mouth, like a fish hook and showed him her teeth. She put her other finger on one in particular. "You see this tooth? It's a false tooth. You knocked that tooth out, remember? Remember that night? I sure as hell do. So get this straight—I'm here to listen to whatever it is you think is so important, but other than that, there's nothing. You got it? Nothing."

"All right, I'll tell you why I'm here, but you should understand this—I'm telling you because I still love you." He paused, as if waiting for her to say she loved him, too. She remained silent. "I think this guy wants to hurt you, and I don't want to see that happen. It's as simple as that. I'm trying to help you."

"You can help me by leaving me alone, okay? I've moved on with my life, and you should, too. Now—I'm leaving if you're not going to tell me why I should stay."

"Okay, okay. You might think I'm stalking you, or some shit like that, but what I want you to know is that yes, I am watching you, but only because I know what Flanagan has up his sleeve."

"And what is that?"

"He's trying to frame me. He wants it to look like I killed Mark Cherneau."

"He says you *did* kill him. I think I might believe him."

"He wasn't my favorite person in the world, but I didn't kill him. I couldn't kill anyone."

"You certainly gave it your best shot with me."

"You know me, Sandy. I have a problem when I drink too much. All them times I hit you, I was stone drunk. Didn't even know what I was doing."

"Spare me the bullshit."

"I ain't saying it's an excuse; I'm just explaining it to you. But what I'm trying to say is that I ain't no murderer. I couldn't plan out something as nasty as this. Hell, if I were going to kill Cherneau, I probably would have just taken my gun and shot the bastard. Ain't that right? You know it is."

"Maybe so. What I'd like to find out, though, is why you think Tom wants to frame you for it."

"He killed Cherneau. Look at him and look at me. Who do you believe? Him, right? I guess I don't blame you. I don't think anyone would take my word over his. And he's counting on that. He's a cop, and I'm a drunk who used to beat his wife. If he comes after you and... does something to you, who do you think the cops are going to come after? This guy could do anything to you and get away with it, and you're letting him into your apartment late at night. Whenever he wants, really. Don't you think it's a bit strange that he's been coming to see you without his partner? Without anyone?"

"Okay, I'll play along. Let's say Flanagan did kill him. Why would he pick you, specifically?"

"Because I know something about him that other people don't know. Something about Flanagan that he doesn't want known. He figures that if he gets me locked up, he kills two birds with one stone. I'm someone who can do him damage, so if I get life, he gets rid of me for good, and he gets away with murder. That's how I see it."

"Are you talking about his homosexuality?"

"You knew he was a fag? How did you know that?"

"He told me, Phil. He told me that was your big news, and that he didn't want that known around Logan because he thinks it would jeopardize his job. Yeah, he told me you'd say that. Now, is that all you were going to tell me? Besides—if, like you say, no one would take your word over his about a murder, why would they believe your word about his being gay? Why would he be so concerned about you?"

"See, that's what you have to ask yourself. Why am I a threat to him? It's because I know what I know, and I know that it's true. If I were just blowing smoke, you think he would give a shit what I say?"

"I think maybe you killed Cherneau. Maybe you're trying to pin it on Tom Flanagan because he's gay. You've always hated gay people, and you can't stand the thought that he is going to be the one who brings you in and arrests you for this."

"Come on, Sandy. It's not that. What, you think that just because he's a queer that it's okay to be alone with him? You think he wouldn't hurt you because he's gay?"

"I don't think he'd hurt me because *he's* a decent human being, which is more than I can say for you. Is that really it? You think that because he's gay, he's a criminal?"

"There's more to it than that."

"So tell me what it is, exactly. Why is it he would want to frame you?"

"Because it's not just that I know he's gay."

"What, then?"

"Tom Flanagan used to be in love with Mark Cherneau."

Chapter Seventy-Seven

Karen checked her voice mail at five o'clock and got the message. It was from Janice—she was ready with the list.

She hadn't thought that Janice would be willing to do such a favor, risking her job for Karen, even though they'd been pretty good friends.

Karen got to Dante's in Lancaster at ten after seven. She took her briefcase in with her. Janice was sitting in the lobby.

"Did you just get here?" Karen asked.

"Yeah. The guy said it would just be a few minutes to get the table ready."

Karen sat down next to her. "So how've you been?"

"Okay. How's it going with you and Bill?"

"Terrible, as usual. You know how they say that an affair by a spouse is just a symptom of something that's wrong in the marriage? I think that's probably true. When I think about it, I guess this was bound to happen. We've been going through the motions of being married for years now; there's no real feeling left. Even when we have a 'fight,' it isn't what you would think of as a fight. We don't speak; it's not even worth it. We're just...tired."

"I think that happens a lot in marriages. Things become stale."

"Yeah, but with a lot of those marriages, the partners are *content* to be stale, you know. Tired is okay with them. This is different."

"Maybe Bill has some things he's tried to resolve on his own and couldn't. I think when a man has an affair, he might be trying to bury his past and create a new identity. Now, that past might include you and it might not."

"I'm not sure I follow," Karen said.

"What I'm saying is that maybe it's nothing you did. Maybe your marriage was doomed from the start."

"Great. That makes me feel so much better."

A waiter took them to their table. He told them the specials, which included the salmon. Karen and Janice smiled at each other. They told him they didn't need to see the menu. He left and brought back glasses of water.

"Last week I had to go home for a minute," Karen said, "and I got the mail. I found a letter to Bill that had no return address. There was a woman's handwriting on the envelope. It had to be from her."

"Did you consider opening it?"

"I didn't have enough time. As soon as I saw it, Bill was walking up the sidewalk. He was acting really strange when he saw the letter."

"Strange how?"

"Guilty. He took the letter and left. We had a small fight, but like I said, we're too tired to care."

"People say 'love and hate' like they are opposites, but at least with hate, there is still some emotion left. Some passion."

"I think our marriage crumbled a long time ago. Now we're just wandering around the rubble. I've been thinking about how it could be saved, and I haven't got an answer. Maybe it's best if we get it over with and end it now. Maybe there's nothing worth saving. I mean, why should I? We're like burdens to each other. He can be with this girlfriend of his and I can get on with my life."

Karen looked around the restaurant. There were no empty tables. She remembered the first time she had been to this restaurant; it was four years earlier, with Bill. She had wanted to go dancing afterwards, but Bill didn't want to. He had given her a lame excuse that he was too full from dinner to dance. They had settled on a movie instead. Karen tried to remember what the movie was, but couldn't. Even the memories of the good times were fading. There was nothing left to salvage. It was in that quiet moment that Karen decided that she would leave her husband.

"Karen?"

"Huh?" Karen said, as if from a trance.

"Thought I lost you there."

"You did."

"I just asked if you wanted the files now or if we should wait until later."

"Files?"

"Of all the women Bill counseled." She opened up the book bag and took out a manila folder that was half an inch thick. "There are files in here of all thirty-seven women he saw in the last two years. Each file has a page or two, with the profile form that each woman filled out about themselves." She handed the folder to Karen, who took it and quickly flipped through the pages, then put it in her briefcase.

"I really appreciate this, Jan. You didn't have to stick your neck out for me, but you did. If I can ever return the favor, you know I'll be happy to do it."

"No problem. What are friends for, right? I just hope that you find what you're looking for. Sorry there aren't pictures. You could have just looked through them and picked out the prettiest girls and that would be a start. I might remember some of them, so if you have any questions, let me know."

"Thanks."

"I would like to ask you one question, though," Janice said.

"Shoot."

"Once you find out who it is, what *are* you going to do? I mean, you're not going to hurt her, right?" Karen laughed at this. "You're not going to lock her up and throw away the key?"

"Ha ha, Janice."

"My question is—if you're going to leave Bill anyway, what difference does it make who the bimbo is?"

"I don't know, Jan. It doesn't, I guess. Not if you look at it logically. I just want to know, okay? Maybe I want to see what kind of woman Bill would leave me for. Maybe I want to know what she has that I don't. He's been in a...daze for the past few months. He sleeps all the time, never says anything, he essentially quit his job, and when he is awake, he sits in front of the TV like a zombie. I don't know if I've seen him smile in at least a month. Clearly, this other woman has consumed him. She must be all he ever thinks about. It's like he's almost under a spell or something. I'm just curious what kind of woman could have such power over him."

Chapter Seventy-Eight

Sandy was not expecting what she had just heard. Tom Flanagan, in love with Mark Cherneau? No way. She looked at Phil. She didn't know why he would lie about this, other than to shift the suspicion away from himself.

A young man with white pants, a white shirt and a red-and-white striped vest came to their table with two plates of burgers and fries. He set them down on the table and came back a second later with the strawberry milkshake that Sandy had ordered extra thick.

Sandy realized she wasn't hungry. Not with Phil sitting across from her. "You know what I think? I think you're making this all up. Now I think you did it more than ever. I think you'd like to see the blame go anywhere but at yourself. You know what the strangest thing about it is? I think you're jealous. You know he's been over to my apartment late at night, you know I respect him, and even though the man is gay, you're jealous!"

Phil was eating his cheeseburger, not looking at her. He seemed almost more interested in the sandwich than what she was saying.

"You're funny, Sandy," he said with his mouth full, "you come up with the craziest schemes. Everything has to have some reason, some big complicated reason, and you can't just see it for what it is."

"Which is what?"

"That it's simple. The guy was in love with this other guy and the other guy didn't want nothing to do with him, so he killed him. Why don't you just accept that?"

"I can't accept that just because you tell me to. I need to know the whole story. Besides, I don't think Tom would do something like that."

"Why, 'cause he's queer? What, you don't think that some fag can do violence? I tell you, from what I heard, he can be nasty when he wants to be. He's been pickin' fights with me ever since I been a suspect. But anyway, you want the story, so I'll go on and tell ya.

"Now, I don't know if you know, but him and Cherneau were good friends in high school. Flanagan didn't play baseball, because he was a damn beanpole and he had no coordination. In school, though, Flanagan was always playing some kind of joke or another. And he didn't give a shit if he was caught or not. Now, hanging around the guys, Flanagan would act like he liked girls—he'd look where his friends looked, make comments on which girl had the nicest ass—just like his buddies. But from what I heard, Mark Cherneau and him were good enough friends that Cherneau knew that Flanagan was gay."

"From what you've heard? These are all rumors. I suppose the next thing you're going to tell me is that, in high school, they were lovers, right?"

"No, I never heard anything like that. As far as I know, Cherneau was straight as an arrow. What I'm saying to you is that Cherneau knew his friend was gay, and that he never told anyone about it. He kept it a secret because that's how Flanagan wanted it."

"I don't believe this. This is crazy," she said and sat back in her seat.

"Hey, I know it's hard to believe, but I heard it from someone who wouldn't lie about this. Me and Cherneau never saw eye to eye, that's for sure, but we did have some mutual friends."

"Friends?"

"She was a friend of mine," he said, looking at her while he finished his coke. "A relative of his."

"Are you talking about his sister?"

"Lisa told me the whole story herself. You know she never much liked her brother. I guess that was why we were friends. She was never popular like her brother, wasn't as smart as her brother, and she was never the athlete he was; Lisa was just plain ordinary next to him. That's what we had in common. We've talked on occasion at the bar; we've even had ourselves some long talks about her brother and the Gay Detective."

"What did she say to you?"

"That through high school, Mark knew Tom was gay and didn't say anything. Protected him. Not long after graduation, though, Tom started spending much more time around Mark, always calling him asking him what he was doing, things like that. She said that Mark was moving on with his life, with his career in baseball. Now I don't know if you know this or not, but when Mark was just out of high school, he got real serious with a girl. He spent almost all his free time with her. He had girlfriends in high school, but nothing like this. As far as he was concerned, he had no time to spend with anyone else. It was then when Tom started showing real signs of jealousy. He kept talking bad about her to Mark whenever he could, and this didn't help. He would constantly keep track of where Mark was, would tell him that he was whipped, and that Angela was controlling him. It got to a point where Cherneau wouldn't return Tom's calls. He tried to be polite about it, but he didn't want anything to do with Tom Flanagan. Finally, Tom gave up and stopped calling. It was soon after that that Cherneau went to Akron to play baseball, and then to Maine."

"You're telling me that Tom Flanagan was in love with, *obsessed* with, Mark Cherneau? Come on."

"Is it so hard to believe? Come on, you know Flanagan's gay, right? You also know that he and Cherneau were good friends. All the women loved Cherneau, so why is it so hard to believe?"

"I don't know. Maybe it's not that hard to believe. So what happened when Cherneau came back to Logan last year?"

"From what I hear, Flanagan contacted him a couple times, trying to get together. Cherneau never called him back."

"And that's a reason to kill someone? Because they don't return your calls?"

"If it's someone you're madly in love with, maybe so." Phil sat back and put his hands in his lap. "Sandy, I've done a lot of nasty, horrible things to you in the past. I know that. I know I can't make up for it. But I can't help it; I still care about you. You know that. You know I never lied to you, or at least when I did, you could always tell. You were always smarter than me. There's no way I could fool you. That's why I had to see you in person; if I told you this on the phone, you wouldn't be able to tell I'm telling the truth. But look at me. Can't you tell I'm not lying? I have to tell you this to warn you. I don't know this for sure, but maybe he killed Cherneau because Cherneau was gonna stop holding back the fact that Flanagan was gay. Maybe that's what pushed Flanagan over the edge. I mean, jealousy is a nasty thing—I should know, right? It can make you do crazy things. Now I think Flanagan's after me. He wants me dead, or at least locked up far away from Logan. He's setting me up; he's been doing it from the start. Maybe he saw Lisa and me talking and that was enough for him to think that she was telling me the story I just told you. He visited my house the other day and threatened to kill me if I told you what I just did. If you're going to see him, at least make it in a public place. And it would help if he had his partner with him. Don't see just him."

Sandy sat there, unable to speak. She looked at Phil, the man who was still legally her husband, the man who had nearly beaten her to death, but still she had to admit it.

What he had just said made complete sense.

Chapter Seventy-Nine

Tom Flanagan sat in his car outside Rockin' Robin in Columbus. He had been out there the whole time. He had followed Phil Oliver, the idiot, the whole way from Logan and Phil didn't have a clue. Tom refused to let this bastard just do whatever the hell he wanted. Phil was a murder suspect, and it was Tom's job to watch him. Of course, it was more than that. Much more. He was violating the law, sitting there talking to Sandy. Tom decided he would let the restraining order violation go. That was a lesser charge; Sooner or later, Phil would go a little too far. He knew Phil couldn't stand to be looking at her, talking to her and not to be physical with her. That was just something in his makeup. It was a compulsion with him, and eventually he would have to feed it. And when it happened, Tom would be there to haul his ass in. Attempted murder two, at least. He would make Phil pay.

Tom had been sitting there for the better part of an hour. He was parked close enough to see them in the booth by the window, but far enough away to not be recognized. What in God's name could they be talking about for so long? Old times? They would be talking about him. What were they saying? At times, it seemed as if she was angry with Phil, and she would shake her head. Whatever he was telling her, she wasn't believing, and that was good. But as the hour progressed, Tom saw in Sandy's face the look of a young girl, a girl who loved the man across the table from her, no matter what he had done to her. Come on, Sandy, he thought. You can't be that stupid. The look on her face was one of interest, of contemplation. She was silently staring at Phil, arms crossed, as if she didn't want to believe what he was telling her, but did anyway. He spoke for a long time. He wasn't sure because of the distance, but when Phil stopped speaking, he could have sworn he saw her nod.

Phil finally walked out of Rockin' Robin, stopping on the curb as the cars passed in front of him. He scanned the parking lot, looking for his car. He spotted it and crossed the street. Tom had parked far away so he wouldn't be spotted. After he watched him get in his El Camino and drive away, he looked back inside the restaurant at Sandy, who was still sitting in the booth. Her vacant stare was interrupted by the young man who had waited on them. He made change for her and placed it on the table as they exchanged smiles. Soon after that, she was walking to her car. He got out of his.

"Sandy!" he yelled to her and waved. She was clearly shocked.

"Detective! What are you doing here?"

"I couldn't let you be alone with him like that. It could have been dangerous for you."

"The restaurant was crowded—I think I was pretty safe."

"I followed that dumb-ass all the way from Logan and he didn't even notice me—can you believe that?"

"Yeah, I can," she said. "Phil doesn't pay much attention when he's driving."

"You got that right. He almost ran off the road a couple times on 70. So, tell me—what did you two talk about?"

"Not much. We talked about his trying to give up drinking and how he was sorry that he was so abusive. He kept trying to get me to come back with him, saying he would stop drinking and hitting me."

"Yeah, right. Not in this lifetime. Guy's a pathetic loser, and he'll never change. You can bet on it. Now come on—I know you talked about me. I want to know what he said."

"He said you were gay, but he was pretty shocked when I told him that I already knew. He said that there weren't that many people in Logan who knew. He said that if you keep harassing him, he would tell everyone in Logan that you're gay and that you wouldn't have a job soon after that, not the way people in Logan are, that's for sure. He said you want to get him locked up so that he can't say anything."

"I want to get him locked up because he killed Mark Cherneau, and probably Dale Parker, too. Sure, it's true I don't want the people of Logan to know I'm gay. He's right; I probably would be out of a job. But even if he did talk, I don't think anyone would believe the town drunk before they would believe me."

"It's funny—he said the same thing."

"So was there anything else?"

"Nope, that was it," she said. "Were you expecting something else?"

"No, just wondering. So are you going home now? Maybe we could talk about how to get him locked up. We still haven't talked about that, you know. I have a plan if you're willing to go along with it."

Sandy looked over at the movie theater and saw all the people going in. "Actually, I'm meeting a friend tonight. We're thinking about seeing a movie. Why don't I call you in a couple days; we can talk about it then."

Chapter Eighty

Bill Summers knew that once he saw Julianne there would be no turning back. He would lose himself in the pale beauty of her face, and his decision would not only be made, but also irrevocable. Maybe that was why Bill, now that the time had come to leave, was having trouble going through with it.

He tried to imagine the guilt he would feel—how long would this affect him, and how long would the feelings linger? Maybe it would be easier than he thought, and he could just put it behind him and never look back.

He almost felt his marriage was a job, and he was quitting. It had become a job he no longer liked, and one he no longer hated. He felt nothing for it, and he detested his ambivalence.

He had once felt passionate about everything in his life, and lately, he felt passion for nothing. He missed his younger self, when he cared about things, and felt his life served a purpose. Julianne had reminded him of these things, and her enthusiasm sparked something in him that had been dormant for years.

He sat at the rest area with a six pack on the floor of the back seat. He had never been much of a drinker, but he had the notion in his head that leaving his wife might be easier if he were drunk. As he opened the first beer, he tried to figure out what the hell he was doing. Why was he trying to get drunk? This wasn't like him, was it?

By the time he had reached his fifth beer, he had gone to the restroom three times. He was tired and confused. He wasn't sure he could drive a car, much less find the campsite. He felt like a failure; the things he had held to be important in his life, his marriage and his job, were now gone. So many marriages had been through so much worse and survived, and here he was, not able to handle his own. He felt the sting of irony that he couldn't help himself when he had helped so many others. Karen must have been disappointed with him when he took that leave of absence. She hadn't said anything about it, but Bill could feel it—she thought he was a loser. He had slipped away from her, and the further he got, the less she seemed to care. He had gone down a dark road, not knowing his destination. Until now. He looked around the rest area. It was cool and breezy, almost midnight. No one else was around. There was one semi parked at the end of the lot, and Bill supposed there was a guy in the rest area who was there to maintain the place. Other than that, Bill was alone here. *This* was his destination, he realized. Here in this desolate place, without anyone. He kept telling himself there was someone who cared, someone waiting for him. She was out there, and she was beautiful, so why didn't he go to her now? Julianne had been in a desperate situation, and anyone other than Dale probably seemed like a prince to her. Bill would go to her tomorrow, but for now he was drunk. He felt paralyzed, not being able to go back to Karen, and when he thought of going to Julianne, now that the time had actually come, he had a sinking feeling. He knew what he was doing was wrong, morally wrong, but he couldn't stop himself.

As he opened the sixth beer, he decided he was too tired to do anything tonight. He wasn't going anywhere.

Chapter Eighty-One

It was late Friday night, and Julianne waited in the woods for Bill. She was hoping tonight would be the night he would come, but maybe it wasn't. She had sent him the letter almost a week ago—he must have received it by now. A terrible thought crossed her mind, one she hadn't thought of before—what if his wife had gotten the letter first? What if she read it and never gave it to him? Then she realized, though, that they were probably looking for her, and her being a police detective, they would have come and taken her away. No, Bill had received it, all right. Maybe he just had to take care of some things first. She hoped he wasn't having second thoughts.

The wind swept against the tent, blowing harder tonight than normal; maybe there was a storm coming in. She had been lucky so far—it had not rained at night since she'd been out here. The trees rustling disrupted the peace of the forest. She wished Bill was there with her. She needed him so she could be free. He was the last crucial element to her mission—to putting all the bad memories of her past aside and beginning anew. Bill Summers was an intelligent, attractive and honorable man, not some redneck who made knives in his basement.

She thought of all the men in her life, all the rotten things they had done to her, and she thought that Bill was almost too good to be true. She had seduced him, it was true, and now she felt like her whole relationship with him was a trick she was playing on him, one she hoped he would never figure out. She didn't want him to see the real Julianne, the ugliness that was there, the stain that had been on her for so many years now, a stain that could not be removed without him.

Chapter Eighty-Two

Tom Flanagan knew tomorrow would be the day. He sat in the recliner in his living room, a room lit only by the small yellow lamp that was on the end table next to him, drinking a glass of water. He'd had two glasses already and was still thirsty. There was no television in this room, and the book that sat on the end table, *Journey Into Darkness* by John Douglas, lay closed.

He went over it again and again. How far was he willing to go to get Phil Oliver locked up? The plan was fairly simple—Tom would put himself and Sandy in a situation where he could arrest him for attempted murder.

He felt the cool water slide down his throat. Sandy would be in town tomorrow to go to dinner at her mother's house. He had looked up her mother's address earlier that day. It was written on a small legal pad on the end table beside the book. He would let her eat dinner with her mother and her family and then he would pay them a little visit. She would want to know what he was doing there, and he would tell her something to get her away from them. Something simple. From there, he would take her in his car and drive her out to a remote area. He would pitch his idea to her, but she wouldn't go for it. She wouldn't want to put herself in danger. But this was what she had to do if she wanted to be free. Tom would convince her of that.

From there he would drive to Phil's house. Making sure it was vacant, he would break in (with no signs of forcible entry, of course) and take her down to the basement. He would tie her up and tuck her away somewhere. She would be in some pain for a little while, maybe even bleed a little, but he knew for her it would be worth it. For himself, too. From there, a simple anonymous tip would take care of Phil, and it was up to

Tom to determine for which crime Oliver would be convicted—attempted murder, or murder. He could silence her too, if he had to, but that probably wouldn't be necessary.

In the end, she would thank him for what he did.

Chapter Eighty-Three

Karen and Janice finished dinner at Dante's at about 8:30. They entertained the thought of going to a movie, but went to Burdine's, the local ice cream shop instead. It was a nice little place, and they spent over an hour talking about movies they'd seen or books they'd read. Janice and her husband Sam were thinking of having a baby, and they talked about that for a while. She kept saying how scared Sam was, but the more she talked, Karen could tell that she was just as scared. They didn't leave Burdine's until they closed at ten.

When Karen got home at a quarter till eleven, Bill was gone. The TV was turned off, but the lights in the living room were on. She thought he must have left in the last few hours, otherwise he wouldn't have turned the lights on. He certainly wouldn't have done it as a courtesy to her.

She looked in all the rooms. What was she looking for, though? His car was gone. Was she looking for the letter? She went upstairs and saw one thing that was out of the ordinary. She turned the hallway light on and saw that the door to the linen closet was open. She thought of weeks earlier when she had come home and he had been standing there, in front of it without any clothes on. Something had struck her as peculiar about that incident, and something was strange about this. She walked up to the closet, and saw that the bottom part was a mess. The blankets and towels were unfolded and laying on the floor, some still in the closet and some out in the hall. He had obviously been digging in here, but for what? What was in here other than blankets and towels? Did this have something to do with whatever he had been doing weeks ago, when he had looked so guilty?

She went downstairs and turned on the news, then went and got her briefcase. She put it on the coffee table in front of her and opened it. The news spoke of another murder that had happened in Zanesville the day before. The media had moved on from the Cherneau case. They were no longer mentioning it, not even to mention there was nothing new. Karen began to think that too much time had passed without a lead of any sort in the biggest case of her life. She began to think that she might never solve this case, and that it would weigh on her for the rest of her life. Tom had told her about the famous FBI profiler John Douglas and how he'd been haunted, thinking they'd never catch the notorious Green River Killer until, almost 20 years after the first murder, he was arrested.

She picked up the manila folder. If she couldn't solve the Cherneau case, she could at least solve who the hell was screwing around with her husband.

She opened the folder and saw a long list of names. Beside each name was a case file number. She went down the list from the top: *Teresa Adkins, Kaylee Anderson, Stephanie Bailey,, Michelle Bender*—and then Karen's eyes skipped over the next few names. They were drawn to the name she had heard, spoken and thought of so many times in the past two weeks. There it was in black-and-white: *Julianne Case.*

Karen was astonished. She had never considered that he could be involved in the case, and now she needed to determine where he fit. He had been distancing himself from her for months now. She had to admit she didn't know her husband anymore, or what he was capable of. Obviously, he had been going through some problems. She expected that if he had wanted to talk about them, he would have. But he never did.

It was still possible he didn't know everything, but there was no doubt he knew something. She had so desperately sought scraps of information for months now, and he had kept things from her. He had deliberately let Karen go through the toughest case of her life, caring so little for her as to not tell what he knew. But that was the thing—how much did he know, exactly?

Obviously, he would have known that Julianne was being sought for questioning, and if there was nothing between them, he would have turned her in. Wouldn't he? Was he that selfish—that not only was he having an affair, but also that he would keep this affair a secret, even if people's lives were destroyed in the meantime?

Maybe they had been working as a team, or at least together on the murder of Dale Parker. Maybe she wanted to get rid of her abusive boyfriend, but didn't know exactly how. So she seduces a man she thinks she can control, and gets him to kill Dale in an act of chivalry.

Karen thought more about this theory and decided it was improbable. Another scenario, as hard as it was to accept, was that Bill had done this on his own volition. He had heard so many abuse stories, and had been in an abusive home growing up. Maybe one day he decided he wasn't going to stand for it anymore. Maybe he fell in love with Julianne Case and that pushed him over the edge. He had always been so involved in the well-being of his patients. Karen could remember many stories he had told about some husband abusing his wife, and in telling the story, Bill would get so angry that he would start shaking. Still, she was having an extremely difficult time accepting her husband, a man who had never actually done anything about anything in his life, as a killer. Hell, maybe it was all some sort of coincidence. Maybe Julianne Case wasn't the other woman, and Bill had just kept his mouth shut in an effort to not get her in trouble. He had heard of whatever cruel things Dale had done to her, and maybe he was glad that she had killed him, and maybe his silence was his way of helping her get away with it. She hoped that was all there was to it, but she doubted it.

She thought of going out at this late hour to search for him, but had no idea where to start. First, she wanted to get proof that he was involved in this murder, concrete evidence of some sort. What could be done? Then it came to her.

The phone only rang once before Tom picked up the phone.

"You up?"

"Yeah. What's going on?"

"You have a friend in Trace Evidence, right?"

"Brian, yeah."

"Does he do fingerprints?"

"You kidding? He's the best in the division at matching a print. Why? You got something?"

"I might. Now I need you to keep this a secret for now, okay? I want you to call him and—"

"Right now?"

"Yes, right now. Tell him to bring whatever computer gadgets he needs to run a match on the partial we found in Parker's house. And don't bring anyone else, all right? Just you and him."

"Okay, Karen. Where are you now?"

"I'm at home."

Chapter Eighty-Four

It took Tom and Brian nearly an hour to get to Karen's home. Brian had been sound asleep when Tom called him, and he didn't seem to understand why this couldn't wait until morning. Tom didn't make a convincing argument because he knew nothing. After ten minutes of begging and pleading, Brian gave in. He did take, however, his own sweet time getting his gear together and driving over to Tom's house. The first thing he said to Tom was, "This better be important." He had assured him it was, otherwise they wouldn't be asking him to do this in the middle of the night. When he mentioned that what they were doing was secret, and that no one in the p.d. or homicide knew about it, Brian seemed to wake up a little.

Arriving at two-thirty in the morning, they didn't even have to knock. Karen had been waiting by the window, watching for them. Tom introduced Karen to Brian, even though they had seen each other around the office more than a few times.

"Guys, thanks for coming. I know this is a strange circumstance."

"No problem," Tom said. "We're a little more than intrigued, though." Brian, who was carrying a laptop and some other gear over his shoulder, nodded in agreement.

"Have a seat. Let me show you what I just found." The two men sat on the nearby couch. Karen sat in the chair across from them. She opened the manila folder. "Now I take it that both of you can keep a secret. I don't want this getting out."

"Absolutely," Tom said. Again, Brian nodded in agreement.

Karen looked at Brian. "Tom already knows that my husband is a social worker and a licensed therapist. For a few months now, I have suspected that he's been having an affair. I didn't know who with, and I wanted to find out. Now, I know that Bill is, or was, very involved in his job. It has happened before where he has gotten a little too involved. I wanted to know who it was, so I was able to get a list of all the patients he's had in the last year."

"Isn't that list confidential?" Brian asked.

"Thank you, Brian. That's not the point."

"Karen, I know you didn't drag us out in the middle of the night to hear about Bill having an affair," Tom said.

"Take a look at the list," Karen said and handed it to him. He looked at it for just a few seconds, and then he saw it.

"Oh, my."

"What is it?" Brian asked. Tom pointed to the name on the page and showed it to him.

"Oh, my," Brian said.

"You think this is who he was having an affair with? Is he upstairs? Have you asked him?"

"I haven't seen him all night. I got here around eleven and he was gone. But look—the Dale Parker murder case has been all over the news, her name's been reported in the coverage, and he never once mentioned that he knew her. Why else would he keep that quiet? I think he's been having an affair with her, and that maybe he's working with her on this."

"You've got to be kidding me," Tom said. "Bill? In something like this? You told me yourself he was sort of wimpy when it came to confrontation, and now you think he's involved in a murder?"

"I don't know. I do know he's not been acting like himself lately. I didn't want to bring this to the chief before I knew for sure, and I think there's a way to prove whether or not he's involved."

"I suppose that's where I come in," Brian said.

"Exactly. I want you to find a print of Bill's somewhere in the house, and see if it matches the one we found on the doorknob of the linen closet in Dale

Parker's house. If we get a match, then we can report it. But I don't want to jump the gun here. If it doesn't match, then this never happened."

Part Three

SATURDAY
8:45 a.m.

Bill woke when a nearby car door was slammed. Three children came out of the back seat of a Ford Explorer, two girls who looked between ages seven and nine and a young boy, who was probably no older than five. The girls took a look at Bill and then looked at each other and giggled their way to the bathroom. The boy waited for his mother to get out of the car and they walked up to the bathroom together.

Bill had been reclining in the front seat, and now sat up. He grabbed the steering wheel as the pain shot through his forehead. His head felt caught in a vice and his vision was blurred. The taste in his mouth, the stagnant morning taste combined with the bitterness of the beer, made him sick to his stomach.

The Explorer door shut and Bill watched the man standing there, watching his family go into the building. He seemed happy. Bill stared at the dashboard in front of him and searched his soul for that feeling, scanning for it, through all the aspects of his life. The only thing that registered was Julianne.

The man from the car next to him pulled out a canvas bag and put it on the hood of the car. He pulled out an apple, leaned on the hood, and took a bite.

Bill got out of the car and took in the fresh, cool air. The man eating the apple glanced in his direction and smiled.

"How you doin'?" The man said.

"Hey," Bill said. He became aware of his haggard appearance.

"We got a three hour drive ahead of us," the man said, "and we were on the road for twenty minutes when the boy goes 'I have to go to the bathroom!' What can you do, though? You can't say no. When you gotta go, you gotta go. Hey, you want one?" He reached in the bag and produced another apple. He held it out to Bill.

"No—thanks. I couldn't."

"Go ahead. My wife brought a whole bushel of these things, I think. I don't know how she expects us to eat them all. Go ahead, if you want."

Bill smiled and took the apple. "Thanks." Bill took a bite.

"Rough night?"

"Yeah."

"Had my share of 'em, believe me."

"You seem pretty happy now."

"I don't know about that—you ever had three kids under nine on a three hour trip in the car?" The man laughed. "My goal is to just get there with my sanity intact."

"Where you going?"

"Their grandparents' house in Toledo. We go up there a couple times a year. How about you—where you going?"

Bill took a bite and watched the sun peeking over the tops of the trees behind the rest area. "I'm not real sure."

The man had finished his apple. He looked at Bill, puzzled. It seemed Bill's cryptic response had made him uncomfortable. "Have a good one. Gotta use the head." The man started walking away. "Good talking to you."

"You, too." Bill raised the apple to him. "Thanks." The man put up a hand and went up to the building. Bill also needed to use the facilities, but he would wait until after the man had left. He got back in his car and watched the two girls, the mother and son come out of the bathroom. The girls were laughing and looking at the boy, like he had said something or done something funny. Bill suspected they were having some fun at the boy's expense, because he was not laughing.

Soon after that, the man came out of the bathroom and walked quickly to the car. He opened the driver's door and looked at Bill. He smiled and nodded. Bill nodded back, and then watched as they drove away toward Toledo.

The sun was higher now, making Bill's headache worse. He wondered if he had any aspirin, and bent across the seat to check in the glove compartment. When he opened it, he saw Sandy's gun. He'd forgotten it was there. The barrel of the gun was pointed at his stomach, and Bill slowly pulled it out and set it on the passenger floor. He looked through the glove box, but didn't find any aspirin. There were some papers from getting oil changes, insurance papers, and an old checkbook. Seeing the empty checkbook reminded Bill that he had planned on going to the bank.

He felt on the edge of something, and although he didn't know what was beyond it, he was preparing to jump. All the ties in his life would be broken, and after he ran off with Julianne, he would never look back. It was for this reason, he supposed, he wanted to see Sandy one more time.

10:37a.m.

After going to the bank and withdrawing $1710 out of their $3420 checking account and the entire $149 in his own savings account, Bill went to Columbus hoping to see Sandy.

He knocked on the door, and for a moment, there was no sound in the apartment. After a second ring of the doorbell, he heard the footsteps and the sound of the deadbolt unlocking. When the door opened, she was wearing sweatpants and a t-shirt that was too big for her. He thought that she could wear a suit of armor and look good.

"Bill, what are you doing here? It's good to see you!" She put her arms around him. Bill felt her breasts push against his chest. He held her for probably a second longer than he should have.

"Did I wake you?"

"No. I was awake. What are you doing here?"

"I came to say goodbye. I'm leaving Karen and moving."

"Oh my God, you're kidding! What happened?" She waved him into the apartment.

"We haven't been close for a long time. It was a bad situation and it was only going to get worse. I just wasn't happy."

"That's sad. So where you moving to?"

"I don't know where we're going." He saw the confusion in her face. "I met someone and we're leaving tomorrow; that's why I wanted to come see you and tell you goodbye. I also wanted to give you this thing back." He reached around the back of his jeans and took out Sandy's gun.

"No, I don't want that. I gave that to you to keep. I told you, I have no reason to have one of those things in

300

my house. It scares me more to have it than to not have it. I know that sounds crazy, but it's true."

"You should take it, because I feel the same way about guns. The thing's been sitting in my glove box since you gave it to me." He held it out to her. "Here, take it. You can take it to a pawn shop and get some pretty good money for it."

"Nope. If you don't want it, you take it to the pawn shop. You can keep the money; I don't care."

"Sandy, I insist. It's your gun, and I can't have it in my possession any longer. Just take it."

She took the gun and put it on the coffee table between them. "I guess I can take it back this afternoon. I can't have it here another night, that's for sure. I can take it back before I go over to my mother's house later."

"You going back to Logan?"

"Early Labor Day get together. No big deal—just my mom and a few of her friends."

The two sat down and talked over old times, some of the light-hearted moments they had shared.

"Bill, how well do you know Tom Flanagan?"

"A little, I guess. Why?"

"Do you think he would be the kind of guy who would try to set someone up for something *he* did?"

"I don't know; I only met him twice, and Karen was there both times. It's not like we ever talked very much. Why do you ask?"

"Don't tell anyone this—"

"Are you kidding? I'm leaving town tomorrow."

"It's just that he's been someone I trust. I let him in my house whenever he comes by, and now I'm not so sure he is what he presents himself to be. I talked with Phil yesterday—"

"You're kidding me."

"I know what you're thinking. I made sure it was in a public place. Anyway, Phil thinks...well, Phil made a pretty convincing case, let's just say that."

"A case for what?"

"He thinks it was Flanagan who killed Mark Cherneau and that other guy."

"Oh you've got to be kidding me. I don't know why he would say such a thing, but you have to remember that he was always able to convince you of just about anything."

"That's true, but this I think is different. I mean, just because he's trying to convince me of something doesn't mean it isn't true, right?"

"I guess not. Just be careful."

He walked to the door then, and she followed.

"So, tell me about this woman you're in love with."

"She's a few years younger than me, very beautiful—" then Bill stopped. "But it's more than that. It's her approach to life. She enjoys everything she does—doesn't matter what it is—going to the grocery store, riding in a convertible, whatever. Even when she talks about things that are painful, she has this optimism that is addictive."

"And you're hooked."

"You could say that. I never had this kind of outlook in my life with Karen."

"I'm happy for you."

"Thanks. I'll always care for you, you know that," he said.

She smiled a little and gave him a hug. "I know. I feel the same way." She kissed him on the cheek, and he kissed her on the forehead.

Contrary to all the rumors, it was the only time they had ever kissed.

10:41 a.m.

Phil had been awake for almost ten minutes, but he was still in bed. He felt like his blood was lead, and that he weighed 500 pounds. He stared at the ceiling, at a place in the plaster that was cracked. It was cracked when he and Sandy had first bought the house. He'd been planning to fix it for so many years now, but had never gotten around to it. He didn't know anything about fixing anything anyway. When they were initially going through the house with an inspector, the inspector had said that the crack may or may not be a problem. He had said that he couldn't tell from looking how deep the crack was, and he didn't know how long it had taken the crack to form. He had said that the ceiling could come down in two weeks, or it could stay exactly how it was for another twenty years. Phil was glad it looked as if it was the latter.

Those years just after they had been married were the best. He hated his love of alcohol when he saw what it had caused. Before he was an alcoholic, he'd had a steady job, had more energy, and the sex with Sandy was incredible. She was still in her late teens then, and early twenties, and she was willing to try anything, and to do anything. She had looked forward to him coming home, to making love to him.

And now look at me, he thought. He lay on the bed, with lead running through his veins. He had slept for ten hours and still felt like shit. He was dehydrated, and his tongue felt like it had passed its expiration date.

He was convinced that her return to him would turn things around, and that keeping her with him would be all the motivation he would need to give up drinking and become *real* again. It was easy to fall into despair when no one was around. He had tried to stop drinking on his own, but couldn't. His whole world was the bottle, and if not for drinking, his life was not only empty, but unbearable.

He would see her tonight. This would be the first step of his recovery. She would have to go back to him. He would convince her of his love and his commitment to stop drinking. Her mother was on his side, and that would help.

She would have to go back with him. One way or another, she would. He couldn't see beyond tonight without her.

There was no other way.

Karen sat impatiently at her desk. Brian had been working in the fingerprints lab for the better part of three hours. They had taken five of the best prints they could find of Bill's, and now all she could do was wait to see if her husband was involved in murder.

Brian came out once, telling her it would take a little longer because the one they had found on the doorknob in Dale Parker's house was only a partial.

Ten minutes later, Brian was at her desk with a folder. He motioned for her to walk with him into the hallway so that they could have some privacy from the other officers sitting at their desks.

In the hallway, Karen opened the folder. She saw the blown up pictures of the prints, red triangles marking points of reference. She was too anxious to read the findings.

"Just tell me, are these the same fingerprints or not?"

"The computer kept saying 'inconclusive,' so I had to do a lot of it manually." He took one of the pages from her and pointed to the two prints, side by side. "You see the two points here on the one from the murder scene, and they match the print we got from the refrigerator in your house, but the computer usually requires a third point to match. Here, the murder scene print is incomplete, and we could only match it to two. I'll tell you, though, and I know you don't want to hear this— but that print you had from Parker's house and the one from your refrigerator are the same print. Sorry, Karen."

"Yeah, me too." She paused. "Are you sure? I mean, if the computer can't tell, how can you?"

"Just from eyeballing it. I've been doing this for fifteen years, and I can tell a matched print when I see one. The print was partial so it's gonna come up inconclusive. But I can tell you this—if that print you had was complete, this would have come up as ninety to ninety-five percent probability."

The disappointment was clear on Karen's face. Her husband had deceived her. He'd made her look like a fool. He probably knew everything. As much as she hated to admit, he may have even been the one she'd been looking for. This whole time she had been driving herself crazy over finding this murderer—had she been living with him all along?

Tom came into the office and went to Karen's desk. She was cleaning up paperwork and putting it in a briefcase.

"What's going on?" he asked.

"Prints came back—it was a match."

"I'm sorry."

She was on the verge of tears. She looked up from her briefcase at Tom. "Why is everyone consoling me like there's been a death in the family? My husband has taken off with some girl who might—no, who is *probably* some deranged killer, and all you two can say is 'sorry'."

Tom looked away. "It's hard to be rejected. You shouldn't be ashamed to be crying."

"Why do you think I'm crying?"

Tom put his arm around her and rubbed her arm. "Look, this doesn't mean you're not strong. Even the toughest people are allowed to cry. And you're one of the toughest people I've ever met. It's not easy to have your marriage fall apart and find out your husband is involved in a homicide in the same day."

"First of all, my marriage fell apart a long time ago. I'm not crying about that. Secondly, I am upset with my husband for whatever he has to do with this case, but I'm not crying about that, either."

"What are you crying about, then?"

"He was there, under my nose this whole time, and I didn't see it. He kept asking me about the case, and I let myself think he was just trying to be supportive. I'm upset because I should have known. I let myself get tricked. I'm upset because he saw the pain this case was putting me through, and he didn't care. He didn't care." She fought back her sobbing, but when Tom put his arms around her, she let go. She released it all—all the love she had for Bill, all the stress the case had caused, all her

307

rage that there was a killer out there who was always a step ahead. It had been years since she felt so alone, so vulnerable. But this was no time to be weak.

She pulled back from Tom's arms. "I feel like an idiot," she said, wiping her eyes.

"No way. I'm not gonna let you feel like an idiot. Why don't you go home, take the rest of the day off."

"Absolutely not."

"What are you going to do, then?"

"I'm going to search for my husband."

Tom took his keys out of his pocket. "Get your coat, I'll drive."

"I'm going alone."

"No, I'm going with you."

"We'll do better if we investigate separately," she said. "We'll get twice as much done that way. Trust me."

"You got any ideas where he might be? Anything you want me to do?"

"I don't have a clue where he is. Comb Dale Parker's house for any shred of information that might give us a lead. Tear that place up if you have to."

As Karen was leaving, she was stopped by Jared Wilson.

"What's happening with the Cherneau and Parker cases?"

Karen cast a sideways glance at Tom. "Nothing new to speak of, Chief. We're going through Dale Parker's house again, to see if there's anything we might have missed the first time. Doubt it, but it's all we got."

"Keep at it."

Tom walked by the two of them. "Karen, I'll call you later if we get anything. Let me know if there's anything you need." He left the station. She walked the same direction.

"Where are you going?" she asked.

"I'm going to check on a possible lead," he said, and took off before she could ask.

3:49 p.m.

Sandy got into her car. She took a look around the parking lot. There was no one. She opened her purse and took out the .38 snub-nose revolver and held it in her hands. It was nickel-plated, and its shine gave it a certain beauty. It was a beauty that Sandy thought ironic, given that its singular purpose was to kill.

She put it in the glove compartment and started the car. Manny's Pawn Shop was downtown, which meant it was out of her way, but that was okay. She wasn't supposed to be at her mother's until six.

As she drove down 315 south, she thought of Bill. He was leaving Karen, something Sandy thought he'd never do. He wondered what this other woman was like, and why she was better than herself. What could this woman have that she didn't? Not that it concerned her that much—she had gotten over Bill long ago. Part of her being able to get over him, though, was that she thought he would never leave Karen. So she had just put him out of her mind. Now he had left her. What had changed in him that made it possible for him to leave? Bill and Karen never had seemed to be compatible, but she figured it was an 'opposites attract' sort of thing. She didn't get it, though—Karen never seemed to be that nice of a person. Maybe he finally came to his senses.

Twenty minutes later, Sandy was stuck in gridlock. There was an Ohio State football game that started at 3:30, and there were still many cars which were making their way toward the stadium. She inched along, cursing herself that she had forgotten, that she had taken the worst possible route to downtown. Normally, this was the fastest, but not when there was a home game.

After fifteen more minutes, she was able to get going again, and within another ten minutes, she was on Third Street downtown. She got a parking spot that was close to Manny's. She got in the glove compartment and took out the gun and put it back in her purse. She wondered if Manny would recognize her. She didn't care what they gave her for the gun. Whatever they offered, she would take it. She just wanted to get it over with. She had tried to be the type of person who could carry a gun, but she knew in her heart she wasn't. This didn't upset her; in fact, she was kind of glad. She never liked people who carried guns.

She got out of the car, locked it, and walked up to the door. There were no lights on inside. Sandy groaned in disappointment. There was a metal fence pulled across the front doors, and a sign next to the door. It said, "Store Hours—M-F 9 to 5, Sat 10 to 3, Sun Closed."

"Shit." Sandy just stood there. She hadn't even thought they might be closed. All that traffic she had gone through, and the store had been closed since before she left. She looked through the metal fence; there was no one inside. There was nothing she could do. She went back to her car.

She sat there for a moment, thinking of anywhere else she could sell the gun. There were pawn shops all over this area of town. She had even seen one on her way here. She hadn't noticed if it was open, though. Finally, she decided she didn't want to go to another place. While Manny's was probably no safer than any of the other pawn shops around, at least she had been there before, and it seemed okay. Manny himself had been pretty nice to her. She didn't want to take her chances with some unknown place.

She put her purse on the passenger seat and started the car. She thought of going back to her apartment, to leave the gun there, but she didn't want to fight the traffic again. She took the gun and put it in the glove compartment and left for Logan.

4:00 p.m.

Julianne walked through the woods, making her way home. She had been out since nine this morning, exploring. She liked her daily walks, the silence of them. Her senses had become much more receptive in the three weeks she had been out here. Everything—the cardinal hiding in a tree seventy yards away, the far off caw of the crow, the smell of rain coming. The smell of autumn.

She looked forward to getting to her campsite and taking a nap. There was something to be said for a late afternoon nap. She would get up at dawn, and by the time four o'clock rolled around, a nap was a perfect thing. And she liked perfect things.

Some nights she would eat nothing more than the berries she had picked that day, and some nights she would make a fire and cook some beans and rice. She would definitely be building a fire tonight—this would be her last night here, and she had quite a bit of wood left. Besides, tonight Bill was coming. In the back of her mind, she wondered if maybe he wasn't in love with her. She wondered if he was like all the rest. The other men in her life had taken so much from her, always take, take, take. But Bill wasn't like that. Bill was gentle and giving. When they made love, it wasn't like with other men. He had almost seemed afraid of her. To think of it! He was an important, intelligent man, and he had treated her with respect, something she had never received and never expected.

4:45 p.m.

Phil closed the car door and walked up the drive-way. By the time he got to the door, Vera Mullen was there, opening it for him.

"Sorry I'm a bit early." He walked in and stood in the middle of the living room.

"No problem. I just finished baking the apple pie."

"Smells great. Wouldn't be a Labor Day picnic without apple pie, now would it?"

Vera smiled. "Looks like rain, though. We'll have to eat inside. Anyway, it's good to have you here, Phil. I think Sandy needs you more than she lets on. Out in that big city when she should be here." Her smile faded, and she went out into the kitchen.

"You want anything to drink?" She called out.

He thought he could use a beer. "Nothing right now."

He sat and watched TV, which was showing a talk show that he had never seen. The word 'mute' was on the screen in green letters.

"I told Sandy six, so it'll probably be a while until she gets here," Vera said, coming into the living room, wiping her hands on a dish towel. "Gives us a chance to talk, though." She sat down and looked at the screen for a minute.

"I'm kinda worried what she's gonna do when she sees me," he said. "You didn't tell her I was going to be here, did you?"

"No. I know you didn't want me to, and you're right, she might not have come. But I think once she's here, with her family and friends, she'll warm up to you."

"I hope so. I miss her."

"Don't worry. I can't see how she can live in that Columbus without knowing anyone—having no family

312

or friends. It's got to be lonely. Everything she needs is right here."

Vera stood and went to the table, making sure everything was set.

"So who else is coming?" He noticed there were eight spots at the table.

"Let's see—besides the three of us, there is my friend Laverne from the beauty shop, Ed and Cindy from across the street, Alice Baker, a friend of mine who's coming in from Athens, and Anna Mullen, Melvin's sister."

"You two get along?"

"Oh, yeah. She knows what a stubborn man her brother was. She and I trade stories about Melvin all the time. We get a kick out of it. Strange, I know. But just because he had some problems, and sometimes didn't treat me so well, doesn't mean I have to stop being friends with his sister. You'd think Anna and I wouldn't get along, but like I said, she knows Melvin could be a real bastard. I guess families are just funny that way."

"I guess so."

"It's like you and Sandy. She took off for Columbus and left all her responsibilities behind. Her ties to you are very strong, and I always knew she'd come back to you. A woman can't just leave her husband and expect those feelings to just go away. She's stubborn, like her father. That's why we have to help a little by having the two of you over for this party. She just needs a little push."

"Thanks for having me over. A lot of people wouldn't understand, but you do. I just want things the way they were when we first got married."

"I know you had some problems, and it seems like those days are behind you now. She needs to understand that you can't run from every little problem that comes up in life."

"Hopefully tonight I can convince her of that."

5:04 p.m.

Karen knew Bill wouldn't be there, but she went home anyway. She didn't have a clue where he could have gone, but this was the only thing she could think to do. As she walked around the house in the uncomfortable silence, she couldn't seem to focus on what she was supposed to be looking for—a clue that could lead to the whereabouts of a suspect. All she could see was her own life, and wondered what had happened to it. It had slowly crumbled around her, and she hadn't noticed. She'd never seen her own home in this manner before— each painting, each piece of furniture, resembled a memory from her life with Bill. The pictures on the refrigerator from vacations long past, the wallpaper that Bill didn't really like but said he did because Karen liked it so much, the iced tea stain in the carpet that happened one humid summer day when they had made love on the floor—these were the things Karen couldn't get out of her head, things she seemed to have forgotten and were now coming back. But she also looked at them with fresh eyes, the eyes of a detective. They were all possible clues.

She grabbed the mail and assorted junk that was always kept on top of the microwave and took it over to the couch. She began sorting through it, hoping for a scrap of paper, anything out of the ordinary. There were bills, pay stubs, coupons, but nothing to point to where he could have gone.

She walked upstairs, hanging on to the rail. She was emotionally as well as physically tired. She wished she could just get in bed and sleep for days, and when she woke up, none of this would be happening.

She reached the hallway and saw the linen closet door open. What had been in there? Did he find whatever it was he was looking for? The bottom of the closet had always been a mess—there were blankets, old sheets, and not much else, really. Whatever he'd been doing in there, she didn't know what it was.

She went into the bedroom and called the station.

"Doris, I need you to put out an APB for me, okay?"

"Sure, Karen. What do you got?"

"It's a red Chrysler Sebring convertible, black top, with the Ohio license plates '975 MRH'." There was the sound of typing on the other end of the line, and then the typing stopped. "Bill Summers?" Doris asked. "323 Fairview—this some sort of joke, Karen?"

"I wish."

Tom took two men from the forensics crew and three from evidence to search Dale Parker's house again. The men approached the door. There was still the yellow police tape forming an 'X' across the door frame, plus a sticky tape sealing the door to the frame. He didn't think they would find anything; they had already been through the house once. He could tell when he talked to Karen that she wanted to be alone—that was probably why he had been sent here to do another search.

This was good for him. He had wondered what type of excuse he was going to use to get away—it would happen tonight. He would lay his trap and wait.

Jeff Singer was one of the men from evidence. He and Tom played racquetball every other Saturday.

"Did she give you any reason why we're back here?" Jeff said.

"Not really."

"Any specific area of the house we should be looking at?"

"No. She didn't say anything."

"Then why are we here, Tom? On a Saturday night?"

Tom strolled through the house with his hands in his pockets. He looked around the house like a potential buyer would. "I think she's pretty desperate. We've got nothing to go on; all leads have been exhausted. Just do your thing for a couple hours and we'll call it a night. I'm not gonna keep us here if there's nothing to find. But we have to say we tried."

Tom and the other men split up into three pairs. Two were instructed to start in the living room, two were told to check out the kitchen, and Tom and Jeff took the bedroom where the crime occurred. Tom wanted to examine every inch of the room himself. If they were to find anything, it would be in here.

Over the next hour and a half, the men searched with a less-than-passionate effort, and found what they had expected to find—nothing. In forensics, however, it was never that simple. There was always something to be found; sometimes you just had to dig deeper. They had taken samples of hair, some fibers, but in the end, they knew it was not much, and would probably come up inconclusive. Getting results in forensics was · hit-and-miss, and required patience.

Patience, though, was one thing that Tom didn't have. He looked at his watch. Almost seven-thirty.

The two men who had been in the kitchen came into the bedroom and told Jeff and Tom they had finished. Tom looked at Jeff. "Did they check the basement the first time through?"

"Checked the whole house," Jeff said. "Place was a mess, but they didn't find anything."

"Frank and Jim done in the living room?" he asked the other two.

"They said they have about another ten minutes," one of them said.

"Why don't you two just check out the basement again. Jeff and I are almost done in here. If you don't find anything by eight or so, just go on home. All right, guys? Thanks." The two men left for the basement.

Tom knew that Sandy would be at her mother's, but he didn't know for how long. The picnic they were having started at six, and Tom didn't want to miss her and let her go back to Columbus. Getting her tonight would be key to the success of his plan.

"Listen, Jeff, I'm gonna let you finish up here," he said, standing up.

"What, you're leaving?"

"Yeah. I forgot I have to be somewhere. But like I said, you guys can wrap it up by eight if you don't find anything."

"Okay. If you say so."

"Thanks, Jeff. I'll see ya."

"You want us to call you if we find anything?"

"Sure," Tom said, already down the hallway.

6:16 p.m.

Sandy turned off Carmont onto West Case Road. This was the road home. It was still another quarter mile, and as she drove the straight but hilly road, she looked to her right. There was the cornfield that belonged to Rufus Weaver, whose friends jokingly called 'Doc' because he had flunked out of his first year of medical school.

Sandy's mother lived across the street from the Weaver's, just down the road. Mrs. Mullen's backyard sloped upward, meeting the forested hills beyond her property line. Sandy's mother maintained her four acres impeccably, and it was a full-time job. She had rose bushes which, by this time of year, were pretty much dead, and other small bushes along the front and sides of the house. The large front yard had been a cornfield while Mr. Mullen was still alive, but he had died of lung cancer in 2005. The grass Mrs. Mullen had planted over the corn had come in nice and full, and you could no longer see any signs that the land had ever been farmed.

She got closer to the house she grew up in, and noticed the black El Camino in the driveway. For the slightest of moments, she felt like she was eighteen again, when she still lived at home, when seeing that car in the driveway was a common thing.

But now the sight of it brought nothing but bad feelings. It reminded her of the beatings, the feelings of being suffocated by fear. It couldn't be, she told herself as she turned in the driveway.

But it was. It was Phil's. What the hell was he doing here? She sat there for a moment, still in her car. She didn't want to get out, but she knew she would. It was such a confusing sight. Why was he here? Her mother had always liked him, even when Sandy talked bad about him, she would always try to defend him. 'I'm just trying to make you see his side of it', her mother would say.

'Communication is the most important thing in a marriage.' Then the strangest thing crept into her thoughts—had her mother invited Phil? Was she that naive?

When she walked in, she saw Phil sitting there in her mother's favorite chair. Her mother sat on the couch, next to two women that Sandy recognized, but couldn't name. They all seemed to be having a good time.

"Hi, dear," her mother said. "How was your drive?"

"Okay," she said, unsure of what else to say. "It was okay."

"We're just about ready to eat—why don't we go into the dining room and I'll start bringing it out."

Everyone said 'okay', and when Vera went into the kitchen, Sandy followed.

"Mom, what is he doing here?" she said, keeping her voice low.

Vera put a spoonful of margarine in the serving bowl of corn. "It was his idea. He wanted to see you, honey. I didn't see any harm in it, just a little picnic with family and friends. Besides, I thought it was a good idea. Doesn't some little part of you want to see him, too?"

"Mom, I don't think you realize what he put me through! Didn't any of what I told you sink in?"

Vera stirred a pot of baked beans. "That he hit you? Yes, I know. You told me, and Phil told me. That was over a year ago, and I honestly think that he has grown up a lot since then. He had to face a lot of things when you left him. Did you know he stopped drinking?"

"You believe that just because he told you? You always believed whatever he said—I can't believe how you can take his side on everything!"

"Sandy, dear. You may think I take his side, but I'm on whatever side will help put your marriage back together. That's what's important to me."

"What about me? I would think I would be more important. Maybe I sugar-coated it to protect you when I told you before, but when he would get drunk and start hitting me—he almost killed me, mom!"

Vera kept cooking and preparing, slicing the ham on the kitchen table. Her voice was shaky. "Don't be so dramatic. I'm not defending what he did, I'm just saying that he had some problems, and if I'm any judge of character, he seems to have worked them out. Have you even spoken to him since you left?"

"You make it sound like I abandoned my marriage."

"Well, didn't you?"

"I escaped is what I did! And I *have* spoken with him recently, as a matter of fact."

"Doesn't he seem like he's changed? Grown up?"

Sandy didn't respond. She was running out of patience.

"Here's the way I see it, Sandy." She wiped her hands on a dish towel and turned her attention to her. "You got into this marriage too young. Your husband had problems, you probably had problems, he hit you, and times got a little tough, and you left. You *quit*. Life is tough, okay? And you don't solve your problems by running away. Your father and I had problems all our lives, but we stuck it out. We took responsibility for the choices we made, which is something no one seems to be doing today, especially younger people. People your age blame their parents, their teachers, their employers, they blame God—and never, not once do you hear someone say 'it is my fault, I take responsibility for my life.' You never hear those words—"

"But I am taking responsibility! I took my life back when I left him."

"You're not honoring your commitment to him. You were only married for two years, and you took off at the first sign of trouble."

Vera put an arm on her shoulder. "Look. I know this all sounds like I'm telling you to go back to him. I'm not. I'm telling you to give it an honest try. Give him a chance to prove himself to you. What's done is done. Just try to have an open mind, and at least consider what I'm

321

saying. Maybe once you talk to him, you'll see what I mean. Did he ever hit you when he was sober?"

"No, he didn't."

"What was he like when he was sober?"

She couldn't look her mother in the eye. She looked out the window to the back yard, watching the trees sway in the evening breeze. "When he was sober…I loved him."

Vera gave her a little pat on the back as if that settled it, and began taking the trays of food out to the dining room through the swinging door.

As dinner progressed, Sandy found that she didn't have much of an appetite. Occasionally, she would glance across the table at Phil, and more than once, he had caught her doing so. Each time, he would smile politely.

"Sandy, why don't you tell us all about Columbus? Are you still working at the law firm?" her mother asked.

"No. That was just a temporary sort of thing. They told me they didn't have enough in the payroll to keep me on, but they did tell me to give them a call after I graduate. Columbus is a lot bigger than what I'm used to, that's for sure. I think I've adjusted well, though. I moved again about a month ago," she said, looking at Phil, still wondering if he had been the one that broke into her first apartment, "to a really nice place."

"Did you move for any particular reason?" one of the others asked. Sandy looked at Phil.

"No, just wanted a change. This place is nicer and it's about the same money. Better security."

"If that law firm doesn't want you, it'll be their loss," Phil said. Just his speaking made her uneasy. "They should have appreciated what they had." He looked at her then, and Sandy struggled for something to say. She looked at her mother, who was smiling and looking back at her as if to say, 'see, I told you.'

"Thank you," she said to him.

From there, the topics ranged from trivial to the downright boring—how Mrs. Peterson down the road

322

didn't have the nice flowers that she'd had the year before, and how the stifling weather this past summer could have had something to do with it; how the leaves were starting to change already, and what the Farmers Almanac said about the long winter ahead; how Betty Abelson's grandson had sprained an ankle riding his bike in her care, and how awful Betty had felt about it, as if she could have done something to have prevented it.

After dinner, they all went into the living room and sat around the television which still had the sound turned down. Sandy helped her mother as long as she could in the kitchen, and when they were done, she went to the sliding glass door that faced the backyard. It was overcast and breezy. It looked colder out than it actually was. She looked at her mother's garden and saw that there was a small wire fence around it.

"When did you put that fence around the garden?"

Just then, Phil came into the kitchen, holding his glass.

"Did you want some more Pepsi?" Vera asked.

"No, thanks. I was just bringing out the glass to you in case you were running the dishwasher."

"Sandy was just asking about the fence."

"Oh yeah?"

"Yep. Phil put that fence there for me."

"Your mom was having trouble with—what was it, you think? Raccoons?"

"I'm pretty sure it was raccoons. Earlier this summer, I think I saw one out there. Why don't you take her out there and show her how you made it? He also put up the trellis there and the bird bath on the other side—go have a look at it. It's amazing what a few little things can do for a garden to make it look like a *garden*, not just a bunch of weeds in the back of the yard."

There was a silence then, waiting for Sandy to speak.

"Come on, just a few minutes," Phil said.

"All right," she said, and opened the glass door.

Phil walked with his hands in his pockets, and Sandy had her arms folded. They both looked at the ground in front of them. Soon, they were at the garden. He told her all about putting in the metal stakes, and how he attached them to the wire fence. He took her around the garden and showed her the bird bath. Then there was nothing else to say.

"Sorry that we sort of tricked you by not telling you I was going to be here."

"You're breaking the law, you know. The restraining order."

"I know, I know. I just wanted to have this chance to tell you how sorry I am to have caused such pain in your life. You were right to have left me; I know that now. I don't deserve any second chances with the way I treated you, but I want you to know that I've changed. I don't drink anymore. Not like I used to. I've got some job opportunities lined up, too. I want you to know I still love you, probably more now than ever. You were always the only good thing in my life, and you still are. I have to be honest—you were a big reason why I was able to get my life back on track. I did it to prove to you that I'll do anything to get you back. I have to have you in my life again."

"You know that can't happen. I have my own life in Columbus now. If you've gotten your life together, I am genuinely happy for you, but I can't let you into my life again."

"You don't have any feelings for me at all? We're still husband and wife, you know. By law."

"Yeah, well, I'm working on that."

He looked at the forest behind her. "I think we were meant to be together. Your mom thinks so, too."

"You've got my mom fooled. You tell her that you're sober now, and she believes you. You do a little work around her house, and you're her golden boy. I don't buy it."

"Buy what?"

"That you're this totally different person. That you can just become someone else overnight."

"I'm not trying to fool anyone. I'm trying to become a better person, and to put the past behind me. I just wish you'd do the same."

The two men who had been examining the living room at the Parker residence, Len Davis and Mike Richardson, were the last to finish. Len had heard the other men walking downstairs earlier, and now he went down to see what was going on.

As he descended the stairs, Len noticed the drop in temperature and the musty smell so common for basements. He walked over to the three men, who were standing in front of a pile of boxes, going through them one by one. He walked up next to Jeff and nudged him.

"What's up? Where's Flanagan?"

"Took off."

"Took off? Where did he go?"

"Don't know. Just said he had to be somewhere and that we should check the basement. He said if we didn't find anything by eight to pack everything up and go home."

"So what do you want me and Mike to do? You need a hand?"

Jeff looked at his watch. "It's only about fifteen minutes. This shouldn't even take us that long. Just get everything set to go and wait for us."

Len looked around the basement, which had a number of small rooms. Two small windows at ground level provided little light. "Okay. I'm gonna take a look around down here, if that's okay."

"Be my guest."

Len went through room after room, finding Dale's workbench and his vast collection of knives, and another room that was full of tools lying around and assorted junk. At the other side of that room was a door. He negotiated the junk on the floor and walked over to the door. It opened inward to blackness. He reached along the wall, trying to find a light switch, but there wasn't

326

one. From the little light that came into the room, he could see it was nearly empty. He took a step inside and could still see nothing. He thought there might be something in the corner, but couldn't make it out. He walked back to where the other men were still going through the boxes.

"Hey Jeff, where's the light to this room over here?" he said, pointing.

"There's a pull chain in the center. Here, I'll show you. You gotta see this room."

When they got there, Jeff walked to the center of the room and reached up and pulled the chain. What Len saw was strangely pristine, especially taking into account how messy the other rooms were.

The four walls were painted white, and so was the floor. In the back corner of the room stood a three foot statue of the Virgin Mary. It was made of plastic, and as Len touched it, he saw the cord running out of the bottom. It was a Christmas lawn ornament, hollow and very colorful. To either side of the statue were votive candles. Laying in front of it was the strangest thing of all—a white dress spread out across the floor, with rosary beads across the chest. Len didn't know what to say.

"Something, isn't it?" Jeff said.

"Yeah, something." Len squatted down and picked up the rosary beads.

"Didn't exactly expect to find a place of worship when I turned on the light, did you? We gave it the once over—it's clean."

"Man, it's just...odd, you know? What do you think she did down here?"

"Who knows with some people, Len."

He stood up. It seemed so out of place, this pristine room among the dirt and junk surrounding it.

He went upstairs, and saw Mike sitting on the couch with his eyes closed and his head back. "Wake up, Mike."

"Just resting my eyes. I still don't see the point of us being here. Why would Karen Summers think we missed something?"

"You ever misplace something, Mike?" Len asked.

"Misplace something? Sure, who hasn't."

"Ever lose something, like your keys, and first you look where they should be, and they're not there. You look in other places where they could be, and they're not there, either. Pretty soon, you're looking everywhere, even in places where they would never be, right?"

"Yeah, and?"

"And what happens when you still can't find your keys? Usually, you go back to that first place you looked, the place they should be. You can't understand why they aren't where they should be, so even though you know they're not there, you look again. Doesn't make sense, but that's what you do. And then there's other times, maybe one percent of the time, when your keys actually are where they were supposed to be, and it's just that you didn't look hard enough the first time through. You get lucky every now and then. That's what we're doing here, Mike. We're looking again, hoping to get lucky."

"I know you're right. It just seems pointless. Even the first time through, they found next to nothing. The only thing they found was that other set of prints."

"Yeah, that's right. Did they ever find out whose prints those were?"

"I don't think so."

"They were found on one of the closets, weren't they?"

Mike pointed down the hall. "That linen closet down there on the left."

Len started down the hall. Mike stood up. "Hey, what're you doing?"

"I'm just gonna take another look."

7:59 p.m.

Tom had everything set up like he wanted—the plan was to pay a visit to Sandy's little family get together, be the ever-charming Tom Flanagan, and shortly thereafter, he would take her out to Hooligan's, an upscale bar. There he would propose his plan—he would tell her that, with her help, he could get Phil put away for a long time. Sometime when Phil was gone, they could somehow get into his house, tie her up in the basement until he came home, and then, with other officers, Tom would show up. When she would hear the door knock, Sandy would know to scream, thus giving the officers probable cause to search the premises. They would all run to the basement to see a tortured ex-wife.

It was as simple as that. Phil would never know what hit him. He would carry on about how it was a set-up, how he had been framed by Flanagan, and this was exactly what Tom wanted. It would only serve to make Oliver look more guilty. Sandy could describe, in detail, how her ex-husband had been stalking her in Columbus, how he had broken into her apartment, and how she even had to get a restraining order.

Kidnapping was a lock; he knew he could get that. Attempted murder was more tricky, but he could probably get that, too. The history was there; the motive was there; all they would need to convict would be the actual crime. Tom Flanagan was prepared to provide that—at least the appearance of it.

He drove up the small two lane road to Sandy's. The day was dimming, but it was still light enough that he didn't have to turn on his lights. Besides, he was almost there.

As he got up to the house and turned in the driveway, he saw two people standing in the backyard. They were at the back, by the tree line.

He sat for a minute trying to comprehend what he saw. He kept telling himself that it wasn't Phil that Sandy was talking to, but it was. What's wrong with her?! he thought. Why would she be talking to him?

Tom turned the car off. He took his gun out of the holster, which was laying on the passenger seat. He tried to contain his anger, but he couldn't help it. Phil Oliver had no respect for the law, and no respect for Sandy. He had no respect for anything. He had blatantly disregarded what Tom had told him.

He got out of the car and closed the door as quietly as possible, trying to press it shut. He walked up the driveway and around the right side of the house, the gun down at his side. He watched them arguing behind the small garden. He couldn't hear what was being said, but he could see Phil with one hand on her shoulder, like he was trying to make her understand something.

As Phil was trying to convince Sandy, Tom started walking toward them. His pulse quickened, and he raised his gun.

Sandy saw him first. She put her hand to her mouth, making Phil look up.

"What the hell are you doing here?" Phil asked.

Tom steadily aimed the gun at Phil's head. He got to within twenty feet of them and stopped. "I should be asking you the same thing," he said. "You're under arrest."

But before he could finish, Phil was already running up into the woods. Tom quickly followed, and behind him was Sandy. They were running up a steep path, and the branches reached out as if trying to slow him down. He heard Sandy behind him, and knew that he didn't need the distraction of her being in this. Without taking his eyes off Phil, Tom yelled back to her: "Go back to the house and call the police! Go now!"

Tom continued to run. He wasn't losing ground on Phil, but he didn't seem to be gaining either. There were a couple times when he had a clear shot, but he didn't want to risk stopping to shoot, missing, and then falling farther behind. Tom felt a pain run through his left ankle, but he could endure the pain as long as he had to. His plan to set Phil up was long gone now, but this would do. He could kill him out here and be done with it forever.

The two men, some fifty feet apart, weaved through the woods, ducking branches, jumping over fallen trees. Phil seemed to know where he was going, but did he have a destination? Every now and then, one of them would slip, and the gap between them would get smaller or larger.

Under the trees, there was no sky, and the darkness that surrounded them told Tom that if he let Phil get too far ahead of him, he would lose sight of him, and it would be over. The path was getting narrow and it was slowing them down.

Tom heard a thump and quickly lost sight of Phil. He continued to run, but now there was no path to speak of. He saw the fallen tree trunk in front of him and beyond it, Phil lying on the ground. As he approached, Phil struggled to get back up. When he did finally reach his feet, it was obvious that he had sprained or possibly broken his right ankle. He hobbled along, but Tom quickly caught him.

Tom reached out with his left hand and pushed him. He hit the ground hard. Standing at his feet, he pointed the gun at Phil's head. Phil was wincing from the pain in his ankle, and he reached for it. He started to sit up, and Tom put a foot square in his chest and pushed him back down.

Both men were breathing heavily, and Tom exhaled the word, "Gotcha."

"Fuck you, Flanagan." He lay there on his elbows, his chest rising and falling.

"You should have known you couldn't outrun me. You're out of shape. I mean, *way* out of shape. And now it's just the two of us. Isn't that convenient for me. Let's see—I can tell them whatever I want to, and they're gonna believe it. You're a bad guy, Phil. And bad things happen to bad guys."

Tom could tell he was in a great deal of pain. "I don't know exactly how I'll explain the gunshot but I'm sure I'll think of something." He raised the gun and pointed it at Phil's head.

"You have the right to remain silent." Tom fully extended his arm.

"No!" The voice cried out from down the hill. Tom looked down and there was a flashlight pointed at him. It was Sandy. The flashlight pointed at Phil, then back at Tom.

She was clumsily pointing her .38 with one hand and the flashlight with the other.

"What are you doing?"

"Don't shoot him, Tom."

"This is what you wanted! This is what we both want! Think of your life without him around to terrorize you. He's done nothing but harm to everyone he's ever known. I've got it all worked out here. And now you can back me up."

"I won't lie for you. I won't cover up a murder. You should do the right thing, Tom. You can arrest him if you want, put him in jail—but don't kill him."

"Are you defending him? Is that it?"

"I just want you to do what's right."

"You know, if I arrest him, he'll get out one day. Probably sooner rather than later, and then we'll have to deal with him all over again. He'll do his time and we'll be right back where we started. I say we end it right here." Tom raised his gun.

"Tom, don't! Don't make me do this!" The silver plated gun shook in her hand, as did the flashlight. She took another step toward the two of them, now ten feet away.

"I know you're not going to shoot me, Sandy. Deep down you want me to kill him. You'd rather see him dead than me. Hell, I'd let you shoot him yourself, but I know you're not the type to shoot anyone, so I'll have to do it. Not that I have a problem with it. I'm gonna enjoy it, actually. You can thank me later."

8:09 p.m.

Vera Mullen had watched from the kitchen. She had seen the strange man chase Phil up into the woods. None of the others in the living room had seen, though. She had seen her daughter come running down the hill, and around the house to her car. She watched now as Sandy ran through the backyard. She went out the sliding glass door and yelled to her. It wasn't until Sandy stopped and turned around that Vera saw what Sandy was carrying. She ran over to her.

"What are you doing with a gun? What's going on?"

Sandy was out of breath. "Go inside and call the police. I don't know what's going on, exactly. Just tell them what you saw."

She watched as her only child started to run into the woods.

"Sandy!" She could still see her and Sandy came back down long enough to yell, "Call the police, Mom! Do it now!"

And with that, she disappeared into the woods again.

She ran back inside, and by this time, everyone in the house knew something was wrong. They were all in the kitchen, looking up at the forest. They tried to get her to tell them what was the matter, but she didn't speak to them. She dialed 911. When the woman answered, Vera explained what had happened. The woman on the other end of the phone told her that officers were on their way. She tried to keep Vera on the phone, asking again what had happened. She told her to calm down and go slowly, take deep breaths. Just as Vera was starting to retell it, though, she cried out. She hung up the phone.

Her daughter was up there, and she had just heard a gunshot.

8:17 p.m.

Bill took the first right, just like the girl working in the campsite booth had said. The overcast day was fading fast.

The gravel road had no signs indicating this was the place to park for the primitive site, but soon enough he saw the cars parked in the open clearing. He recognized the old truck sitting there in the corner of the lot, its front end pulled into the weeds. He pulled into a spot between a station wagon and an SUV, which were the only other vehicles in the lot.

He got out of his car and took the sleeping bag out of the trunk. He put the bag on the ground and took out Julianne's last letter to him. He made sure she was staying at site number four, then folded it back up and put it in his pocket.

He started down the five foot wide path. He had waited so long for this moment, when he could feel he would leave this life behind and be reborn. He took deep breaths to try to smooth out the nervous excitement that was like an electrical charge inside him.

He passed site one, and saw a big tent and a campfire, but couldn't see anyone. In the tree above the tent there was a net which held their food.

Site two was on the other side of the path, and farther off it. There was a tent that was either gray or faded army green; he couldn't tell which with the fading light. There was no campfire and no signs of movement. Maybe they were sleeping already.

As he continued up the path, he thought of how he had loved camping as a child, and even into his late teens. Somehow, it had gotten away from him over the years as his life had become more complicated. First college, then Karen, and then his job had surrounded him. Maybe it was laziness on his part, but he just never seemed to have the time for camping. There had always been something more pressing.

He passed site three, which was vacant.

He didn't know what he and Julianne would do or where they would go. He didn't know how they would survive. None of that concerned him, though. Not as long as he was with her. With her in his life, he would face the future without fear.

He reached the post which had the number '4' painted on top. Underneath was a clip that had a piece of paper which read: "9/6."

Tonight was her last night here.

This was it.

8:19 p.m.

Karen had spent all evening calling Bill's friends, former co-workers, and his only remaining family—a brother he hadn't spoken to in three years who lived in Chicago. No one had heard from him, and this came as no surprise to her.

She drove around because she couldn't just sit at home. She wasn't the type. Periodically, she would check the station to see if anything came of the APB they had put out for his convertible, but so far nothing.

Then Doris came over the radio and asked if she'd heard from Tom.

"No. What's up?"

"He was with some people from forensics out at the Parker residence, and then he left. They just called wanting to know where he was. Said they couldn't reach him but that they had found something major."

"They say what?"

"No, but they said to let you know if I couldn't reach him."

"Okay. Tell them I'm on my way."

Karen stepped onto the porch at the Parker house. Two men were outside smoking a cigarette. She recognized one but not the other. They greeted her with a nod, and she nodded back.

She walked inside and at first didn't see anyone. She took a look down the hall and saw Len and Jeff talking to another man who was on his knees in the linen closet.

"So where's Tom?" she said as she walked to them.

"We don't know," Len said. "He took off, and told us to call him if we found anything. We sure found something, but he's not answering his cell."

"What'd you find?"

Jeff was in the closet, moving things around to clear the way. There had been a lot of blankets on the bottom of the closet, along with a sleeping bag and a comforter. Now they were lying in the hallway. "Karen, you have see this for yourself. We didn't want to move them before a detective got here."

She stepped into the closet.

"You see that bottom shelf?" Jeff said.

"Yeah."

"Underneath that shelf, back against the wall is a thin piece of plywood. If you knock on it, you can hear that it's hollow. Now, we put it back how we found it. All that junk out in the hall was in front of it. Go ahead and take the piece of plywood out of there."

She put a hand out on the corner of the piece. She turned to Jeff. "Nothing's gonna jump out at me, right?"

"No. Nothing like that."

She took off the plywood. From the deep hole in the wall, Mark Cherneau's hands reached out to her.

"My God. She killed them both." She stood up and wondered if Bill knew he was with a murderer. There was still the possibility that, for whatever reason, he had been in the house before the murder took place, touched the closet door, and didn't have any part in this. She hoped that was the case. "Go ahead and take them out of there."

Two men opened a bag and crouched down in the closet. She took Jeff aside. "How did you know to look there?"

"It was Len. He and Mike were just waiting for us to finish in the basement. Hey Len—come over here a second."

"Excellent job, Len," Karen said, "How did you know to look there, though?"

"I just thought there might be something special about that closet since they found the prints on it. Did they ever find out whose prints those were?"

"No," Karen lied.

"Anyway," Len continued, "When I was a kid, the closet in my bedroom had a little compartment like that one. I would put whatever I didn't want my mom to find in there. Firecrackers, girlie magazines, whatever. Just lucky, I guess. Once I had a Playboy centerfold in my sleeping bag and when we went on a family camping trip I forgot it was in there. I unrolled it when we got there and it came flying out and my mom saw. Not exactly the way you want to start a fun family vacation."

They all were laughing and Karen slipped away. She'd gotten to the end of the hall when she stopped. She turned and looked back at the men. Len was re-enacting his boyhood faux pas, waving the sleeping bag and then quickly rolling it back up.

That was it.

The sleeping bag.

She mentally transported herself to the linen closet in her own house. The picture in her head showed towels, sheets, blankets strewn about.

But no sleeping bag.

That's what was missing.

She opened her cell. "Doris—I need you to call all the campgrounds in the area—"

"Karen—"

"Check on the car description, but also check the names of campers within the last—"

"Karen!"

"What?"

"I already have something. A girl who works at the state park had a man ask her for directions to the primitive campsites. She said the man had dark hair and was driving a convertible. She couldn't remember the color, but said it was a dark color."

"The primitive sites? Where are they in relation to the regular ones?"

"They're about a mile past them, up the hill on Stevens. Where are you now?"

"I'm at the Parker house on Whitman Road. Do I take 419 to get there the fastest?"

"There's a shortcut if you keep going down Whit-man to Perry. That'll come out on Stevens."

Bill walked up the narrow trail, and saw the flames of the campfire. Beyond it was Julianne, sitting at the picnic table. She had seen him first and was smiling.

As he walked around the campfire, she stood up. She put her arms around his neck. He dropped his sleeping bag to the ground. He slid his arms around her thin waist like a snake, coiling her. He looked into her dark eyes, so warm and loving. She kissed him, and he felt as if he could kiss her like this forever. If he could take one snapshot of his life and keep the feeling for eternity, it would be this moment.

"I'm so glad you're here. I knew you'd come."

"I love you Julianne. I want to be with you forever."

"You will." He couldn't take his eyes off her. He had abandoned everything for her, and was glad he did.

"Would you like some tea? I just was heating up some water."

"Sure, that would be great."

The last remnant of light in the sky was gone now, and Julianne took the two mugs of hot water into the tent.

"You want me to come in there?" he asked from outside.

"Stay out by the fire where it's warm. I'll just be a minute. Earl Grey or Constant Comment?"

"Either one—I'm not much of a tea drinker."

Julianne dug into her backpack. She took out a plastic baggie containing both types of tea, and a silver sheet of pills. There were ten to a sheet, and one by one, she popped each of the pills out of its seal and into the mug. She put in fourteen pills in all. That was two more than she'd given Mark Cherneau. She didn't want Bill to feel a thing. He was the nicest of them all and deserved mercy. She took a spoon and stirred the hot water until she could no longer see any evidence of the pills. She dipped two tea bags into the mug, pressing the spoon against each bag, then added two sugar packets to counteract the bitterness of the pills.

After making her own tea, she stepped out of the tent. He was sitting on the picnic table with his arms folded and his feet only a couple feet from the fire. She handed the mug to him. He took it eagerly.

He wrapped both hands around the mug. "Cold out tonight. Has it been this cold every night?"

"It's been pretty cold lately." She looked up at the trees, watching them sway. "At least the trees are shielding us from most of the wind. You get used to it, though—sleeping outside. The way it is out here is nothing like sleeping indoors. You'd think that by sleeping outdoors you wouldn't feel so...confined. Maybe it's just me; maybe I'm claustrophobic, sleeping in that little five by seven tent. Out here, it's a deeper black than you can imagine, and it's quieter than you think silence can get. It can get to you. The loneliness is almost overwhelming at first. But now that I'm used to it, I like it. I almost need it. You have to get used to the cold just like everything else; I guess I have."

"The tea'll keep me warm." He took a sip. "So where do you want to go tomorrow?"

"I don't want to think of tomorrow. I only want to think of right now. I have to tell you something before we move on."

"Okay."

"This is really important to me. I need to confess something to you so that I can start fresh. I have to purge my sins so that I can leave them behind. Do you understand?"

He didn't look as though he did, but he nodded and took another sip.

"My father was a very cruel man. He abused me sexually. He was the first person that ever—you know. I was with Mark and then Dale and that's it. Until you."

Bill remained quiet, sipping the tea.

"I ever tell you how my father died?"

"You only told me that you felt relieved after."

"'Relieved' is a nice way to put it. I was glad the abuse had stopped. My father was killed in a farming accident. He was only 39. He was so strong—in the prime of his life, really. Sometimes, when I'm lying there in that tent, nearly freezing, I think of him. In the six years since the accident, I've visited his grave a few times, and even though his birthday is in December, I never go then. I always go in the summer. You know why?"

"Why."

"It's kind of hard to explain. I can't go to his grave in the winter because I don't like to think of him down there in the freezing ground. I mean, I know he's dead and he doesn't feel it, but I can't get the picture of him down there out of my mind. Just thinking of how that would be, and me standing six feet above him, on top of the frozen ground, makes me shiver. It's creepy."

"I guess you should just try to remember him like he was when he was alive."

"He was a bastard when he was alive. I like him better dead."

She stared into the campfire and then shook as if she had come out of a bad dream.

8:50 p.m.

Tom Flanagan felt the pinch in his side before the sound or sight had even registered. His knees buckled and he hit the cold ground. The entire right side of his torso felt as if it had been deflated, and as much as he pulled, he couldn't get enough oxygen. His suffocating body panicked, like a swimmer needing to surface. Only there was no surfacing for him now, just short gasps as his body would not allow him the time to exhale. The pain in his chest was becoming overwhelming, and he tried to lift his head to look at the gunshot wound in his side. He couldn't see it. His head dropped back to the ground with the force of its own weight.

His mind raced—feelings of regret that his life had gone unfulfilled, that he hadn't done or said the things he'd wanted, and now it would be over. He was unprepared. No one would ever know who he truly was; it would be like he'd never existed.

He would die without ever having gray hair, without ever feeling old, shot and killed by a woman he had been trying to protect. He heard her voice now; it was muffled, but he could hear her saying "You stay there, and don't move. I have to help him!" Then he heard Phil's voice: "Just leave him! We have to get out of here!"

"*We* don't have to do anything! I'm gonna help him and you're not going to stop me!"

He could see Sandy pointing the gun at Phil. She appeared above Tom and got down on her knees. "Oh my God, oh my God," she kept saying. She bent over and put her ear to his mouth. Tom tried to speak, he wanted to tell her to forget about him and pay attention to Phil, but the blood was filling in his lungs now and he couldn't. His eyes began to flutter, and he felt her hands pressing against his chest. "I'm sorry, Tom, I'm so sorry." She was sobbing now. "Would you get over here and help me, God damn it! He's gonna die if we don't get him to a hospital!" Tom saw flashes of light, and he saw Phil approaching Sandy from behind.

He felt the weight of Sandy falling onto his chest. The last thing he saw was Phil Oliver wrapping his arm around her neck, pulling her away.

8:57 p.m.

Sandy saw stars after she took the blow to the head. Had Phil kicked her? She landed on top of the dying Tom Flanagan, and when Phil wrapped his arm around her neck, she felt the gun, *her* gun, pressed into her cheek.

"What are you doing?" She asked, being dragged farther up the hill. They moved slowly as Phil was hobbling on one leg. "Where are you taking me?"

"We gotta get out of here. Cops'll be here any minute."

"Why don't you just go? Let me stay and help Tom."

"You can't help him now. Besides, I need you." Her eyes weren't adjusting to the darkness; maybe that was because of how hard he had kicked her, but it also seemed that he couldn't see, either. He was behind her now, with one arm still around her throat, and the other holding the gun to her head. He steered her into trees as they ascended the hill.

"Why are you doing this? What is this going to accomplish?"

"Nothing. This is gonna accomplish nothing. How do you like that?"

"But I saved your life back there! He was going to shoot you, and I saved you!"

"Did I ask you to save me? Did I!? You think I give a shit whether I live or die?"

"Yes, I do. I do."

He stopped a moment. "Okay, listen. This is what we're gonna do. Hank Peters lives about a mile down the road. We can borrow his truck and get the hell out of here."

"I don't want to go anywhere with you."

344

"Trust me, Sandy. It can be the way it used to be, if you give it time. We could use a new location. Fresh start. Don't worry; I'll get us out of the mess you made."

"If you think I'm going anywhere with you, you're wrong."

"You're going with me, all right. You either go with me or die, understand? I made my best effort with you, to try to show you I've changed, to show you how much I love you. I opened my heart and all you did was spit on it. You think you're too good for me now, is that it? Well, you ain't. Never gonna be, neither. You're mine, you got me?"

She suddenly flashed on all the horrible things he had done to her when they were together. She couldn't bear to think of them, but hard as she tried, she couldn't push them from her mind. His body weighed heavily on her backside as they staggered, and she felt like she might pass out. As they reached the top of the hill, she turned and saw the lights from town in the distance. The night seemed so quiet amid the chaos. Phil stopped to rest. He was breathing hard now, harder than Sandy. She felt repulsed as his lips touched her neck.

"Tell me you love me," he said. "You know you still do, otherwise you would have let me die back there. Now tell me you still love me."

"I still love you."

"That's what I wanted to hear, sweetie. You know, I can't wait until we can get away from here, someplace we can disappear. We can start our lives over, you and me."

She threw an elbow into his side that should have hurt him. He let out a groan, but his grasp around her throat only got tighter.

"*Don't do that.* I'll shoot you right here and now, I swear it. Do you believe me?" Sandy didn't say anything. "I said, do you believe me?"

"Yes, I believe you."

"Then don't try any more of that shit and we'll both have a much better time."

Phil kept the gun pressed against her cheek, but released his forearm from around her neck. He grabbed at the back of her shirt collar. She then felt the gun pressing against the back of her head.

They started their descent.

Bill finished his tea and asked for another cup. Julianne emerged from the tent with another tea bag. She poured the hot water into the mug and took it out to him. She sat next to him on the picnic table and put her mug down. She ran her fingers through his hair and kissed him. It wouldn't be long now.

"You look tired," she said. "How do you feel?"

"Okay, I guess. I had a rough night last night, and today was pretty emotional."

"I remember you telling me that your father caused you a lot of pain, too."

"He did. I guess I've worked through it. My mother did a pretty good job of raising me," he said.

"My mother left when I was nine. She told me, 'You will always have Mother Mary watching over you.'"

"Nothing can replace your own mother."

"That advice was the best my own mother could have given me, though—to watch yourself because you were being watched by someone else. Mary got to have it both ways. She got to be both a mother and a virgin. How that must feel to be a mother and to be *innocent* like that? I mean, to be able to enjoy having a child but not to have your innocence taken from you, *ripped* from your body, is to be twice blessed!"

"I'm not sure I follow you," Bill murmured. "I'm sorry. I think I drifted off there for a minute."

"It's perfectly all right. I've kept you long enough. I'm sure you could use the rest."

9:25 p.m.

A light mist began to fall and Karen turned on her windshield wipers. She was still on Whitman Road, passing the '45 mph' sign at well over seventy. She tried to push back the fear in her mind that she was already too late, that for whatever psychotic reason, Julianne Case may have already murdered Bill. Her tie to Dale Parker was an obvious one, but how she was connected to Mark Cherneau she didn't know. Her name had certainly never come up in the Cherneau investigation. If Bill was in love with this woman, could he be so naive as to not see that she was insane? Was she so shrewd as to not be detected by a trained psychologist? Did he see it, and was he trying to help her? Was he blinded by his obsession?

All were possibilities, but one even more terrifying was that he had been in on it the whole time. Maybe the two of them had killed those men and planned to run off together.

She saw the green sign up ahead, and when she got close enough, could see that it was Perry Drive. The two lane road curved through the hills like she had remembered. It was in good condition and there was no one else around, so she was able to make good time.

The mist turned to rain so she rolled up the window. Karen wiped the drops of rain off the side of her face. She supposed they felt like tears, and she asked herself: *If he dies, will you cry for him? Will you be able to cry then?* She turned the wipers from intermittent to their regular speed. There was one other possibility as far as Bill's involvement in the murders, one that she could hardly allow. Bill may have been the one who killed them both. If he was in love with Julianne Case, there was certainly the motive to kill Dale Parker. He would have known the details of the abuse Dale inflicted on her. Maybe Mark Cherneau had abused another woman that Bill had been in love with. He had never spoken well of Phil Oliver, and she knew how Bill had felt for Sandy. If this was true—if Bill was the murderer, then it would be Karen who had been naive.

She had been on the road two minutes now, and was beginning to wonder how long it would be until it hit Stevens. She hoped that Doris had been right about the shortcut. It may have been a shorter distance, but she wasn't able to drive very fast around the curves, and the road was mostly curves. She started thinking that it would have been faster to take 419.

As she pulled around a wide curve, she saw two people scrambling to get across the road. They were five hundred yards in the distance, and just off the edge of the road as she had come around the bend. There was a man who was limping and woman he was dragging by the arm. He was yanking her into the forest to the right of the road. The man was wearing a white t-shirt and holding his right hand to his stomach. At first, Karen thought the man was injured, but then saw his hand down at his side and the shiny glint of a small handgun, possibly a knife. Karen turned on her brights, and the two began to run faster.

While they ran, the man took a look back at the headlights. Karen only got a glimpse, but she knew it was Phil Oliver. And he had Sandy. She was wearing a gray sweatshirt, and it had stains on it. The sleeves were pushed up, and her hands were covered with blood. Karen wondered whose blood it was.

As she got closer, she watched the two from behind as they ran along the road, toward a small, white one-story house. She was still behind them as they ran around the back of the house and disappeared.

9:32 p.m.

Bill is such a trooper, Julianne thought. He was sitting there beside her, trying so desperately to stay awake, to pay attention. She could tell, though, that he was already somewhere else. Quite possibly, his mind had shut down altogether and he was nowhere at all. She watched as his head nodded, his eyes nearly closed.

She put her arm around him, supporting him. She knew how far gone he was when she felt the weight of him, and realized that she practically had to lift him herself. She put him on the hard packed soil, less than ten feet from the fire. His head rolled to one side, away from the flames.

She got down on her knees, and swung a knee over him, straddling him. She pressed her crotch to his, and felt nothing. She leaned over him, putting her face close enough to his to feel his gentle breath. "Bill? Bill, you there?" She softly smacked his face with her palm, and his face didn't so much as twitch.

Mark Cherneau had been halfway gone from the alcohol alone by the time she had seen him that night. He had been drinking with friends, but to Julianne, he still looked alone. By the time he staggered out into the parking lot, she had her plan. She would erase her past. He could be gone just like her father.

They had been in the parking lot, and as Mark stood at the end of the lot, pissing into the grass, she had opened the can of beer and added the pills. When he got into her car, she offered it, and he took it without either of them saying a word.

It had been that easy. Once out in the woods, Mark had begun kissing her hard, pressing his mouth onto hers so much that she could feel his gums. The foul stench of the beer entered her lungs, polluting her. He had grabbed her butt and squeezed hard enough that there had been a bruise a week later.

Mark took his shirt off and lay on the ground. She stood up.

"Wait," she had said. Mark looked at her, confused. "I've got something in my car you're gonna love."

"What is it? Just come here."

"I want to get a blanket, too. I don't want to roll all over the ground like some animal."

"Sounds good to me," Mark had said.

Although her car was less than a minute away, Julianne had taken nearly five to come back with the duffel bag. When she came back, Mark was sleeping, passed out, or knocked out—possibly all three.

She took out the only things she could find in the trunk of her car—six tent stakes and an old saw.

She grabbed a nearby rock and pounded the stakes into the ground, two for each knee, and one through each pant leg at the ankle.

She sat there for what felt like hours, watching him in the blue night. She watched as his stomach rose and fell with each breath. His skin was so white, so smooth, like porcelain. Her original plan had been to just slit his throat, but as she looked at him, her eyes had been drawn to his arms. He had fondled her for the first time with those arms, had stuck those filthy fingers into her, and more than once, he had slapped her with those hands.

Suddenly, it struck her how ridiculous he would look without his arms. The terror of having your arms amputated! To know that, in a matter of minutes, most of your precious blood would be flowing out of you and into the soft dirt below!

She had known then that she could do it, and that the look on his face would be worth it.

At the first sign of a groan from Mark, she began cutting. The old saw did not work well—it snagged in the skin. Then she put the back part of the saw, the part up by the handle, firmly into the shoulder. She pulled back the blade toward her, firmly and quickly. The blood helped to lubricate the blade and Julianne didn't stop sawing until she reached bone. Mark's eyes did not seem to focus, and rolled back into his head. A barely audible gasp escaped him. His other arm reached across his body in a weak attempt, but Julianne was able to easily push it away.

She had sawn down through where the bicep meets the deltoid muscle. When she reached bone, she grabbed the hand and stood up. She yanked and twisted until it pulled loose.

The other arm was just as stubborn, and by the time it came off, Mark was already in shock. She searched his face for any sign that he knew what was happening to him, but didn't see one. He was no longer someone with a mind or a personality, no longer the person who had made her dirty inside—it was just a thing that was quickly dying in front of her.

9:42 p.m.

Phil pulled Sandy around the back of the house and watched for the headlights.

"Just shut up and don't move," he said, his mouth against her ear.

Phil looked at the green Chevy pickup in the driveway. It was parked just outside the detached garage. With Sandy in tow, he ran to the truck and tried the door. It was locked. The garage door was open, though, and before heading to the back door of the house, he grabbed a crowbar from the workbench. As they got behind the corner of the house, the headlights on the road grew bright.

He tapped on the window to the kitchen and waited for a response. He tried the door but it was locked. "C'mon, Hank! Where are ya?" He knocked on the back door. There was no time for this bullshit. He took the crowbar, opened the screen door, and jammed the curved end into the door jamb. He pressed the bar toward the door, the gun in his hand making it difficult. After the bar popped loose a couple times, he was able to wedge the bar far enough into the door to open it. The wood splintered and cracked, and he put the crowbar down and threw his shoulder into the door. The door flew open, almost causing him to fall down.

The kitchen lights came on, and standing there with a shotgun in his hand was Hank Peters. Phil grabbed Sandy and held her in front of him. He put the gun to her head.

"I think you better drop it, buddy," Phil said. "You know you couldn't hit me without hitting the lady, too." Phil pointed the gun at Hank. "I'll shoot you right now if you don't drop that fucking thing!" Hank put the gun on the kitchen table.

353

"No, put it over there on the floor," Phil said, pointing to the far corner of the kitchen. Hank did.

"Good to see you, Hank."

9:50 p.m.

Karen's mind was racing now, asking the question over and over again—what do I do? When she listened for an answer, there was silence. She didn't know what to do. As her car approached the house, she slowed considerably. Light rain covered her windshield, and was wiped away. She slowed to a stop, still in the middle of the road. Her foot held the brake, her mind bouncing from one thing to the other. There was Phil Oliver with a gun, who seemed to be running from something, and there was Julianne Case, who had been camping out all along, waiting for her prey.

She shut off her headlights and turned into the driveway. The house was only about fifty feet from the road, so she was now very close. She watched silently for movement, and listened for noises. There were neither.

Her breath was short now, and she drew her gun from its holster, checking the clip. She rolled her window down a couple inches so that she could hear better. She heard three quick raps at what sounded like a window. She looked but didn't see anything. They were behind the house.

She took out her cell and dialed Tom. It rang three times, and then an automated voice said: "The cellular phone you are dialing is either not turned on or out of service." She needed her partner now.

She picked up the radio.

"Doris, I need you to send everyone available to 1278 Perry Road. I just saw Phil Oliver holding his ex-wife hostage. He's armed. They ran behind the house. I think he might know the person who lives here and they're trying to hide."

"Karen, we just sent everyone we could to that area. We had a report twenty minutes ago of a shot fired at 2033 West Case Road."

355

"Who reported it?"

"Vera Mullen."

"That's Sandy's mother. The shots were from Phil Oliver and he's fled to this address. Tell them to get over here as quickly as they can."

"What the hell are you doing? Sandy, you OK?" Hank Peters asked.

She nodded.

"She's not okay," Phil said. "Sandy went and shot somebody and it's important that we get her the hell out of here right now. We need your truck."

"You gotta be insane. You think I'm just gonna give you my truck?"

Phil raised the gun. He didn't point it at Hank, but at the ceiling, as if to show it to him. They stood on either side of the kitchen table. "I'd think you'd want to help out a friend in a desperate situation. C'mon, now—be a sport and hand over the keys. I'll bring it right back. Couple days, tops."

"I think, whatever you two have gotten yourselves into, you better give it up. If you go running from the law, when they catch up to you, they'll kill you."

Phil lowered his gaze. "They gonna kill me anyway, boy." He raised the gun and pointed it at Hank's head. "Now where's those keys?"

"On the table by the front door."

Phil pushed Sandy in front of him and they walked to the front door. Phil picked up the keys and looked out in the driveway.

"Shit. Hank, I want you to turn off all the lights in the room. TV too." One by one, the lights in the room were turned off. Hank came over to the window and looked out at the car in the driveway. "Who's that?"

"Cop. God, of all the fucking luck—she had to be on this road tonight." The three of them stared out the window, waiting for something to happen.

Nothing did. The car in the driveway sat there for a few minutes, and now it was backing out.

"Whoa, what the hell is this?" Phil asked. "What is she doing? Where's she going?"

"Looks like she's leaving," Hank said.

"You don't know this cop like I do. This is a damn trick, I know it. This woman's got it out for me. Got it out for Sandy, too, doesn't she, *honey*?"

"You've lost it," she said.

"Sandy here was banging that cop's husband last year, weren't you, dear?"

"No, I wasn't."

"Now she's got it out for the both of us. My fault, I guess. Can't seem to keep my woman *in line*!" He pushed her into the door. Hank took a step back as Phil pointed the gun at him. "Don't try anything, Hank. Don't make me shoot you.

"Okay, I want you to sit there on the couch and don't think of trying anything. I've never fired a .38 and I'm starting to wonder what kind of feel it's got. Go sit on your fat ass and don't move a muscle. That should be easy enough, right?"

Hank nodded and sat on the couch.

"I want you to sit down too," he said to Sandy.

"Don't you think you better get out now while you got the chance? You got the keys to the truck, and the cops'll be here any minute. Just get the hell out of here!"

"Don't try to outsmart me, buddy. You and I know this is some sort of setup. You think you can trick me into just walking out the front door so I'll get shot?! Cops're probably already out there! 'Course you can't see 'em, but I'll bet they got the cross hairs on the front door as we speak! You just keep your mouth shut, understand?

"And you—" He pushed Sandy into the chair next to the couch, and aimed the gun at her nose. "You know you can't run from me, don't you? You ran away that night last year, and you ran away to Columbus, but I found you. I'll always find you. I guess it's just the Good Lord telling you that we should be together." He took a step closer, pressing the gun into one of her eyes. "Tell

358

me, dear. Tell me you're not stupid enough to try to run. Promise me you won't run."

He pressed the gun to her head. "I want to hear you say it."

"I promise I won't run."

He lowered the gun and smiled at her. "Thank you. Stand by your man, just like the song says." He lowered his head to her's. "Give me a kiss," he said, and pressed his mouth against her tightened lips. He stood up and stared at her.

"I'm gonna kiss you again, and this time, you're gonna kiss me back—you understand?"

Phil pressed his lips against hers. Once again, she grimaced.

"Fucking bitch," he muttered, and put the gun in his left hand and pressed it against the side of her head. He put his right hand underneath her chin and pressed her cheeks forward, forcing her lips to pucker. "That's more like it," he said, and pressed his lips onto hers.

Just as he was starting to pull away from her, Hank crashed into him, knocking the two men to the floor. Hank had both hands on Phil's elbow, trying to knock the gun away. His upper arm pressed against Phil's throat.

Sandy got out of her chair and ran through the kitchen and out the back door.

"I'll fucking kill you!" Phil said. The gun finally was knocked free. Hank stretched out for it, but Phil grabbed at his shirt and pulled him back. They rolled away from the gun, and now Phil was on top, pressing his hand against his throat and punching him in the face again and again. Phil dove off him and lunged for the gun. He grabbed it and, lying on his back, turned in Hank's direction. Hank got up to his knees, and Phil fired a bullet into Hank's chest.

Hank fell to the floor, his arms outstretched and landing on Phil's legs.

Phil got up and ran after Sandy.

"Get back here, you bitch!"

He ran through the kitchen and out the back door.

Sandy swung the curved end of the crowbar at his head as hard as she could. He was stopped in his tracks, being knocked back into the screen door. She had gashed his head, almost knocking him unconscious. Phil slowly began to raise the gun, but before he could, she swung again, this time lodging the teeth of the crowbar into his eye socket. The bar lodged in his skull and he dropped dead.

"I told you I wouldn't run anymore."

10:00 p.m.

Julianne sat on the ground next to Bill. He was unconscious. She looked at his sweet face. This had to happen, though. This was what she was destined to do. She would have to stay focused; she would have to be brave.

The rain fell in big drops off the leaves overhead. She put his head in the crook of her elbow and lifted him up. She pulled the jacket off his left arm and then down over his right. She threw the jacket toward the tent. She then pulled his brown sweatshirt over his head. Finally, she took off his undershirt. She lay the shirt out on the ground so that his back wouldn't get dirty. She put him back down, and when his head hit the dirt floor, he groaned. The cold rain fell on his bare chest now, and after watching it accumulate for a minute, she put her hand on his stomach and rubbed upward, all the way to his neck. She put her hand around the back of his neck, leaned down and kissed him for the last time.

She stood and went into the tent. The duffel bag was tucked against the side. She kneeled and started to undo the buckle but stopped. She rested her forearms on the bag filled with clothes and closed her eyes.

Her fingers interlaced, she said, "Holy Mother Mary, please help me on this journey. Help me see clearly and do what it is I am meant to do. Do not allow me to interfere with my own destiny. Do not allow anyone to interfere with my mission. I will be a Virgin soon and carry Jesus like you before me and create a new world where no one will put the stain of sin on my heart. Amen."

She turned on the Coleman florescent lantern. The artificial light hurt her eyes. She opened the duffel and looked inside. Pulled the wooden handle out of the bag. She had cleaned the saw since the last time, but there was no shine to the blade. There was only the flat gray and rust that had accumulated over the years. She pressed her finger into the jagged edge. It was dull.

She put the saw down and felt at the bottom of the bag. She could hear them clanking against each other. Her arm wasn't long enough, though, to reach the bottom, so she just turned it upside down, spilling the contents. Landing on top of the pile of clothes were four metal spikes she had found in Dale's workshop. She grabbed the saw and the spikes, turned off the light in the tent and went back outside. Bill was lying there, motionless. The forest was still, and the light rain made the only sound. The campfire's flames were getting low and the darkness that had surrounded the clearing was now closing in.

She knelt beside him, and took one of the metal stakes in her hands. She grabbed a nearby rock that was the size of a softball. She pulled at his jeans, so that there was a spot at knee level where she could drive the stake. She did this on the outside part of both knees. Bill murmured incoherently. She had two more stakes, one for each ankle. She placed the spikes over the pant leg and hammered them into the ground. He was ready.

She straddled him, leaned over and picked up the saw. As she sat up, she saw his right arm lift off the ground. Julianne was scared by what she was seeing. The arm raised slowly, like a zombie's. It reached for her; she felt the hand sliding up her arm, and over her shoulder. His eyes didn't open—there was still no movement in his face. The hand seemed to be acting on its own.

The arm straightened as the hand wrapped around Julianne's throat. There was no pressure to its grip, and the corners of her mouth turned slightly upward. She took his hand and pulled it down. She tucked the arm close against his side, her left knee trapping it in place. She took his other arm and stretched it out away from his body. She put her right foot over the wrist and began cutting.

10:09 p.m.

Karen practically jumped out the car when she got to the primitive campsite lot. She saw the red Sebring convertible and as she ran toward the path she checked the license plate. It was his.

She drew her weapon and made her way up the path. Although she wanted to keep running, she slowed, keeping her eyes and ears tuned.

The sky was gone now—obscured by the ceiling of trees. Karen could barely distinguish the black branches against the dark blue sky. She moved forward, passing the third site, looking left and right. She heard a woman laugh in the distance and walked faster toward the sound. She had been about ten feet past the fourth site when she heard a sound she could never forget.

It was the sound of her husband screaming.

The sound had come from her right, and to the back. She ran back to the signpost for the elevated and obscured site four. She ran up the narrow, winding path. The actual campsite was much further removed than the first three, which were in plain sight from the normal path. Leaves brushed at her face; branches snagged her forearms. Her shoe struck a root hard, and Karen felt herself falling. She put out one hand on the path and continued.

She saw the dim light from the fire first. It shown against a picnic table. Bill was lying there with a puddle of blood around his left shoulder. She heard a rustling in the woods on the other side of the clearing, but didn't see anything.

She checked the tent, and made a 360 degree turn, her shaking gun hand outstretched.

Julianne Case was gone.

Karen turned her attention to Bill, who was now unconscious. She put two fingers against his throat. His pulse was rapid and faint. She tried to rouse him by giving him little smacks on the side of the face. "Bill! Honey, wake up!" she said, in what was both a whisper and a scream. "We have to get you out of here—honey, wake up!" She felt an enormous pressure on her lungs then, breathing shallow, on the verge of hyperventilating.

She stood and considered dragging him out of there, but decided that she would have to pick him up. The blood was quickly running out of his shoulder. She got on his left side, and knelt down beside him. His shoulder was a bloody mess. The arm dangled from the socket, ready to drop. She pulled the metal stakes out of the ground, and put her left arm under his knees. She put the other under his neck. She picked him up carefully, making sure his wounded arm was pressed against her chest. Keeping the gun in her right hand, she turned and started down the narrow path leading to the larger path. She turned and walked sideways so that the leaves and branches wouldn't get in the way as much. She felt the blood soaking through onto her chest. Her mind told her to run, but she knew she had to be careful; this rough terrain could barely be called a path, and she knew by the way it twisted when she had picked him up that Bill's arm was barely attached.

Karen was exhausted by the time she reached the flat five-foot-wide path that led back to her car. Her biceps and shoulders burned, but she wouldn't let herself stop for even a moment. Her pace steadily grew as she stumbled down the path. Her mind was searching for the route to the nearest hospital when it happened.

Before she could react, there was an explosion of leaves to her left, and Karen was knocked to the ground. Bill fell on top of her, and lay across her like a wrestler pinning his opponent. She couldn't get her arms up to defend herself. She looked up at Julianne Case, the rain pasting straight black hair to her ghostly pale face. The eyes held nothing behind them.

364

A boot pressed against Karen's throat, and she felt her airway closing. She tensed all the muscles in her neck, but the pressure only got worse. She was practically standing on her throat, and then, when her body felt as if it would implode, the foot raised, and hovered over her. Her throat still felt closed, and she had to struggle to pull air into her lungs.

She was able to breathe once before the boot was forcefully brought down on her neck again. She was stomped twice, and her vision started to blur and fade.

With Bill laying across her stomach, Karen bent her arms up, rolling him over her upper body and neck. She couldn't see and she could barely breathe, but she held the gun up and pointed it backward behind her head and to the right. She fired two shots; after the second one, Karen heard her cry out.

She twisted onto her side and was able to get out from under him. She got up on two knees and watched as Julianne was trying to escape up the path. She was hunched over and staggering.

"Stop and turn around!" the words were barely audible escaping Karen's mouth. To her surprise, Julianne turned and began walking back toward her. She was mumbling words that Karen couldn't decipher. She got closer and Karen could see that she'd shot her in the stomach. The words became more clear, and as she got to within twenty feet, she could hear that Julianne was repeating something. Blood ran from her mouth down her chin.

"Separate me from my sin," she was saying. She continued toward Karen. She got to ten feet.

"Stay where you are."

"Separate me from my sin. Take this stain from my heart." She continued walking slowly, her arms still and at her sides.

"I said stop, Julianne."

She tilted her head. "How do you know my name?" she asked in what sounded like the voice of a child. She held her stomach now, as the blood streamed over her hands.

Julianne fell to her knees. Her eyes glossed over as she sat on her heels. Her body started shaking and she fell to her side. Karen could no longer see her face, only the back of her head. She watched Julianne going into shock. For two minutes, the body in front of her convulsed, a living being in its final stages. A faint voice in Karen's mind told her to go for help. She ignored the voice and watched with morbid fascination, a vengeful thirst being deliciously quenched.

She walked on her knees to her and put her hand against her throat. She felt with two fingers on one side and her thumb on the other.

Karen felt nothing.

There was no pulse.

SUNDAY
1:01 a.m.

It had all happened so fast. She had driven the 18 miles to the nearest hospital at 80 miles per hour, and pulled up to the ER. From there, the doctors had fired questions. No, he's not allergic to penicillin. No, she didn't know his blood type. No, she didn't know how long he'd been unconscious, but she did volunteer that he'd been sedated with a heavy dose of benadryl.

They rushed him up to surgery. She was told to wait downstairs. It was an awkward feeling, this utter helplessness that Karen had been enduring for the better part of two hours now. Her adrenaline had been pumping then, and suddenly the control she had over the situation had come to a screeching halt. She tried to slow her adrenaline by leafing through the women's magazines on the table, but her efforts were futile.

After alternating between standing and sitting for an hour, a doctor came out, telling her that it was still too soon to tell. The doctor said they were trying to stabilize his condition and to repair his arm. He spoke to her calmly, almost in a casual tone. At first, Karen thought this tone was one of indifference. She reminded herself, though, that they were professionals, and it was important they remain calm. The last thing anyone needed was an hysterical surgeon.

She looked down the long white corridor, and saw Detective Randy Myers walking toward her. She had spotted him when he was two hundred feet away, and by the time he got to her, Karen knew something was wrong.

"What is it?"

He sat down next to her on the vinyl couch. "How's your husband?"

"Don't know yet. Lost a lot of blood. He's in surgery. What's wrong?"

Randy took a breath and held it for a second. "I've got some news, Karen. Some very *hard* news. Have you seen Tom at all tonight?"

"I haven't been able to get in touch with him. I don't know where he is."

"Karen, Tom apparently had been following Phil Oliver today. He followed him to Vera Mullen's house, where he kidnapped his ex-wife at gunpoint. Tom chased him into the woods. We're not exactly sure what happened, but Tom was shot."

"Oh my God," Karen said, putting her face in her hands.

"He's dead, Karen. I'm sorry."

She didn't make a sound; didn't take a breath. She drew in air only when she had to, and once she did, she began sobbing. Through her tears, above the sound of her crying, her mind screamed *No! It isn't fair!* and there was the sting of regret—she should have been with him. She could have helped him. She could have prevented this. She would have given anything at that moment to go back in time, go back just one day, so that she could erase this tragedy that now surrounded her.

Randy stayed and comforted her, put his arm around her, and they sat in silence for five minutes.

"Did they catch Phil?" she finally asked.

"They found his body. They went over after you called it in, but by the time they got there, he was dead. Hank Peters—it was his house—he was dead too."

"How?"

"From what Sandy said, Phil was holding both of them hostage when Hank and Phil started fighting. Phil ended up shooting Hank, and Sandy had run out the back door. She found a crowbar, and when he came out after her, she hit him twice with it. The second time was fatal."

"And she's OK?"

"She's shaken up, obviously, but she's fine."

Karen tried to take comfort in that, but her thoughts drifted to Bill. She couldn't lose him tonight, too.

Finally, at five minutes past two a.m., a different surgeon came out and introduced herself as Doctor Bickham.

"We have good news," she said. "Your husband made it through the surgery intact. He is still in serious condition, but we expect him to be stable by morning. Unfortunately, there's bad news, too. We weren't able to save his arm. Muscle fibers were shredded, nerves completely severed. We had no other option. I'm very sorry."

Karen tried to picture Bill without the arm, to prepare herself. "Can I see him?"

"He's still groggy. The drug he was given had long been absorbed into his bloodstream by the time you brought him in, so pumping his stomach would have done us no good. We'll monitor his progress, but for now, we have to let the drug run its course."

"When do you think that will be?"

"At least tomorrow morning. He probably won't be fully awake until sometime in the afternoon."

"Can I just briefly see him before I leave?"

"Sure."

With Randy waiting outside, she went in the room, and her eyes went to the face of the man she had once loved. She stood ten feet from him. She didn't know why exactly, but she was afraid to get close. He looked weak. She asked herself if she still loved him. After searching her mind for a clear, definitive answer, she didn't know. Wasn't what she had done tonight proof that she loved him? The fear that she felt, not knowing if she would get him to the hospital in time—wasn't that proof?

Or was it just her job?

A grapefruit-sized bandage capped his shoulder. Although her mind knew better, Karen kept looking for his missing arm, thinking he was somehow laying on it or that it was tucked under the sheet. He had wires coming out from the neck of his hospital gown, and an oxygen tube in his nose. She noticed the dryness of his lips, and how unusually still he was. He had always been a light sleeper; always tossing and turning. Now he was somewhere beyond sleep, beyond the restlessness he was used to.

She stepped closer to him. It hurt her to see him *broken* like this. She touched his remaining hand and wondered if he could feel it.

Chapter Eighty-Five

Karen didn't wake the next morning until eleven. She had gone home, went to bed, but couldn't fall asleep. Her body, as well as her mind, was exhausted. She craved sleep but it wouldn't come. She had undergone too much stress to be able to put it all aside and succumb to sleep. When she closed her eyes, if she didn't see Bill lying there in a pool of blood at the campsite, she saw Julianne Case jumping out of the woods at her. Beyond that, she could only imagine what Tom had gone through, dying alone in the forest.

Ironically enough, Karen had no other choice than to take a Benadryl in order to fall asleep. When she finally woke, the previous twenty-four hours felt like a horrible dream.

Now she walked down the stairs to the County Coroner's office. What had happened was most certainly not a dream.

When she got to the room, there was no one there. She tried not to, but looked anyway at the two gurneys on either side of her and walked straight back to the end of the room. Under one of those white sheets lay her partner.

She looked through the window to the other room and saw Dr. Barnes performing an autopsy. The only part of the corpse she could see from her angle was the long straight black hair.

She took a step back and looked at the floor. She needed to pull herself together. She concentrated on taking slow, deep breaths. She was startled by the sound of the door to the autopsy room opening.

"Detective Summers—what are you doing here? I heard about what happened; you should be taking it easy. Is your husband all right?"

"They say he's going to be fine. I'm going to the hospital later. He should be stable by this afternoon."

"That's good news. I'm so sorry about your partner." He nodded toward the white sheet behind her. She turned her head halfway back and stopped. She wanted to look, but she knew she couldn't bear to. If that meant she was weak, she didn't care.

"Did you already do the autopsy—is that your first of the day?" She asked, looking into the other room.

"Yes, that's the first of the day."

"Could you just speculate a cause of death on—" she turned and indicated Tom—"on him?"

"Detective Flanagan was shot once in the upper quadrant. We won't know the exact angle of the bullet until after the autopsy, but from what I could guess, the bullet probably punctured the right lung, causing it to fill up with blood. He probably lost consciousness soon after. You can take at least some comfort knowing that he probably died in a matter of minutes."

Karen nodded, but didn't say anything. She didn't think there was any comfort to be found in any of this. She had come here, in part, to find out more about Tom's death, but now that she knew, she didn't know if it was a good idea. It almost hurt more; at least when she was in the dark she didn't have to picture his lung filling up with blood.

"So you finished with her?"

"Just finished a few minutes ago."

"Cause of death?"

"You should know, detective."

"I know, but what is the official cause of death?"

"Massive internal bleeding as a result of a gunshot wound to the stomach."

She started to ask and then stopped herself.

"What is it, detective?"

"Do you think she could have been saved? I mean, do you—"

"Don't think like that, Karen. You have a big heart, but there is nothing you could have done for her. The other police officers told me she was dead when they got to her, and they came along soon after they heard the gunshot. Did you check for a pulse before you left?"

"Yes. There was none."

"Then there was nothing you could have done."

"They couldn't have...revived her, or anything."

"No. Absolutely not."

She nodded, trying to convince herself. She began to walk away. "Thank you doctor."

"Detective? Could you wait a second? There is one more thing I have to tell you." Dr. Barnes walked over to her, standing closer to her than he had stood before. She could see that he was uncomfortable.

"Detective, what I'm about to tell you can stay between us. You just say the word and I can make it go away forever."

"What are you talking about?"

He took a long breath and let it out slowly. "During the course of the autopsy, I found a fetus. It was about the size of my thumb. Miss Case had been pregnant, about three weeks."

Karen felt her knees weaken and folded her arms. She couldn't look him in the eye; the black and white linoleum tiles under her seemed to vibrate and she felt light-headed. She put a hand on an empty metal table and told herself to look professional.

"If you want, I could take a tissue sample. I could run some tests, maybe—"

"No, that won't be necessary. You don't have to do that."

"Like I said—just tell me you want this buried, and it's gone."

After a moment of silence, she said it, the words barely audible:

"I want it buried."

Chapter Eighty-Six

Bill emerged from the haze not knowing where he was. His vision was like looking through a windshield in the rain without the wipers on—the colors all blurred into one another. His throat felt dry, and when he tried to summon a nurse, the word 'hey' came out more like a scratchy cough than speech.

What happened? He was trying to remember. Last night he had gone to see Julianne—and then it came to him, the way seeing something can trigger a forgotten dream from the night before.

He remembered drinking the tea. He remembered adoring her, giving himself to her, completely submissive. He remembered the unnatural way sleep had flooded his mind and forced itself on him. It had pressed on his brain, and his body shut down soon after. There were the sounds of the forest, the light rain on his face, and Julianne talking about the Virgin Mary, her voice pulling further away, fading. The dark silence had enveloped him.

And now he was here. He looked down at himself, at the white blanket covering him. He tried to lift his arms. He couldn't move his left arm, and soon realized he couldn't even feel it. It was numb the way it sometimes got when he would sleep on it wrong and wake up in the morning not being able to make a fist. He would cut off the circulation all night to wake up and feel the blood rushing to the tips of his fingers, and after a thousand tiny needles, the feeling would return.

This time was different, however. He hadn't been sleeping on his side, and there was no sensation of blood running through his arm. He lifted the sheet and saw the large bandage on his shoulder.

His arm was gone.

"Couldn't be saved." A soft voice from the corner of the room.

Startled, Bill turned his head and saw Karen sitting in a chair by the window. He hadn't even known she was there.

She stood and went to his side. He saw the redness in her eyes. "Nerves were completely severed. Muscles shredded."

"I'm so sorry," he said. The lump in his throat made it hard to swallow. "She tried to kill me."

"You're sorry she tried to kill you or you're sorry you were going to run away with her?"

"Both, I guess." There was a silence then, and after holding it in as long as he could, Bill said, "You don't love me anyway, though."

"You're wrong about that. You're wrong. I carried you for a quarter mile, your arm gushing blood all over me. I risked my life to save you."

"You were doing your job. You would have done the same for anybody."

"That may be true, but I was terrified. Not that I was in danger, but that I might lose you." She went to the corner of the room and pulled her chair to his bedside. "I hate you for what you've done, but it doesn't mean I want you dead. I need you, whether I want to admit it or not."

"Thank you for saving my life."

Karen started to respond, then simply nodded.

"Did she kill Mark Cherneau?"

"Yes. She killed Dale, too." She put her hand on his chin and turned his head toward her. "Unless you killed him."

"He was dead when I got there."

"Why were you going there that night?"

"I was going there to kill him."

She let go of his hand and walked over to the window. She looked at the hills in the distance. "You'll be interested to know I shot Julianne. Shot her in the stomach as she was standing on my throat."

Bill stared at the little black holes in the white ceiling.

"She's dead." She turned to face him, without getting closer. "How does that make you feel?"

Bill closed his eyes.

He didn't know how it made him feel.